Marion Harland

Sunnybank

Marion Harland

Sunnybank

ISBN/EAN: 9783337105136

Printed in Europe, USA, Canada, Australia, Japan

Cover: Foto ©Andreas Hilbeck / pixelio.de

More available books at **www.hansebooks.com**

BY

MARION HARLAND,

AUTHOR OF "ALONE," "HIDDEN PATH," "NEMESIS," "MIRIAM," ETC.

NEW YORK:

SHELDON AND COMPANY.

1867.

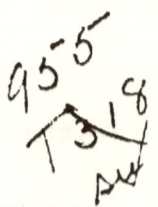

MARION HARLAND'S WORKS.

Each Work complete in 1 vol. 12mo.

ALONE,	$1.75
THE HIDDEN PATH,	1.75
MOSS SIDE,	1.75
NEMESIS,	1.75
MIRIAM,	1.75
HUSKS,	1.75
HUSBANDS AND HOMES,	1.75
SUNNYBANK,	1.75

THE CHRISTMAS HOLLY,
A new and elegantly illustrated book for the holidays.   Ready in October.

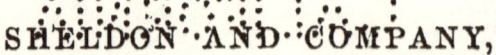

SHELDON AND COMPANY,

498 & 500 BROADWAY, NEW YORK.

Stereotyped at the Boston Stereotype Foundry,
No. 4 Spring Lane.

TO

M. C. H.,

IN MEMORY OF THE AFFECTION BORNE HER BY MY DEAD

AND HER LOVING KINDNESS TO MY LIVING CHILDREN,

AS IN GRATEFUL ESTEEM FOR HER CHARACTER AS WOMAN AND FRIEND,

𝔗𝔥𝔦𝔰 𝔙𝔬𝔩𝔲𝔪𝔢 𝔦𝔰 𝔇𝔢𝔡𝔦𝔠𝔞𝔱𝔢𝔡.

TO THE READER.

I HAVE the vanity to believe that the many readers of "ALONE"—whom I account my friends—will not be sorry to recognize, here and there, an old acquaintance as they turn the leaves of this volume. I hope—less confidently, perhaps, but earnestly—that they will like the familiar faces none the less for the years that have gone over them since their last meeting; which have added matronly dignity to Ida's carriage and speech, left sly lines upon Ellen's arch face, and frosted Charley's beard.

For the characters, plot, and general machinery of the story, I am responsible. But bearing, as it does, the date of an era of political convulsions and civil conflict, it was inevitable that these should have a certain influence in determining the complexion of the narrative. Whenever I have treated of such topics, I have adhered strictly to the truth; have stated only what I knew, for myself, to be fact. Every incident, however minute, relative to public affairs, or military operations, is authen-

1 *   (5)

tic. While I would have the interest excited by these subordinate to that felt in the development of character and personal history, I have yet striven, conscientiously, to present a faithful portraiture of the daily life and experience of those who bore the heat and burden of that fearful season. A Virginian myself, — one whose attachment for her native State is second only to that she feels for her Country, — I have infused nothing of partisan bitterness into the simple record of what I love best to describe — home-scenes in the Old Dominion. If I know my own heart and motives, I have written every line — to borrow the grand, immortal words of another — "WITH CHARITY FOR ALL; WITH MALICE TO-WARD NONE"!

MARION HARLAND.

SUNNYBANK.

CHAPTER I.

ELINOR.

February 26, 1861.

VIOLETS always bloom earlier at Sunnybank than they do anywhere else north of the James River. I found the first white blossom, a frail, frightened-looking darling, upon the southern border, a fortnight since, and the double purple English ones are now in full blow. The whole garden is unusually early in awakening from the winter's sleep, this year. Everywhere, within its bounds, there are tokens of the stealthy but sure advance of Spring. Tufts of grass are shooting up along the edges of the gravel walks, and my flower-beds boast quite a brave show of crocuses, jonquils, and snow-drops. The leaves of the hardy rose-creepers have put on a more tender green, while those of the two stately magnolias on either side of the gate shine as if newly varnished. The Florida honeysuckles are darkly verdant, and hale as though they had never known a touch of frost; the verbenas are budding, while thyme and lavender are none the less fragrant for the light snows that have powdered them since their last flowering. Beyond the garden fence the hill-sides are fair to behold in their covering of wheat and young clover, and the forest that girdles the landscape has assumed the " grayish-green livery of Spring." To the southward, this is relieved by a roseate tinge that tells me the maple swamp has hung out its millions of crimson tassels.

(7)

Oh! our Virginia is a bonnie state, and Sunnybank is a very gem upon the breast of the dear old mother. Perhaps an artist's eye would see little comeliness in the quaint building under the roof of which I drew my earliest breath, nineteen years ago — the same roof that had sheltered my mother's cradle twenty-seven years before I opened my baby eyes upon this bright world. But I love every brick and every beam of the pile — even the steep eaves and the odd belvidere that towers above all. For more than two hundred years men of our race have cultivated the broad acres which our first American ancestor won from the wilderness. I like to think that none save those of our blood and lineage have ever pressed the soil with a master's foot. The domain is passing beautiful, as seen in the hazy light of this warm afternoon. I can imagine nothing more lovely than the view from my chamber window; nothing in climate more delightful than the balmy air that fans my cheek; no earthly peace more perfect than the rest that possesses my spirit.

For I am happy! I say it lowly and thankfully, folding my hands above my heart and looking up to the soft blue sky — softly radiant still, although the tears gently fill my eyes to overflowing, as I gaze, and think of the mercy and loving kindness that have followed me all the days of my life up to the present hour of full content. I do not know how it is with others of my age and sex; but for me, I feel that the history of my woman's life dates from yesterday; that my nineteenth birthnight set the seal upon the free, careless girlhood, now swept into the past like some bright, uncertain dream; that another door is set open for me to enter; another path appointed me to tread; almost as if another, a deeper, richer nature were given me, one more capable of enjoying an existence, the wells of happiness in which are yet unsounded. Yes! my girlish days have flown forever, and if I sigh at their flight, it is not in sadness. At best, the joys of that transition stage were fleeting, its views shallow and limited, its aims undefined. My face is set steadfastly, hopefully, confidently towards the future of action and promise. Not that there is anything in my past which I would blot out of memory if I could — a dark page I would destroy — even a passage I could wish were erased. I should be ungrateful were I, by such desire, to cast a slur upon the tender mother-love ; the watchful care of my father ; the abiding affection of my brothers that has surrounded me with an atmosphere of comfort and cheer from my infancy. It may be that hundreds and thousands of others have the like agreeable conceit concerning their respective households, but I certainly think there is no happier family upon the globe than ours.

This came into my mind with peculiar force, night before last, when we sat down, an unbroken band, about the supper table, all glowing with delight at the arrival of my twin brothers, and anticipating the celebration, on the morrow, of their birthday and mine. We were just two years apart, to a day. They were twenty-one yesterday. One smiles incredulously in passing from the survey of their tall figures and manly features to Mamma's smooth forehead, abundant brown hair, and steady, bright eyes. It seems absurd to believe her the parent of three grown children. We are to have Lynn at home altogether now. Having finished his law studies in town, he will enter into partnership in his father's practice ; in time will succeed to the whole of it, should his life be spared. I have heard Mamma say that she never dared, during the first ten years of his life, to hope that he would outlive his boyhood. It has been this delicate state of health, this ceaseless dependence upon her maternal cares, and the need of constant vigilance on her part, that have contributed largely towards rendering him, in a peculiar degree, the mother-child of her band. His love for her verges upon idolatry, while she pets him — I do not say loves him — more than she does the rest of us. He merits it all, for he is noble as gentle, and beautiful as good.

Yet if I have a favorite brother, it is Ross. People call him the image of his father, and they have the same height and complexion ; both have black eyes and hair ; both are erect in figure, broad-shouldered and deep-chested, and the son has inherited the rarely-sweet smile that warms and colors the father's grave features like a burst of living sunshine, also his step and voice ; but the animated, sometimes impetuous speech, the lively play of feature, the mobile mouth, and thoughtful brow, — these were the mother's gift. With this combination of attractions he could not fail to become a splendid specimen of manhood ; nor could I fail, in beholding these, to grow very proud of my handsome, brilliant brother.

Shall I soon forget how shocked, silly I was, — how disappointed my wiser mother appeared, — when we received the letter written at the close of his college course, announcing his choice of a profession — the same letter that brought us the news that he had carried off the highest honor of the institution, and Lynn the second?

"A merchant ! " I said, aghast. "What use has a shopkeeper for Latin, Greek, and the higher branches of mathematics?"

For an instant, as I have said, Mamma looked disconcerted. Then, as Papa read aloud the boy's reasons for his preference of a mercantile life, her countenance cleared, and at the conclusion she said, quietly, with no show of reluctant conviction, —

"There are truth and force in what he says — do you not think so, love?"

And the matter was decided by my father's hearty assent.

I found that letter, written two years since, in my desk yesterday, and took it down stairs to show it to Mr. Wilton. He, too, after receiving a liberal education, has become a merchant ; and I felt that Ross' emphatic sentences embodied the views of his friend as well as his own. That same brother of mine has a tolerable command of strong English where occasion calls for the use thereof.

As for example, I copy from the letter before me : —

"The state is surfeited with doctors — glutted with lawyers. As you can testify, our own county has two of each of these public benefactors to every square mile of her territory, and we are no better, nor worse off, in this respect, than are the counties to the north, east, west, and south of us. Professional men hover over and alight upon our worn-out fields like a swarm of

lean, hungry grasshoppers. Where one makes a decent livelihood, fifty others would starve, were it not that famine is averted
by a slice of the patrimonial estate, or a few lusty negroes, the
dowry of the brides who would scorn the idea of allying themselves with ' tradespeople.' As to ambition to excel in pur-
suits which are in themselves noble and elevating, these followers
(afar off!) of Galen and Cicero have none. What is there in
their daily life to stimulate them to intellectual effort beyond the
paltry, wearing considerations — ' What shall I eat? what shall
I drink? and wherewithal shall I be clothed?' There is no
room for, or incitement to expansion of ideas and desire. They
dwell continually in the shadow of their grandfathers' tombs,
'alking largely of keeping up ancient landmarks, the value of
old blood, and the corrupting tendencies of innovations. Like
the trees in Pope's quincunx grove, —

> ' Each alley has his brother,
> And half the *county* just reflects the other.'

" You, father, have a fine estate, and have, moreover, by your
talents and diligence in business, placed yourself at the head of
your profession in your section of the state. My proposal is
this : Take Lynn in as your partner, when he has passed at
the bar, and suffer me to accept the offer made me by ' Dana
& Co.' of a bookkeeper's place in their house, with the prospect of promotion, in due time, to a share in the name and
profits of the firm. The day is coming when our commercial
princes will rule the land ; and I find in this prospect the more
cogent reason why *gentlemen*, intelligent, cultivated men, should
enter a profession which has been too long given up to the illiterate or self-educated toilers after wealth for wealth's sake."

He carried his point. It is rather a habit of his to have his
own way. I sighed then over his victory — was so weak as to be
eager in my explanation of the motives that had urged him into
this particular walk of life, when the denizens of the region opened
eyes and mouths in astonishment at his " extraordinary taste ; "
some presuming to intimate that we, his family, must be sadly
chagrined at this " waste of money and talents." Setting aside

the benefit and pleasure to him that have already attended upon
his pursuit of his chosen profession, it would be worse than
ungrateful in me to repine at the course affairs have taken. So
far as man can judge, had he studied law or medicine, he would
never have become intimately acquainted with one whose friendship he prizes beyond that of any other associate, and I might
never have met him at all.

Eighteen months ago Ross wrote home for permission to
bring an invalid friend, just convalescent from a tedious fever-
spell, to Sunnybank, during his summer vacation. Pursuant to the
prompt and cordial invitation forwarded in reply, he introduced
to us Harry Wilton. Since that time he has been a frequent
and welcome visitor. Of course he accompanied my brothers
when they came up to the birthnight fête. He has never
seemed like a stranger to any of us; but I have not appreciated
before, as I have done during this visit, as I did, especially, last
evening, what a restful confidence, what quiet happiness, I
have come to feel in his society. He is not a brilliant talker in
the sense that Rolf Kingston is; he is less of a "ladies' man,"
as the phrase is popularly used, than Ross or Lynn. I suppose
that he would be considered by most strangers as less handsome
than any one of the three I have named. I met with a word, the
other day, in reading a new book, that struck me instantly as
being most expressive of the effect he produces upon me, and I
imagine upon every one else who knows him well — "masterful!" Master of himself — in thought, impulse, passion, and
exerting through this self-command, this stanchness of principle,
and stability of purpose, a wondrous control over those with
whom he is brought into close intercourse. Yet his manner is
invariably courteous; his voice full and pleasant, in ordinary
conversation subdued to gentleness that is very winning.

I felt it, or the general influence of his presence, to be full of
calm, last evening, when he appeared, from some unknown
quarter of the room, at my side, while Rolf Kingston was weary-
ing me with protestations and entreaties. I am afraid, or I ought
to fear, that I angered the latter gentleman by my expression

of relief and ready response to Mr. Wilton's introductory remark, to the effect that he had been commissioned to ask me to sing; for he, Rolf, looked black as night when I laid my hand within the other's arm, and left him to the undisturbed enjoyment or malcontentment of the corner in which he had contrived to catch me. If he were displeased, the sensation was not a novel one, for I had offended him deeply, an hour before, by declining to accept the bouquet he tendered.

"Knowing my passion for flowers," he stated, he "had ordered this three weeks in advance of the festal eve."

He verges upon the pompous, sometimes, in his set speeches.

"Some of the flowers were brought from Savannah, in compliance with my desire," he added.

"My passion for flowers!" He must have detected a gleam of it in my eyes as they rested upon the surpassing loveliness of those he held. A pink japonica bud formed the heart of the cluster, and about it were grouped rare and exquisite exotics, the like of which had never greeted my sight until that moment. I uttered an exclamation of delight, but was recalled to my senses, before putting out my hand to take them, by the expression that flashed across his face.

"You should have had musk-roses from Damascus and lilies from the valleys of Judæa, if they could have been transported safely!" he said, in a low tone, that brought back to my mind another scene and other words.

The reminiscence put me upon my guard.

"I have lilies-of-the valley already, and roses sweet as those of Damascus," I answered, playfully, holding up my bouquet.

"Very neat!" he said, condescendingly. "Are they the product of the Sunnybank conservatory?"

My reply was an imprudent negative, for the question was unexpected.

"Your brothers probably procured them in the city?" persisted he, with a slight but unpleasant emphasis upon the two first words.

I was vexed to feel myself coloring — more vexed that I had

2

not words ready with which to reprove his impertinent queries without satisfying his curiosity.

" It is enough for me to know that they are here, and mine," I managed to say, after the lapse of a few seconds. " I have not asked where they grew."

" By which you would imply that it is sufficient for *me* to know that you have no use for other *gages d'amour!*" he said, bending towards me. " I comprehend, and I will remember."

" Has that fellow been annoying you, Nellie?" asked Ross, approaching, as Mr. Kingston quitted me in a mute but towering passion, carrying off his ill-fated nosegay with him.

" He is mortified, I fancy, because I could not conveniently manage two bouquets," I rejoined, in as careless a tone as I could assume.

Ross is high-spirited and jealously watchful of my comfort, and I am often overtaken by a nervous fear least ill-will should arise between these two on my account. My brother glanced at the flowers in my hand, and smiled, rather mischievously.

" If he persecutes you, give me a hint, and I will rid you of his attentions."

As if this alternative were not more to be dreaded than passive submission to the said attentions ! And that is saying much. I experience positive mental nausea and bodily faintness whenever Rolf nears the oft-forbidden subject.

"A suit no longer — but a *pursuit*," said aunt Ellen to me, the other day. "My dear Brownie ! *can't* you say, ' No '?"

I could not tell her how frequently I had said it, seemingly in vain.

He sought me again, then, later in the evening, cleverly manœuvring to entrap me in the angle formed by the piano and the wall, and began the dialogue by apologizing for his undue warmth in the flower episode. I did not affect anger, for I felt none, although the words, " other *gages d'amour*" still made my cheeks burn whenever I allowed myself to dwell upon the insinuation. We chatted in a friendly strain for a while. He can be very entertaining when he likes, and except when he introduces the one obnoxious topic, I really enjoy his society.

"My poor gift found more favor in Miss Lamar's eyes than in yours," he said, directing my attention to Agatha, who stood not far off.

"And appears to better advantage than if I had been the recipient," I returned, gayly. "She has fine taste ; and allow me to say that you showed yourself to be as appreciative of the beautiful in animated as in floral nature, when you bestowed your flowers upon her."

"I deserve no credit for discrimination in this case. Others have eyes as keen as mine where she is concerned. Her beauty does not blush unseen. And that reminds me — this Mr. Wilton, this piano-playing, French-speaking storekeeper, this Yankee Damon to Ross' Pythias, is likewise a friend of Miss Agatha's — is he not?"

"Mr. Wilton was well acquainted with her before she came to us," I tried to say calmly, while my ears tingled with disgust and shame at his ungentlemanly language. "He was very kind to her father during his last illness, and she feels very grateful to him in the recollection of this."

"That is evident!" was the sneering reply.

"What do you mean?" I asked, looking up steadily into his eyes. I began to suspect that he was the worse for wine.

"Just what I said, Miss Elinor — that Miss Agatha has a feeling heart, and is duly grateful to her early benefactor. If there were any further significance in my remark, it may have been born of a passing thought that the soul of this venerable patron, no doubt, swelled with compassion at sight of the woes of his interesting *protégée ;* and we all know to what pity is akin."

The aim of this innuendo was so palpable, the spite of it so thinly veiled, that I laughed outright.

"The love which is so nearly allied to compassion is hardly the kind which Agatha would value. I would not advise you to repeat the substance of that remark in her hearing, unless you have a fancy for being consumed by the lightning of her magnificent eyes."

"It is not likely that I shall ever choose to discourse to her upon any phase of this important theme," he responded; and before I knew what he was doing he had glided into the one odious channel.

I will not recollect this to-day. It seems such a petty annoyance, when compared with my wealth of mercies — the gifts of youth, home, friends, love!

I have written the last word with a firm hand, although I know that it means more, far more, to me than it did twenty-four hours ago. There is no wild fluttering of pulse or heart when I remember the brief quarter of an hour during which we stood together, apart from other eyes, beyond the hearing of other ears, and the sound of other voices, than our own. Each incident and word of the interview is distinctly stamped upon the memory, that will hold them while reason lasts.

Ross and Lynn had brought, as a birthday present for me, a fine colored photograph of the two, beautiful as to execution, life-like as to resemblance. This lay upon Papa's study-table, and aunt Ellen, in extolling its merits to Mrs. French, asked me to send for it. Partly because I feared to intrust it to a servant's care, partly because I was weary, and heated, and dizzy, after spending three hours in the heart of the crowd, I slipped from the room, and went for the picture myself.

I remember going slowly up the broad staircase, leaving the murmur of the assembly below me; stopping an instant at the window upon the landing to look out at the moonlight, and pluck a sprig from the orange-tree set there; and with this in my fingers I entered the study. There was a bright fire on the hearth, and the reading-lamp upon the centre-table was burning. But the great easy-chair was turned away from this, and in it sat Harry Wilton, his head resting upon his hand. I must have come in very softly, for he remained motionless —as I imagined asleep — until I touched the table.

"Excuse me for disturbing you," I said; "I came for this," taking up the framed photograph.

"You can never interrupt me, Brownie!"

He had never called me by my pet name until now; and the grave sweetness, the inexpressible gentleness of his tone, dispelled my trifling embarrassment.

"And least of all times, just now! for I was thinking only of you."

"Of me!" I was about to echo, wonderingly; but before I could speak, he took my hand in his, and looking up into his face, I knew all!

"I must have you, Brownie! I cannot live without you!"

This was all he said for a little while.

I can shut my eyes now and renew the impressions of that interval of stillness; hear the low song of the blazing wood upon the hearth; inhale the odor of the orange-blossoms, growing more and more powerful in the warm room; feel the tightening clasp upon my hand.

"I said that I was thinking of you as you came in," he resumed. "May I tell you my thought?"

"Yes!" I said.

"It was a wish which I have cherished for a year and a half —a wish which has grown into longing; a longing which has become a part of my being. The wish and longing are that I may, some day, call you by the holy name of 'wife.' May I add to these hope?"

Was I unmaidenly? No! I will not insult his betrothed by the thought! His open avowal, simple and frank as his own nature, merited like candor from me. The strength of will, or character, of which I have spoken, constrained a direct and truthful reply.

"Yes!" I said, again.

He detained me but a little longer; and before he let me go, he took the spray of orange-blossoms from my hand, divided it into two parts, one of which he returned to me.

"This I shall keep for myself!" he said. "I shall never give you up until you send that back to me!"

But he said it smilingly, and leading me to the door, opened it for me, and we parted.

At the foot of the stairs I met Agatha — the glowing exotics in her hand, and heightening into gorgeousness her dark beauty.

"Children of the tropics!" I stopped to say, touching her crimson cheek, while I pointed to the blended gold, white, and scarlet of her bouquet. "How gloriously you are looking to-night! Your *rôle* shall be that of a priestess of Isis!"

Her answer was a laugh and a nipping pinch of my brown arm.

"Can you tell me where Mr. Wilton is?" she asked with the pretty imperiousness she assumed sometimes. "He has hidden himself from vulgar sight for half an hour and more! I want him!"

"I found him in the study, just now, when I went up for this," I answered, showing the picture. "I suppose he is there still."

"You suppose he is there still — like the old woman who lived under the hill!" mimicking my quiet tone. "What a demure, discreet Jenny Wren it is!"

And with another laugh she ran on up the steps.

I believe that I did not blush at her bantering tone any more than I had done at her direct question. All that had passed between Harry and myself belonged to an inner existence, so sacred, sealed so far away from the chance touch of the careless or curious, that I was fearless. Within ten minutes I had learned to live two lives — one for and to the world — the other all his.

We have not exchanged a syllable relative to this matter to-day. I was busy helping Mamma in the forenoon; but aunt Ellen, Agatha, and the servants were within hearing most of the time, and I could not speak to her of what lay nearest my heart. Just before dinner, I met Papa upon the landing of the staircase, in company with Mr. Wilton. They had been closeted for an hour in the study — engrossed I knew by what subject — when I caught a glimpse of Harry's countenance. He passed me with a silent bow and a smile, and descended the stairs with a fleet step, that told the story of a glad heart. Papa stopped, put his arm about me, and kissed me twice, without speaking — a fervent caress, more expressive than words. Neither could I speak. I only laid my head upon the breast that has been my broad shield against danger and distress from my babyhood up, and nestled there as a bird might rest under her parent's wing — as lovingly and securely.

This was by the window on the landing-place where the orange-tree still stood. We had not spoken or moved, except that he was stroking my hair gently, — his own gesture, that means a world of sweet things to me, — when we heard a door open and footsteps in the upper hall. Then he kissed me again.

"This is for Mamma!"

The words swept the last shadow of doubt from my mind. I had dreaded telling her that I had promised to leave her. The footsteps that had interrupted us were Agatha's. She probably did not observe us, or, with her accustomed tact, forbore to intrude upon our confidential talk, for she stopped at the hall window, and seemed to be gazing down into the yard with such intentness as not to notice me as I passed.

I meant to speak with her after dinner, for so faithful a friend deserves to have a share in all that interests me ; but she has been suffering with headache all day, and she sent down a request to be excused from coming to the table, or appearing below again until evening. She will allow no one to see her while she is a prey to these terrible attacks of neuralgia, which our good doctor pronounces constitutional. When she first came to us, the room assigned her adjoined mine ; but she entreated so earnestly that it should be exchanged for one more remote, lest her moans, at night, while these spasms racked her, should disturb me, that Mamma gave her the large chamber quite at the other end of the hall. I have never told her, or any one else, how often I have wept outside her locked door, at the sound of her sobs and stifled cries, not daring to request admittance or to summon help. Poor girl ! the agony must be excruciating that wrings audible expression from her brave spirit ! Without the sanctuary of that locked chamber, she never utters a com-

plaint — never hints of present or past suffering. Only her wan
complexion and swollen eyes testify to the severity of the ordeal
which she has borne in solitude.

"It is past now!" she says, when I would inquire into the
nature and extent of this. "We will not live it over again!"

She carries out this principle, courageously and consistently,
in her daily life. No cloud, from those early years, so heavily
overshadowed, is ever allowed to dim the brightness of my
existence. I wish, oftentimes, that she would accept my
sympathy; yet there is something grand and heroic in this
silent endurance — this resolute cheerfulness. Everything about
Agatha is on a grand scale — from her strong, intense nature,
her fire of imagination, and deep capacity for love and sorrow,
to her Juno-like face and figure. "Dark and rich" were the
adjectives that arose to my lips, at first sight of her, upon that
midsummer day, two years ago, when she alighted at our door,
and throwing back her crape veil, as my father presented her
to my mother, acknowledged the introduction to *her* mother's
"early and best friend" with a melancholy sweetness of voice
and manner that was an instant passport to our hearts. Since
then, our home has been hers; the adopted daughter of the
household has been cherished almost as fondly as the real one.
I have no sister near my own age. Wee Carrie, although the
darling and plaything of us all, is but a baby as yet — just four
years old last month. It was a kind providence that gave to me
this older and wiser companion, when I was beginning to feel
the need of such a friend. I love Agatha with an affection
which it seems to me that sisters seldom bear to one another.

The sunset grows more golden — the air more fragrant.
There is a slight cloud of dust far down the road, and across
the fields I can catch, now and then, a tone that I recognize.
Papa and uncle Charley drove over to the village post-office,
this afternoon, accompanied by Ross and Mr. Wilton on horseback. Lynn acted as escort to aunt Ellen in one of the long,
long walks which she says are essential to the preservation of
her health and vigor. I clearly discern the forms of the return-

ing equestrians. It may not be becoming in me to say it — but nobody is any the wiser for my opinion excepting yourself, dear, discreet Journal — and I *do* think them a pair of the finest-looking men I ever beheld!

I do not care now one whit for Rolf Kingston's saucy hit about Damon and Pythias. I exult in the fact that each has no dearer friend than the other — again, through grateful tears, I thank the good Father of us all for the triple love that at once makes and guards my happiness — the love of parents, brothers, and betrothed!

CHAPTER II.

AGATHA.

LET me try to set it down just as it happened.

I had dressed for the treble birthnight party, and no prevision of coming woe passed between me and the image reflected in my mirror. When I was ready, fully equipped from slipper to head-dress, I sent the maid away, and, leaning my elbow upon the toilet-table, studied the picture before me long and intently. I should be a dull scholar indeed if I had not learned ere now that I am handsome. The flattering tale has been told me, directly and indirectly, — in broad, blunt praise; by graceful implication; by admiring glances and gaping starers, — ever since I could run alone. My truthful glass now but treated me to a later edition of the old story. The amber silk robe, with its black lace *berthé* and flounces, became me marvellously. Mrs. Lacy's taste is indisputable, and her expenditures upon myself are liberal beyond the limit of any expectations which a penniless dependent — her daughter's foil and humble companion — has the ghost of a right to entertain. Therefore my new dress, — her selection, and presented by her; as, indeed, my very stockings and handkerchiefs also are, — my new robe, then, was crisp, lustrous, and heavy — three requisites in a really excellent silk. The purplish-black of my hair was lighted up by a cluster of yellow sweetbrier, which Elinor has been nursing into premature bloom during ever so many weeks for this distinguished position; and the lace fall across my bosom was festooned by my one valuable ornament — a diamond brooch presented by my benefactors on my birthday, last November.

I had always an unreasonable and presumptuous hankering after diamonds, pearls, and the like perquisites of wealth ; so I accepted the gift with a pleasing show of gratitude and humility, feeling to my heart's core the covert meaning of Mrs. Lacy's reply to my modest objection, that it should have been Elinor's instead of mine.

" Elinor is too youthful in appearance, and in reality, to wear diamonds. When she is one and twenty, I shall have mine reset for her."

An adroit means of reminding me that *my* mother had no precious stones to bequeath to her only child. If she ever had any, — and I have a faint recollection of hearing her speak of a set of pearls and rubies which were the wedding gift of this same Mrs. Lacy, — they disappeared before I understood what their value really was.

" Brownie is too *petite* and *riante* for anything so dignified and fine-lady-like as diamonds," added my favorite detestation, Miss Ellen Morris, whom the gods, in punishment for some unconscious, yet enormous, sin of mine, have sent hither to pass the winter.

" Poor me ! " cried the spoiled pet. " With what may I make myself beautiful, then, Aunt Ellen ? "

" Wild-roses and holly-berries yet awhile, you elf ! " was the answer. " What business have mocking-birds with jewelry more expensive than dew-drops, I should like to know ? "

If there is any one habit indulged in by this family which irks me oftener than another, it is the superfluity of pet names bestowed upon this, the elder, and for many years the only, daughter of Castle Sunnybank. True, the father and the mother, in speaking of her in the third person, invariably style her " Elinor ; " I suppose to deter retainers and mere acquaintances from unwarrantable familiarity : but, with the brothers, she is " Our Mocking-bird," and " Nellie, sweet ! " or " Nellie, darling ! " while Miss Morris never, by any chance, calls her by her right name. " Birdie," " Fairy," " Pet," " Rosebud," and a score of other diminutives, slip from her glib tongue *ad*

infinitum, and, to me, *ad nauseam*. One and all address her as
" Brownie " — a title that suits her well.   She is a brown little
witch, brown as to hair, eyes, and complexion, even to the
dainty fingers ; to the graceful tapering of which down to the
tips of the rosy nails, Miss Morris once directed my notice, as
an unmistakable sign of gentle blood.   Elinor has, moreover, a
small, spirited-looking mouth, white teeth, and a dimpled chin.
Riante, Miss Morris said ; but *piquante* would better describe
her physiognomy.   " Mocking-bird " is almost as applicable to
her as " Brownie."   Gay or pensive, in thought or in frolic,
she sings with the spontaneity, the sweetness, and, I honestly
believe, the unconsciousness of the wildwood songster from
which the sobriquet is borrowed.   She warbles, like him, because it is so natural for her to sing that she cannot help it.   It
is the fashion of the family to applaud this habit.   It reminds
me disagreeably of a chamber-maid chanting her roundelay to
the accompaniment of dust-pan and broom.

I heard her last night, as, having completed my critical and
impartial survey of myself before my mirror, I heaved a hopeful sigh at the wish that I might appear to one other pair of
eyes as I did to my own, and turned to go below.

I paused outside the parlor door to contemplate the tableau
at the other end of the long room.   The apartment is handsomely furnished, — for the Lacys have taste as well as ample
means ; and, on this occasion, it was decked like a summer
bower.   The choicest treasures of the green-house had been
reserved to grace this *fête*.   The window-seats were filled with
fragrant shrubs and pots of flowers — roses, mignonette, and
violets.   Creepers floated downward from hanging baskets
between the window-curtains, and from brackets hung against
the walls.   At the farther extremity of the room was Elinor's
masterpiece.   I give her credit for the conception, although I
pricked my fingers and wearied my spine in assisting her to
carry out the design.   It was a miniature Temple of Liberty,
with fluted pillars of greenery, crowned with blossoms, flooring of moss, and a vine-covered roof.   Upon the wall behind it

was a monogram, also of evergreens, blending the initials of the twin brothers; and over this drooped two silk flags, one bearing the coat of arms of Virginia; the other, the stars and stripes of the Federal government. It appeared that the latter hung too stiffly to please the architect of the edifice; and, with her usual impetuosity, she had mounted upon a table close at hand to coax the offending folds into easy curves. Standing thus, she steadied herself by resting one hand upon Ross's shoulder, while with the other she adjusted the drapery. The light from a bracket overhead fell upon her uplifted face. Her lips were apart; her eyes were large and eager; her smooth, brown arms were a study, in curve and moulding, for sculptor or artist; and the rose-color of her dress cast warm reflections upon neck and cheek. I, of all women living, have least cause to depreciate Elinor Lacy's charms. I frankly aver that my eyes never dwelt upon a more enchanting picture.

A group composed of her father, mother, and brothers, Mr. Charles Dana, and, of course, Miss Morris, watched her between interchanged glances of proud delight. A flower dropped from the cipher under the flag, and she staid to replace it, warbling the melody I had heard in my room above: —

> " And the star-spangled banner in triumph shall wave
> O'er the land of the free and the home of the brave."

Ross breathed, rather than sang, a subdued base accompaniment. The Lacys are noted for their fine voices.

Miss Morris ended the impromptu duet with her distinctly accentuated speech: —

" Very sweetly sung, young people; but the melody is one I never admired. I suppose a fiery Union-lover, like yourself, Brownie, will brand me with treason for saying it: but this be-praised national ballad belongs to what I call the gilded gingerbread order of music. Moreover, it has been worn into threads, or crumbs, by organ-grinders. And, while I am shocking you all, I may as well ease my mind of an observation, uttered confidentially, that, in my humble judgment, this display

3

of boundless devotion to a bit of bunting, streaked with red and white, and bedizened in one corner with tawdry stars upon a blue square, that inevitably reminds one of a boy's pocket handkerchief, is very absurd, if it is not wicked idolatry."

"Perhaps the stars and bars would suit your taste better!" rejoined Ross, sarcastically.

"I don't deny that I had as lief make a pagan of myself for the sake of one as the other," said the gay spinster. "I feel more enthusiasm at the sight of a pretty silk dress-pattern than I could arouse by staring for an hour at the biggest and brightest star-spangled rag that was ever woven, even if fifty brass bands were clashing away all the while with "Yankee Doodle" and "Hail, Columbia!"

> "'A primrose by the river's brim
> A yellow primrose was to him,
> And it was nothing more,'"

repeated Elinor, stepping down from her elevation, and surveying her completed work with a pleased smile.

I must grant her the credit of possessing a generous and equable temper. Even to-day I will do her justice, if I can.

"Aunt Ellen, you are an incorrigible political heretic, and I would get angry with you if I could. The only reason why I do not cast you off utterly for your treasonable and sacrilegious utterances is, that I have contracted an obstinate habit of caring for you — affection second in degree only to that which I feel for our glorious old flag."

As she kissed her hand saucily to the banner, and nodded laughing defiance at the critic, a voice said in my ear, —

"She *is* a stanch little patriot! Heaven bless her!"

I must have been unaccountably interested in watching the scene within the room not to have noticed that Harry Wilton was standing behind me all the while.

"Come into the porch: the night is lovely," he continued.

I took his proffered arm, and we made two or three turns of the long piazza in silence. Still I was unprepared; so free from dread and dismay as to please myself, childishly, with the sweep and "swish" of my ample silk skirt against the balustrade, the glitter of my diamonds in the moonlight. I gnash my teeth in remembrance of my insane unreadiness for what was to come.

When I can syllable the shock of an earthquake, or the rush and roar of the tornado, I may be able to recall and recite the precise words that told me of his love for Elinor Lacy. I have written it, and read it over since it was penned; and yet I am aware that I do not believe it. Her lover! *hers!* when, for four years ——

But let me keep to my story. It helps to steady my reason to write it out in full. Even my nature must have some outlet for its confidences, and I have found voiceless paper a trustworthy repository for these.

When my brain began to recover its equilibrium, my first rational thought was gratitude for the obscurity of night; my second, self-gratulation that neither sigh, groan, nor word had escaped me while the torture was being applied. I have endured, dumbly, smilingly, too much and too long to be surprised into outcries by mortal agony itself. But I think — I say it calmly — that, if I had held a dagger during the moments immediately succeeding his confession, I would have struck it home to his heart with a resolute hand, and then sheathed it in my own. I am thankful that I was unarmed, except with womanly pride and its swift ally — woman's wit. Together, these braced me up to say, —

"This is no news to me."

A lie! Of course it was. Had I never told one before, this would have arisen as promptly to my tongue. Was there ever a woman who would have uttered the truth in the circumstances that compassed me then? If she ever existed, she should have been burned alive by a committee of her own sex.

"I imagined as much," he responded, affectionately. "I felt sure that you, my wise, good sister, long ago divined who

was to me the chief among the many attractions of Sunnybank."

The many other attractions of Sunnybank, no doubt, included
me, along with the fruit, vegetables, and healthful breezes of
this charming country-house! His " good, wise sister " secretly
recognized and appreciated the compliment, and, while doing
thus, said, pleasantly, —

"You are assuredly not the chief of dissemblers. I deserve
no credit for my discovery."

"I have not tried to dissemble in this matter," he returned
in the firm, even tones that never fail to control me in my wild-
est moods. "I have sought perseveringly to win Elinor Lacy's
affections from the first week of our acquaintanceship. I told
her father as much six months ago, and obtained his permission
to avow my feelings to her when she should have passed her
nineteenth year."

Her nineteenth year! and this was her birthday! O, this
was terribly sudden!

"And you mean to avail yourself of this permission?" I
said, still without faltering.

"If my life is spared three days more."

"To-night?" I asked, boldly.

"Probably. Will you not bid me God-speed?"

"Who would suspect you of being so impatient a lover?" I
remarked, half bitterly, while I would have been playful, and
still " sisterly."

"You forget that I have waited six months. But will you
not give me your good wishes for my success?"

Did some shadow from my begloomed spirit reach his, that
his tone had an anxious inflection? At any rate, it warned me
to aim after more thorough concealment.

"I do, most heartily," I answered, looking up fearlessly;
"and may you find in her, love as faithful as has been your
friendship for me!"

"Thank you."

There was no suspicion now of a hidden meaning in my

words. He was too much in earnest to question my ingenuousness.

Two, maybe three, maybe four hours later, I missed them both from the parlor, and started to seek them. I met Elinor coming down stairs, a spray of orange-blossoms in her hand, and a dreamy light in her eyes that told me all was over, despite the contrary evidence of her composed voice and features, — tranquil even while she answered my inquiry as to his whereabouts. I fancy that I pinched her, as I returned some silly raillery; and then I went on, not towards the study, where she had informed me I would find him, but in the direction of my own room.

As I flew along the hall, I heard him call me softly, but clearly, —

" Agatha ! "

I did not mean to look around; but I am so used to obeying him that I halted and turned my head, involuntarily. He stood just without the study door, smiling, and holding out his hand as to a petted child whom he suspected of waywardness. I went back to him like a fawning spaniel — to him who would, I knew, wound me to the quick, perhaps unto death. Before I reached him, I saw that he too had a cluster of orange-flowers, the counterpart of those I had seen in Elinor's hand. These served me as a text.

" Auspicious omens," I said, pointing to them. " Will you give them to me ? "

He drew them away from my touch with something very like a shudder, although he smiled in shaking his head.

" Not in exchange for all these ? "

I held up the richly-rare bouquet which Rolf Kingston had thrown away upon Miss Elinor's humble friend, after it had been rejected by that disdainful damsel.

" Not in exchange for a king's diadem. Come in — won't you ? "

He pushed the door open, passed in after me, and set me a chair near the fire.

3 *

"A new and pretty version of the broken sixpence?" I interrogated, again looking at the flowers instead of his face.

"You have guessed it. Sit down for a moment."

I could not support loverly rhapsodies in my then frame of mind, and I pleaded the necessity of my speedy return to the company below.

"I am on severe duty to-night," I was foolish enough to add. "The halt, the maimed, and blind — in other words, the dull, silly, and bashful — are apportioned to me by the Lady Manager of the feast. This is one of the methods in which I pay for my keeping."

"Agatha!" — he frowned, and his rebuke was sternly uttered, — "will you never dismiss these morbidly unjust fancies, — unjust to yourself as to the friends whose constant effort is to make you happy? Few orphans find a home so pleasant as is yours; few adopted daughters receive love so free and fond as is lavished upon you. I wish I could convince you of this, once for all," he said, softening as he proceeded. "To-night my heart is so full of grateful joy that I would have all the world happy, especially those whom I love as I must ever love you."

And just here — I can laugh now when I think of it — the door swung inward again, and appear Miss Morris at the threshold. We were standing upon the rug, and Harry had taken my hand in his fraternal grasp in uttering his last sentence. My face was bent over my flowers; and I doubt not that the picture was a striking one. Evidently, it was the reverse of agreeable to the intruder; for she honored me with one of the sharpest of her sharp looks.

"I beg pardon! I thought this room was empty," she said, in retreating.

"I must go," I said, hurriedly, and escaped after her.

None are so desperate, so reckless of others' opinion, as the truly miserable; and, for the rest of the evening, I was extravagantly gay — positively impudent in the hardihood of my bearing towards my particular friend, the single lady aforesaid. She sought to transfix me with her keen eyes whenever I approached her; was merciless in retort upon certain of my pert speeches, and actually savage in animadversion upon divers of my expressed views. I laughed in her face more than once, and met every thrust with apparent good humor. But for the counter-irritant of this skirmishing, which kept my wits upon the alert, I must have gone wild, or possibly betrayed myself as ridiculously as did Rolf Kingston his sense of discomfiture, when he glowered gloomily upon his unfeeling lady-love from a corner, gnawing his gloves as the Furies were biting at his heart-strings.

Is it to gain a like respite from this cruel weight upon brain and spirits that I find myself now dwelling upon the particulars of the breakfast-scene, in which Miss Morris enacted a prominent part? or is it a kindred impulse to that which influences him who fears he is losing his reason to count the panes of glass in his window, to assure himself that one faculty of his mind is still intact?

I went down stairs, this morning, languid, unrested, heavy-lidded; went down, because I dared not avoid the observation of the family and their visitors. Mr. and Mrs. Lacy, Ross, Lynn, Harry Wilton, and little Carrie, were already assembled about the table; and Elinor entered just as I was replying to Mrs. Lacy's queries regarding my headache.

"We need ask no questions about *your* health," said Ross to his sister, in undisguised fondness.

The regards of all being directed to her by this remark, she blushed as redly as did the geranium-blossom of her breast-knot. For myself, I stared at the girl in amazement. I had not believed it possible for even a cold-blooded, unromantic woman to enjoy such child-like, refreshing slumber, as had evidently been hers on the night succeeding her betrothal to the man of her heart. Her eyes were clear and soft; her complexion, fresh; her smile, frank and ready, color though she did. Her dress is always neat and tasteful; but, this morning, she had undoubtedly studied the effect of her costume upon her appear-

ance. A pearl-gray cashmere wrapper, with a wide border of
crimson palm-leaves, was bound about her waist with a crimson
cord ; and the single bright flower at her throat comported 'perfectly with this Oriental costume. I have an eye for *minutiæ*,
and jealousy is more quick of vision than love ; yes, than such
love as I saw flash from a pair of eyes opposite mine, as I
glanced across the table — eyes that were not directed towards me.

Why should he or anybody else care to look at me? I was
olive-green from sleeplessness and pain ; my black orbs, lustreless ; my lips, livid. There was no need for me to torment
myself with thoughts about the apparel which no one would
notice ; so I wore a plain black alpaca dress, severely simple as
a conventual robe. Thus thinking, and thus contrasting myself
with my rival, I slowly sipped the cup of black coffee, without
cream, poured out for me by my mistress. It is the next best
thing to opium for toning the nerves. My Lady Lacy knows
my moods and habits well enough to supply me with this tonic,
without being asked, when I come down to breakfast with one
of my silent headaches.

"Why, Agatha, dear!" exclaimed Elinor, catching sight of
my countenance as she took her seat at her father's right hand ;
"not a neuralgia day, surely?"

I was never glad before to see Miss Morris ; but I was actually grateful to her for rustling her silk *peignoir* into the room
at that precise instant ; furthermore, relieved that the babbling
stream of her talk effectually prevented me from making any
rejoinder to the inquiry relative to my insignificant self. But
nobody noticed the omission, or prosecuted the discussion of a
subject so unimportant. As the spinster passed her pet's chair,
she gave her a tweak of the ear.

"You malicious little sprite! how dare you look so pro-
vokingly full of life and spirits, when I am jaded, and yellow,
and cross? I detected two new crows-feet about my eyes, this
morning, and a gray hair over my left temple. It is Nature's
revenge for my dissipation last night. She is a vindictive bel-

dam. She treats me as a step-mother might, and a viragoish one at that. No coffee, thank you, Ida! Miss Agatha's panacea for disordered nerves is my bane. A cup of weak black tea, if you please. Don't tempt the fallible flesh, Lynn, with those ravishing waffles. I must take a piece of dry toast. Yes; I know the matchless flavor of Sunnybank broiled chicken, Mr. Lacy; but I am doing penance. An egg, did you propose, Brownie? I will try it, my love, provided it was laid to-day, and it is boiled just right."

Then, weary of the ridiculous twaddle, I ceased to listen, and, having quaffed my coffee, stirred the slight sediment in the bottom of the cup with my spoon, and thought over my own bitter fancies until the antiquated belle's ringing voice addressed me, and summoned my wandering wits to their post.

" Are you reading your fortune in those coffee-grounds, Miss Agatha?"

" Yes, ma'am," I replied, in grave-simplicity.

" And what is the result of your incantation, may I ask?"

" I find only sparkle and sweetness," I answered, lifting my spoon to show a morsel of sugar upon the tip.

A smile went around the board, and she made another attack.

" I hope your *preux chevalier*, Mr. Coleman," — a rich and very "fast" bachelor, who had followed me like my shadow the evening before, — "reads the like flattering tale in his morning cup."

" Of coffee?" put in Ross, demurely; and this time there was a laugh.

" You indiscreet boy!" scolded Miss Morris. " Who knows what mischief your impertinent and uncharitable insinuations may do! I had not looked for so unkind a hit from you. In love, more than in anything else, a fellow-feeling should make one kind. Ask pretty Miss Hall, when you pay your next call there, if I am not right."

" You have made a trifling mistake," said Mr. Lacy, who, dignified as he looks, likes to take his part in family fun; " she is Lynn's inamorata. Is not that so, my boy? I remarked to

Mamma, last night, that the signs of the times indicated a movement in that direction."

"It is scarcely fair, sir, this putting a fellow into the confessional so publicly," returned his son, lightly; but his cheek took a warmer hue, and his eyes strayed, accidentally, perhaps, to mine, leaving them as suddenly.

Miss Morris sneered, loftily, —

"Lynn! he is the most flinty-hearted boy I ever beheld. I do not believe he was ever in love for a moment in the whole course of his life."

This time he did not look at me; but something in his manner impressed me as being queer, jocose as was his reply.

"Mistaken *there*, at all events, Auntie! I have adored you from my babyhood, when I wore pretty little frocks of your embroidery. It is my constancy to you which renders me insensible to the charms of others."

"My precious child, a man may not marry his grandmother; and the love that leadeth not unto the altar of Hymen is voted Platonic folly, ethereal humbug, in this practical age. In classic phrase, — for slang has become classic in this same era, — it does not remunerate. Ask your brother, and his commercial friend over there, if what I say be not solemn, practical truth."

I caught the drift of this apparently thoughtless rhodomontade, if no one else did. She had overheard the latter clause of Harry's remark to me, the previous evening. "I must ever love you" savored to her too strongly of sentimental flirtation, when she took into view the speaker's relation to her favorite. He dared not trifle with the daughter of the house of Lacy, protected by father, brothers, social position, and wealth: *ergo*, he must be amusing himself at my expense; and, much as she disliked me, she would give me warning to this effect. Love, such as he professed to feel for me, could not lead unto the altar of Hymen; therefore it behooved her to open my eyes to my true standing.

I hope it is not a deadly sin to hate a fellow-woman: if it be, then, in respect to this one, I transgress beyond the hope of forgiveness.

I have asked no questions about family secrets to-day, and no one has volunteered any information ; but my senses of sight and hearing have served me well. I know that the betrothal has received the parental sanction, and that, if the brothers have not been already taken into confidence, Ross will be during his ride to the village with Wilton. Lynn has gone to walk with his patroness, Miss Morris. She worships that boy — I imagine for the sake of his name. It belonged to her dead lover, — so Elinor once whispered to me, — dead upwards of a score of years ago. I do not relent towards her when I think of her grief at his loss, — of her twenty-five lonely years, filled with sadness and ineffectual longings. I am glad to believe that she has thus suffered ; that, underneath her gay mask, she suffers still. I feel no pity for any one : least of all do I seek pity for myself.

CHAPTER III.

ELINOR.

A QUIETLY happy Sabbath. I never desired so earnestly before to go to church. I know that He who smiles upon His children's bliss, as truly as He comforts them in their affliction, is really no nearer to the seeking soul in the sanctuary reared in His honor by mortal hands, than elsewhere; but something within urged me to enter His courts with my thank-offering for the new and great joy He had given me.

I rode to church in company with Mamma, Aunt Ellen, and Agatha. I suppose that I was unusually silent, — maybe grave in seeming, — for Agatha once accosted me as "Little Nun." It was a foolish whim of mine to dislike the term, but I did wish that she had not used it. I tried to laugh off the impression; to scold myself for thinking of it a second time; yet, after I was seated in the church, even as I bowed my head in prayer, the phrase recurred to me, and the mocking tone in which it had been uttered.

Led by these, my thoughts strayed off, during the interval of quiet preceding the commencement of the public services, into a strange and not a bright track. A nun's life — so I mused — must be chill and gray as it is self-denying and unalterable, unless it be varied by sharp conflicts with rebellious will, with tastes and aspirations after — alas! not hopes of that to which woman's thoughts and desires tend as naturally as rivers seek the ocean — home and home-loves. Nature, strong in all humankind, is doubly powerful in our sex. I do not believe that so many are led into this untempting path by religious en thusiasm as driven by sorrow, goaded to the irrevocable step by disappointment.

"Women have an innate proclivity for self-sacrifice," I once heard Aunt Ellen say, in her half-sad, half-jesting way. "If Isaac had been a girl, she would have quarrelled with the officious ram for not running his awkward horns into some other and distant thicket. And Iphigenia, no doubt, congratulated herself, on the way to the sacrificial pile, upon the fine thing she was about to do."

What change in outward circumstances, I asked myself, could induce me to resign, utterly and forever, the bright hopes that now seem inseparable from my existence, to bury all thoughts of personal happiness, and take upon myself, voluntarily, deliberately, a cross the pressure of which I must feel every hour until I laid it down with life? Was I cowardly? Did it prove me to be no heroine, that every instinct of my nature shrank from the long, weary task of self-denial, of continual warfare? Am I, then, an ease-loving, spoiled child, unfitted by constitution and education to cope with the severe realities which others meet bravely, endure uncomplainingly?

Agatha has, for the past year, occupied the position held for many years (since the erection of the building, in fact) by Mamma — that of performer upon the small but sweet-toned organ that accompanies our music on Sabbath. Still, the selection of voluntaries and tunes devolves upon Mamma, as of old. And when my distrustful, ungrateful reverie had reached this point, I felt her touch upon my shoulder, and saw her finger designate in the music-book before me the sentence she had chosen as the opening piece of the day.

"*Cast thy burden upon the Lord, and He will sustain thee, He will comfort thee!*"

It was like the pointing of an angel hand. Doubts, fears, the nameless pain that was striving in my heart, were gone before I joined my voice with Agatha's in the introductory duet. When the more timid utterance of the sentence arose into sublime

4

confidence in the chorus, and Harry's deep, fervent tones blended with those of my brothers, bearing up mine into exultant strength, I thanked GOD and took courage in the persuasion that He would sustain me under the blessed burden of a trust so dear and holy as the charge of another's happiness — a care so precious that I might well fear to assume it unassisted by divine grace. He who bestowed the gift, and who best knows its value, can alone rightly understand how the mere imagination of losing it should shake my soul to feebleness.

Something of this I confessed to Harry during our walk in the garden this afternoon. It is becoming easier, every hour, for me to tell him all that is in my heart. If I have a wise and strong, I have likewise one of the gentlest of tutors. He listened kindly to my stammered story, and then talked, as I thought no other man besides my father could do, upon such topics as the Christian's hopes, the Christian's duties, the Christian's reward in this world and that which is to come. My noble, noble Love ! mine, whatever else of change may betide — mine in time and eternity !

There is no lovelier spot upon the Sunnybank plantation than the burying-ground at the bottom of the garden. This evening, when we reached the low wall enclosing it, we stood for a long time surveying the peaceful scene before us, speaking lowly, now and then, of those who slept under the turf. The giant weeping willow in the centre of the small cemetery is a landmark for miles around. It was planted more than forty years since to mark my grandfather's grave. Twelve years later his wife was laid to her rest beneath its shadow. I told Harry how my mother, then a girl of fifteen, an orphan, with neither brother, sister, uncle, or aunt, in the world, passed a whole night beside the freshly-made grave, praying, in wretchedness of desolation, that she might die and have a home in this village of her dead, so abject was her sense of loneliness.

"Do you know, dear Brownie," was his comment, "that we as often have reason to thank God for not answering our prayers, as for vouchsafing a speedy reply to our requests?

'Not as I will, but as Thou wilt,' should be no idle form of speech when coupled with our petitions. You remember what is the mission of ' God's kindest angel,'—

> ' To make our own our Father's will.' "

I could not but glance, as he spoke, at a green hillock near my grandmother's tomb. The head-stone set over against it is ·far whiter that any of the rest, and is wrought with greater skill. The design is, to my taste, very beautiful. A stem from which droop lilies-of-the-valley, and below the name of the little sleeper the words, " *My Beloved is gone down into His garden to gather lilies.*"

Dear little Morton! his father's namesake, and the most lovely in feature and disposition of us all! He was my junior by two years, and died in his fourth summer. Therefore I have a distinct recollection of his appearance and many winning ways. His loss was my first, my only real sorrow. My eyes filled now as I reverted to the day when both parents knelt beside their dying child, and besought the Father to spare the precious life. Here I had to stop, and there was a pause in our talk — not an unfeeling one, for a hand had sought mine as it lay among the ivy on the top of the wall, and folded it warmly and closely; but the quiet of the hour and place, which was still even to the flexile weepers that swept the marble stones, and chastened thoughts of the great mystery of mortality of which the heaving earth, on either hand and in front of us, was the token, held us mute. By and by I felt a light, loving touch upon my bowed head.

" Nellie, love ! " said low, sweet tones, but sad as sweet, " weep not for the dead — neither bemoan him ! He is safe ! Whatever may befall her other sons, your mother, *our* mother, has felt the last pang of solicitude she can ever know on account of him who sleeps here. Heaven grant —— " Checking himself abruptly, he added, " The air is growing chilly ! We must not forget that this summer weather does not belong of right to the earliest days of March, and that it is liable to be withdrawn at any hour. I fear that you will take cold if you stand here longer."

Mamma met us in the hall, as we entered the house.

"Were you uneasy about her?" asked Harry, smiling.

"Not at all!"

Question and reply were commonplace enough; but I saw the glance of trustful affection exchanged as these were said, and it sent me off to my room to weep in very gladness.

Yet I feel very humble to-night, — oppressed by a sense of my unworthiness of the abundant mercies with which my young life is crowned. I float in the flood of light that has streamed along my pathway for many happy years, as an insect does in the sunshine that has steeped him from the beginning of his ephemeral existence, — a mite in the boundless universe of the good Father, — but a mite all a-thrill with the bliss He has given. My heart has grown more large and tender with the incoming of this tide of delight. This is but the legitimate effect of an all-satisfying affection. I do not like the term "absorbing love." It conveys an implication of selfish indifference to the welfare and griefs of others. I pray earnestly that my wealth of blessings may never cause me to enter less heartily into the gladness of those who rejoice; to feel sympathy less lively with the sorrowing — those who are bereft of that which makes me rich.

This brings to mind my meeting with Aunt Ellen, yesterday forenoon, near the greenhouse. I had been busy for an hour with the gardener, rearranging the plants borrowed from his shelves for the birthnight party, and stopping just outside the door to gather a bunch of my English violets, I encountered Aunt Ellen. She was equipped for a walk, and I asked if she wished me to go with her.

"No, Pet! I am frumpy and disagreeable to-day, and decent company for nobody except my very objectionable self."

"The idea of your being 'frumpy'!" I laughed.

And thoughtlessly — these thoughtless tricks warn me constantly what a light-minded child I am still — I held up my flowers to her face, saying, "They are the sweetest breath of Spring!"

I was shocked to see her recoil and change color at the touch or odor.

"I cannot bear it, dear!" she gasped — catching her breath between each fragment of a sentence. "I have a strange antipathy — not so strange either — but the scent of violets overpowers me! I smelled them once — sweet and powerful — as they lay within a coffin! Since then I have never handled one except when I go, every March, to lay them upon a grave. But that is a penitential pilgrimage!" •

She uttered this with rapid incoherence, like one striving to recover strength or self-possession; then the blood returned to her lips and cheek, and she slipped her hand under my chin and raised my face nearer hers, smiling fondly, although her eyes were less steady and bright than it is their wont to be.

"I haven't many old-maidish notions, Brownie, if I *am* a single lady of an uncertain age; but this is one, and you must not tell tales upon me. I have been slightly unstrung for a couple of days. This unseasonably warm weather is enervating, besides reminding me of other days and other scenes; but an hour's walk in the open air will bring me up to concert pitch."

"Dear Aunt Ellen!" I could not help saying, as I wound my arms about her neck, and gazed into the face that has ever looked lovingly upon me, "I never think of you as being subject to the fluctuations of spirits that trouble other people. I wish I could comfort you, — could share with you my affluence of happiness!"

For I so pitied her in this my first insight of the darkened undercurrent of the life that appears to others a clear, sparkling stream, neither deep nor turbid!

"My blessed girl! I believe you! I know that you mean what you say — but I would not rob you of one ray of sunlight. Nor do I want you to disturb your affectionate little heart with thoughts of the days of darkness, which are many,

4 *

that have been apportioned unto others. Your mother is wiser and better than I — poor earthworm that I am! and she preaches of the necessity of cloudy days. Perhaps it is best — it must be, or it would be ordered otherwise, I suppose — that with some, November should last the year round. If the prayers of a sinner like myself are heard, your glad, bright May will be unending. Forget everything else that I have said ; and, now, good by for a little while ! "

She kissed me upon the lips and then upon my eyes, and passed on. I watched her as she trode down the walk with her swift, even step, looking neither to the right nor the left ; through the lower gate of the garden, past the burying-ground and along the lane beyond, until her figure was lost to view in the woods.

Just so she holds on her way through the world, and those who see her day after day and year after year, count her among the lightest of the light-hearted. Her remark touching Mamma's preaching referred to a quotation the latter had used that morning at breakfast-time — ".There is no cloud the shadow of which is not needed." This incident gave me a half hour of very sober thought — soberness that steals in again upon me in the review of it. Were the violets she spoke of in the coffin of her dead betrothed — the Lynn Holmes — handsome and gifted — in loving memory of whom my father and mother named one of their twin-boys? Five years ago, I mentioned him in Aunt Ellen's presence, knowing of him only as a child might from hearing my mother allude to her early friend and adopted brother, when questioned as to her reasons for bestowing upon her son a name which strikes most people as singular. I did not observe Aunt Ellen's countenance, having no suspicion that she was interested in the subject, but I did notice that she instantly quitted the room. When I was next alone with Mamma, she cautioned me against a repetition of the blunder by confiding to me enough of the sad story to enlist my sympathies in the early trial of the friend whom I had been instructed to call " aunt," who had herself taught me to love her as well as if she were in truth nearly allied to us by blood. Do days of darkness come to all? Are — not shadows merely — but clouds, heavy and fraught with storm — necessary to the healthful growth of the soul?

Then, Father, be near me when their gloom shall creep upon my track. Help me to say from the heart, as with the lips, " Not as *I* will."

In casting my eyes upon the above page, they were arrested by three words— " Her dead betrothed ! " And yet she lives and smiles, and, so far as man can judge, finds pleasurable interest in life ! while, at the suggestion of such a woe, my weak woman's nature is aghast. " God forbid ! " is all I can say. O Thou who art the Preserver as Thou art the Giver of life, let *his* be very precious in Thy sight, and fit me to share it !

CHAPTER IV.

AGATHA.

"Has it never occurred to you, Ida, that you may be doing an unwise thing for your own children in keeping Agatha Lamar here?"

I was writing at the desk in Mr. Lacy's study, and the door leading into the adjoining chamber — Miss Morris's — was very slightly ajar. This was an uncommon circumstance, this means of communication between the rooms being very seldom used. I had known, for, I suppose, twenty minutes, that Mrs. Lacy and her guest were having a cosy confabulation over their needles, but had not troubled myself to listen until I heard my own name. Then I laid down my pen, and stepped nearer to the wall, that I might hear yet more distinctly what was to follow. I am aware that this act would be esteemed dishonorable by most people; but to myself I do not pretend to play the honorable. Self-preservation is my first and last law, and I had been directly attacked. It behooved me to collect what materials I could for my defence.

"What do you mean?" was Mrs. Lacy's reply, uttered surprisedly, and in doubt as to the import of her crony's question.

"Just this. I have studied the young lady pretty closely, now, for a couple of months, and I believe that I have formed a tolerably accurate idea of her real character and plans."

"Take care, Ellen," interposed Mrs. Lacy, yet more seriously. "Remember that you have never liked her."

"And prejudice is a bad medium through which to make an impartial observation, you would add," said the other, coolly. "Granted, my dear. Granted further, that, being a firm believer in hereditary traits — especially where these are taints as well — I was never disposed to regard old Pinely's grandchild with much favor. But until this winter she has worn her mask wonderfully well. Lately she has become careless or desperate. I have caught her off her guard once or twice, and if you will promise not to be angry, I will give you the benefit of my discoveries. Firstly, she has all along cherished a *penchant* for Harry Wilton — how far comprehended and encouraged by him, it is not for me to say. Secondly, her black eyes are doing execution upon our Lynn's great, tender heart, and if he were to throw himself at her feet to-morrow, she would marry him to obtain a husband and a settlement — Mr. Wilton being out of the question now."

I hearkened for Mrs. Lacy's reply in perfect agony. If she turned against me, what was I but a worse than beggared wanderer?

"I should be greatly shocked and pained could I believe these assertions," she answered, and her calm voice brought me hope. "Her relations toward Mr. Wilton are somewhat peculiar. You must have heard ——"

"Yes, yes; how he chanced to take music lessons from that dissipated scamp of a Lamar, and became interested in the bright-eyed daughter, who spent her days up in the garret back room, sewing, cooking, washing, practising on the rickety piano and violin; sometimes at the point of starvation, pawning her clothes off her back for bread; at others locked up, for two or three days together, in the wretched chamber, while the brutal father was on one of his drunken sprees abroad; — how Mr. Wilton secretly stimulated her to keep her face clean; to study the books which he brought her, and to perfect herself in the one branch of knowledge Lamar could teach her — music; how he spoke of her case accidentally to Charley Dana, who recognized the name of her promising parent as that of poor Laura Pinely's husband, and after satisfying himself that this was the identical individual who had robbed you of your charity-school teacher, wrote to you a statement of the affair; and when, a month later, another letter arrived, informing you that Lamar had drunk himself into a fatal fever, and that his only child was an orphan, how Morton posted off to New York to offer her a home and parents. I was teetotally opposed to the Quixotic scheme from the outset, and I have never changed my mind."

"Ellen! Ellen! is not your enumeration of the miseries endured by the unhappy child before she found that home sufficient to move the hardest heart to pity and to charitable judgment? I am not so blind to Agatha's faults as you think me. I recognize with pain the truth that there are grievous blemishes in her character. But when tempted to dwell upon these, I recollect that she was left motherless at thirteen, and how little there was in the wild Bohemian life she led afterwards to foster the seeds of good which I must believe poor Laura tried to implant in her daughter's heart; and then come such thoughts of my own desolate orphanage, and its attendant trials of uncongenial associations and lack of moral and religious training, that I redouble my efforts to overcome for her, by present happiness, the hateful memories which must haunt her, seldom as she refers to them."

"And preciously you pamper her among you all!" exclaimed Miss Morris, angrily, yet laughing — "from Mr. Lacy down to Brownie, who looks up to her as to a sublunary saint, made sacred by virtue and misfortune! Wait until you have her for a daughter-in-law, and she will show her true colors. I wouldn't care so much if Ross were the destined victim. He could manage her, perhaps. But Lynn could never be stern to one he loved, or otherwise than chivalric in his gentleness to a woman. The prospect may not appall you; but dearly as I love the boy, I had rather close his eyes with my own hands to all earthly scenes than see him the husband of that designing adventuress."

"I should regret such an event more than I can express," rejoined Mrs. Lacy. "I do not think them suited to one another, and while I do not go so far as you do in my dread of

hereditary taint, I frankly confess that I should not like to
receive as a daughter, Lamar's child, or the grandchild of Pompous Pinely."

And she laughed in pronouncing the odious nickname.

" Poor Laura ! " she resumed. " I shall never cease to regret that unfortunate summer at the Springs, where she met
this handsome stranger. Yet how bright and happy she was
when she came home with tidings of her approaching marriage ! "

" She was shamefully obstinate, shamelessly ungrateful, in
persisting in consummating her engagement before Mr. Lacy
could make proper inquiries about the fellow ! " said Miss
Morris, severely. " Another proof that bad blood is not easily
gotten rid of. Her father's predominant trait, next to his self-
conceit, was ingratitude. I have no patience with any of the
race ! You picked Laura up out of their pigsty of a hovel,
educated and clothed her like a lady, and she requited you by
throwing herself away upon the first graceless villain that addressed her. And her daughter takes every favor showed her
as composedly as if it were her due ! receives my darling
Lynn's homage as royalty might the service of a subject ! I
tell you it is an evil stock — root and branch."

" I shall not cast off Laura's child until she forfeits my favor
by some unpardonable transgression," said Mrs. Lacy, firmly.
" I have offered her a home while she chooses to keep it, and
my promise shall not be recalled."

" More shame to her that she accepts it ! " cried Miss Morris,
testily. " If she had one spark of true, worthy pride, she would
not remain the beneficiary of a stranger's bounty. Were I in
her place, I would teach, take in needlework, be a domestic
drudge, — yes, pick stones upon the highway, — before I would
live a dainty do-nothing, an elegant pensioner — dependent upon
charity for the very gown I wore and the bread I ate ! There
you see old Pinely, over again ! He would tease your negroes
to lend him — which meant to give him — fourpences and nine-
pences, sooner than he would work for an honest livelihood."

Here the outer door of the chamber opened to admit a servant, and the draught of air shutting the inner one, I left my post and came noiselessly away to my distant room.　＊　＊　＊

I have written out the above detailed account of the interview between my benefactress and her dear friend with a circumstantiality, an avoidance of intemperate comments, an absence of vituperative epithets that in another would amaze me. But for myself, I understand what is the meaning of this still heat — the white glow of intense, consuming wrath. Yet I knew all that I have just heard long ago — knew better than they could describe or imagine the horrors of that dark era — the cheerless middle age of my never-bright career. My defamer spoke lightly of starvation; of solitary confinement; of servile tasks performed by the lonely, neglected child. Did she guess at tales of cruel beatings and words yet more cruel? of crushed affections and insulted delicacy? of scenes and language that made cold, hunger, and darkness a welcome relief in comparison? If she had surmised aught of these, would her spirit have been moved to kindlier judgment of the grandchild of a worthless pauper, the child of a wicked adventurer? I do not believe it. She hates me not quite, — that could hardly be, — but nearly as bitterly as I do her.

Yes, I knew it all before — the pretty tale of my antecedents. Not from the Lacys. They have affected a profound reserve with respect to my mother's early history, — dating their accounts of her beauty and virtues from the period of her entrance into their service. They have a grand style of ignoring whatever they do not care to remember or to tell. My mother taught a species of charity-school founded by my Lady Bountiful while she was Miss Ida Ross, maiden *châtelaine* of Sunnybank. For this position " poor Laura " — as the cronies in council invariably styled her during their late interview — was educated by her youthful patroness, and she occupied it creditably to herself and her employers until she committed the heinous sin of falling in love on her own responsibility, and wedding the man of her choice. My lady shook her doubting

head over this folly ; but she nevertheless provided her late servant with a liberal *trousseau ;* Milord put a store of bank-notes
into her purse, and they sent her on her way with prayers and
blessings (verbal!) enough to have warded off the malign fates
for years to come. Only, nowadays, this sort of talisman is
wofully dubious in value. Indiscreet neighbors and gossipping
servants — and even the Sunnybank menials, will tattle — have
been less reticent than my mother's patrons and mine. From
these I have gathered how my grandfather — familiarly known
as Pompous Pinely — was in his youth the intimate and equal
of Mrs. Lacy's father ; how he managed, by drinking, gambling,
and horse-racing, to squander a handsome fortune, and after living with his family upon the charity of former friends until the
eldest child was eighteen years old, perished miserably, while
drunk, by falling into the fire upon the hearth of the hut he
called home. There are always benevolent people to repeat the
like agreeable stories to the persons most nearly interested therein. So much for the Pinely ' stock ' !

My father was, I doubt not, what Mrs. Lacy styled him — a
handsome adventurer. Music, language, drawing, and dancing-
master, by turns, he must have been a highly educated and
accomplished man, Miss Morris' assertion that he could only
teach the first-named of these branches, to the contrary. I,
also, am a believer in blood, and I know that the swollen tide
that throbs painfully through my veins at this instant, is of a
strain as rich and old as they can boast who dread to mingle the
current with theirs. And my beauty is of a nobler type than is
that of their irreproachable offspring. It likewise is an inherit-
ance. I have said that my father was a handsome man. My
mother, as I recollect her, — and the picture is as vivid in feature and coloring as if I had seen her die but yesterday, — was
lovely as an angel. But gently! I must not think of her
when I would keep my brain clear — my will steady.

So, Miss Morris, I am the chosen beloved of your prime
pet and *protégé !* a fact I might have been slow to suspect but
for your imprudent tongue. I credit the story — not because

5

you have told it in my hearing, but because it is corroborated by my own recollection of certain looks, words, and actions of your favorite which I passed over thoughtlessly for a time, in preoccupation of mind with other and weightier concerns. The Fate which it is the fashion of this pious household to denominate Providence has not thrown this information in my way without designing that I shall make use of it. If it serves no better purpose, it will enable me to persecute my persecutor. But with his mother on the *qui vive*, and his spinster guardian ever at hand to defeat my moves, it is well that I should be wary. I have the advantage of a thorough acquaintance with the boy — for boy he is, when compared with my mature womanliness and virtual old age of experience in the ways and wickedness of mankind. Beside these, he is a tender daisy of innocence — a guileless lamb.

Yet it is a noble youth! pure as a girl in life and thought. Heaven knows how much purer than some women whom the worlds call good and spotless! yet in courage and intellect beyond the suspicion of effeminacy. I have always liked, if not admired him more than I do his brother. There is a steadfast, searching look in Ross' eye which irks me when I am the object honored by his attention, and his blind devotion to his sister causes him to regard other women with indifference. I think that he neither quite likes or trusts me, while Lynn, if Miss Morris' testimony is admissible, adores me. Me! the Pariah, whose touch is contamination, in the estimation of his adopted aunt! the Bohemian, as his mother was pleased to designate me! the slighted woman whom another man has cast aside, as a tiresome bauble, for a girl whose character and affections, when contrasted with mine, are like milk-and-water to living fire! Shall I let him go on loving me? shall I lure him on to adore me yet more fondly? shall I — I do not say try to love him in return. That can never be. Would that it were not an impossibility! But shall I verify my well-wisher's prediction by *marrying* him?

Marrying! How well I recollect the first time the idea

occurred to me except as a vague dream, that I might escape
poverty, degradation, brutal unkindness, by becoming the cherished wife of one who loved me, — have a home, neat, cheerful, happy, — I cared not how humble, — that should be *his* and
mine! It was one spring Sabbath afternoon, bright and mild
— such March weather as rarely visits northern latitudes. My
father had arrayed himself in his least shabby suit, and gone
out, I could divine upon what errand, and sure of a few hours
of quiet, I had made our dingy little parlor as tidy as I could :
and put on my best gown — a delaine — black ground with a
tiny rose and bud upon it — I have a bit of it now laid away
with a lock of my mother's hair. It fitted me well, although I
had made it myself. I fastened my collar with a knot of
bright ribbon, and the purple-black braids of my thick hair
were wound like a coronet about my head. I studied the effect
in the mean little looking-glass between the windows, and decided that I was growing prettier every day. The conviction
made me feel better and happier. I fancy that most people are
better for being happy. While the good — or comfortable —
fit was on me, I took out my mother's Bible from the drawer,
and sat myself down to read. I promised her on her death-
bed that I would sometimes do this and think of her. While
thus engaged, I heard a knock at the door. I unclosed it cautiously, lest the visitor should prove to be one of my father's
boon companions, and saw, instead, Mr. Wilton.

"I called by to leave these with you," he said, offering me a
bunch of white hyacinths.

"How lovely!" I exclaimed. "And how fresh! Where did
you find them?"

"One of my Sabbath-school children gave them to me, — a
poor little lame girl, whose only garden is a row of boxes in a
garret window."

"I had forgotten, when I asked the question, what day it
was," I answered confusedly. For when I said "find them,"
I meant "buy them."

"Have you not been to church to-day?"

He said it gravely, but kindly, and the blood mounted to my temple as I returned a negative.

"May I talk a little while with you, when you have put my little Annie's flowers into water?" he continued yet more kindly, coming in.

I assented, and with the perfume of the hyacinths stealing toward me, and the strange calm of the Sabbath afternoon shutting us in from the world, I listened to his solemn, faithful teachings; his enumeration of the gifts with which nature had endowed me; the responsibilities imposed by these, and the duties which I, and I alone, should perform. It was not a lecture, but such honest, affectionate persuasion as moved me to tears.

"Do not think me harsh, Agatha," he said, seeing this. "But it grieves me to see your talents abused; your nobler traits of character perverted; your opportunities of doing good despised. You are a very proud sufferer; but I know that you do suffer much and often. I am nine years older than you are, my child, and I can foresee, more truly than you are able or willing to do, the heavier trials that lie in wait for you. You are motherless, and high-spirited, and ambitious. You will be beautiful, and you cannot fail to be admired. I would have you strengthened to meet sorrow and temptation, with the one infallible strength for fallible mortals. Forgive me if I have wounded you, and set it down to the sincere interest I have felt in you from the hour of our first meeting."

Then saying simply and fervently, "God bless you!" he left me.

I laid my head upon my mother's Bible, and cried yet more heartily, when he had gone. But they were not all sad tears. I had loved him dearly before. I felt that I could die for him now. I understood the purport of his warning, so delicately conveyed. Of all my father's pupils, he was the only one who behaved to me as if my poverty and unprotected situation were incentives to respectful treatment, instead of excuses for bold admiration and unseemly flirtation. His demeanor to me was courteous and modest, as if I had been a queen in disguise. He liked and esteemed me. Might not warmer feelings come with time and the development of such characteristics as he approved in me? It was a preposterous dream, but I had it out. I saw no more the poor room; the close streets; the foul, ill-ventilated city; the drunken father reeling home to heap abuse upon my head, and to meet sarcastic recrimination by curses — perchance blows; no more the godless household where heaven and religion were never named but with jeers and oaths; where poverty joined hands with guilt, and want was intensified by surly discontent. I painted a cottage among trees and flowers, and wide, green fields; myself redeemed from the debasing associations of my early life, elevated to the position of the mistress of this paradise, and deemed worthy of sitting at *his* side, his honored wife, in the sight of men and angels!

Oh! I did mean then to be good! to struggle upward through the deadly fogs that enwrapped me towards the light he had kindled in my sight. My Maker — if I have a Maker who can read hearts — knows how I tried to battle with inward evil and outward temptations. Yet here I am, to-night, suffering the torments of the lost, who, standing upon the shore of the great, fixed gulf, gnash their teeth at the spectacle of the bliss of the happy ones upon the other side, — envy, and hate, and blaspheme!

I have been raving, I believe! I will go back to the word that threw me off at a tangent. Marry him! become the wife — wedded and sure — of Lynn Holmes Lacy, Gentleman, of Sunnybank, a lineal descendant and honorable representative of one of those famous ornaments of our Republic — the first families of Virginia. It looks well and sounds well. This state, I am led to believe, I may take upon myself, whenever it pleases me to smile encouragement upon my, as yet, undeclared suitor. We would not be an ill-looking couple. I, with my dark beauty, would set off, and with advantage to both, his slender figure, chestnut hair, hazel eyes, and rather delicate, high-bred features. And she who holds his heart-strings may

5 *

lead him at will. His love for the mother who nursed him through a sickly childhood is wonderful, and others say very beautiful to behold. It would be a rare sight to witness, were he to turn a deaf ear to her solicitations, and take to his bosom the woman in whose hearing she has declared that such an alliance would make her wretched. In common with the rest of Milord's children and underlings, he looks up to his father as the embodiment of earthly wisdom and goodness ; accepts his highest expressed wish as a mandate ; resents any dissent from his opinion and will as an approach to sacrilege. Yet I am vain enough to fancy that I could work upon him to defy this supreme ruler of conscience and action. As to Miss Morris, when was ever a *passée* belle, however pert of tongue and quick of wit, an equal match for a beautiful, determined, and not over-dull girl, provided the umpire were a young man with love in his heart, and warm blood, instead of ice, in his veins?

I write it down, therefore, as a tolerably well-assured fact, that I can thwart my enemies, cover my tormentor with confusion, and win for myself an enviable worldly position by effecting this union. Maybe accomplish still more — maybe sear into insensibility this pulsating heart-nerve, the sharp agony of which is enough to drive one to distraction. I have heard of such results. The experiment may be worth trying. Now for a glance at the other side of the case. Milord took occasion, the other day, in the presence of his assembled household, to compliment my practical sagacity — my " excellent common sense," his lordship was pleased to say. Let me bring it into play by weighing the question fairly. I remain here, a humble dependant — since, *soit* my grandfather Pinely's aversion to ungentlemanly toil ; *soit* my father's taste for luxury and the fine arts ; *soit* my own decided disinclination to governessing, clear-starching, and road-mending, joined to divers recollections of the coarse drudgery which I have known by experience, and my censor from hearsay ; *soit* any one or all of these, the truth unquestionably exists that I infinitely prefer luxurious leisure — the opportunities and facilities for cultivating my personal and intellectual gifts — to ignoble and ill-paid toil. Honorable independence is a fine thing upon paper; but I love the ease of the flesh. This old house, with its lofty rooms, quaint nooks, and indescribable but delightful flavor of antiquity, suits me well; ditto the well-bred tone and habits of its inmates. I like to wear handsome dresses, rich silks, fleecy muslins, cobweb laces, and soft wools. I find that the thousand and one refinements and comforts which wealth can procure accord as well with my inclination, agree as admirably with my physical and mental health, as they do with those of the spoiled favorite of fortune, my benefactress' daughter. The better, doubtless, for I view each and all of them against a background of want and woe, such as she, soft, simple, sweet, innocent, never dreamed of. Soft and simple she may be, but she has had the art to win that to secure which I would have gone back to my former estate of destitution of bodily comfort, and reckoned myself rich if this were borne for and with him I loved.

I remain here, then, I was saying, a humble hanger-on of the Lacys, in unambitious singlehood, and grateful, make-one's-self-generally-useful dependence, and see the happy couple married; should she desire it — for she always gets whatever she takes it into her small brown head to covet — I may enjoy the high privilege of making myself as useful to Mrs. Wilton as I have done to Miss Elinor Lacy.

"To him that hath shall be given, and from him that hath not shall be taken away even that which he hath!" "*Even that which he hath!*" And for this I am expected and enjoined by the affluent pietists about me to be devoutly thankful! to revere and worship Him who has permitted the robbery of the weak and poor! to love the wealthy tyrant who has wrested from me my one precious possession.

CHAPTER V.

ELINOR.

"NOBODY talks anything but politics nowadays!" said Agatha, to-night, as I imparted to her, in an "aside," my dissatisfaction at the turn the conversation had taken.

This is true to a great extent. The discussion of national disorders has become the principal topic of fireside talk, as of popular harangues. As the Republic is a government of the people, — a joint-stock company, wherein the meanest citizen has his share, — so this unhappy rupture between North and South is regarded as the people's quarrel. Instead of leaving the settlement of the affair to rulers and statesmen of tried probity and acknowledged wisdom, men, women, and children are eager to thrust officious fingers into the wound, further to inflame and to tear it wider. Up to to-night I have had little anxiety as to the final result of the battle of words and newspapers. All that I know of the merits of the conflict I have learned from my father. He maintains that the Federal Union is the essence of national life, and while he looks with pain and pity upon the secession of the far Southern States from the great body of the united whole, he is yet, in common with most others of his party, sanguine as to the peaceful adjustment of the difficulty at no very distant day.

I have seldom heard Papa speak in public; but this morning, we ladies, instigated by Aunt Ellen, presented a petition to be allowed to accompany the gentlemen of our home-party to the Court House, where a meeting of the citizens of the county was to be held to decide upon the nature of the instructions to be delivered to their delegates in the Convention at Richmond.

The day being bland, we foresaw that the convocation would be upon the Court House green ; and Uncle Charley had privately engaged an upper room in the hotel overlooking this. Papa demurred, in doubt or modesty ; but we insisted, and carried the motion triumphantly.

Mamma sat at the same window with me, and I pleased myself with the fancy that one of the speakers of the day remembered who was concealed behind that blind. As I saw her eye gleam and lips part in breathless attention, heard her quick, irregular breathing during the more animated portions of the address, and when her hand closed upon mine, and a tear softened the brightness of her smile at the burst of applause that marked the conclusion of the oration, I comprehended what a mighty and beautiful thing was wedded love ; two hearts beating the same measure ; two souls welded into one, each interlink making the united twain stronger, happier, holier. It must have been a proud hour for the wife, when I, the child, felt such exultation in my father's success. I have never marvelled at his influence in his neighborhood and county. This could hardly be, when I have witnessed from my birth the potency of his mild, beneficent rule in his home ; yet I was unprepared for the ardent spirit, rising into enthusiasm, that characterized his eloquence. I had looked for calmer, more dispassionate argumentation throughout. How gloriously the patriotic fire leaped forth ! renewing his youth and thrilling his audience with electric sympathy !

Virginian in heart and soul he has ever been, but he seemed more proud than ever of his birth-state as he pictured the part he believed she was destined to play in the present emergency ; the noble stand she would take in resisting the aggressive wave of treason. He saw in her, he said, " the Great Pacificator, who, strong in the right, and determined to maintain it at all hazards, should yet speak, in calm majesty, to the fierce sea of national faction, and it should be still ; the Mother of States, who, unrolling the record of her illustrious sons, — the statesmen and warriors whom, in their lifetime, their brethren had delighted

to honor, — should command, in their name, the cessation of
the unnatural strife; and, bearing the olive-branch of compromise, — saying to the North, 'Give up!' and to the South,
'Keep not back!' — should win for the nation length of days,
and peace that should endure forever and ever, and for her own
head a crown of unfading glory." Brave in all things else as
we knew him to be, it was evident that he spoke truly when he
declared that he dared not contemplate the reverse of this picture. In a few brief, reluctant sentences, he portrayed the
vision of a gallant Commonwealth hurried, by an overstrained
and false sense of honor, and the flattering lures of specious
politicians, into a rebellion which she, at her yet loyal heart,
condemned and abhorred; her soil drenched with the blood
and swollen with the graves of her bravest sons; the Aceldama
of the Union, foul and horrible, spread widely over territory
where the fairest germ of that Union had been nursed into life
— a spectacle so monstrous in ghastliness of woe as to wring
from the spirit of every patriot who once gladly claimed Virginia as his birthplace a cry of bitterness like that which rent
the Saviour's heart as he wept over Jerusalem the doomed.

I have said that there were tears in Mamma's eyes when he
closed his appeal, and my own were brimming. I was not
ashamed of the weakness when I turned to find Harry at the
back of my chair, his face full of sympathetic emotion.

"You may well be grateful for such a father, Brownie," he
whispered. Then, to Mamma: "Mr. Lacy has done the cause
good service by this morning's work, my dear madam. I con-
gratulate both you and him."

I could smile, after this, at Aunt Ellen's theatrical exclamation, —

"'Almost thou persuadest me!' I will never listen to another Union speech while I live. As Sydney Smith said of
reading books prior to reviewing them, 'It prejudices one's
mind so horribly.'"

Escorted by Harry, we returned home to dinner. The rest
did not follow us until evening. Rolf Kingston came with

them, and supped with us. I was secretly sorry to see him; yet I had never felt more kindly toward him, — more disposed to make what reparation I could, by friendly words and actions, for the pain I had given him in the past. Surely, in the plenitude of my happiness, I can afford to bestow thus much pleasure upon one to whom I can never grant more.

After supper we were all gathered in the parlor — a large semicircle around the fire; for the night had brought a chill rain. Aunt Ellen opened the ball by one of her gay attacks upon my father.

"I always said that Ida, here, had married a tolerable copy of the Admirable Crichton; but if I had doubted it up to this morning, I should repeat the assertion confidently to-night. Is there anything which you cannot do, may I ask?"

"One or two things," answered Papa, with the indulgent smile that usually responds to her raillery.

At heart, he really loves and esteems her, as she does him; yet they are continually sparring.

"Such as what?" asked she.

"Such as reforming the heretical opinions of several good friends of mine upon certain subjects. Ida, dear," turning to Mamma, "did I tell you there was not a pound of rice to be found in any one of the three stores? West expects a supply to-morrow, he says. Ellen, you are versed in mediæval lore: do you know whether the Admirable Crichton purchased the family groceries in person?"

"History is silent upon that head," was the reply. "But, reasoning from common sense and analogy, I should say that he performed such duties as gracefully as he twanged his lute, and rode down his adversary in the lists. Your turn for practicalities amazes me. When your wife selected you as a partner in the dizzy waltz of life, I was decidedly of Beatrice's opinion with respect to Don Pedro — that, had I been in her place, I would not have married you unless I might have another for working-days. You were too costly to wear every day. You have disappointed me most agreeably. Do you know," re-

proachfully to Ross and Lynn, " what hindered my enjoyment
of your respected parent's distinguished effort of this forenoon?"

" Contrariety of sentiment," suggested Ross. _

" The sensation of being in the wrong," put in Uncle Charley,
taking his cigar from his mouth just long enough to utter the
sentence.

" I will finish *you* presently," retorted Aunt Ellen, nodding at
the latter. " But, as I was remarking, I could not rightly
enjoy the eloquent oration, because of the obtrusive regret that
neither of you degenerate boys will ever be half so handsome
as your father."

Papa bowed in mock confusion, his hand upon his heart.

" Certainly not," rejoined Lynn. " That would be an act of
disrespect incompatible with the general dutifulness of our behavior."

" Yes," pursued Aunt Ellen, meditatively ; " I highly approve
of your following your estimable patriarch's lead in everything
except his politics : they are behind the age."

" Mr. Lacy is too wise not to yield, in time, to the logic of
events," said Rolf Kingston, pleasantly. " We can afford to
wait until these shall work out his conviction and conversion.
The mail, to-day, brings news of the addition of another State
to the young Confederacy. The cause is gaining ground."

" There has been nothing to equal it in mad folly since the
devils entered into the herd of swine, and they all ran violently
down a steep place into the sea." Uncle Charley filliped his
cigar impatiently. " The demon of Disunion has entered the
masses, and they are on the stretch for the precipice. Let
wise men stand from under."

He returned his Habaña to his lips, and puffed in the long,
slow way peculiar to him when thoughtful or troubled.

" Oppression, robbery, and the threatened subversion of
cherished liberties, are stinging goads, which have, before now,
irritated men and nations to madness," said Rolf.

" I challenge you to produce a single man, between the
Alleghanies and the Chesapeake, who has been impoverished

or maltreated merely because he is not a Yankee and an Abolitionist," rejoined Uncle Charley. "This hue and cry about Anti-slavery fanatics and Personal Liberty bills, and violation of the Constitution is the clap-trap of thwarted politicians, ravening after the loaves and fishes upon which they have fattened for so many years."

"The Constitution!" repeated Rolf, catching at the word. "After all, therein lies the chief obstacle to the independence of the South. John Randolph says of the doctrine of consolidation, 'The Constitution was in its chrysalis state. I saw what Washington did not see: but two other men in Virginia saw it — George Mason and Patrick Henry — *the poison under its wings!*'"

"There is no use in attempting to disguise the truth that the ablest men of our state did, at the very time this Constitution was framed, foresee the danger that now hangs over us," said Lynn, candidly. "Hear Grayson in reference to this weak joint in a harness otherwise proof against repeated and violent attack — 'My greatest objection is, that it will, in its operation, be found unequal, grievous, and oppressive;' and he goes on to shadow forth, with amazing fidelity, the precise condition in which prominent southern leaders aver that we are now placed — the domination of the manufacturing and commercial section over the agricultural; burdensome taxation without adequate representation, — in short, the numberless encroachments of the North upon the prerogatives of the South. The whole article reads like a fulfilled prophecy."

A dead silence succeeded this observation. It had taken us all by surprise. I sat upon a low stool between Papa and Harry; and while the hand of the former only rested more heavily upon my shoulder, where it had lain since Uncle Charley's first remark, I felt Harry start and turn towards the speaker, as if uncertain whether he had heard aright; Ross gazed straight into the fire with a settled, gloomy air; Aunt Ellen and Mr. Kingston looked pleased, while I was almost sure that a swift, bright glance went from Agatha's eyes to Lynn's.

Mamma interfered, with her usual tact, to alter the saddened tone of the conversation.

"I have faith to believe that order will come out of chaos before long. At present, I do not deny that to me the political world seems bent upon enacting, upon a gigantic scale, the comedy of ' Much Ado about Nothing.' After diligent study of the newspapers of both sections, and much and tedious reading of speeches and manifestoes, I am yet in the dark as to what constitute the overt tyranny of the North and the wrongs of the South. As Stephen Blackpool says, ' it is a muddle !' "

" So were the waves after the case of wholesale *felo de se* to which I alluded just now," said Uncle Charley.

Whereupon, Mr. Kingston felt himself called upon to set forth at length the unrighteous dealings of the Government with the down-trodden Slave States and the exceeding beauty and justice of Secession. He spoke well and more temperately than I had feared he might do, for moderation is not his forte. His climax was an anathema fulminated against the outrageous iniquity of the election of a candidate by the votes of a faction, dominant, for the time, by reason of the lack of unanimity among the opposing party.

" You, too, had your sectional candidate !" My heart trembled as Harry entered upon the discussion of the dangerous theme. " What if he had been elected? "

" There is a radical dissimilarity between the cases," began Rolf.

Lawless Uncle Charley took up the sentence. " Yes — the case rivals that of the celebrated hypothesis of your bull goring my ox, and my enraged Taurus inflicting the like damage upon your peaceful domestic animal."

Rolf was evidently irritated by the smile that went around the circle.

" It is not in the nature of Southerners to submit to impertinent dictation, to interference with their property and opinions, especially from their inferiors," retorted he, hotly.

" 1 was not aware that the plaintiffs had suffered the latter indignity," replied Uncle Charley, with quiet contempt.

" For more than seventy years," — Harry's voice was low and calm, his enunciation deliberate, — " for more than seventy years, the South has lived and prospered under the Constitution that, according to the renowned authorities just now cited, harbored poison under its wings. Hers have been the chief places in our national councils, and the most lucrative offices in the gift of the Government. It is her boast, in the words of your most popular journal, which I now hold in my hand, that ' she has, since the organization of the Union, held the balance of power, as *it is her right to do*, her citizens being socially, intellectually, and morally superior to those of the North. But —' the editor goes on to say —' our whilom servants have, of late, strangely forgotten their places. They now aspire to an equal share in the administration of the Government. They have presumed to elect from their own ranks an illiterate, base-born, sectional tool, whom they rely upon to do their foul work of subverting our sovereignty. It is high time that the real masters awoke from their fatal lethargy, and forced their insubordinate hinds to stand, once more, cap in hand, at their behest.' "

" That is infamous ! — the ravings of a foolish or drunken blackguard," cried Ross, impatiently.

" It is mild abuse compared with the vituperations of one of to-day's orators," answered Harry. " Not an hour passes, when I am in the city, in which the substance of this paragraph is not uttered in my hearing. It remains to be seen whether the General Government — I do not use the word Yankees — for I speak of North, East, and West — twenty millions of freemen — whether these will bow their accustomed necks to the offered yoke, or —— "

He stopped.

" Well, sir ! Go on," urged Rolf, imperiously.

Harry fixed his clear, grave eyes upon the angry face of the other.

" Or, whether Law, Justice, RIGHT shall be triumphant ! "

"As it must be always," rejoined my father, emphatically, breaking his long silence. "I cannot believe that the Just Judge and Governor of the earth will suffer the vine He has planted to come to shameful nought — to perish utterly and disgracefully. In some portions of the vineyard, the fences are falling fast, and the wild boar of Secession is making sad havoc among the roots; but I am hopeful still."

"Is it not one of the laws of fermentation that it works clearness in the end?" asked Mamma, cheerfully.

"In the long run, it does," said Uncle Charley. "But sometimes the run is wofully long. All Christendom holds the belief that this crooked, crazy world will come out right and straight in the Millennium; but Armageddon and its valley, inundated with blood, must first be waded. I am no alarmist, but my prophetic spectacles are not of the same make as yours, Morton. My constant prayer is, that the horrid tide in which the bridles of the war-horses are to be dipped may not, in our day and sight, be fed by the blood of brothers, drawn by brothers' hands. I may be mistaken. I should be glad to be convicted as a timorous old graybeard and causeless croaker by the events of the next three months."

"I am no seer, although the son of a prophet," said Ross, bowing smilingly to his father. "But I share my mother's hopes of the peaceful settlement of this trouble. The great heart of the nation is yet sound and true. I think" — more lightly — "that the crushing injuries received by me, individually, at the hands of the Yankees, will hardly spur me up quite yet to sharpen my carving-knife for your throat, old fellow," clapping Harry upon the back.

"I predict civil war in less than ninety days," pronounced Rolf Kingston, portentously. "We are ready for it. If our enemies are not, the fault is theirs. Like honorable foes, we have given them timely warning."

"According to your code, what a pink of chivalry is a rattlesnake!" said Uncle Charley. "Do you know, my valiant Sir, what I would do with traitors, if I were President? I would treat them as sane Christians do rattlesnakes — put my heel upon them, and trample rattle and bite out of them!"

Again Mamma interposed to avert open contention.

"You are savage in your similes, to-night, Charley."

"He ate duck for supper. I notice that too much meat at night always makes a heathen of him," apologized Aunt Ellen.

Mamma joined in the laugh raised by this, as did Uncle Charley.

"Armageddon and rattlesnakes are unpleasant things to talk of before going to one's pillow," continued Mamma in the same jesting tone. "To my apprehension, the alarm raised by the blatant fire-eaters is like the shepherd's cry of 'wolf.' I hope that the good old Ship of State will ' sail on strong and great' when our children's children are in their graves."

"I think that I could not endure the agony of a contrary belief and live." Papa spoke abruptly, and with emotion.

He pushed back his chair, and began walking slowly up and down the room. We, left around the fire, looked at one another, surprised and awed by his manner — all feeling that the discussion had been pushed too far.

> "'Dies iræ — dies illa!
> Solvet sæclem in favilla!'"

he repeated, presently, coming back to us and leaning over Ross' chair. "What words of horror and grief are too strong in which to depict a calamity that is now the plaything of a thousand flippant tongues! A bleeding, dismembered Republic! a body of death, crumbling and falling apart, in place of a glorious, united, indissoluble Nation!"

"We, who uphold the right of Secession, declare that each State is a complete living system in itself; that separated from one or all of the rest, it could exist and act freely as before," said Rolf, but very respectfully.

"I have heard of ocean monsters, the fragments of which, when the main body was hacked to pieces, still retained life and

6 *

motion — became, as some affirm, each a new specimen of animated Nature," rejoined Uncle Charley. "But I did not know,
until now, that our Great Republic was a polypus."

Rolf bit his lip. I wish that Uncle Charley were not so
severe upon him. If he undertakes to correct or chastise all
who hold such sentiments as Rolf expressed to-night, he had
better turn the whole of the Southern States into a Reforma-
tory. That would not be a bad remedy for radicalism — confinement until the return of reason to the patient.

Aunt Ellen pretended to hide a yawn.

"More monsters, Charley! We shall have a menägerie
here pretty soon. Good people, one and all, doesn't it seem
to you that we have had 'somewhat too much of this'? It
is worse than folly to talk politics with those who do not agree
with you. By so doing you may possibly strengthen yourself
in your own belief, but there is a moral certainty that you will
establish your adversary ten times more stubbornly in his. I
am a rank rebel myself, but I love my ease too well to be forever raising a dust by attempts to promulgate my notions.
Time will bring you all around to my stand-point by and by.
Why should I fret myself about that which the gray old school-
master will teach you so much better than I could ever do,
even were you amenable to reason — which, allow me to say,
you are not. Mr. Wilton, Birdie, Ross, Lynn — we want some
music to take the taste of this talk out of our mouths."

Harry, long ago, fell into the habit of playing my accom-
paniments, and he was foremost in responding to the appeal.
As we stood together by the piano, looking over the music, he
said softly, "Your faith is not shaken by anything which has
been spoken here this evening?"

"No!" I answered, and added, what I afterwards said to
Agatha, "I dislike such talks excessively. They make me
uneasy and unhappy."

"Politics are an unsafe subject for parlor talk," he replied,
"for the obvious reason that in this day, they lie so near the
heart of every one who takes any interest in the signs of the

times, as to be a matter of vital self-interest. And " — more softly yet — "since they make *you* unhappy, we will have no more of them. I tried to remain quiet, to-night but I forgot myself once or twice. Where is Lynn?"

He was talking to Agatha, bending over her as she sat back, in an attitude of languid grace, upon the sofa. Aunt Ellen was watching them. I begin to suspect that she does not admire some of Agatha's ways, bewitching as I think them; and I had noticed her omission of Agatha's name in summoning the musicians of the party. From his shaded corner Rolf Kingston was regarding us with a fixity of gaze that disconcerted me. I called hastily to Agatha.

"Come, dear! we can do nothing without you."

"I must beg leave to be a listener," she pleaded.

Lynn broke out with an eager remonstrance.

"Do not urge her," said Aunt Ellen. "She does not belong to the class of young ladies who manœuvre to have an honor pressed upon them which they meant from the beginning to accept. Miss Agatha is the soul of sincerity."

"We all know that," I began; but Mamma raised her finger, unseen by Aunt Ellen and Agatha, as a signal of silence.

"My dear!" she said to the latter, "if you are not really indisposed to music, you will gratify us by taking your part with the rest."

Agatha arose instantly with the sweet smile that answers every request from my parents. But this time it was patient as well as sweet, and I found a chance, after a while, to ask her if she were quite well.

"In body — yes!" was the reply, accompanying a squeeze of my hand that made me writhe.

Dear, heroic girl! what can a volatile butterfly like me understand of the depths of a nature purified and strengthened as hers has been by months and years of sorrow? The least mist that comes between me and perfect happiness throws a chill gloom upon my heart. I cannot sleep, now, for the uncomfortable impression produced by this evening's talk I remember, uneasily, Uncle Charley's prognostications; Rolf Kingston's vaunting assertions; most distinctly, Lynn's advocacy of what our father — what we all believe to be the wrong side. I am haunted by visions of the woes shadowed forth by my father's graphic sketch of the forenoon. Mournful accents repeat in my ear, "Dies iræ — dies illa!"

Is this presentiment or girlish nervousness? — or is it that the shadows which checker the sunshine are deeper, more strongly defined, than those drawn by paler, less certain light?

CHAPTER VI.

AGATHA.

THIS is what I call life ! a ceaseless rush of events, that leaves one scanty leisure for reflection upon one's personal grievances.

" It is a sublime thought," said Rolf Kingston to me, this evening, " that we, the men and women of this age, are helping to make history. The time is very near at hand when every brave son of the South may be — not in a figurative sense, but literally — ' a hero in the strife.' "

" The more reason why you should not choose a Yankee poet as your fugleman ! " returned Miss Morris, smartly.

She does not admire Mr. Kingston. *Ni moi non plus !* but it suits me to make use of him, and we have gradually grown to be great friends.

We — that is, Elinor and I — came to the city a week ago. After the breaking up of the birthday party of Sunnybank, I do not scruple to state that the country was to me simply insupportable, the routine of every-day duty and falsely so-called recreation in the homestead the deadest of dead levels, made trebly hateful by the fierce warfare that went on within me. But for my neuralgic days — which at that epoch averaged three per week — I must have broken out into open frenzy — shocked my staid benefactors and their saintly daughter into spasms of holy horror at my outrageous impiety and more outrageous ingratitude. I survived it — thanks to the safety-valves aforesaid ; but the frequent repetition of these attacks aroused Mrs. Lacy's prudential solicitude. An invalid dependant would be an undesirable addition to her *ménage*, and she summoned the family physician. I played the interesting patient cleverly; answered readily and sweetly the questions with which the solemn old goose plied me; hearkened with profound respect to his disquisition upon the exceeding delicacy of the human nervous system; was assured by him that the pain which I thought was in my brain was in the scalp instead; said "scalp being a wonderful network of the finest and most sensitive nerves;" and I would have swallowed, without a grimace, whatever vile potion he had chosen to poison me with, had not my Lady made a suggestion that displayed more sense than his entire harangue.

"I have been thinking, Doctor, that a change of air and scene might benefit her. My friend Mrs. Dana, of Richmond, has written a pressing invitation to me to bring the whole family down this spring to visit her. This is impracticable; but I have considered seriously the expediency of sending Agatha and Elinor to her for a while. The drier atmosphere and more lively scenes of the city may exert a salutary effect upon Agatha's health.

"And Elinor's spirits," I longed to subjoin.

This show of maternal feeling towards her orphaned *protégée* doubtless misled the credulous man of medicine, who, in common with most of the denizens of the neighborhood, is a devout believer in my Lady's virtues; but I saw further into her motives. The "mocking-bird" had piped feebly of late. Her blood is luke-warm, and her nature shallow, but she had apparently missed the pleasurable excitement of her lover's presence. Mrs. Lacy is a fond mother, and because fond, observant. But the proprieties must be observed. Mrs. Grundy might frown, should Miss Elinor make a trip to the town wherein her betrothed is known to reside, unattended by a friend of her own sex. What more plausible pretext for such a movement could be devised than a journey and visit for restoring the health of the humble friend? The matter was adroitly managed. She introduced the subject of the proposed jaunt to Elinor when I was by.

"Mamma!" exclaimed the ingenuous young creature, whose

every look and sigh has entreated this boon for four weeks past. "Dear Mamma!" her breath coming in fluttering pants, and her cheeks like flame. "That would be delightful! But do you really think that it would be quite — that is — al together ——"

"Proper?" supplied "Mamma," with an amused smile. "If I were not assured that it was quite right — altogether proper — I should not propose the plan."

"Aha!" meditated audacious I, in malicious glee. "You tripped there, *Madame Mère!* Just now it was Agatha's delicate state that furnished the mainspring of your scheme. As if I had not known all along, that I might be at death's door for lack of change of prisons ; and if it pleased your daughter's whim to remain at Sunnybank, my only removal would be to the burying-ground over there!"

I wonder, by the way, whether they would desecrate the soil so long enriched by the dust of Rosses and Lacys, by laying there the offspring of a penniless adventurer and a charity-school teacher!

So we came to Richmond, and were hospitably received by Mrs. Dana, the widow of Mrs. Lacy's guardian, and sister-in-law of him who, next to Miss Morris, I most cordially dislike and dread of all my acquaintances — Elinor's eternally-quoted "Uncle Charley." He resides with Mrs. Dana, her daughters being married, and her sons settled in homes of their own. I find myself very comfortable here, being treated in some respects just as Elinor is, and in virtue of my invalidism receiving distinguished marks of attention from the family and regular visitors of the house. Not that I have escaped beyond the atmosphere of the Lacys. I did not hope for that. Only this afternoon, I lay upon a sofa in the library, feigning intense fatigue and drowsiness after a walk, and listened, with closed eyes and placid visage, to Mrs. Dana's talk, two hours long, with Miss Morris, upon the inexhaustible theme — Ida, Ida's husband, and Ida's children.

Miss Morris has spent the day here. Her nominal home is

in a fashionable boarding-house; but she is never there, except
at night. Her proclivity for inflicting her company upon her
friends is absolutely terrific; and since she knows everybody,
and visits everywhere, she is continually upon the wing. Rolf
Kingston made his appearance in the parlor, last evening, very
unexpectedly to all excepting myself. Elinor may imagine
that he has given her up — has, reversing the order of nature,
cast off the plumes of love to humble himself to the shell of
friendship. But my nature owns affinity too close with his —
wild, fervid, strong, in good or in evil, to credit the ridiculous
fable. I saw his eye flash, last night, in alighting upon her,
sitting apart from the rest, by a window overlooking the valley
and opposite hills, and talking with her accepted lover. If that
glance had been a drawn sword in keenness, as it was in glitter, those two lives would have been severed at once and forever
by the death of one of the pair. But sword-thrusts do not often
accompany jealous glances, in this degenerate day.

Like every second man whom one meets on the street, Rolf
came to town, he says, to attend the sessions of the Convention
— the august body of wiseacres sent hither, in solemn mockery,
by constituents as purblind, to decide, in the name of the State
of Virginia, a question the reply to which the Fates have already
written in the sight of the world. But these representatives of
a free and enlightened people seem to derive an infinite amount
of satisfaction from making speeches portentous as to length,
gaseous and fiery as to quality; the Union members stigmatizing their opponents as "traitors;" the Secessionists belabor-
ing them, in turn, as "base hounds of submissionists." Something must be done, I suppose, to while away the time allotted
to the farce. Meanwhile, the real storm of opinion, without
the halls of legislation, if less vociferous, waxes daily more
mighty. From far and near, people flock to swell the living
surges that sweep and dash, and mutter hoarse thunders about
the Capitol walls. It is, as Rolf Kingston says, an era in which
it is worth one's while to live, — whether it be true, as alarm-
ists have it, that the life of a nation is trembling in the bal-

ance, or whether this stupendous collection of combustibles will, after all, have an inglorious ending in smoke and harmless fireworks. It excites me — gives me something to think of besides my wrongs, and that is a wholesome change. I care so little, personally, which way the scale turns, that I can freely enjoy the play of others' passions.

Mr. Dana is cooler and more bitter than ever. Miss Morris and he invariably bring to my mind the famous Kilkenny cats, when they cross arms upon this topic of public affairs. Ross stands his ground tolerably well, although drilling nightly with the military company to which he has belonged since he was nineteen years old. Still he calls himself a Union man, and would probably be terribly incensed were he to happen upon any of the letters which his twin-brother despatches semi-weekly to me — the confidante — shall I say the cause? — of his growing change of political complexion. But decidedly the Unionist, *par excellence*, of our present family group, excluding Mr. Wilton, is the awhile-ago uncontroversial Elinor. I laughed heartily to-night to see her plumage ruffle spiritedly and her face flush at a sharp attack of Rolf Kingston upon the opposite party. It was aimed, I saw, more at Mr. Wilton than at the political opponents of the speaker — abstractly considered ; but the gentleman assailed, being engaged in turning over a book of engravings for the amusement of one of our hostess's grand-children, seemed not to notice the ferocious onslaught of his rival. Elinor sprang to her arms very much as the brown wren, of which she reminds me, might fly to the defence of her brood, and there ensued a lively skirmish, in which she assured-ly was not worsted.

" You are a valiant, but a very silly little thing ! " remarked Miss Morris, stroking the pretty brown head, that has an ex-pression of invitation to the caressing touch of all whom the owner loves. " What difference will it make to you whether the old government stands or falls? You will get your berries, water, and occasional lump of sugar, all the same, whichsoever may be the dominant power."

"Certainly — the South being able to supply all three of these from her own resources," said Rolf, in reference to Elinor's assertion that this section of the country would be the chief sufferer from the non-intercourse of the two.

"Yes, I suppose there would be enough left at the end of a year's blockade to feed the birds of the air," rejoined the simple damsel, with engaging archness. "And little else!" she added, after a second's pause.

"We will never be reduced to such a strait that we cannot offer food and homes to our friends — bullets, powder, and a bloody, dishonored grave to our enemies!" Rolf blazed out, boldly and warmly. "You can tell this to your Yankee teachers, Miss Elinor, at your next lesson."

My heart bounded slightly with apprehension or excitement at this; but a stealthy glance showed me Harry's unmoved countenance, still bending over the prints, kind and genial, as he listened to or talked with his play-fellow. For all that he appeared to know or care, Rolf Kingston and his doughty demonstrations might have been a hundred miles removed from his cognizance.

"Thank you, Mr. Kingston," said the miniature duchess, drawing up her wee figure with cool *hauteur*, that gave her a marvellous resemblance to her lady-mother. "But I employ no teachers who would be the wiser for any information that I could offer. Their vocation is to impart, not receive, instruction. Uncle Charley!" as that individual made his appearance at the door, "you are impatient for your game of chess, I see. I am ready to give you your revenge, for beating you so frightfully last night."

"And I will have mine, some day!" said Rolf's black eyes, as he champed the ends of his mustache.

Catching my look, he colored — then returned it with one full of meaning, and crossed the room to where I sat.

"You and I ought to have a verbal understanding, instead of the tacit sympathy that has existed between us for so long," he said, in a guarded undertone, drowned by Miss Morris's chatter with Mrs. Dana, the rattle of the chessmen, as they were arranged in opposing rows, and Jeannie's merry prattle.

"I have no objection," I answered, kindly; "that is, if my counsel or sympathy can benefit you."

"You are too clear-sighted not to perceive the position in which I stand just now," he said, hesitating a little, as if the disclosure were an awkward or difficult one to make in words. Rallying, he dived *in medias res.* "I have loved her ever since I was fifteen and she ten years old. I have offered myself to her four times. I shall never give her up until she is married to another; and then,"—drawing in his breath hissingly,—"unless I am bound hand and foot, I shall kill him!"

Fortunately, I am not easily scared, and the tawny glare in his eyes, the desperate resolve expressed by feature and tone, merely sent my blood a trifle faster through my veins,—thrilled me, as a slight electric shock would have done. And this while I felt that his talk was not all gasconade,—that he had made up his mind to pursue the girl who had set his wild nature on fire, up to her wedding-day, and then murder the man who had robbed him of her. Nice, agreeable discourse this for a respectable elderly widow's respectable parlor, within earshot— did they choose to play eavesdroppers—of said widow, and an equally respectable elderly bachelor, to say nothing of an any-thing-but-respectable-and-steady tattler of an old maid! I showed, because I felt, no symptoms of fear or faintness at the sanguinary picture.

"Behold how great a matter a little fire kindleth!" I answered, in pitying jest. "I should hardly have expected that one like her could have stirred your heart to its depths. But"—more seriously compassionate—"I see that this is so!"

He stared at me—half-soothed, half-affronted.

"One like her! Miss Agatha! Her equal has never yet been created! She is a diamond without a flaw! the brightest, love-liest, purest fairy, that ever a base mortal, such as I acknowl-edge myself to be, dared worship and woo! I am not worthy of her now, — I can never be her peer in virtue and goodness; but she could mould me into whatever likeness she wished. I would submit to any probation — any length and severity of novitiate — if I had but the hope of final reward — her love — held up to me. I am here to-night, because it has become next to impossible for me to live out of sight of her. And what does she care for this entireness of devotion — this ardor of affection which time, and slights, and coldness, and actual repulse have not availed to cool? Less — much less than she does for the liking and good will of that snarling old cynic whom she is now amusing!"

This was downright fatuity, and threatened to degenerate into drivelling whimpering over the lost dolly which those cross-grained beldams, Miss Atropos and sisters, had refused to give into his embrace. I respected him less than when he had talked of murder with malice prepense.

"Excuse me for the hint," I offered with amiable reluctance. "But it strikes me that your behavior to her is often the reverse of conciliatory. I have reason to believe that it pains her when you address her as you have already done twice this evening. Do not be angry, while I tell you a little story of a custom prevalent in one of the South Sea Islands. When a youth becomes enamoured of a maiden there, he goes to the spring to which she is in the habit of repairing for water, and lies in ambush until she appears. Then, approaching her unseen, he knocks her senseless with a club, and carries her off in triumph to his home. Custom reconciles. one to many odd fashions; but this one is not likely to be popular in civilized countries."

He did not smile, but neither did he seem offended — only sad and meditative.

"Is this so? Am I then an unmitigated brute — a rough, coarse barbarian, where I would inspire love and confidence? And to *her* — poor tender Birdie!"

Now, I respected him least of all! I could have laid a horse-whip soundly over his comely shoulders for his boyish wanderings. What is there about this deer-eyed russet-skinned elfin girl, with her bird-like chirp, and swift, skimming gait, that so fascinates all who behold her, with the solitary exception of my stony-hearted self? Upon this subject, Rolf Kingston might and did talk like a fool; but in other respects, I knew him to be the reverse of a blockhead. This master-passion of his soul, measuring its age by decades, is not the blind adoration of a raw country lad for a moderately pretty face and sweet smile. His natural abilities are fine, and they have been improved by travel and cultivation. He has seen fair and wise women in this and in other lands; yet he turns aside from all to prostrate himself before this insignificant specimen of femininity with spirit as abject as was simple Harry Foker's when he prayed that French weasel, Blanche Amory, to put her foot upon his neck.

Rolf shook off his reverie, with an effort to regain his manliness, after the repentant ejaculation last recorded.

"You cannot understand how I am wrought up to say things that sound to others unkind and ungentlemanly!" he pleaded, deprecatingly. "Just now, for instance, it nettled me to hear her quoting the Submissionist cant which I was certain she had caught from that confoundedly cool hand over there" — motioning slightly towards Harry. "I want you to be perfectly frank with me. Do you believe that she is engaged — that she will ever be engaged to that — that ——"

"Gentleman!" I finished the sentence.

He smiled — or rather sneered. "I suppose that we may as well call him by that name whether he is entitled to it or not! Will she ever marry him?"

"Never!"

I was not conscious that I intended to utter the word, until I heard the hollow echo of a voice that did not sound like mine, and saw the blended surprise and relief portrayed upon his visage. Did devil or prophetic angel speak through my lips?

"Thank you! You are a better judge than I — not merely because you have more and better opportunities of observation,

7 *

but you are more impartial. Jealousy warps the perceptions fearfully!"

"You need not tell me that!" I returned.

He absolutely laughed now — like a boy from whose mind a great load had been lifted.

"I dare say I have made myself ridiculous in your eyes. Nor do I expect you to comprehend the extent of the service you have done me. The day may come when you can understand it better than you do now. If it should, I hope it may be in my power to testify by my deeds how grateful I am for the sisterly sympathy, the wise advice, you have given me."

"It is little to give, but sympathy is all I have to offer my friends in their trouble or their joy," I said, tremulously. "You recollect the fable of the lion and the mouse. I cannot offer to gnaw asunder the meshes of the net Love has thrown over you. You would not thank me for the proposal or the act. Still, exigencies may arise in which I can be of use or comfort to you. If so, command me! For the present, be sure that you have my best wishes for your success — for your final happiness."

His conceit did not strangle at the huge sugar-pill. I marked, with wicked glee, his bow of grateful acknowledgment of his puissance and my impotence, — as a king might bend to a pretty peasant who restored a fallen pocket handkerchief to his Majesty.

As if I did not hold his most precious heart-secret in my hand, untrammelled by promise of safe-keeping! as if I had not read him through, during this brief dialogue, as easily as a child does a primer, — his weaknesses, his hopes, his dreads, — while he was ignorant of my hidden history as "swart Paynims" of the missal to which poor Keats likens his Madeleine's heart! Men are massive machines, but the works are generally ridiculously simple in structure and arrangement. A woman's eye and hand are seldom long in detecting and regulating the motive power.

Luckily for my enjoyment of the evening, Mr. Kingston had

an engagement elsewhere, and his departure left me free to join Harry and Jeannie at their remote stand. We turned over the engravings, happily, for a season. I am learning to control myself outwardly in his presence. I copy diligently the gentleness which he once told me was one of his betrothed's chief charms. I guard sedulously against the morbid outbursts which he has also told me — more than once — pained and repelled him, — I infer from the connection in which the remark is usually made, because this same pattern for the unimportant remainder of her sex never yields to such sinful repinings, such injurious doubts of her kind. It would be strange if she did. If no one had ever treated me cruelly; if I had never looked vainly into a human face for love and smiles; if poverty, dependence, and enforced sycophancy were to me matters of far-off hearsay, the probability is that I should be on excellent terms with myself and the world at large. But my conduct has been exemplary recently, and my hero has repeatedly signified his approbation of it. He is extravagantly fond of children, and they always love him. There was more reality than pretence in his semblance of content as he sat apart with his young favorite. When I drew near, she vacated her chair, and remained standing beside him, her arm about his neck, her sunny curls mingling with his dark locks. Now and then, while we talked, her hand stole up to his cheek in timid caressing. He smiled the second time this happened, and detaining the shy fingers in his, pressed them silently to his lips.

It is Harry Wilton's nature to love all things innocent, helpless, and affectionate; and in observing this fresh proof of this trait, the thought smote me suddenly and sharply, as though it had never pierced me until then, that Elinor's winning, artless manner, her *naïve* sprightliness, her ready smile and frank speech, had, by appealing to this his vulnerable point, beguiled him into the belief that she would make a congenial companion for life. The oak invites the vine to cling, — takes pleasure, maybe, in its soft clasp and bright leaves; but when the storm bows its proud head, the monarch needs a mate more stanch and hardy, whose boughs, interlaced with a grasp like the death-hold, may stay him against the blast. Would the self-deceived man ever awake to a knowledge of his error? and if so — when? Revolving these things in my mind, I smiled sweetly, talked dispassionately and sensibly, as I might have done with my great-uncle. By and by, I saw his face light up with a smile of peculiar radiance, — a gleam my gayest sallies and most engaging wiles have never called forth, — and I knew, before I felt her lean over my shoulder, who had approached us. Harry arose, disengaging Jeannie's arm from his neck, although he still kept her hand in his, and offered a chair to his fair one. She declined it. She "preferred to stand — was tired of sitting," and he, perforce, must stand also.

"You were the victor in both games!" he said, gently, con-gratulatorily.

How had he known this, when they had been divided by the width of the room, and I had not seen him glance once towards her?

"Yes! Poor Uncle Charley!" she laughed; "his hand is losing its cunning!"

This to her late opponent, who had followed her.

"Say, rather, that yours has learned new tricks!" was his rejoinder; "Yankee tricks, I suspect!" menacingly, to Mr. Wilton.

The chess-board is often an accessory to, or diversion from, the love-making of the engaged pair; so it was quite *en régle* that Mr. Wilton should smile proudly down at his pupil, and that she should return the smile by a blush.

"Are you weary of victory, or can you play one game more?" he asked, next.

She moved off with him, with dutiful alacrity, toward the table she had lately quitted. Mr. Dana took the chair next mine, and Jeannie's grandmother sent her to bed. I, left with an old bachelor and a picture-book upon my hands, withdrew next, upon plea of my health. Ten minutes later, I heard Miss

Morris leave the house under Mr. Dana's escort, and Mrs. Dana passed my chamber on her way to hers.

Those two are alone in the parlor now, — looking into each other's eyes and each other's hearts, secure from angry and jealous observation ; the outer world, with its strifes, its changes, and its passions, swept far away from sense and thought. I may, at times, lull the pang that is ever eating into my heart, by picturing to myself the awakening that may, that ought to come to him, but I do not delude myself with the fancy that it has begun yet. His infatuation is greater this hour, than when he first declared his love. I see it — I feel it — and I live ! I sit here in the lone night-watches, and await her appearance in the room we together occupy. I know, when she gives me a good-night kiss, that her lips are warm and quivering from the pressure of his ; that his hands have held hers ; that the happy murmurs I hear in her dreams are repetitions of his fond tones.

" The day may come when you will understand this subject better than you do now ! " spoke Rolf Kingston, out of the pitiful pool of his experience.

Will it?

CHAPTER VII.

ELINOR.

April 16.

IT is over! For two days, the air had been thick with rumors of war and bloodshed. For two days, the eyes and thoughts of the Nation had been fixed upon that fire-girt Southern Island, with its brave, but feeble garrison, — the Representative of that Nation's majesty, — testifying in the defiant boom of every cannon's answer to the rebel bombardment, that resistance to armed treason is henceforward to be learned as one of the Nation's laws. For two days, thousands and hundreds of thousands of loyal hearts, all over this broad land, had cried mightily unto our country's GOD to avert this last and direst trial, — the humiliation of our flag by hands that once helped to rear it in the sight of the world as the beloved ensign of National faith. But under the whole expanse of heaven there was no answer to these prayers except the reverberation of the cruel guns. On Saturday — the 14th of April — the end came!

I had promised to walk with Harry, and, equipped for the excursion, was entering the parlor, where he awaited me, when the breathless calm, that had brooded over the city for twenty four hours past, was broken by the sullen roar of a cannon. Another and another followed.

"Seven!" I exclaimed, sick and shuddering.

The signal was unexpected, but I interpreted the dread significance of the number of the revolted States.

Harry caught my hands, and led me to the sofa.

"It must be true, dearest! The fort has fallen!"

Then he dropped his head upon the arm of the sofa, and was

mute. I knelt before him, praying him to be comforted; but my own spirit was bowed to the lowest dust. While I spoke words of hope and resignation to him, my rebellious heart was crying out, "Hath the Lord forgotten to be gracious?"

"Poor, trembling darling!" Harry said, presently, lifting a countenance pale, indeed, but steadfast and even smiling, as he addressed me. "I ought to be ashamed of myself for failing you at this moment! We will be courageous now, love! Will you wait for me here, while I go out to learn the worst?"

"I will go with you!" I answered; and in two minutes more we were in the open air.

The scene there presented will be with me while life remains. The street was alive with people; Secession flags blossomed in rank luxuriance, in windows and from roofs; were waved from doors and porches by girls and women; carried aloft, in mad exultation, by boys along the sidewalks; hung upon lamp-posts and stretched from side to side of the thoroughfare. Joy, intoxicating and unbounded — riotous delight — was manifested everywhere, by all classes. Staid citizens threw up their hats and hurrahed that Sumter had fallen, and ladies elegantly dressed and refined, in feature and carriage, sounded the same refrain from the balconies of stately dwellings. It was a carnival scene — bewildering, exciting, frantic. Harry spoke but once in our hurried passage along the route to the Capitol Square, whither we were swept by the stream of jubilant pedestrians. In the porch of a handsome house stood a lady whom we both knew — a young and happy wife and mother. She held her babe, a laughing boy of ten months, aloft in her arms. With both chubby hands he grasped a flag bearing the stars and bars, and upon his bosom was pinned a rebel cockade.

"Hurrah, my little man! Sumter is down, and the Yankee nation will soon follow!" she cried, in the shrill accents of intense joy, as we passed.

"And you may bemoan this day in tears of blood!" uttered Harry, low and huskily. "Is the world going mad?"

One might have thought it, from the spectacle presented in

the square. Every avenue leading to it was thronged. The
beautiful grounds were filled, and upon the southern terrace was
the park of artillery that had fired the salute. The Governor's
mansion was beleaguered by a moving mass of figures, and, as
we entered the upper gate, a long procession issued from the
western door of the Capitol, and descended the steps.

"The Convention has adjourned for the day," said Harry.
"Stand back here out of the press until they have gone!"

They went by in groups of two, three, and more; some
striding on in haste or excitement, talking loudly and gesticu-
lating gleefully. Others were grave and slow, deep in conversation that reached no ears except those for which it was
intended; others yet, — and these were easily distinguishable as
prominent Unionists, — with depressed heads and visages set in
wordless sadness. One of these, recognizing Harry, approached
us, and with a brief apology to me, drew him a few paces apart.

Withdrawing my eyes from them, lest I should glean something of what was evidently a confidential conversation, I
discovered that I was standing at the base of Crawford's monument — his last and greatest work. Above me towered the
colossal equestrian figure of WASHINGTON, and the tearless sorrow, that already hindered respiration and made speech impossible, nearly choked me as I gazed upon the almost divine
sweetness and dignity in the countenance of the Father whom
Virginia had given to a united people. Was the dear name,
"Patriæ Pater," to be from this day a forbidden word? Harry
and his friend still conferred apart, and leaning against the
pedestal of HENRY's staute, I turned my thoughts from the scene
before me to the other and far different one conjured up by
memory.

Three short years before, I had seen collected here statesmen,
orators, and poets — honorable men not a few — and a mighty
concourse of citizens from North, East, South, and West, to
unite in doing homage to the names of the great ones whose
deeds and virtues were commemorated by the enduring marble
and bronze. EVERETT, WISE, and YANCEY had then joined

hands and proclaimed, in stirring strains, their perpetual brother-
hood; had sat, side by side, in the view of admiring thousands,
in the august semicircle that held SCOTT as the hoary and
majestic keystone of the arch. *Now* — O, it were meet that a
pall should hide the magnificent pile from the light of heaven,
since upon our National Ensign had been written — "Ichabod!"

A cheer from the crowd called my attention to the Capitol —
and I saw, with horror and indignation I cannot describe — the
rebel flag floating from the roof!

Harry came up to me instantly. He was whiter than when
he had left me, and the rigidity of his features was like that of
the bronze visages above us.

"I cannot breathe here!" he said. "Take my arm, and let
us get out of the crowd!"

Not another word passed until we were far beyond the tumult,
in quiet, embowered streets, the inhabitants of which seemed to
have forsaken them for the lower parts of the town; where the
sound of our footsteps was strangely distinct, as we loitered along
the pavement, and the narrator's voice was lowered, lest his story
should be audible to chance listeners behind the blinds of the
still houses.

Such a tale as it was! There is no need, in this generation,
to write the details of the fight. They are stamped, as with
fire, upon the memory of the youngest child, who knows, to-day,
how Sumter was assailed, and how it fell. I — a southern
woman — will never set down the shameful record, although it
may be that no eyes but mine will read this page.

"There are two rifts of light in the cloud!" I remarked,
when Harry was through.

I tried to say it cheerfully, for he had grown paler and more
sorrowful with every word.

"What are they?"

"First, the lives of the handful of brave, true, soldiers have
been mercifully — I might say, miraculously — preserved."

"GOD bless every one of them!" interrupted my listener.

"Amen!" I said, fervently. "Then, again, this overt act

of treason on the part of those whose watchword, until now, has been peaceful separation; the barbarous attack upon those whose only crime was fidelity to the charge committed to them by their government and ours; the outrage offered our dear old Flag,—must open the eyes of all wise and good men to the real *animus* of the rebellion. If there is a spark of patriotic fire left in the hearts of those who have, until now, wavered between treason and loyalty, this must fan it into a flame. To-day's work will decide the great question in Virginia. She cannot hang back now."

"I believe that she will not! But let us dismiss politics once more, Nellie! I am heart-sick, and I would like to forget the whole hateful subject—if I can! Here is our favorite view, and it was never more lovely."

We were upon the summit of Gamble's Hill, overlooking the armory, the river, Belle Isle, and the surrounding islets,—each with its willow grove,—the flashing rapids, and the verdant slopes beyond. To our right lay Hollywood, beautiful in its wooded hills, and streams, and peaceful valleys, with their sacred treasure of peaceful sleepers. To our left stretched out the city of the living,—noble and fair,—and, in the distance, as still as that of the dead. I heard my sigh echoed yet more heavily by my companion, and my hand was pressed closely to his side; but I felt that it was not the time to attempt further spoken consolation. I let the lovely landscape, the bright, soft afternoon, the solemn, soothing monotone of the river, do their own work upon his perturbed spirit. At last he raised his arm, and pointed northward. A long, low line of cloud hung upon the horizon,—dun, with brassy edges,—sullen and dense, save where a rainbow, vivid with emerald, rose-color, and gold, spanned the murky vapor—a happy smile, cast by the sun's last rays.

"Fair weather cometh out of the north! With the Lord is terrible majesty!" repeated Harry clearly—triumphantly. "After all, darling, He reigns!"

This one thought I have kept folded to my heart all through

the Sabbath.   So unlike a Sabbath it seemed, amidst mutter-
ings of sedition and organized resistance to governmental punishment, with the marked omission, in every pulpit, of the
prayer for the Chief Magistrate and others in authority; with
scanty congregations in the sanctuary, and throngs of earnest
talkers at the street corners!   I have remembered it all through
this day, when the mutter has waxed into a roar of revolt at
the proclamation from the President, calling out an armed force
of seventy-five thousand men to quell the rebellion.

This afternoon, the only Union ensign displayed in the city
since Saturday — which had streamed in solitary beauty from a
flag-staff in the garden of a wealthy and influential citizen — was
hauled down.   For the present, until the heat of the popular
indignation shall subside, the stars and stripes are banned!
The night is cold and dark, as no other night has ever been,
when I think upon this; but I hope still.   By the order of the
Governor, the Secession flag has been removed from the roof of
the Capitol, and in its stead there streams the banner of our
grand, brave, old Mother, reminding the vacillating and faint-
hearted of her worthy deeds of yore, her consistent adherence
to the cause of Right and Freedom, and, with her sublime " Sic
Semper," bringing comfort, hope — to me, at least, assurance.
It cannot be ——

*   *   *   *

RICHMOND, Monday Evening, April 16, 1861.

DARLING ELINOR: I wrote those two words half an hour
ago, since which time I have sat gazing at them, like one
stupefied, not knowing how to go on with what I have to say.
I told you, this morning, that I would, if possible, come to you
this evening.   Several circumstances combine to keep me away.
I am very busy.   Work that would require a month for its
proper accomplishment, must be done in less than two days.
Yet, if I can take time in which to write, I might as easily
spare it for a personal interview.   This I *dare* not do!   This is
the plain truth.   I never thought myself a coward until now,

when I find that I am afraid to look into your eyes, and speak what you must nevertheless learn from me — me alone.

I love you, — I do not declare as man never loved woman before, — but as I never loved anything else upon earth. I believe that you love me, and I prize this belief as I prize nothing beside, excepting my hope of heaven. Yet, while this knowledge is fresh and new, — when I have just come to a full appreciation of how sweet it is, and how rich I am, I must leave you — leave without a definite appointment of reunion, — the pain of parting softened only by my faith in you and trust in the Good Father of us both! My precious love! my almost wife! this is very bitter! No wonder that my soul refuses to receive the consciousness as truth! Let me explain my meaning briefly and simply as I can. The convention, as you may have already heard, went into secret session this afternoon. I have believed, since Saturday, that this would be its next act; have known what the object of such action would be, viz., to shield from the fury of the populace such members as should cast their votes against the ordinance of Secession. That this must now pass is beyond the shadow of a doubt. You understand this, dear? The passage of the ordinance is a foregone conclusion. You said truly to me, the other day, that your state must now assume a decided position. She will side with her southern sisters — not because they are right, but because they *are* her sisters. This done, Richmond nor Virginia is any longer a place for me. I have no option in the matter. My sentiments — which cannot change — with respect to the political heresy of disunion are too well known for me to be overlooked when the victorious party shall come into power. If protest, if martyrdom, would avail to check the tide of evil, I would stand my ground and abide the result. But the sacrifice of liberty and life would be useless. Like most desperate diseases, political and physical, this will run its course. Already I have received friendly warnings, as well as threatening notices, to the effect that " men of my stripe " — that is the phrase — " had better depart speedily from the midst of the faithful."

I am not a Virginian by birth or breeding; but you will bear me witness — you, to whom I have laid bare my every thought — how fervent is the love I have for my adopted State. If for no other reason, I should prefer a residence within her bounds to any other location, because here is your home. I shall return to New York, and there begin my business life anew. Pecuniarily, I sacrifice much by the removal, for this revolution has taken me by surprise, and, in a mercantile point of view, at a disadvantage. I hope that I shall be able to meet all my liabilities promptly, and leave behind me an untarnished name, at the same time preserving my credit at the North; but this will spare me very little available capital for future operations. I tell you all this, my love, as if you were, in truth, my wife. You deserve this frankness from me. It may be a year — it may be more — I pray that it may be less — before I can offer you a home; and then it will probably be very different from that I had planned for my " mocking-bird." But it will be ours — yours and mine — and you will come to it. Something within me assures me of this. Buoyed by this promise, I shall work hard, very hard; and if, at times, my heart is faint with longings for a sound of your voice, for a ray from your dear eyes, the angels of love and hope will not let me be utterly cast down.

I will not wound you by asking you to be true, or by assuring you of my continued constancy. Such useless vows would mock the holy union of our souls. You are mine, Brownie, "until death do us part." I shall call early in the morning, and during the two days that yet remain to me here, I trust to be much with you. I had not known how I dreaded to make this revelation to you, until I felt that I could not do it by word of mouth. Now that all is said, I torment myself with fancies of the probable effect of the tidings upon you. That it will shock and sadden you, I know. Your sweet face will be pale to-morrow, and the great, brown eyes will have a look of patient suffering I have never before seen in them. I feel like an inhuman wretch when I think of this as my work — my doing — when,

8 *

all the while, I would joyfully bear your share of the burden with my own, if I could!

I wrote to your father, last night, confiding to him my fears and plans. He will take care of you for me. This knowledge lessens my weight of sorrow. Blessed is he who can commit his choicest treasure to the keeping of such a father! And our mother will be more tender than ever to my lonely-hearted girl. These reflections comfort me; but dearer than all other consolations is the thought of our mutual love and truth. Sustained by this, we will meet the parting bravely; will wait, with the patience the gracious human Saviour will surely grant us, for the dawn of better days. Forgive me the pain I have unwillingly caused you. If I have erred in selecting the mode of making this communication to you, attribute the fault to my judgment — not to my heart. .

For my sake, try and sleep to-night, that your heavy eyes may not reproach me too sorely to-morrow.

Your own

HARRY.

CHAPTER VIII.

AGATHA.

I HAD been out to make a call upon an acquaintance last Monday evening, just a week ago to-night. Mr. Kingston, who, since our confidential confabulation No. 1, has taken me under his gracious patronage, was my escort. We returned to Mrs. Dana's about ten o'clock, and being, by this time, slightly *ennuyée* of my friends' talk, which ran chiefly upon the perfections of Miss Elinor Lacy, I said, as I rang the bell, —

" I suppose that Elinor is invisible by this time. She retired to her room with a headache before we went out."

The *ruse* succeeded. He bowed himself off without entering the door, which was opened by a servant.

" Has everybody gone to bed?" I inquired, struck by the stillness that reigned in the lower part of the house.

" Mistress has!" was the reply. " She was very tired, she told me to say to you, and hoped you'd excuse her, and make yourself at home. Mars' Charles ain't come in yet."

" And Miss Elinor?"

" She is in the library, I b'lieve, ma'am."

" Alone?"

And to my surprise the answer was, " Yes, ma'am — leastways, she was, awhile ago, when I took a letter to her that had been left at the door."

A letter and no visitor! This was queer, for I knew she expected her betrothed that evening. I dismissed the servant, and proceeded forthwith to the library. I knocked once, twice — thrice, without receiving an answer. I unclosed the door, and advanced into the room. Elinor's writing-desk stood open upon the writing-table. I had seen her busy at it when I peeped into her sanctum, just before I went out. She sat in the arm-chair beside it, where I had left her, apparently asleep now, an open letter lying in her lap. A step nearer showed me that her unconsciousness was not the result of natural slumber. She lay against the cushioned back of the chair, in a dead faint — colorless and breathless as a corpse. Most women would have shrieked, or dropped into a swoon themselves at the sight. But I am not made of the same stuff as are other women, and my primal act was to try and discover what all this meant. I picked up the letter that had fallen from her relaxed fingers. The hand was familiar. It was also clear, round, compact. A very few minutes sufficed to put me into possession of the contents.

Harry Wilton was going away, — self-exiled, because of his political opinions; going in less than two days; going perhaps never to return! During the remainder of his stay in Richmond, he meant to be much with *her*. In a year, perhaps in less time, he would come for her to take her to his home; for she was to be his until death parted them. But there was not a word, not a thought, of me! His soul overflowed with tender compassion and love for her; while for me, whose heart bled in hot, leaping gushes at every phrase of endearment lavished upon his puny, babyish idol, — for me, who would have gone with him to the world's end as a bond-slave, defiant of poverty, defiant of public reprobation, defiant of shame, — he had not so much as a commonplace message of remembrance such as he might have sent to the acquaintance of a day!

I have read, in old legends of the Norseland, of the Berserker rage, — a blind, deaf, unreasoning frenzy to which their most valiant heroes were subject, — a seizure always frightful to behold, often premonitory of bloody or scandalous deeds. A cognate fury it must have been that possessed me, as I stood above that motionless form — wilted by the first sharp wind of adversity, like any other summer flower, and felt — not reflected — for it scorched my brain — a lightning flash — what a barrier she was to my happiness, — the blight she had been to my life. But I did not touch her. I left the brown head lying helpless against the cushion, the long lashes drooping upon the bloodless cheek, — just as I had found her. Only, as I went out of the room, the officious whisperer, which good people call conscience, said humbly, —

"Is it not dangerous to neglect her? What if she should never revive?"

"So much the better!" I said aloud, and dropped the curtain upon the tableau of love in distress, *à la mode.*

Still pursued by the Furies, I walked out of the house, without summoning a creature to her assistance, and staid not for thought or plan until I had rung the bell at the door of Harry Wilton's boarding-house. Something then — I think it was the tame tinkle of a piano in the parlor, suggesting the proprieties of society, reminded me to draw my veil over my face, to adjust my shawl about my shoulders, and compose a formula of inquiry to the footman who answered the summons.

"Is Mr. Wilton in?"

"I believe so, ma'am. Will you walk in?"

"Not there!" I said, when he would have ushered me into the common drawing-room of the establishment. "I am his sister. I will go directly up to his room."

I smiled in stating the relationship I bore to him whom I came to see. Was he not over-fond of calling me by the title I now assumed to answer my own purposes? The man led the way up to the second story, through a long hall, and would have knocked had I not prevented him by a hasty gesture. Another wave of the hand bade him go his ways, and when he was at a convenient distance, I tapped for admittance.

"Come in!" answered the deep tones I had expected to hear

I raised my veil as I obeyed. I have a hazy recollection that the apartment was of fair dimensions, and was fitted up neatly — perhaps handsomely. Had it been spacious as a royal saloon, and furnished with more than regal splendor, I should have seen nothing at entering save the table, littered with papers, and standing by it, with the air of one disturbed from engrossing reverie or study, the figure of the proprietor. This at the first glance. A second showed me the slight frown of impatience or inquiry, the look of expectancy exchanged for active alarm.

"Agatha! what has happened? Is Elinor——"

Up to this moment I can recall, with tolerable distinctness, the various steps of this affair; but here I lose the connection. I infer from this phenomenon, that I had until then maintained some semblance of composure, and, in reality, remained, to a certain extent, mistress of my words and actions. With what exclamation I interrupted his inquiry, and what avalanche of protestations and reproaches followed, I do not remember with sufficient accuracy to write them down; but I have within my mind perfect daguerreotypes of the fluctuations in the counte-nance of the listener to my nightmare ravings; the incredulity that succeeded wonderment; the grave rebuke of the gaze that marked the passing of disbelief in the evidence of his own hear-ing; the cool contempt that, at last, like a dash of cold water, brought me back within reach of my senses. There was no indignation, no symptom of wounded feeling. I ponder upon this as the cruelest stroke of all. I was not worth it!

My pen cut through the paper with that last sentence. This is absurd in one so tranquil and impartial as is the narrator of this act of the melo-drama. If "once upon a time"—a cen-tury or so ago—(it seems longer!)—I was precipitated by passion—by a turbulent *émeute* of my hereditary traits (*vide* Miss Morris)—by what my Lady would reprobate, as "ill-regulated affections," into that preëminent horror of proper ladies—a scene; am I not ready to cry, "*Mea culpa!*" with the prescribed smiting upon the breast, and pledge my sacred word never again to suffer myself to be unduly excited by any-thing?

I will write it over and round every letter with lingering pre-cision. I was not worth it! He appeared suddenly to tower into a giant of moral rectitude, — a snow pinnacle, a crystal shaft, an obelisk of ice, or anything else pure, lofty, and freezing, while I grovelled in the mire at his feet.

"I will see you home!" he said, in chill, measured accents. "You are not fit to be trusted to go out alone — especially at this hour of the night."

He took up his hat.

The revulsion of feeling produced by his manner and words was too much for me. My brain was saved by a burst of hysterical tears. Until now he had not offered me a seat; but as my sobs became violent, he brought forward a chair, and bade me sit down until I should be more composed. He remained standing still at a little distance from me. In the height of my agitation, I appreciated his tacit denial of my claim to the character of a guest. Humanity forbade him to turn me out of doors, but protest against my presence there was written in every lineament, spoken in every movement.

Presently he brought me a glass of water.

"It will do you good!" he said, briefly, but more gently than he had before spoken; and mastering my sobs, I dared look up at him.

"You despise me!" I said, piteously. "But I am very wretched — very lonely! and to-night I am wild at the thought of your going away. I have no other friend in the world; and you used to seem to like me!"

I was interrupted by a tap at the door behind me. Wilton frowned, bit his lip, and then unlocked it cautiously, just far enough to enable him to see who was there.

"Excuse my intrusion!" said a gentleman's voice, "but my sister is just going home, and she would like to have the book you promised to lend her."

"I will get it."

Closing the door in the face of his latest visitor, Mr. Wilton took down a volume from the book-case, and went out into the hall with it, shutting me in. The panels were thin, or my ears were preternaturally sharpened. I heard, as distinctly as if she had been at my elbow, Miss Morris say, —

"Thank you, Mr. Wilton! I will take great care of it, knowing you to be scrupulously particular with your books as with all other precious things!"

I almost believed that she would have appended a sarcastic clause — "Your reputation included!"

For by this time it had begun to dawn upon my beclouded apprehension that I had done a dangerous as well as a silly thing.

"I feel as if I had been walking in my sleep!" I said, with a foolish laugh, when Mr. Wilton returned, and, this time, locked the door upon the inside.

"I wish I could persuade myself that *I* had been dreaming for the past fifteen minutes!" he rejoined, seriously.

He had resumed his stand upon the hearth-rug, keeping, as before, at a respectful distance.

"I am willing," he continued, "to ascribe much that is reprehensible in your feelings and conduct to the defects in your early education. I know that your impulses are strong to violence, and that they are imperfectly disciplined. But, admitting these extenuating considerations, your behavior to-night has been blameworthy — inexcusable! Passing over the insane outbreak with which you commenced this scene, — an attack which I scorn to try and convince you that I have never provoked at any period of our intercourse, past or present, your coming to this place alone, and at this hour, was imprudent in the highest degree. You have lowered yourself in my esteem, and, should your visit be suspected by others, your standing in the eyes of the world would be seriously damaged. Now that you are calmer, we had better go. Every minute of your stay here increases the chances of detection."

He had often lectured me, in days gone by, but never in such stern, dry fashion as this. Angry as I knew I ought to be with him, I could not resent — I was even disposed to admire this new phase of his character. Yet it was hard to accept the position in which he held me by his severity.

"You judge me pitilessly!" I ventured to say, rising to go. "You contrast me with Elinor ——"

"If you please, we will not introduce her name in this connection!".

He made a slight, it seemed an irrepressible, but most expressive gesture, in saying this. It was as if he would guard something spotless and priceless from the risk of pollution — would snatch a pearl from beneath a profaning foot. Nothing that preceded and followed that tone and movement would have been more insulting to a woman who retained a vestige of self-respect.

"Are you ready?" he added, in a business-like style.

When we were out of doors, he spoke again.

"You had better take my arm. The streets are full of disorderly characters in these times."

Another blow at my improper conduct in having traversed them alone! I had opportunity in which to collect my scattered ideas during the walk. My escort might have been a galvanized iron statue, for all the effort he made to entertain me. Looking back upon the adventure, as I strive to do with the eyes of a third person, who, thoroughly conversant with its several stages of attack, repulse, and inglorious retreat, has yet no individual interest in the affair, I ought to smile at the grim silence in which we stalked along the pavement — silence unbroken except by the echo of our steps; the answering ring of an occasional passing footfall, and the flapping of the Secession flags overhead.

There was still a light in the hall when we reached Mrs. Dana's respectable abode.

"I have a pass-key!" said my companion, with no abatement of his distant gravity; and I understood that he meant my return to be accomplished secretly, if possible.

What I had to say must be spoken before that key touched the lock. I caught his hand. "I believe that I promised reform — that I professed repentance — of what I have no conception now; but I could not endure his anger. I am

9

certain that I supplicated pardon, for he softened slightly at that.

"I am not angry with you, Agatha," he replied. "But you have grieved and disappointed me! I am seriously uneasy as to your future, and the future of those with whom you may be associated."

"You will not betray me!" I said, quickly, thrown off my guard by the threat of disclosure I fancied was implied by this remark. "I should be ruined for life were the Lacys to know of this mad freak!"

"Therefore you should know *me* better than to imagine me capable of 'betraying' you!" he returned, freezingly as ever. "A woman should live above the risk of degrading revelations. If I speak plainly, it is you who have forced me to do it. Your secret is safe. I have still too much regard for you to injure you, unless justice to others should compel me to tell a story I should be ashamed to repeat. Good night!"

He wrested his hand from me, not roughly, but impatiently, unlocked the door, motioned me to enter, and drew it to again as if he were my jailer. A lady and gentleman were passing at the moment. Was it my heated fancy, or did the ray of gas-light flashing from the half-open door show me the visage of my arch-enemy, Miss Morris? I believe that woman is ubiquitous. I am fast learning to look upon her as the emissary of the Evil One set for my destruction.

I crept up stairs very softly; turned the knob of the chamber-door without creak or rattle; glided in, and saw, kneeling at the bedside, a figure clad in white, with long brown hair rippling over her shoulders. The broken-hearted damsel had recovered from her swoon, unaided by mortal ministrants, and having very sensibly come up to bed, had assumed another dramatic *pose* before retiring. Some people are fond of indulging in this sort of private practice. The situation would, doubtless, have been vastly effective in the sight of the — to me — relentless judge from whom I had just parted; but it was thrown away upon me. We women understand the machinery of each other's wiles.

She remained motionless for several minutes after my entrance, apparently so absorbed in holy meditations as not to note my presence. I went on quietly with my preparations for my nightly repose, interrupted but once by a stray glimpse of white set features and a pair of blazing eyes, caught accidentally as I passed the mirror. Warned, by the apparition, of the necessity for circumspection, I stole on tiptoe into the dressing-room to bathe my face. Then, loosening my hair, that it might serve further to hide, by its friendly screen, the traces of my late folly, I repaired to the bedroom. Elinor had lain down meanwhile. Stepping still like a cat, I crossed over to the bed, and stood beside her before she knew that I.had come back. Her eyes were closed, as I had seen them in her fainting-fit; her countenance was as much like tinted marble now as then; but as I gazed, one large tear oozed from beneath the shut lids, and rolled down upon the pillow. Nothing hysterical or ill-regulated *there!* Then she languidly opened the " great brown eyes," as he called them in his letter, and stared at me.

I had braced myself to witness a flood of weeping; to be the recipient of a string of lamentations; and the sooner this was gone through with, the better. So I put my cold hand upon her forehead, which was almost as chill, and smiled encouragement to whatever she had to say.

" Ah, Agatha, dear! When did you get back? Have you had a pleasant evening?"

" Delightful!" I returned, with saturnine facetiousness, which she took for dead earnest.

" I am glad to hear it. Is Mr. Kingston down stairs?"

" No. It was growing late, and I was growing tired; so I did not press him to come in."

" What time is it?"

I consulted my watch. " Just eleven."

" Only eleven!" with a little piteous, patient sigh.

I interpreted it silently into the old, old cry, heaved by aching human hearts in all ages, when the night of sorrow is long and dark, " Would GOD it were morning!"

" Are you not well? " I inquired, with a tolerable counterfeit of tenderness.

" Yes," — rousing herself, — " only, like yourself, rather tired. I shall be better in the morning."

She turned her face away, folding her hands in the childish way she always has when composing herself to sleep.

" I am afraid you have been lonely this evening ! " I ventured a step further.

" O,. no ! I have been writing ! I am rarely lonely, you know ! "

She held up her pale lips for a good-night kiss, and I gave it. The charitable readers of human nature who contend that hypocrisy is not innate with our charming sex are not familiar with such exhibitions of our characteristic as was afforded by the trifling interview just described.

I did not sleep until near daybreak. By two o'clock Elinor was breathing easily and naturally. Up to that hour she was as broad awake as I. I detected this by her perfect stillness of body and limb — her sometimes impeded respiration — more surely still, by the sigh that occasionally struggled into life. This was her first grief, and, Sybarite that she is, it filled her with dismayed surprise, perhaps because it showed her that she was not to be exempt from the common lot of humanity.

When I awoke from the heavy slumber that finally seized upon me, she sat by the window, with her Bible upon her lap, giving, I shrewdly suspected, one peep at its contents for ten down the street in the direction from which her knight was to come. She was dressed carefully and becomingly, but her utmost efforts could not hide the heaviness of eye he had begged should not reproach him at his appearance, nor restore the bloom to the rounded cheek. If she thought that his loverly impatience would bring him to her before breakfast, she was disappointed, for we had nearly finished that meal when the message came that he was in the library.

" Why does he not come in here, as usual ? " wondered Mrs. Dana. " Charley ! go and invite him to take a cup of coffee with us."

"I will go, Aunt Dana!" returned Miss Elinor, composedly. "I have finished my breakfast."

"My dear, you have eaten nothing!" expostulated the hostess.

Her brother-in-law shot her a look from behind his newspaper that silenced her.

He is an autocrat in his odd way, which I can never entirely understand. This signal, however, I did comprehend. It meant that he was in Wilton's confidence.

An hour later, Elinor came to our room, and told me, in an unsteady voice and with swimming eyes, a piece of news she would not distress me by communicating the night before, "knowing how sincerely attached I was to my old friend." Mr. Wilton was going North again to live.

"I can but like and respect him the more for his heroic adherence to his principles," she said. "I am sure that he is doing right. But we shall miss him sadly!"

This was the sole expression of regret articulated in the anticipation of parting, for many months, perhaps for all time, from the man with whom she had but yesterday looked forward to passing the rest of her life! I was aghast to her lukewarmness, I dare say, for I was stricken dumb for full a minute and a half.

At length I said, "I heard a rumor of this, last night, dear; but I thought it best to wait for confirmation of it before harassing you with the story. As you say, we shall miss Harry sadly. But courage! it will all come right in the end!"

At that she kissed me, and called me a "blessed comforter," and departed for a walk with "Aunt Ellen." While they were out, I confided to Mrs. Dana the fact that one of my horrible headaches was coming on, and craved permission to "have it out" in a certain lonely third-story room, which no one visits twice a week. The old lady protested vainly against my proposed regimen of darkness, solitude, and a cup of coffee, and as uselessly recommended her family physician, "who had made the treatment of neuralgia a speciality." I was in no mood for

9 *

temporizing, and I had my way. I transported myself and my surreptitious vial of morphia to the comfortless dormitory, and locked my door. When I was well enough to be down stairs again, Harry Wilton had gone. He intrusted a note for me to Elinor.

DEAR AGATHA: If I was harsh in my dealings with you at our last meeting, you will forgive me. I confess that I was disappointed and shocked at what passed then; but now that it *is* passed, let it be forgotten by us both. Life is too short, and real friends are too few, for us to nurse unkind remembrances of those in whose fidelity we can have faith. There is much that is dear and lovely in my reminiscences of our intercourse; much that I shall ever cherish gratefully. As to my sentiments with regard to yourself, you cannot be at a loss. I must ever think of you with sincere and affectionate interest. May you be blessed with an abundance of Heaven's best gifts — hope, love, happiness!

Faithfully,

H. M. WILTON.

It was a single drop of water to my parched tongue, — but it was ice-water at the best, the thawing of the snowy pinnacle aforementioned, — a frosty touch, that made thirst and pain the more intense a moment afterwards.

Thirst and pain! I am gnawed by both, despite my reckless affectation of gayety; an affectation I would keep up to myself as to the world, in the idea which sometimes is plausible — sometimes absurd — that practice may perfect me in this as in other hypocrisies. Thirst and pain! and to assuage these I feed upon dust and ashes, gnash my teeth upon stones in lieu of bread! Hate is said to be the half-brother of Love. I begin to believe this. There are seasons when I am inclined to think that this ceaseless dwelling upon one image, this perpetual renewal, to my sick fancy, of the looks, tones, and language of one person, and that person one who has wounded me as no other has ever done, insulted me as none besides would dare do, —

may be the work of the vindictive half-brother rather than that of his blind relative. Yet I discover that the schemes which employ my restless brain have all one obstacle. How to strike at the one I knowingly hate, — hate for her seductive arts; hate for her affluence of love while I am beggared; hate for her wealth and popularity while I am worse than poor, and by many less than liked; hate for her happiness, and, sometimes, because she is so fond of me; hate as only a woman can loathe a successful rival she feels to be her inferior, — how to reach and punish her, without touching him!

CHAPTER IX.

ELINOR.

It has often been jestingly said to me that our mother had brought us up to believe in the infallibility of our father as religiously as Roman Catholics do in that of the Pope. With all my love and veneration for him, I never knew what a tower of strength he was until upon the morning of my last and only sad ride with Harry. I saw him standing at the window of Aunt Dana's parlor, watching for our return. His face told that he knew everything. If it had not, I must yet have felt this in the embrace into which he lifted me from the carriage. Still holding me with one arm, he held out the other hand to Harry.

"You ought to go! You can do nothing else," he said, in a moved voice.

Harry's was not more firm, as he responded, "Thank you for saying that! I thank you yet more for coming for her!"

They made it as easy for me as such sorrow could be made. One or the other was with me through all my waking hours; their loving vigilance noted every motion and look; averted from me every possible annoyance. I should have been sinfully ungrateful had I not tried to emulate this unselfish affection. After the earliest shock had passed, — I am thankful that no one knows how weakly I sank under it, — after the numb agony was over, my duty lay out clearly before me. Harry had too much to suffer already, and too much to sacrifice, for me to add a feather's weight to the load. Whether or not, in the future, I was ever to be a helpmeet to him, the opportunity was offered me to sustain and cheer him now. I prayed hourly that I might be strengthened to put far from me the dismay that might enfeeble

my resolution to aid him ; the despondency that might cloud the
countenance I would have him remember as beaming with trustful love in this, the darkest hour of our experience. I had to
struggle, too, with my impatient jealousy of the claims of necessary business and other friends upon his time. I was certain
that he would keep his promise to devote to me every minute he
could snatch from imperative engagements ; and when I kept
before me the fact that upon the fulfilment of these depended
his prosperity and fair name, I reproached myself that I was
rebellious.

But the hours — then the minutes — were so few, so brief, so
precious ! At length the last hour arrived ; and when my heart
seemed sinking into death with the thought, Papa proposed that
we — he and I — should accompany Harry through the first
stage of his journey, taking the return train to the city. It was
like him ! so Harry and I said, when we found ourselves seated,
side by side, in the northward-bound car, at sunset, with the
hope of one more and a long heart-talk before we separated.

" You are not a refugee yet, Mr. Lacy — are you ?" asked a
gentleman, laughingly, in passing my father, who sat just across
the aisle from us.

" Not exactly," he replied in the same tone.

I glanced up, involuntarily, at Harry. He smiled, but the
muscles about his mouth stirred as with pain, hardly kept down.

" Yes, dear ! that is what they will call me now — what I
am ! "

As Uncle Charley parted from the traveller, he stooped to
whisper something in his ear, but not so lowly that I did not
hear it.

It was, " Look out for me ! "

I had no idea of what he meant, yet it augmented the depression that deepened insidiously within my spirit ; which I sought
to relieve by giving my attention to what was going on around
me. I noticed, not without an undefined sensation of alarm,
the unusual number of strollers that lounged up and down the
neighboring sidewalks, and loitered about the train, some of the

latter evidently listening to the guarded undertones to which the voices of all — even the rudest of the loungers — were modulated. And with this shade of uneasiness, there grew upon me a strange, indescribable sense of the unreality of all that I saw and heard. The familiar streets and houses were seen as through the bewildering vapors of a dream; men and women glided by like phantoms, and there was a shimmer of purple and orange light in the air — the reflection of the glowing west, vague and dazing — not dazzling.

Ross lingered until the car was in motion.

"Good by, old friend!" he said, wringing Harry's hand. "Write to me soon! Think of me affectionately — always — if you can! And believe that nothing can change my feelings toward you!"

He sprang from the train without waiting for a reply.

"What did he say? What did he mean?" I asked, perplexedly.

"To assure me of what I did not need to have confirmed — his enduring friendship!" returned Harry, composedly. "We have a pleasant evening for our journey!"

The dialogue languished after this. I was unaccountably indisposed to talk, and this feeling seemed to pervade the whole company. The dreamy state fell upon me again. The ladies' car was very full, but very quiet. The languorous hues of the west swooned away into the paler twilight, and here and there a star peeped through the gray sky.

Just when the blending of day and the slowly-falling darkness was most confusing to the eye, the train halted for an instant, and several gentlemen entered the car. Harry touched my father's arm lightly as they passed us, and, attracted by the motion, I scrutinized them as closely as the imperfect light would allow. One of them, I thought, I recognized as Mr. Carter — well-known to every visitor of the Convention as one of the most conspicuous Union leaders. It seems remarkable, now, that the circumstance of his quitting the city before the adjournment of the Convention, and just at the most critical period of their deliberations, did not stimulate my curiosity; but I accepted it then as a feature — and not a startling one — of my dream.

On through the gathering gloom rolled the ponderous train — the only moving thing abroad upon that enchanted night! Within it there was none of the hum of social life. The passengers were not drowsy, for every figure was upright; and the few faces, made dimly visible by the faint glare of the lamps sparsely scattered along the walls, were wakeful — one might have imagined, uneasily watchful. Had it not been that my hand lay in Harry's warm, living clasp, and that the outlines of my father's stately figure were in my sight, I might have believed myself to be indeed dreaming, or that the motionless shapes and anxious countenances about me were bodiless spectres.

By and by, the spell was broken, rudely — to me terribly. At one of the principal stations along the line a crowd had assembled, to await the arrival of the train, which was there to take in wood and water. It was a tumultuous gathering, whose chorus of queries and exclamations raised a Babel din in the breezeless night air. The railway officials were curt, and apparently unsatisfactory in their rejoinders, and received a variety of uncomplimentary observations in return. All at once a movement was made in the direction of the ladies' car, in which we were seated. Eager and angry visages, dusky in the shade or ruddy by torch-light, were pressed against the closed windows, and thrust impudently through those that happened to be open.

" Three cheers for the Southern Confederacy ! " shouted a stentorian voice from the platform of the depot.

And not three only, but three times three, yells of triumph deafened us.

" Three cheers for Jefferson Davis — the savior of southern liberties ! "

Again a burst of wild acclamation that made the windows rattle.

" Three groans for Carter ! "

I awoke from sleep, often, in the dead of night, with that cry sounding through my brain — its emphasis of malignant exultation, even the broad provincial accent of the speaker, and the drawl of the last word.

" Three groans for *C-u-a-a-*rter ! "

It gave me an impression of brute ferocity that stopped the beating of my heart for one awful moment. From the crowd went up a responsive bellow — it was not a shout of execration and derision.

" All aboard ! "

The hoarse call and the shriek of the engine were welcome music to the travellers' ears. As a stream of hisses was directed at the moving line of vehicles, a window directly behind us was raised violently; a man threw himself half out of it, and shaking his fist in the faces of the crowd, poured forth a volley of anathemas, in which the terms " blackguards," " traitors," and " cowardly villains," were the mildest employed. A half minute sooner his temerity might have cost him his life. Fortunately, the instant rush toward him was foiled in its aim by the quickened speed of the car; but the howl of rage and chagrin at his escape was like that of a pack of hungry wolves.

" What did you gain by that demonstration ? " questioned Harry, over his shoulder.

" I feel better ! " was the rejoinder, growled in a deep base ; and the irate Unionist was left to recover his breath and temper at his leisure.

The episode may appear ridiculous in the retrospect; but it bordered upon the tragic at the time of its occurrence.

" Don't be frightened ! " whispered Harry, chafing my nerveless fingers ; " I had not expected this, or I would not have consented to your coming. You understand what it all means — do you not ? "

" I suppose that Virginia has, at last, apostatized ! " I answered, bitterly. " I ought to have been prepared for it, but I am not ! "

I could see that he smiled at my sudden heat.

"Hush, love! such things are not safe to say, even here! I may, I do, love you the more for your patriotism; but others may feel differently. The ordinance passed to-day in secret session; but the fact is more than suspected by the populace, as you have seen. To-morrow the news will be published far and wide. Brownie!" — with an abrupt show of passion totally foreign to his ordinary bearing, — "I wish we could leave the country! go abroad and forget this miserable commotion! I could brave the storm for myself, but you were not made to support trouble such as may befall you, — if you remain at the South!"

How thankful I have been since that I did not yield to the temptation presented by this appeal to my heart! Union, in place of speedy separation; peace instead of the reign of terror of which I had just beheld the inauguration; a long, bright day of love and happiness, a glance at which made the lowering present yet more gloomy. Nor can I tell what helped me to stand firm when my weak, selfish will seemed about to fail. I was very full of rebellious, of wicked thoughts; doubts of GOD's goodness, and mercy, and fatherly love, in that His children were called to pass through those swollen waters of trial. I did try to send up one cry for strength and light before I spoke.

"That would be unworthy of us both," I said, falteringly, I fear, but I could say it — and to him. "I should be a trammel, not a help, to you, even were it right to leave my parents at this juncture. But you have duties yet more solemn to bind you to your native land. Your country has need of all good men and true in her extremity of peril. She cannot spare you!"

He was so slow in answering that I began to dread lest I had wounded him. Then he thanked me for my "courage and honesty; for the right counsel I had given, when he was almost beguiled from the path of duty." I was glad that he had spoken this, and thankful, as I have said, that I had held fast to his integrity and mine, and I was careful that he should not suspect how much sharper was the pain of parting after this dazzling temptation — but it *was* sharper!

If there is no cloud the shadow of which is not needed, the need must have been great and urgent which called for the darkness that enwrapped my soul as I stood upon the wharf that night and marked the approach of the steamboat that was to take from me my best beloved. It was beyond my power now to utter words of consolation or hope of our common Future. I could only endure dumbly my great woe; only forbear to add to his grief by weak wailings over what was beyond remedy. There, under the star-lit heavens, the river rolling darkly by, each dash reminding me how soon it would divide us, he took me in his arms, prayed our Father to have me in His loving keeping, kissed me again and again, and gave me back to my father.

We returned to town that night. The evening of the next day saw us at Sunnybank. Agatha remained with Aunt Dana for a fortnight longer, by the advice of her physician, and at my request. My home is very beautiful; the dear ones within it are more than kind — sympathizing and tender to a degree that brings the tears with the words of gratitude I would speak in acknowledgment of their abundant goodness. Yet the cloud has not passed. There is a vast blank in my life, an unceasing yearning in my heart. There have been many sources of disquietude besides Harry's absence. Every breeze is freighted with the horrid noise of civil strife. "Sumter!" is the battle-cry with which a mighty army, at the North, have suddenly started to their feet, and rushed to the defence of the National Capital. "No coercion!" "State sovereignty!" "Defence of our homes and firesides!" are watchwords that have banded together the men of the South as by a sacred oath. Lynn went down to Richmond, last week, ostensibly to escort Agatha home. We expected them yesterday, but there came, instead, letters from both my brothers, announcing that Lynn had joined the company in which Ross is a lieutenant. This company was mustered into "the service of the State of Virginia" the day preceding the passage of the fatal ordinance, — mustered in without the knowledge of, at least, half the members of the corps. Ross knew nothing of the formal act until he read in the morning's paper an order to the men to appear at their barracks that evening, with their knapsacks packed and lettered. This was the hidden significance of his farewell address to Harry. He was aware that, at that very hour, he was regularly enrolled as a soldier of the Southern Confederacy. He rejects this title, positively. I quote from his last letter: —

"I am a son of Virginia. I owe allegiance to her — since her withdrawal from the Federal league — to her alone. I wear her uniform. I will fight her battles upon her soil, should an invading foot cross her boundaries, let the invader be British, French, or Yankee. The action of the Commonwealth, as a free and sovereign body, has taken the responsibility of decision out of my hands. A month ago, I would have said, and sincerely, "May my arm be palsied if ever I lift it against the old flag!" But before and above all other claims came those of State and home. Do not censure Lynn. Every loyal Virginian must bear his part in the approaching struggle, and he prefers to fight at my side."

My mother is a brave woman; yet I thought, for a time, that this letter had been her death-blow. It was directed to Papa but he was with me in the garden when it was brought in, and, ignorant that he was so near, impatient for news of her absent children, and uneasy at the delay in their arrival, she opened it. Summoned by her one wild scream of horror, Papa and I ran to the house. She met us in the porch, pale as death, clutching the letter, and sobbing, hysterically, "My boys! my boys!"

Papa lifted her as he would have done a child, and carried her to her room, said a soothing sentence or two, and obeyed the gesture that entreated him to read the paper. He turned from her to do this; but I could see his face — saw the anxiety depicted upon it change to displeasure, deep and stern. Then I guessed what had happened, although I had not dreamed of it before.

"I had rather they were ——" he commenced.

Mamma sprang up in time to put her hand upon his lips.

"Do not say it, Morton! They are our children! GOD
only knows how soon we may be called upon to mourn because
they are not! My boys! my noble, fond boys!"

She was very ill all night. It was late when the doctor left
her, and Papa watched with me beside her until morning — a
sad, sad vigil. He looks older to-day by ten years than he did
yesterday. Although he says little of his personal affliction in
the event that has wrought the change, I can see that there are
other emotions besides parental solicitude at work; that his
hopes for and pride in his sons have had a shock. He called
me into his study, this forenoon, while Mamma was sleeping,
and asked me to read a letter he had just finished in reply to
those received yesterday. I was surprised and relieved at the
mild tone of it, — the absence of everything like reproach, — while
it was full of affectionate regret at their precipitate action.

"I have written as their mother would have me do — not as
man to men!" he said, when I expressed this feeling. "For
myself, I say nothing except that I am disappointed. Having
conscientiously and carefully formed my opinion of what is lawful and right, I cannot alter it at the bidding of the cabal at
Montgomery, or be convinced against the dictates of reason and
conscience by the arguments of Beauregard's Paixhan guns.
If Secession was treason a month ago, it is treason still. Those
who wish to shirk the issue may plead that their geographical
position determines their politics. My principles rest upon
other and less variable data."

"But you will not deal severely with Ross and Lynn, dear
Papa!" I begged. "They have but followed the example of
thousands of others. What can two men do, in opposition to
the multitude that is pressing in the contrary direction?"

"What martyrs in the cause of truth have done in all ages —
stand up valiantly for the right; if need be, die for it!" was
the response. "But, my child, do you not see that if those who
thus unwillingly swim with the tide, I do not refer to such as
have been, from the beginning, temporizers and trimmers, but
to those who professed and really held Union sentiments up to

the 14th of April, — if these had maintained their ground firmly, that the opposing current would not have been irresistible? that it might perhaps have been stayed until the country regained some symptoms of sanity? The law of necessity is always a potent plea; but one should be very sure that it has application to the case in point before he avails himself of it. There is no other behind which cowards and sophists are so apt to skulk."

He folded the sheet, put it into an envelope, and wrote Ross' address upon the back, I watching him with mingled reverence and love, while my heart ached for the affectionate sons, the heaviest punishment of whose misdeeds had, from childhood, been their father's disapprobation. Was our happy family to be rent into factions by this sectional strife? Were the days of unspeakable tribulation at hand when every home should be a scene of war, and a man's fiercest foes be those of his own household?

Papa looked up at my sober countenance, and smiled, in stretching out his hand to draw me close to him.

" At least, I am sure of this loyal little ally — of this clear, wise, not-very-little brain!" tapping my head.

It may appear vain in me to set this down, but praise from judges like him is dearer to me now than of old; I think because I belong to Harry, and value whatever commends me to really competent critics, the more that it makes me worthier of him.

" I am glad that I can be a comfort to you," I said. " And remember, Papa, what answer came to poor discouraged Elijah, when he fled for his life."

He repeated it, in a dreamy, mechanical way : —

" ' Yet I have left me seven thousand in Israel, all the knees which have not bowed unto Baal, and every mouth which hath not kissed him!' I shall descry the consolation in that, by and by, love. I am unusually dispirited to-day; am rather in the mood to sympathize with the hunted prophet, in his weary moan under the juniper-tree, and afterward, at the mouth of the cave. ' _I_ have been very jealous' for what I believed — what I still believe — to be a righteous cause. It has been my hope that I might be instrumental in establishing it in permanence and beauty, and the Lord has showed me the vanity of my help. He needs it in nothing. My prayer was, that He would accept this, my work; but he knows best. His will, not mine, be done!"

I bent my head upon his; kissed the still luxuriant locks, with their honorable interlining of silver — silent reminders to me of the treasure of wisdom and experience he had collected during his fifty years of life. But profound as was my respect for the humility that put all these out of sight, and bowed meekly to the will of Him who had decreed that his counsels should come to nought, I had no language ready to convey this. His last words had taken me back to the holy, happy Sabbath succeeding our betrothal, when, over little Morton's grave, Harry had talked with me of kindred themes.

"'Not as I will, but as Thou wilt,' should be no idle form of speech, when coupled with our petitions," he had said, in the simple, impressive way that gave a charm to his most trivial observation.

Then — a sad, salt wave breaking upon the faint sparkle of this — came another memory of that hour.

"'Weep not for the dead, neither bemoan him!'" He had broken off the quotation there, with gentle consolation for the loss of my baby-brother. My thought continued the mournful strain : —

"But weep sore for him that goeth away. He shall return no more, nor see his native country!"

CHAPTER X.

AGATHA.

October 9, 1862.

THE first storm of the autumn; which has, up to this date, been singularly pleasant. I played the dutiful parasite all the forenoon, which seemed to me interminable. For Mrs. Lacy and Elinor had their sewing, and I was expected to sit by, also decorously industrious, while Mr. Lacy read aloud to us from that agreeable fiction — "Motley's History of the Dutch Republic;" a stained and shabby volume in paper covers, which was left here by the literary lieutenant in charge of the reconnoitring party of Federals who visited us last week.

A new book is an event in our life nowadays — a more uncommon one than such calls as that I have referred to. Although removed to what one might suppose was a safe distance from the theatre of active operations, hardly a week passes without the appearance of a squad of blue or gray-coated soldiers at our gate, generally soliciting hospitality in a style that leaves us little choice of a reply to their request. These calls have ceased to terrify — almost to excite us. Thus far, the stampede of half a dozen worthless negroes; the sensible depletion of the family larder, including the prospective contents of the same, in the shape of pigs and fowls; the loss of several cords of firewood, and more than several panels of fencing, which were more convenient to the troopers' hands than growing timber, — this has been about the extent of the detriment sustained by Milord from the ravages of war. After all, the card he has played from the commencement of this noisy and somewhat tedious game, has not been a bad one for himself. By some unexplained method of communication, the invading forces, or such of them as honor us with their society, have generally been made acquainted with the secret — which is anything but a secret — in this vicinity, that he still cherishes a hankering after the flesh-pots of Egypt; that is, for the defunct Union party, now buried forty fathoms deeper than were Pharaoh and his crew in the Red Sea, by the redder current that has, within the past fifteen months, rolled in smoking billows over Virginian soil.

Manassas, Williamsburg, Fair Oaks, and Malvern Hills have failed to convert the Unionist from his obsolete errors; and this, while his twin sons have trampled those bloody fields breast to breast, their swords sent contributions to the gory sea. I am no partisan of either school; but if I were in his place, I feel that I could not help doing as my neighbors and fellow-citizens had done, — thrown myself, heart, soul, and fortune, into the popular cause. Yet, as I have intimated, his policy has, thus far, proved safe enough. His sons are widely and favorably known, in their branch of the service, as gallant and daring soldiers. Both have been promoted for distinguished bravery in action. Ross is now captain, and Lynn lieutenant, in the same company. They have shielded their obstinate parent from the punishment which the Confederacy is not backward in dealing out to such as set at nought its authority. The tables are turned very effectually and ludicrously to a mere looker-on. The traitor of two years ago is esteemed the embodiment of enlightened patriotism to-day, and *vice versâ*. What would then have been reckoned an unpardonable transgression against a righteous government is now the height of pious virtue. Indeed, it is a question in the thoughts of our praying, hoping, boasting members of what is, without figure of speech, the church militant, whether one can be saved who is not ready to swear that there is no divinely-appointed government except the Confederacy, and that Jefferson Davis is the Heaven-ordained President.

Owing to this somersault in popular opinion, Milord Lacy is no longer Milord in church or county, save by courtesy; and

this courtesy is showed mainly on account of his sons. They
may fairly be accounted the salt that saves the family from
becoming an offence in the nostrils of the community where
erst their piety and good deeds were a sweet-smelling savor,
and the manorial estates — the dust and bones of mercy knows
how many generations of buried ancestors, inclusive — from confiscation. For confiscation — the lawful appropriation of the
goods, chattels, and lands of those who were once high among
the saints, but have become, without altering so much as a
single by-law of their creed, the chief of sinners — is now the
order of the day. With a large majority of the free and
enlightened citizens of this sovereign Commonwealth, it would
be sheer fatuity to withhold their allegiance from the "powers
that be." St. Paul is mighty popular in these latter days. I
wonder how many times I have heard that text, "The powers that be are ordained of God," descanted upon, in the pulpit
and out of it, during the last two years! We listened a Sabbath or two ago to a remarkable "improvement" of it from the
mouth of a wandering chaplain who officiated in the nearest
vacant church, — "vacant" in ecclesiastic phraseology, in
consequence of the preference showed by the late pastor for
carnal weapons above the sword of the Spirit, etc. He has
been in the army for six months and more.

Said our chaplain, "The powers that be are ordained of
God. Of course they are, my brethren, or they wouldn't be!"

But what do I care for all this? And to what purpose have
I let my pen stray on in derisive comment upon the fantastic
tricks which the solemn mountebank we dignify by the title of
Man — that anomaly among puppets — one that believes in his
own acting — is deceived by his own laborious imposture —
is daily performing in the sight of angels and his fellow-
worms?

I am tired of everything! Tired of life and the society
of those with whom my wearisome lot is cast; of this gigantic farce, when one considers the provocation and probable
results; this frightful tragedy, if one pauses to examine into

the waste of blood and treasure requisite for carrying it on.
Tired of this stupid country house, with the commonplace
river, more commonplace fields, and most uninteresting hills
that make up the landscape. Tired of the moaning wind and
plashing rain; — wearied to impatient disgust by the song that
arises to my locked chamber-door from the great hall below,
where Miss Elinor is walking, in default of her accustomed out-
door exercise. She takes jealous care of her *physique*. Is it
that health may prolong her day of youthful good looks?

> " When the night wind bewaileth
> 　The Fall of the year,
> And strips from the forest
> 　The leaves that are sear, —
> I wake on my pillow,
> 　And list to its roar;
> And it saith to my spirit,
> 　No more, nevermore ! "

The power and expression of that girl's voice are positively
wonderful. The prolonged crescendo of that "Nevermore!"
fills every nook and cranny of the old house with wild pathos.
I listen against my will — still I listen.

> " But the tender grace of a day that is dead
> 　Can never come back to me ! "

That is what the music means to my spirit, as each wave
breaks and dies around me in melancholy sweetness. There
is something infectious in the weather and that unutterably
lugubrious plaint, which I would give anything in reason — or
out of it — to silence. We hangers-on of great people — court
jesters or useful machines as we may chance to be regarded —
cannot afford such expensive luxuries as vapors, or I should
assuredly indulge myself in a spell on this, the dullest of une-
ventful afternoons.

Hark! the music has broken off abruptly, and there is a
growing hubbub below. It is welcome — even though it be a
posse of Confederate guards, with writs of arrest for the entire
establishment, or the Federals in force !

Instead of which, the Fates have brought us Captain Rolf Kingston and Lieutenant Lynn Lacy, C. S. A. Furloughs are not easily obtained now, but the gallant captain is nearly allied to divers of the mushroom magnates who are now the "powers," and he has exerted his influence to procure for his friend leave of absence. They are friends, intimate and firm; and if this end be a desirable one, I am entitled to the credit of bringing it to. pass.

"I was first attracted to him by his sincere and cordial appreciation of you," said Lynn to me this evening. "His attachment to you is warm and disinterested."

The last adjèctive was pronounced rather carelessly — on purpose, of course. It is highly probable that their friendship would be founded upon any other than disinterested affection which the gallant captain should profess for me!

I did not show unseemly haste in descending to the parlor. The officers had had abundant time for drying their clothes and making themselves ready for feminine inspection before I appeared. It was but just and becoming consideration for the comfort and pleasure of the lieutenant and his relatives that I should allow them opportunity for an hour's uninterrupted conversation, instead of intruding upon family confidences. I was kind and true to my ally in arranging for him an inevitable *tête-à-tête* with his fair one, since, while the brother talked to his parents, the sister must, in politeness bound, devote herself to him. Apparently my *ruse* had worked well; for upon my entrance to the now well-lighted drawing-room, I beheld the captain's fine figure bending toward Elinor, at one corner of the mantel, deferential and devoted, and utterly indifferent to everything and everybody else alive; while Lynn sat upon an ottoman beside his mother, his elbow upon her lap, and his chin resting in his hollowed palm, gazing up into her face, even while he replied to his father's questionings. Her hand toyed with his fair hair; her whole aspect testified to her pride in and love for her boy. Radical dissimilarity of political belief has not yet changed or restrained the current of natural affection in this family. Wounded to the quick, as father and mother must have been by the defection of their sons from the creed in which they had been nurtured, their meetings have not been marred by useless wranglings. I believe that, if the truth be told, the mother never held them one half so dear in the olden days of peace as in these distracted times, when any hour may bring her news of the death of one or both.

I halted, involuntarily, upon the threshold. The scene was so replete with tranquil enjoyment, such a fair representment of domestic concord, that my instinct warned me not to interpose a disturbing agency — to take my untoward presence away and leave the quintette to their brief hour of pleasure. I did not obey said instinct. I rarely do when its dictates conflict with my predestined policy. I stepped into the room, and walked slowly up its length, with what Elinor styles, flatteringly, my swan-like motion. I am glad that I do not frisk like short women of my ardent temperament. Thus floating over the carpet, I was within three feet of Lynn before he saw me. If I had coveted a display of my power over him, I had it. He was upon his feet with a spring that struck his iron heel smartly against the hearth.

" Agatha ! "

The word uttered in that tone was enough without the richer mantling of the bronzed cheek, the rapturous flash of the eye. For myself, as I yielded my fingers to his fervent clasp, I recollected the description which that dainty demoiselle, Pauline de Bassompierre, gives Lucy Snowe of her love-letter to Dr. Bretton : " A morsel of ice, flavored with ever so slight a zest of fruit or sugar." For was not his lady-mother looking on with those far-seeing orbs that invariably stimulate me to wary and consummate circumspection? If he was at once chilled and fired, pleased and pained, she was the cause — not I. I took care that my reception of Rolf should be frank, warm, sisterly — a glass of generous wine — full of glow, perfume, and sparkle, that the exceeding frostiness of the frozen confection might be more palpable. This accomplished, I sat down in Mrs. Lacy's shadow, as demurely as might a duenna of fifty, to whom the companionship of handsome young officers was a prohibited entertainment. But Lynn did not return to his low seat and his loll upon his mother's knee. He went around to the back of his father's chair, rested one arm upon it, and tried to talk with him of army and home news, while he looked at me. I knew this the while I never once, or only once, returned his beseeching glances. That once was when supper was announced, and he stepped up to my side to offer his arm. Mrs. Lacy was in advance of us; Rolf Kingston's tall form hid me from his partner's observation, and I ventured to steal a timid, yet passionate look into his eyes. It was not difficult to achieve this expression, for I was really pleased to see him. It was a refreshing variety in my humdrum life to feel myself again the object of absorbing interest; and while it was not a part of my programme to fan the flame openly, a secret drop of oil would keep it from flickering.

I cast him one ray, therefore, like a flash from a concealed magazine, then drooped my eyelids heavily, as though unshed tears weighed them down, and walked submissively beside him. He hung back in the hall to let his sister and her escort pass before us.

"I return to camp to-morrow," he whispered, hastily. "I *must* see you to-night! When and where?"

With a bewitching tremor, I directed his attention, silently, to his mother, now visible at the upper end of her bountiful board, and shook my head in mournful negative. I saw and divined the purport of his impatient, even imperious gesture, in protest, and began, forthwith, to prepare myself for an *éclaircissement*.

Not that I dreaded it. The prospect warmed my blood; braced my nerves refreshingly. A cleverly-managed love-scene is no bad diversion upon a rainy autumn evening, particularly if one has spent the morning in yawning over a scrap of needlework, and listening, or seeming to listen, which is

11

almost as bad, to " Motley's History of the Dutch Republic."
Elinor goes into ecstasies over the book, I may remark here,
but she had always a taste for the dry and solid in literature.
She has, during the last year, returned to her girlish habit of
studying several hours of each day with her father.   I date
the revival of the custom to Harry Wilton's praise of her pro-
ficiency in the Latin classics.   I never said that the girl was a
dunce, so far as intellectual acquirements go.   I candidly admit
that her attainments in this line are above those of the average
of well-educated young ladies.   She distances me in Greek,
Latin, and French, not to mention English standard authors ;
but I have more worldly wisdom in the tip of my little finger
than she has in her entire corporeal frame.   In witness thereof,
take the fact just named of her adherence to a plan of severe
mental discipline in order to perfect herself in that which she
imagines helped commend her to her absent lover.   When, in
reality, if she had not been able to frame a grammatical sentence,
or spell correctly a single column in the dictionary, he would
have fancied her every whit as well, so long as her eyes were
bright, her mouth a cleft rosebud, and her voice a dulcet pipe.
" What fools these mortals be ! "

I have called Mrs. Lacy's a bountiful board ; but the sober
verity is, that the viands displayed thereupon are less choice
than of yore.   Coffee is no more an every morning institution,
nor has the tea the aromatic flavor that used to greet the olfac-
tories as it was dispensed from the silver urn.   The sugar is
whity-brown, and the increasing scarcity of the commodity
induces a corresponding decrease in the quantity of cakes, preserves, and the like sweets.   Still, while milk and butter are
plenty, and the poultry-yard is free from blockaders, while the
garden and orchard are in good yield, and the plantation returns
of wheat and corn are fair, there is no danger of starvation.
The chit-chat of the supper-table turned upon the meagreness
of the markets and the alarming advance of prices.

" Better days are at hand ! " pronounced Rolf, confidently.
Fleets and armies may soon have other work to do than shut-

ting up our ports and guarding our frontiers Warlike operations on the part of our foes, if they do not, like charity,
begin at home, may end there."

"You deal in mysteries," I observed, seeing that no one else
was inclined to speak, and aware that the Captain, like most
other remarkably well self-satisfied men, does not like his orac-
ular sayings to fall still-born.

"Another month — perhaps another week — will supply you
with the key!" he rejoined, yet more importantly.

"The North is then to be invaded?" said Mr. Lacy, calmly
interrogative.

"I have not said so!" answered Rolf, pleased, nevertheless,
that his intimation had been understood.

"Very true!" was the reply. "Brownie, dear, will you give
me another slice of that bread?"

She complied with alacrity. Evidently it was a relief to her
to have a resting-place for her eyes and occupation for her
hands. Her cheeks were tinged with carmine; her fingers shook
violently. Ascertaining, by one swift glance around the table, that
my trick would escape detection, I contrived to catch Rolf's eye,
and carried it with mine to her agitated face. He is quick of
apprehension, and I was satisfied when I saw his complacent
visage cloud darkly and fiercely. Said Sydney Smith of Mrs.
Siddons in private life, "There was too much of the high
tragedy about her! She stabbed the potatoes!" The Captain,
in his truculent anticipations of bearding his rival in his hall, —
alias counting-room, — drove his fork into the leg of chicken
upon his plate, as if he were impaling his foe with his trusty
sword. I bent my head to conceal a smile, and Lynn said, in
a dissatisfied tone, —

"Is that the way you keep State secrets, Kingston? Hadn't
you better divulge the date and route of the expedition while
you are about it?"

"He may be like Harry Percy's wife — may never tell what
he does not know," interposed Mrs. Lacy, with her usual tact
at diverting a conversation from a dangerous channel.

But the Captain's mottled — or nettled — spirit was not so easily appeased.

"Without boasting of my familiarity with State secrets, I dare predict that in less than a fortnight a victorious southern army will have marched through Pennsylvania and New Jersey to the gates of New York. The plan has been laid with a skill that renders success a certainty. We cannot fail when Lee directs, and Jackson and Ewell execute."

"It is easy to fight battles and storm forts upon paper," returned Mr. Lacy, still composedly. "If you please, we will return to the parlor."

"A more rank traitor and submissionist never breathed!" muttered the angry Captain in my ear, as we accidentally fell against one another in crossing the hall. "The Government is too merciful to such! If it were not for his daughter ——"

He stopped, but looked unutterable things. His is a high, and, I suspect, a vindictive temper.

"A woman in your situation would detect an opportunity of making capital, for herself, out of this heterodoxy," I answered, slightly contemptuous.

He stared inquisitively, and I passed on, leaving him to digest the hint at his leisure. We had rather a dull evening, after all — or I did. At nine o'clock I made an excuse to leave the room, and coming up to my chamber, drew out my journal and began to write. Now and then, some sound from without penetrated to my solitude. Evidently the rest of the household were following my example in retiring early. In about an hour there was a tap at my door. I unlocked it, and behold, to my amazement, the Lady Paramount of the domain! She had a lamp in her hand, and I could see that she was paler than she is used to be, but otherwise she appeared tranquil and dignified.

"Agatha!" she said, "Lynn wishes to speak with you in the parlor, if you can spare him an hour."

"Certainly, Madam, if you and he wish it!" I responded,

obediently, and stepped back into the chamber to extinguish my lamp.

She was still in the hall when I came out. I did not care to look directly into her face in passing, which I did with a slight, respectful bow. She stood, as if irresolute, until I was half way down the passage, then turned and overtook me, as I gained the head of the staircase. I experienced an odd sensation when I heard her in pursuit, — the creeping, shivery feeling, from joint to joint of the spine, that one has in the imagination that ghostly shapes are at his heels, as he walks along an echoing hall or staircase at dead of night. She brought me to a halt at the brow of the stairs by laying her hand upon my shoulder. I faced her then, without a tremor. My faculties are generally ready for their work when a real emergency arises. She searched my eyes with hers until, if I had been a coward, I must have quailed ignominiously. She was strangely moved. Her firm lips quivered, and the color returned to her cheek.

"As you deal truly with my boy, Agatha, may the Lord deal mercifully with you!"

"Madam!" I ejaculated in astonishment that was not all feigned.

It was as if the repressed fire and earnestness of the woman's strong nature had defied even her self-control and dazzled me to blindness. She said never a word more, but left me there. This outburst was in bad taste in my Lady, and exhibitions of bad taste always make one uncomfortable. I actually debated within myself whether it might not be best to retreat to my sanctum, and, from behind its barred doors, indite a neat epistle to the waiting swain, politely declining the honor of the offered interview. But while I weighed the matter I still went slowly down the stairs, and as I reached the last of the flight, the parlor door opened, and Lynn appeared to receive me. There was nothing for it but to go on, and in a trice I was closeted for the momentous scene. Another bit of wretched taste in my Lady, — that is, if she desired to beget in me any maiden bashfulness, any of the pretty coyness that a novice would have felt in the like position. I am not a novice. I don't believe that I ever was. Certainly, this business-like arrangement set me at my ease. I was never cooler than when I declined the chair my companion brought forward, and resting my hand upon the centre-table — an attitude I took care should not be ungraceful — asked simply, " Did you wish to speak to me, Lynn?"

" I do, Agatha!" The voice, gentle and manly, had yet in it a quaver of emotion. "Almost a year ago I told you of my love for you, and asked from you a return. You gave me several reasons why you refused me a definite answer then. You were unprepared for the announcement, which therefore seemed premature. We were both young — too young, you thought, to enter into an engagement so important and binding as that I proposed. The unsettled condition of public affairs, joined to the distress which pervaded most families in our State, my own among them, made the consideration of individual interests appear unseemly and selfish. But you laid especial stress upon your conviction that our union would be strenuously opposed by my relatives and friends. I pass over the arguments you adduced in support of this belief. I regarded them then, as I do now, as the offspring of a morbidly sensitive imagination. But I promised to wait, in silence, for one year. You engaged, on your part, to give me an answer at the expiration of that time. I am here, to-night, to ask you to anticipate the date appointed for your decision by a month. As Kingston says, there are indications of a transfer of the seat of war to the Northern States. I may be ordered off at any moment, and I may never return. I would not urge you ungenerously, but —" his forced sententiousness and unnatural composure giving way before the flood of passion — "Agatha, I have loved you so fondly and so long! I have had a free talk with my mother, told her everything, and asked her sympathy in and sanction to my suit. She will receive you as her daughter — as the best-beloved of her son. The decision rests with you — you alone!"

He was beside me; —he had captured my hand, and my

furtive, upward look revealed his handsome face alive with animation,—his seeking, loving eyes. He *was* handsome ; he was noble and good — and he loved me ! Moreover, he believed in me — poor fellow ! I had better write, poor fool !

If, at that instant, I had had offered me a Lethean draught that should insure oblivion of the whole of my checkered Past, I would have drunk it, were it bitter as gall and acrid as aquafortis. I would have laid my innocent head upon the breast of this gallant and faithful gentleman, and blushed my pure happiness in receiving and returning his devotion. I had never denied to him that I reciprocated this. It was one step in my scheming that his mother and friends should become the chief obstacles to the success of his suit. I was assured that he had derived sufficient encouragement from my half-confessions and skilful equivocations to induce perseverance in his quest. For I intended, all along, to marry him. Much deliberation had brought me to the conclusion that I could not do better. If I had been dubious on this head when the matter was first propounded, the bequest of his far-off cousin, but ardent admirer, last winter, by which this, the second son of the family came into possession of a considerable estate, would have put an end to wavering. Should his father see fit to disinherit him on account of his marriage with an obscure and portionless girl, it would not signify much in our domestic affairs.

I considered all this after I put away the crazy longing for the impossible cup of forgetfulness. It is high time I was providing for myself, and leaving out the fact that I have only such a liking for this youth as his excellent qualities and personal gifts might excite in the breast of his grand-aunt, this settlement would be a very satisfactory arrangement. Understand me — discreet and patient paper ! — I did not believe one syllable of my Lady's cordial consent to my wedding her pet boy. That she had promised not to oppose it openly, and to tolerate me, I did credit. This toleration would be of a piece with the rest of her condescending patronage. I could picture to myself how she would carry it on; how I would be recast in the Lacy mould, — trimmed off here, filled out there, and polished after the similitude of a goodly stone in the edifice of her family pride.

All this time my eyes were sinking lower and lower, and my color mounting; but I did not attempt to withdraw my hands from their imprisonment.

"What shall I say?" I faltered, finally, in well-achieved confusion.

"May I tell you, darling?" and without waiting for an answer, he caught me in his arms.

But I don't like to write about it! A sick shudder steals over me when I recollect that I am surely betrothed to this man; that if we both live a year longer, I shall probably be his wife! I suppose this recoil from the thought betrays that I am not wholly depraved; that there are still remnants of womanly feeling about me, sedulously as I have striven to subdue instinct and impulse by will. We sat together a long time — or so it was to me — upon the sofa, his arm about my waist, his impassioned breathings in my ear. It was not easy to look happy and conscious at first, but I mastered the art better after a while. I stopped upon the landing to throw him a kiss from my finger-tips, he watching me from the parlor door. His glowingly happy face, his proud, tender smile, come between me and the paper when I review the scene, and what used to be a heart smites me.

"As you deal truly with my boy, may the Lord deal mercifully with you!" said my uncomfortable Mamma-in-law, that-is-to-be. She meant it as a curse or a threat. I have dealt truly with him in one sense. I have pledged myself to marry him, and I intend to abide by the contract. Heigh-ho! I ought not to be *ennuyée*, but I am. The rain and wind hold on, and my windows rattle a castanet accompaniment to their requiem over the dead and gone summer.

> "And it saith to my spirit,
> No more! Never more!"

The wailing echo rings through the chambers of memory like a benighted Banshee's cry. Why should it set me to dreaming about my mother? her loves; her hopes; her fate? I could believe that there are sobs and moans of human suffering in the air. If the woe of which the world is full had audible expression, the lament would reach the very stars.

I will not listen! I will not sentimentalize! I will keep steadfastly before my mind's eye — and let them fill it — two naked and positive facts, — first, that my mother married for love; secondly, that her child means to do a wiser thing.

CHAPTER XI.

ELINOR.

October 13.

THERE is a vast deal of expression in staircases.

If any one doubts this, let him try the experiment of spending a week in such a house as I once had the misery of visiting — a building that had no upper floor; an extensive mansion, and in other respects pleasant and convenient. I never understood, until then, the dreariness of a dead level. I envied the very sparrows upon the house-top, and the swallows under the eaves. Since then, I have held the more tenaciously to my idea that much of the character and the poetry of a house depends upon the staircase. And in how few dwellings is this unhaunted to loving imaginations by shadowy figures that still glide up and down, as they were wont to do in months or years agone? figures that on lonely nights awaken echoes the heart can never forget, although, with our fleshly ears we are to hear them no more? Childish forms it may be, with halting, uncertain feet and tiny fingers clinging to the balusters, and chubby faces peeping through the rails; or shapes stately in mature grace, with firm, resounding tramp; or others, bowed with age, feebly climbing, or warily descending, in fear of that which is high. Happy, happy abodes are those wherein the dwellers can sleep through gusty midnights, or awake in the ghostly gray of the dawn, without dreams or memories of heavier and more measured foot-beats upon the main stairs; the march of those who bear man to his long home, and the little procession of mourners who are henceforward to go desolate about the streets and chambers which are to know him no more!

The Sunnybank staircase is a picture in itself. It has its base in the spacious central hall, which, opening upon the front and back porches, and being furthermore lighted by four large windows, forms one of the most attractive sitting-rooms in the house. The steps are wide, low, and deep, and built of solid oak. No carpet has ever covered the boards; and their polished surfaces are the objects of the housemaid's proud care. The balustrade is likewise oaken, and quaintly carved. About two thirds of the way up, this makes a leisurely turn to the left, railing in a landing as large as the boudoir of many a fashionable belle. In the outer wall, at the rear of this, is a window, draped by an evergreen rose-creeper. The window-seat is broad; and I find no other study so much to my liking on this warm October day as this nook; the glossy leaves and late roses brushing my book whenever I turn over to another page. Except for the soft stir of the foliage and an occasional bird-note from the grove, the crow of a chicken or the distant scream of a peacock, the silence brooding through the house is profound. Papa has gone to the village, and taken Carrie with him; Agatha has been invisible since dinner; and Mamma sits sewing quietly in the hall below me. Perhaps she does not suspect my proximity. It is certain that she is disinclined to conversation, or she would call or send for me. I have been watching her for half an hour, and I am sure that I have divined her thoughts. Do they ever, by night or day, stray very far away from the sons from whom she is so sadly separated? High-souled patriot she may be in the National interest, but while the opposing faction counts among its defenders her boys,—while, voluntarily or perforce, they wear the uniform of the Confederacy, and their safety is included in the success of the rebel arms,—mothers', ay! and sisters' hearts must follow the progress of that army with anxiety, that, if not shaped into prayer for the victory of the rebel host, yet cries continually to the GOD of battles to be strength and shield to the beloved ones in the terrible day of warfare.

"If it be possible, let this cup pass from me!" is the voiceless petition of the tried soul of her whose noble face grows paler and graver with each passing month. We can do nothing but sit still and wait —— the lesson which — forget not, O murmuring heart of mine! — thousands of other women, as sorely afflicted, are learning in all quarters of this once happy, peaceful land! One might say that the task should be comparatively easy for me, guarded by such love and care as are showed to me in the sweet seclusion of this old homestead; that contentment, or at least patience, should come without much assiduity of wooing. But to sit through long, hot, still days, and the nights over which a strange hush has come, listening to the echoes ebbing and flowing — a tide that may be felt by my sensitive nerves, although a careless listener would never catch the sigh of the waves — through the corridors, and up and down this ancient staircase, — Lynn's quick, boyish footstep; Ross' agile leap, three stairs at a time, upon the stanch planks that never trembled beneath his weight; another tread, as light and firm, yet more deliberate than either, — this sort of waiting and hearkening engenders feverish longings for the once dear reality — the now unattainable.

These and yet other and older echoes the mistress of this house must hear. Her own shouts of childish mirth, as she ran to and fro through the home that claimed her as sole heiress; the gentle music of her mother's voice; the funeral psalm, chanted brokenly above that mother's coffin, set in the centre of the great hall; the rustle of her own bridal train sweeping the balustrades in her passage to the parlor below, — may be, oftenest of all, the irregular patter of tiny feet, now stilled for all time, lying peacefully under the old willow, the waving plumes of which I can see through the window whenever I lift my head. It is strange how constantly amidst the excitement and changes of this era of our lives, Memory lends eager ears to these voices of the Past.

"Men must work, and women must weep;
And the sooner 'tis over, the sooner to sleep!"

How heavily Mamma sighed last night when I sang that!

Anxiety and suspense are beginning to tell upon her strength and spirits. When the toil, and strife, and partings are at last over, shall we all — the now scattered household — workers and weepers together — be gathered to our fathers in the quiet sleeping-place where no alien dust has ever been laid?

GOD help us all! the shortest day of labor and tears is too weariful and tedious for poor human endurance, and the dreamless sleep is long a-coming!

A day later.

It is well that I was interrupted just here, for my musings were becoming morbidly selfish. I would grow strong — not sad — beneath the continued pressure of the burden which the Wise Father has seen fit to bind upon me. "Wait and hope!" I say many times, daily, to my foreboding spirit. How runs the old rhyme?

> "Beware of desperate steps: the darkest day,
> Live till to-morrow, will have passed away."

To-day *is* brighter than was yesterday; and the brightness comes from the letter, a single page long, lying before me among the leaves of my journal.

"*Via Flag of Truce*," says the envelope. Blessings upon the white-winged messenger! To me it is almost as if an angel had brought me tidings across the dark river of Death of a beloved one gone before. For seven months I had not heard a word from Harry. For seven long, long months, from day to day and week to week, I had looked, and wished, and prayed for some visible token that he still lived in the same world with me. Of his love I have never had a doubt. I say this now with a sort of glad pride; for it shows how well I knew him; how just was my estimate of his constancy. I was sure, moreover, that he had never remitted his efforts to communicate with me; that he had written, not once, but many times.

Of all this, and much more, this one brief page assures me. The handwriting is compact, but clear; the sentences concise.

12

Not a line of space is wasted; and every word tells. The whole letter is so like him, that I smiled through my tears in reading it.

"Do not send me news budgets," he writes. "Tell me mainly of your precious self. Keep a diary which I may read when we meet — for meet we shall, Brownie, in GOD's own good time. Do not let me slip entirely out of the Sunnybank life during this weary separation!"

As if every hour and every minute had not its thought of him, and his name were not a household word as dear and as fondly quoted as are those of the other absent sons!

But to my diary! I was interrupted in my writing, yesterday afternoon, by a visit from Miss Hetty Stratton. She is no favorite of mine. Indeed, to be honest, if I have a *bête noire*, it is she. And I had never seen her so teasingly inquisitive before. I had never been so annoyed by her affectations and impertinent insinuations as on this occasion. I was most displeased by the innuendoes and questions addressed to Mamma. At last I answered her more tartly than was quite polite, and Mamma asked me to see if supper were nearly ready, also to have Miss Hetty's room prepared for the night. These errands I used as pretexts for not appearing before our guest again until tea was served. Papa's presence at the table acted as a check upon her prying queries, although the fact of her volubility remained the same. I further absented myself when we left the dining-room, upon the plea of taking Carrie up to bed. When this was done, I came slowly and reluctantly down stairs, and paused in the front door, drawn irresistibly thither by the cool fragrance and subdued loveliness of the summer night. It was not yet wholly dark, although it was nearly nine o'clock. The air gave up slowly and unwillingly the sunshine that had steeped it through all the golden day. I even imagined that the nasturtium beds and the October roses, curtaining the roof of the porch, emitted a phosphorescent glimmer from the hearts so lately bathed with the fervid rays. A whip-poor-will was singing in the graveyard, and closer at hand, a chorus of

crickets filled up the pauses in his music. It was an evening
one would not voluntarily pass within doors, if there were no
candles in the parlor, and if Miss Hetty had not honored our
dwelling by her visitation.

Thus tempted, and thus driven, I stepped out into the porch,
thence upon the gravel-walk, and strolled slowly farther and
farther from the house, fearing nothing for my uncovered head
from the dry, warm air, and no unwelcome intrusion within
the grounds of my own home. The sky was full of stars, and
I was not solitary in my ramble. I could not but recall the
incidents of one other starlight evening, when I paced these walks
for a short, fleet hour, and the tones that then sang softly, —

> "When stars are in the quiet skies,
>   Then most I pine for thee;
> Bend on me then those tender eyes,
>   As stars look on the sea!"

I remembered — was it very vain? — who had said, "Tender
eyes! That is just the phrase for yours, Brownie! Look up
at me! I can see the starlight in their depths!"

I was singing, —

> "For thoughts like these too sacred are
> For daylight's common beam,"—

when some one very near me said, "Hist, Nellie! don't be
frightened!"

It was hardly a surprise, since, as I have said, I did not feel
alone. I did not immediately recognize the voice, nor could I
see anything of the speaker, except the dim outline of his head
and shoulders above the intervening garden fence. But his
tones were guarded, and I imitated his caution in my reply.

"It *is* Nellie! Who are you?"

There was a slight laugh, and I needed no other rejoinder.

"Uncle Charley," I whispered, seizing the hand he reached
over the paling. "How delighted ——"

"I shall be when I am safely ensconced in your house with
out having been seen by other eyes than yours," he interrupted,

walking around to the gate, and stepping upon the turf at the side of the walk, lest the crunching of the gravel under his feet should betray his vicinity to other ears. "Whom have you in the parlor? I saw a shape that was neither your mother's, nor yet Agatha's, pass the window, just now."

"Miss Hetty Stratton."

"A walking Gazette of neighborhood gossip — isn't she?"

"Something very like it, it must be confessed," I admitted.

"And Rolf Kingston's aunt?"

I answered in the affirmative.

"Humph! you must smuggle me in at the back door, and let me lie in a secret chamber, or cram me up a chimney, until she is in bed. She sleeps at night — doesn't she? Some. of the species are never caught napping. I want to see your father, your mother, and yourself, and I must be astir before daybreak. Will can be trusted to look after my horse, and to hold his tongue — can't he?"

"He can," I replied. "Stay here a minute while I reconnoitre."

As I had anticipated, Papa's study was untenanted. This was the retreat I chose for the unexpected guest. But the parlor door stood wide open, and I must contrive some excuse for closing it. I convoyed my charge to the porch, and left him standing there in the shadow, while I walked boldly into the parlor and shut the door behind me.

"My dear child!" exclaimed Mamma, "why do you close that? The room is too warm already!"

I had foreseen this, and issued instructions to Uncle Charley accordingly. Stammering an apology and laughing at my blunder, I fumbled at the bolt until I thought it was safe to reveal the outer hall once more, and re-opened the door.

"Mamma," I then said, "can I speak to you a moment about a point of domestic economy?"

"Ah! our bonnie Birdie will be the housekeeper of the county, yet!" cried Miss Hetty, airily.

I did not stay to notice her compliment, but followed Mamma

into the hall. A few words explained all that I knew to her, and while she went up stairs to welcome her old friend, I flew to Mammy Rachel's house to take her into confidence, and ask her cooperation in preparing supper and a room for the traveller. Uncle Will sat with her smoking his pipe, and readily undertook his share of the work. But he shook his white head, portentously, as he took down the stable lantern from a nail, while Mammy, less discreet, spoke outright.

"What's the matter, honey, that a good man, like Mars' Charles, who trusts in the Lord and does good to his neighbors, must come a stealing here in the night, like a thief and a robber?"

"I don't know, Mammy," I answered, sadly; for the question had tormented me from the instant of his arrival. "These are strange and terrible days! We must be prudent, and do what we think is right, leaving the rest to Him who is wiser than we."

As I left the house, I heard her groan, "How long, O Lord! how long?" and Uncle Will's voice, the more impressive by reason of the tremulousness of age, in reply, —

"Until the cities be wasted without inhabitant, and the houses without man, and the land be utterly desolate!"

I tried to put the words from me. I busied myself in collecting materials for a substantial repast, and, with my own hands, carried these up stairs in a covered basket, as being less likely than a waiter to attract the attention of Agatha, or Miss Hetty, who were still in the parlor. Uncle Charley was alone.

"I sent your mother back to her visitor," he explained. "Leave me to Rachel's care until Pauline Pry is off guard. She must suspect nothing. When the coast is quite clear, we will have a comfortable family confabulation. Only, Nellie — not a word to Agatha. Let her retire as usual. I have my reasons for the request" — seeing my look of surprise.

During this speech, he had been unbuckling a wallet which he took from the breast-pocket of his coat.

"By the way," he went on carelessly, "have you heard from New York lately?"

. "Not once in seven months!"

I did not mean to complain, but his question was sudden, and my answer sounded to myself like a wail.

"So I feared! It is next to impossible to get a letter through. But a flag of truce boat was sent up the river, the other day, and this came, directed to my care. Now, run away and play the hypocrite to Miss Pry!"

Panting and dizzy with excess of joy, I flew along the passage to my room, holding the precious sheet close to my heart — the envelope directed by his hand; the blessed olive-leaf, borne to me across the raging deluge! I had time to give it but one reading. It calmed me into happy tranquillity. I went below with it hidden in my bosom, feeling as if I were walking upon air. Papa was reading aloud from a newspaper at the centre-table. The rest were listening. The topic of interest was Lee's march into Pennsylvania, and the probable — according to the journalist — the certain and overwhelming defeat of the Federals, in a great pitched battle.

"I am thankful that my boys did not accompany the expedition!" said Mamma, fervently.

Miss Hetty spoke up quickly, but even her indignation — real or simulated — at the want of patriotic self-devotion that could see cause for gratitude in the delivery of one's children from the chances of a bloody conflict, failed to disturb my peace. Agatha looked bored, but civil, and presently put a stop to the harangue by asking me to sing.

"Something patriotic?" suggested Miss Hetty.

"Yankee Doodle, Hail Columbia, or the Star-spangled Banner?" I asked, mischievously. "Which shall I begin with?"

She made a feint of boxing my ears.

"Naughty little puss! You will get yourself into trouble yet, with your Yankee proclivities. If I didn't love you so much, I would assuredly report you to the authorities, and have you arrested. I dare say, if the truth were told, you are, at this very time, in secret correspondence with the enemy."

It was foolish and vexatious, but my cheeks flamed hotly at the coarse thrust, and the letter seemed to pulse back, beat for beat, the throbbings of my heart. It was not cowardice. Still less was it thought of wrong-doing; but my precious secret had been touched roughly, and the manifestation of wounded delicacy could not be restrained.

"I can exculpate her from that charge, Miss Hetty," said Papa, quietly. "All her correspondence passes through my hands. I will be her security."

I covered my confusion by playing a lively waltz; then, a march; then, a medley of fashionable airs,—music which I knew was best adapted to Miss Hetty's taste. Then I sang three sentimental songs, selected by her, and Mamma made a movement toward breaking up the party. Hospitality demanded that I should escort the visitor to her room,—not the one originally designed for her. This, our usual guest-chamber, opened from one side upon the study, and Mammy, instructed by me, had transferred Miss Hetty's hand-basket, hat, and mantle, to another apartment, nearer Agatha's, and in the wing of the house. Fortunately, Miss Hetty had not been up stairs during the evening, or the change of plans would have been more difficult to effect. As it was, she turned in the direction of the room she had occupied upon sundry former visits to us, and opened her light-blue eyes in amazement, when I said, "This way—please!" and led her onward.

"I am quite unfamiliar with this portion of your delightful mansion," she said, when we reached her dormitory. "I am afraid that I shall feel timid in these strange although charming quarters; unless, indeed, my sweet girl, you will make me happy by sharing my room with me. That would be transporting! Indeed, I have counted confidently upon this season of heart-communion with you, my dearest! I told Sister Mary that I did not expect to sleep a wink until late in the small hours. 'For,' said I, 'of course the dear, frank child will have a hoard of confidence to pour into my sympathizing cars. It has been *such* an age since we met!' And, as I said to Sister, and as I say to everybody, upon all occasions, 'If I have a favorite upon *this* earth, it is Elinor Lacy!'"

By this time the enclosure of the long, thin arms about my waist nearly stifled me, or I fancied that it did. I undid then hastily — ostensibly that I might remove the candle from the neighborhood of the curtain, which swayed slightly inward.

"I shall do you a wiser kindness in leaving you to undisturbed repose," I said, civilly. "If you are nervous, however, about sleeping alone, I will send up Jane to stay in the little room adjoining this. By leaving the door open, you can have her within call."

This proposition met with no favor.

"I suppose I am as safe here as I should be nearer to your father's room!" she said, dubiously. "I am always saying how much you are to be envied in having his health and vigor continued to him in these troublous days. No one knows how much or how little his or her life is worth now, when every chinquapen bush may hide a Yankee robber."

"Or a Confederate bushwhacker!" I was so imprudent as to say.

She came up close to me, and put her arm over my shoulder.

"I believe that you are hopelessly infected!" she said, in a tragic whisper. "My precious lamb! do be more cautious in saying these dangerous things! Queer stories are afloat already concerning your family. I contradict them whenever I can; but, as I tell my most intimate friends, in the strictest privacy, everywhere, 'People are *so* obstinate in their prejudices, and you can't convince them that there isn't some smoke where there is so much fire!'"

"Some fire where there is so much smoke, you mean — don't you?" I interrupted.

"Of course I do! I respect your father. I love your mother. I perfectly dote upon you. But my advice — the disinterested advice of a sincere, and tried, and faithful friend, through good report and evil report — is, to *take care !* That is all ! "

This ambiguous warning was made more mysterious by the sepulchral whisper in which it was uttered, and the great eyes and meaning nods that accompanied it.

" You are a Sibyl, Miss Hetty, " I said, laughing, despite my eagerness to be rid of her. " I hope that your solicitude magnifies the perils that surround us. Good night ! and pleasant dreams that shall have in them neither Federal sharpshooter nor Confederate guerrilla ! "

Uncle Charley had finished his supper and lighted his pipe when I returned to the study. Papa and Mamma were with him, making up a group which was so pleasantly familiar to my eyes and thoughts, that my mind refused to credit the near approach of the separation that was to divide these life-long friends for a period, the very indefiniteness of which gave it gloom. It might be for years, — it might be that they would never again look into each other's faces. For by this time I had come to understand — partly by intuition, partly through one or two hints dropped by Uncle Charley himself — that he was an exile. He was in the midst of his story when I entered.

" Thus far I have escaped even the threat of imprisonment by a prudent silence upon political subjects, " he continued, as I sat down upon a stool at his side. " But to be dumb now is to be disloyal. The Government calls loudly for the support of every purse, every arm, and every tongue. And as a general rule, I may remark, that those patriots who are most sparing in the use of the first two are most officious with the last. For myself, my principles have not changed from those I expressed freely, and with impunity, two years ago. But the rest of the world has turned over, and we old fogies, who cannot keep up with these abrupt revolutions, must be pitched off. Sum and rule given — result, self-expatriation, or confiscation of wor'dly goods, and a prolonged view of the inside of a military jail. I am fortunate in being able to select an alternative.

Many a better man and citizen than I, has not the power of making a choice. I made up my mind, a year since, that Dixie would soon be too hot to hold an individual of my luke-warm professions of attachment for the new dynasty. But I have delayed my departure until I should have discharged what I felt to be a sacred duty, namely, making over such of my means as I could not transfer to northern and foreign securities, to John's widow. She has sustained heavy losses lately. All that I have left behind is hers, or it will be within a week or two. I have committed a few final arrangements, which I could not stay to complete, to that *lusus naturæ* — an honest law-yer. (Excuse the slur upon your profession, Morton!) This is one reason why I withdraw from the scene of action so stealthily. There is an underground railroad, at a point I wot of, about fifty miles down the river; and I think that I am ticketed through, having obtained — no matter how — a paper that will enable me to pass the Confederate lines. I hope to go through unchallenged, for a rumor of my flight might put the Governmental ferrets upon the scent after whatever unclaimed . remnants of my property they can lay their paws upon. Don't mention this nocturnal apparition, even to Agatha — at all events, until you hear from Jenny, that she is in quiet posses-sion of everything. By that time I shall be far away — prob-ably in New York — possibly in Europe. I cannot say yet where my journeyings will end."

He looked haggard, while he exerted himself to talk in his accustomed strain, and my heart ached for him and for our-selves. I thought of his love for his home and his native. State, of his popularity in his extensive circle of friends, and how warm was his reciprocation of the affection that had saved his bachelor-life from isolation and dreariness. No light cause, no whim or rash impulse, had wrought him up to this extreme measure; and in the prosecution of this, what peril did he incur?

I asked the question aloud.

"But nothing worse than failure to escape from the State can befall you, if you are stopped."

"Desertion is *prima facie* evidence of defection, Brownie, and I am already suspected of unsoundness in the fashionable faith. One is safe, nowadays, just in proportion as he resembles that eminently worldly-wise animal — the chameleon. My moral cuticle is, unluckily, insensitive. Not that I blame the people, or their rulers. A man in a passion is always a fool, and both parties in this wretched National squabble have lost their tempers and their wits. By and by, the first heat will cool down. Then they will have gone too far to compromise. With Macbeth, they will decide that ' returning were as tedious as go o'er,' and the section which has most money and most men will triumph. But I did not come to Sunnybank to talk politics. Nellie, I will take a letter from you to any correspondent you may have over the border. Write without date, signature, or allusion to local affairs. If I get through safely, I will deliver it with my own hands. If not — why, the perusal will edify nobody else."

Loath as I was to lose a moment of his society, I could not resist this temptation. It was easy to obey the rules laid down for my observance. It was not easy to confine myself to the limits dictated by expediency, and to be satisfied with sending a letter of moderate length. It was the next best thing to a face-to-face talk, and it did my spirit good, like a draught of life's most potent elixir.

The two in the study were still deep in conversation, when this was finished and sealed.

"But this is a selfish gratification!" said Mamma, awakened, by my entrance, to a sense of the lateness of the hour. "You need sleep, Charley, and we have left you but three hours for rest."

"Two would be enough," he answered. "Don't trouble yourself to get up to see me off in the morning. Nellie will attend to that. It will not hurt her young eyes to open them before the chickens begin to crow."

"Loss of sleep will not dim mine!" said Mamma, with a sad smile. "But eyes and heart will be the heavier for this parting. We have been friends for many years ——"

Her voice failed as she laid her hand within that of her adopted brother.

"We have!" he returned, feelingly. "Morton! dear old fellow! we never thought in the days when we were young together — when I played the match-maker and you two supplied the fuel, — I don't say the brimstone, Ida, — we did not dream, I say, that our threefold cord would be untwisted by any such *diablerie* as this war. This is a part of the never-to-be-written history of the rebellion. Wasn't the world miserable, and human happiness unstable enough before, that men must plot to go into the wholesale manufacture of human woe?"

Papa said a few words of comfort — such seasonable comfort as he best understands how to offer, and we knelt together in prayer for the last time.

We were all three up to speed Uncle Charley's departure. I question if Mamma had slept at all. I had only lain down upon the lounge in my room, and counted the hours, with open eyes and busy brain. Uncle Will, true to his trust, brought up the well-groomed horse to the side-door — that being the most distant from Miss Hetty's windows. Mammy had a nice, warm supper ready, which she had cooked in her own room. The traveller was brief in the discussion of this — more brief in his adieux. In the stillness of the hour just preceding the dawn, we stood upon the steps, and hearkened to the muffled beat of the receding hoofs until not an echo came back to us from the darkness that had swallowed up our friend.

CHAPTER XII.

AGATHA.

IN pursuance of my system of daughterly duty, I yesterday afternoon shook off the too-delicious *dolce far niente* that had inthralled me since our early dinner, laid aside Shelley and my luxurious dressing-gown, robed myself decently, and repaired, work-basket in hand, to the summer sitting-room, where my prospective Mamma sat at work.

I had just seated myself near her, and solicited, with becoming respect, the privilege of aiding her in her sewing, when the rattle of wheels was heard in the avenue, and Elinor's voice cried from the landing at the stair-head, " Mamma! there is Miss Hetty Stratton ! "

Instead of coming down to receive the unwelcome visitor, the sentinel who had given the alarm fluttered off in the direction of her room, leaving us to bear the brunt of the attack.

Miss Hetty Stratton is our neighborhood gossip — a very tall, very thin, very dressy, very spry, and not at all pretty spinster of thirty-five, or forty, or, for aught I can affirm to the contrary, fifty years of age. She is high-featured, — particularly as regards the forehead and nose ; her hair is flaxen ; her eyebrows invisible ; her skin is dotted closely with pale freckles ; her eyes are light-blue, prominent and glassy as are those of a china doll ; and she wears a set of very white and very false upper teeth, which, being either too long or too loose, or both, clatter against those of her lower jaw like the dry bones of a skeleton in the wind, whenever she waxes animated. She met Mrs. Lacy in the door with a rapturous kiss and an

13

embrace of her sinuous arms, the beholding of which made my flesh creep.

"My dear friend! it is an age since I have seen you! How d'ye do, Agatha? So I said to Sister Mary, to-day, 'Since Mrs. Lacy has positively taken the veil, and declines visiting her nearest neighbor, I will return good for evil, and invite myself to pass the night with her, just to keep up her spirits and the girls'.'"

"You were very considerate of our comfort, and we ought to be exceedingly obliged to you," replied my Lady, courteously and falsely.

Not falsehood as to the letter, but a lie as to the spirit, nevertheless. She would have led the way into the drawing-room, but the sprightly Hetty resisted.

"Now that I am here, I will not be made company of! How cool and lovely it is in this hall! I was telling Charlotte, one day last week,— that awfully hot day, you remember,— that if there was but one cool spot in the world, it was the great hall at Sunnybank. I will just throw off my hat and duster."

She tossed aside, with girlish *abandon*, a juvenile gypsy "flat," trimmed with buff ribbon, and a flimsy black silk mantle, and then tossed herself upon the antique settee that stands in the hall. She was attired in a grass-green tissue, profusely flounced, and with the lining cut absurdly low in the neck, her meagre shoulders showing sharply through the gauzy veil.

"If there is home-comfort to be enjoyed in the universe, it is assuredly in this house!" she twaddled on. "Everywhere else, a gloom seems to oppress the spirits of the people. One hears of nothing but anxieties about the poor dear soldiers, and complaints of the sufferings of those left at home. But here, all is unchanged. Do tell me, my dearest Mrs. Lacy, when you last heard from those darling, gallant boys of yours."

"Last week."

"And like all other mothers in this region, you are hoping to receive letters from them, shortly, dated from Philadelphia or New York, I suppose."

"At the latest advices from them, their regiment had not changed its quarters," replied my Lady, imperturbably.

" *Inde-e-ed !* I beg your pardon ! I am so shockingly forgetful ! I ought to have known better than to ask such questions of *you*. But it seems so natural to take it for granted that all southern mothers — the Cornelias of this century, as Colonel Ramsay calls them — feel alike on this subject. Brownie ! my bird of beauty ! welcome ! "

Me she had not honored with an embrace ; but the lean arms inwrapped her "bird of beauty" in their snaky folds, and the kissing ceremony was repeated. Elinor has a perfect antipathy to the creature ; and I noted, with malicious glee, that her brown cheek was flushed with disgust, and her lips compressed to hinder the verbal expression of this, as she extricated herself from the feminine anaconda. She retreated to the shelter of her mother's wing, and sought busily, but vainly, in the maternal work-basket for a bit of needlework that might engage her eyes until it was safe to raise them. Foiled in the quest, she betook herself to the occupation of arranging spools, scissors, and the countless et-cetera of woman's labor within the wicker case.

Miss Hetty's pet vanity — one of many — is her long, lean hands ; and to display them she clutches and crawls over everything near her, with her spidery fingers. Her next action, having released Elinor, was to lay hold of a corner of Mrs. Lacy's work ; seizing it with the thumb and forefinger, leaving the second, third, and fourth fingers raised at a graceful angle in the air. A capital manœuvre, if well executed, for showing a handsome ring and the curve of the wrist. She was tolerably well " up " in it, having practised it diligently for thirty or forty years.

" What fresh work of charity engages your attention now, my dear lady ? "

" 'This is a dress for one of Mrs. Young's children," was the answer. " You may not have heard that she is sick, and unable to do much for her family."

"And her husband is in the army! Poor woman! She does her best to serve her country! I trust Providence will make it up to her in a way she doesn't expect! But—" briskly—"why not leave her to the care of those who have a kindred feeling for her in her destitution? in whose hearts her needs would kindle a responsive chord?"

Miss Hetty's style is usually more "highfaluting" than perspicuous.

"I hope that real distress—unmerited poverty, will never appeal to me in vain," replied Mrs. Lacy, still unmoved.

"You do admit, then, that the distress of these poor people *is* unmerited!" the false teeth clattered; "that the sins of the fathers ought not to be visited upon their children! My dear Madam! I have said over and over *and* over again, that yours was a truly humane spirit, and your views more liberal than many of your friends are willing to allow. I shall tell the story of your goodness to the Youngs everywhere! Oh! I assure you that I shall make the best of it! Rely upon me for that!"

"My mother hardly requires that one kind act should be so loudly trumpeted in the county in which she has spent the greater part of her life!" said Elinor, with spirit.

In true feline nature, she ceases to purr, and strikes out with her claws when her favorites are assailed. Miss Stratton reached over to pat her head with her skinny digits.

"Ah! my pet lamb! that shows how limited is your knowledge of poor weak human nature! I am sorry to say it, yet since it is the truth, why should I be? as I told Mr. French the other day, when he was animadverting rather harshly upon this very topic, it is one of the most painful traits of mankind that you may do a person nine hundred and ninety-nine favors for twenty-nine years, and fail in the thirtieth to do him the thousandth, and he will remember nothing except that you have disobliged him."

A bit of homely philosophy, by the way, which she must have filched from some one else. Her brain never concocted anything so true and telling.

"Antecedents are not worth a fig in proving characters," she ran on. "I have asserted once and again, far and near, If Mrs. Lacy would only be a little politic! just adapt herself as she could do, — for she can perform anything she chooses with her own peculiar grace, — just conform outwardly to the opinions and conduct of those about her, there would be less talk of her stubborn disloyalty — I beg a million pardons! the word escaped me unawares! — I would say her disaffection to the prevailing belief, — the universal persuasion of all true Southerners. As I have argued, times without number, If Mrs. Lacy — and there isn't a kinder-hearted woman living — would but overcome her scruples so far as to join with our neighborhood circle in our weekly gatherings from house to house to sew for the soldiers; or, if she preferred to plead domestic duties, or slight indisposition, — for our discussions are perhaps too patriotic on these occasions to be palatable to the ears of Yankee sympathizers, — if she thought it better to send for a bundle of army cloth and cut out and make, — *or* should she object to handling the coarse stuff — for it *is* rough, and the 'fuzz' flies into one's eyes and nose, and the dye rubs off on one's fingers, as my unfortunate hands can testify — just look at them — should she dislike to manufacture the garments herself, she might have them made in her establishment — for a more able corps of seamstresses I never beheld. If she would condescend to conciliate her more loyal acquaintances even so far as this — as I have insisted here, there, and everywhere — tongues would wag less furiously against her and her husband?"

I should have been sorely cheated had I missed the sight of Elinor's face, while this tirade was being poured forth. Held silent by her mother's peremptory eye, she fretted like an unbroken colt in harness. Her cheek was like the ripe side of a Georgian peach; her eyes darted sparks through the drooping lashes; her small hands crushed one another cruelly, and chafed the round, dainty wrists until they were streaked with purple. I was in a state of wicked enjoyment. So lively a tilting-match is not offered to my gaze every day.

13 *

"I am sorry that my conduct has given offence to my former friends and present neighbors," returned Mrs. Lacy. She was too old and wily a combatant to betray one of the outward tokens of emotion manifested by her daughter. "I am innocent of intentional disrespect to them. Much less have I designed to show wilful unkindness toward them. Nor have I obtruded my private opinions of public affairs upon a single person in this community. My crime seems to be that I stay quietly at home and mind my own business, imitating in this, as in all other respects where it is practicable to do so, the example of my husband. Since the outbreak of the armed rebellion, no one in this neighborhood, or any other, has heard from Mr. Lacy a word inimical to the party in power."

"Precisely what I have affirmed, repeated, and *reiterated*!" cried Miss Hetty, her jaws in noisy collision. "I have said in the closet and upon the house-top that Mr. Lacy was one of the salt of the earth. And if he *was* a strenuous Submissionist as long as he dared to be, and opposed the march of the righteous cause up to the very last moment in which it was safe for a man to open his mouth on *that* side — do, for pity's sake, give him credit for keeping quiet now that speech would be dangerous! And if — so I reason with the grumblers — if silence at this vital stage of our dear, beloved South's history *is* treason, is that any just cause why this good man — this elder in a Christian church, and his wife, a model mistress, wife, and mother — should be ostracized and condemned unheard? *Do* the exigencies of the times — and upon this point I dwell continually and forcibly — does the good of the Cause require unsparing proscription? Let us, in tender memory of the dear, noble sons who have cast in their lot with our struggling, down-trodden, bleeding-at-every-pore South, be forbearing, and await the developments of Time!"

At this juncture the teeth became unmanageable, and she shut her mouth; whereupon there ensued a click like the snapping of a spring lock, and she was all right again.

Mrs. Lacy sewed steadily, without a nervous breath or

gesture. Elinor's palms and wrists were bruised almost to blackness, and the veins in her forehead were swollen cords. That girl's habit of obedience to her strong-willed mother is little short of miraculous. Seeing that she would suffocate sooner than speak, and thereby disobey her despot, I slipped in an oily word.

"We are greatly indebted to you, Miss Hetty, for your gallant advocacy of our cause, since it appears to be so unpopular."

"Thank you, Agatha! It is a principle of mine to stand up for my friends, right or wrong — right or wrong — as I had occasion to apologize to a lady, yesterday, for my warm defence of my favorites here at Sunnybank. And I cannot express to you the delight I feel at seeing you, Mrs. Lacy, and my precious girls here at work for the helpless family of a private in the army. There is something so sweet and unostentatious about it! so not-letting-your-right-hand-know-what-your-left-hand-does-y in this quiet, active beneficence, that it actually calls forth tears," — wiping her high-bridged nose, holding her handkerchief with her thumb and finger — second, third, and fourth fingers in a position of extreme divergence. "Oh! I engage that this sign of dawning reformation shall be extensively circulated! Trust me for that!"

"We do!" I said, solemnly.

My Lady gave me a glance of amused reproof.

"My daughter!" she said softly to the mutely-restive slave beside her, — and when she likes, her tones are very musical and tender, — "will you give orders for an early supper? Your father will be home soon now. And see that Miss Hetty's room is ready for her."

As the liberated girl disappeared, the hostess accosted her guest with unflinching politeness.

"Suppose we leave the debatable ground of politics, Hetty, and take a stroll in the garden! Our late flowers are looking finely this season."

I arose and attended my patroness' steps, as she willed I should do; and when we had made the circuit of the flower-garden, and heard Miss Hetty pronounce this "exquisite!" and that "sue-perb!" and the other "so perfect!" we went in to tea. Elinor chatted with her father at the table, and scarcely looked toward the visitor. Mrs. Lacy was dignified, and I played the agreeable generally; "did" the amiable alkali business to the oil and acid of the mixture. Supper was over by eight o'clock, and we had before us the enlivening prospect of an evening of certain boredom. In view of this, Miss Elinor promptly assumed the rôle of the good sister, and offered, with bewitching fondness, to put Carrie to bed. I believe she really likes the monkey; but it was not this liking that induced her particular attentions to her on this evening, and detained her above stairs for an hour and more, while Miss Hetty deluged us with wishy-washy tattle in the parlor.

It must have been nine o'clock when Elinor walked into the parlor, and, in apparent abstraction, pushed the door to after her. She is so prone to do meaningless things that I should not have noticed the action had not her mother exclaimed at the heat of the room, and requested her to unclose the door. She obeyed with a silly simper, and performed what I imagined was her real errand to the apartment; viz., summoned Mamma to a culinary conference in the hall. My Lady was first to reappear. Her placid demeanor and tranquil resumption of Sally Young's unfinished calico created no suspicion of any mystery connected with her temporary absence. But ten minutes thereafter Elinor floated upon our sight, eyes shining like stars, her cheeks suffused with rose-color, and on her mouth a smile of happiness that promised, each second, to break into ecstasy. She was actually transfigured by some new and secret bliss. My instant thought was, that the mail had brought the long-pined-for letter from the thither shore of the —to us—impassable gulf; but a little reflection corrected this. Mrs. Lacy had asked her Lord, in my hearing, "Any letters, my dear?" and been answered, as I knew truthfully, "None!" I have no love for this demigod of the household; but he speaks the truth, or holds his tongue. I tried a shrewd device for divining my young lady's feelings. I sent her to the piano, where she foiled me by playing a string of sentimental fooleries to please the taste of the romantic Hetty.

Well! I am gradually coming to the pith of the matter — the kernel of the nut — the heart of the mystery! I was bored, and tired, and depressed; and I did what most honest Christians are apt to do in similar circumstances, — went to bed and to sleep. So sound was my repose, that when, after what I imagined was a short nap, I was aroused by a tapping at my door, and opened my eyes, I saw that it was already dawn. I got up and drew back my bolt to the untimely intruder, whose agitated tapping irritated my nerves, or temper. There stood Miss Hetty Stratton in a long, white gown and a frilled night-cap with an astonishing border, trimmed with lace.

"Let me in! Let me in!" she whispered hurriedly, her teeth very shaky, as were her limbs with chill or fright. "I *do* believe I am going to faint!"

And down she plumped herself upon my bed, gasping and yawning like a fish upon dry land.

"I will call Mrs. Lacy," I said, moving toward the door.

"Not for ten thousand worlds!" she exclaimed, sitting up with a wonderful return of vitality. "Lock that door, do! and come here! I have had such a fright! such a disappointment! such a disclosure! I must tell somebody of it, or I shall die! Can I trust you?"

"To tell — or not to tell?" I asked, laughing, for my powers of description cannot do justice to the comic scene.

"My blessed child! don't laugh! It is an awful thing — a secret involving, maybe, life and death. Who would have thought it? I am more than ever convinced of what I have proclaimed fifty thousand times — that it is not safe to trust in suspicious characters, however fair may be their professions."

"Doubtful things are proverbially uncertain," I interpolated dryly; "but what have you seen? a ghost, or a Yankee soldier?"

"Hush-sh-sh! not so loud. Put your ear down to me. You

will be discreet, for you are at heart true to the cause — are you not?"

"Yes — yes! but go on!"

"A Yankee spy spent last night under this roof!" she whispered — a horrible, creaking whisper, which suggested the idea that her thorax and epiglottis were ossified, and needed oiling in the joints.

I shivered as I shrank away from her lips.

"I don't wonder you tremble!" she continued. "It is enough to make one's hair stand on end! Lie down here by me, and I will tell you the whole story."

I preferred sitting up, and she agreed that I should do this, provided I sat upon the bed close beside her. She went through her narrative in the same hollow, grating whisper that had chilled my marrow.

She had noticed all the afternoon a restless, unsettled look about the whole family, excepting myself, and her imagination took alarm at this as a sign that some evil was brewing. Elinor's absences from the room, and the frivolous excuses given for these, were further links in the chain of evidence against the dear friends she now stigmatized as "midnight plotters."

"But when the innocent-faced little jade came into the parlor and shut the door, I was sure that something was on foot. My hearing is acute. My friends often tell me that I am a regular Fine Ear. 'Why do you shut the door?' said Mrs. Lacy, thoughtlessly, no doubt, for I am morally sure that she was in the secret all the while. The door was opened, and I heard, as plainly as I ever heard anything in my born days, a man's step upon the stairs."

"One of the servants," I said in all sincerity, for I looked for nothing but the smallest of mice from this travailing mountain.

"Don't you believe it! It was the firm, quick step of a gentleman's boot! As if I didn't know the tread of a gentleman from that of a negro! I could recognize the step of every gentleman of my acquaintance if I were blindfolded by twenty thicknesses of pocket-handkerchief."

When I reflected upon the number of years during which she had been hearkening with anxiety, amounting to agony, for the "coming man," I considered this highly probable; so I said, "Indeed!" and yawned in drowsy inattention she would not comprehend.

"Then that little intriguer"—she evidently took a special pleasure in stigmatizing her late favorite—"that little intriguer took me away to the farthest corner of the house to sleep, in a good-enough room to be sure, but a mile off from anybody else! You needn't tell me there was no design in that!"

I did not remind her that her door was just opposite mine, for what am I but a nobody?

"The room which I suppose you expected to have adjoins Mr. Lacy's study," I explained. "Perhaps they were afraid you might snore and disturb him. He sometimes sits up very late."

I was reckless about angering her. Up to this hour, I had had only the slightest imaginable modicum of condescending notice from her. She was herself a poor relation and a sponge upon her wealthy friends, and naturally intolerant of other parasites. Besides, I knew that she did snore horribly, and was willing that she should be advised of her infirmity.

"*I* disturb *him!*"—spitefully emphatical. Her china blue eyes glared, and she clutched the air with her bony fingers. "Wait until you hear all! I hadn't been in my chamber five minutes when I caught sight of the reflection of a lantern upon the palings on that side of the lawn. I soon made up my mind that somebody was moving about in the stable yard, and considering that it was almost eleven o'clock, and Mr. Lacy is so particular in having his stables locked early, and there are so many horse thieves about, I thought it only prudent and kind to try and find out what it meant. I was afraid to look out into the hall for quite a while, for, as I always shall declare, these long passages are the most ghostly places in nature; but, presently, I became so uneasy that I could stand it no longer, for the light kept waving, and flickering, and dancing up and down, and at last disappeared entirely, and so suddenly I was positive that the thief had gone into the stable. I couldn't reconcile it to my conscience not to give the alarm."

"Dear me!" I yawned again. "What an uncomfortable appendage such a conscience as yours must be! I should have gone to bed without giving the matter two thoughts."

"But you see I couldn't! I am forever saying that if one ever learns to love her neighbor as herself, it must be by forcing herself to take a lively interest in that neighbor's every-day affairs. I threw on a black cloak I found in my closet, and crept out into the entry. It was dark as pitch, but I groped my way to the main hall, and across this to the door of Mr. Lacy's study."

I held up my hands. "In your night-gown, Miss Hetty! What if he had opened the door!"

"I thought of that, and made up my mind not to let him do it. I meant to hold the knob tightly in my hand, and call to him through the keyhole. Just as I stooped to do this I heard voices inside, and ——"

"You listened at, instead of speaking through, the keyhole!" I filled up the pause. "Very proper and natural — inevitable, in fact!"

She took me at my word. "As you say, there was nothing else to do. A *man* was talking!"

"Another man! why, Miss Hetty!" seeing that she expected some comment upon this tremendous announcement.

"Yes — and although the voice seemed to be a familiar one, it did not just then occur to me whose it was. He spoke in a low tone, and I could only catch a half-sentence here and there. The first thing I heard distinctly was, 'There is an underground railroad about fifty miles down the river —' and then —'I have a pass through the Confederate lines.' Next came your name — 'Don't mention my visit to Agatha, whatever you do.' I couldn't quite get the rest of the remark, but

the substance was, that if the story were once in your possession, there was no telling what his fate might be.'

"Now you *are* romancing," I said, scornfully, to conceal the
ridiculous thrill these words gave me.

"It is true as gospel, child! It was hearing this that put
it into my head to tell you the whole affair. When the man
stopped talking, Elinor spoke, in that soft, tender voice of hers
which people think angelic, though I must say, as I have repeatedly whispered to my friends, that I never knew another
girl who, in my opinion, was so egregiously overrated. She
talked very low. It was plain they were in there alone — at
half past eleven o'clock at night; and Mrs. Lacy has the name
of having brought her children up so discreetly! And as sure
as you are born, I smelled hot coffee through the keyhole!
My nose is exquisitely keen."

"Never mind your nose!" I interrupted, impatiently.
"What did Elinor say?"

"I couldn't catch a word — only the tone; but that was
smooth as cream, and sweet as honey. He lowered his voice,
too, in replying, but I heard 'evidences of affection, Brownie.'
And how lovingly he did bring out that 'Brownie!' I vow,
it made me sick to hear it."

I was beginning to feel cold and sick, too. Yet I did not
evince by accent or movement the impatience, the suspense, the
suspicions that tugged at my heart-strings. I was assured, if
one tenth of this tale were true, who was the midnight guest.
But I could bear all that I suffered, and more, sooner than let
this harpy alight upon my vitals, and drag out my secret fester
for the regalement of herself and fellows. I yawned, the third
time, more broadly than I had yet done.

"It was either Ross or Lynn, I imagine" — very sleepily
indeed. "There may have been a military necessity for not
making his coming matter of common talk."

"Ross or Lynn, indeed! As if I did not know their voices
as well as I do my own! What had they to do with underground railroads and passes through the Confederate lines?

14

But I shall never get through if you interrupt me so! I could make out but little more. Once he said, 'The section that has most men and most money will triumph in the end.' And again, 'I did not come to Sunnybank to talk politics.' Then there was a little bustle in the room, as if one or both of them had arisen from their chairs, and I had to run for it. I had just reached the narrow passage, when Elinor came out of the study, and hurried along toward her chamber, I suppose to get something that her visitor needed. At any rate, I considered it best to go back to my quarters, until the house should be quiet. By this time the light in the stable-yard was gone; but I took a seat by my window, determined to watch for more developments of this midnight treason. For, as I have proclaimed, a thousand times, if I have once, these are the days that try men's souls and women's hearts and nerves; and if I do say it, that shouldn't say it, there is the material for a Brutus in my spirit. My nephew Rolf has repeatedly said to me, 'Old girl, you are a frail bark, but you do work like a Trojan. There's the right sort of timber in your sails.'"

"And presently you dropped asleep, I suppose, and awoke just now, with a crick in your neck and a cold in your head." I pretended to wind up the narration to my complete satisfaction.

"Sleep! not a wink has visited my eyelids this blessed night! Before two o'clock, there was a light in Rachel's house, and smoke pouring out of her chimney, warm as the weather is. Then old Will's door opened, and he went across the yard with a lantern, in the direction of the stable; and I saw through it all in a flash — how he had been busy there with the traveller's horse earlier in the night. I set my door ajar, and listened for sounds from below. I heard Rachel come puffing into the dining-room, bringing in the breakfast she had been cooking. There were other noises. You know what a place for echoes that great staircase is. Three people went down it very cautiously — Mr. and Mrs. Lacy and Elinor — for I recognized their steps. Then another door was unclosed, and the stranger walked fast and lightly through the hall, and ran down stairs.

He came from the spare chamber, which *I* was not allowed to occupy. Pretty soon, they left the dining-room, and passed toward the side-door; and it occurred to me that the visitor was to mount there, to avoid the risk of being seen from your windows or mine. I was resolved to get one look at him. His room was empty, and it commanded a perfect view of the side-porch. I slipped along the wall, for it was still very dark, and found the open door without trouble. I smelled the broad-cloth and boots as soon as I was in the chamber. I can always tell when a man has occupied an apartment within the last twelve hours. My patriotic zeal must have given me courage to explore the premises. As I am eternally reminding my sisters, when they wonder at my self-denial, and energy, and strength, under the adverse circumstances that distress and harass us, I can bear and do everything in a righteous cause. I could go to the stake ——— "

" And you explored the room? " I brought her back.

She looked as Virginia might have done at sight of the sacrificial butcher-knife, if Virginia had been a scrawny spinster of forty-five, in a ruffled night-cap, and with loose false teeth.

" I did! I went straight up to the bed, and plunged my hands into it! A man had slept in it; it was still warm, and the pillow smelled of cigar smoke. I then proceeded to the window and leaned out. There was a horse standing before the porch, and several figures were huddled together upon the steps. They talked in whispers, but I could hear a word or two. The stranger's last farewell was to ' Brownie.' ' I wish I dared take you with me! ' he said. Then he got upon his horse, and moved slowly away, taking the turf on the side of the road, that the clatter of hoofs might not give the alarm. When those he had left in the porch turned to come in, I beat a retreat. The floor is covered with matting, you know, and in crossing this, I slipped upon something. It was the envelope of a letter. Here it is. There is light enough now to read it by. I had to wait until the house was still again before I could strike a match and satisfy my burning curiosity."

I accepted the envelope, which she thrust between my fingers, took it to the window, and drew back the curtain. The red rays of the coming sun poured directly over me and it. The cover was torn half in two, but the name was there in full, in Mr. Lacy's handwriting: —

Harrison M. Wilton, Esq.
New York City.

I had taken the precaution to turn my back upon the prying mischief-maker. The instinct of self-preservation is the strongest known to man or woman, and it did not desert me.

When I faced her again, after a protracted study of the fragment, I asked, composedly, "And is it your belief that the gentleman whose name is written here spent last night under this roof?"

"I would wager my life upon it! I can swear to his voice, his walk, his figure! The shameless, impudent Yankee spy!"

I stared at her now, in real bewilderment.

"What do you mean?" I questioned, slowly.

"Mean! That these Lacys have harbored a Yankee spy, and are in secret correspondence with the enemy. I said it last night half in fun. I repeat it in awful earnest. Nobody knows what information they may have given, or how many times that fellow may have been sneaking over the lines, on his underground railroad. I wonder the judgment of Heaven does not fall upon this house, when such deeds of darkness are committed here. But he won't come again, I'll promise you! I will inform the Vigilance Committee! I will arouse the neighborhood! I will go in person to headquarters! I will do something desperate!"

At this climax, the vacillating teeth accomplished a feat of desperation, upon their own responsibility. They escaped irretrievably from the hold of the faded lips, and tumbled to the floor — gums, roof, and, for aught I know, palate, as well. Miss Hetty dived after them; and this element of the ludicrous

being all that was needed to put the finishing stroke to my excited mood, I dropped into a chair, and laughed until I cried.
When I could control myself, I found Miss Hetty standing over
me, mopping my head with cologne.

"Poor thing! poor thing! no wonder you are upset!" she
was saying, snuffling sympathetically meanwhile. "It must
be a shock to discover the baseness of your benefactors."

"Jew! I thank thee for that word," was the quotation that
came to my mind. It steadied me immediately. Yet I feigned
an hysterical sob and giggle, before I entered a protest against
her threatened exposure. I had to deal with a fool, and I
handled her according to her folly. I held up to her view the
consequences to herself of her recital of the events of the past
night; the ignominy that would follow her confession of the
manner in which her information had been gained; the reputation she would achieve as an eavesdropper and a betrayer of
neighborly hospitality. I entreated her to move· cautiously, if
move she must, in the affair. I would not screen my "benefactors," because they were such. I would, from this moment,
mount guard over them, and, should other suspicious circumstances seem to confirm her belief that there was in operation
a systemati˙ correspondence with the invaders, I would assuredly confide these to her. If the public welfare required an
exposure, let it be complete. Patient vigilance might bring
more conclusive or available proof.

I quieted, convinced, and finally I got rid of the prating
idiot. I saw her to her room and to her bed, with my smell-
ing salts within her reach, should her emotions overpower her
anew. Then I went back to my chamber, and darkened the
windows, — the morning was heartlessly bright, — and sat down
upon the floor to think of what I had heard.

I *can* think now, and plan, and resolve. But then I could
only repeat one thing over to my stunned brain and heart, —

"He came for the love he bears her! Nothing else! nothing else!"

14 *

CHAPTER XIII.

ELINOR.

December 29.

We five young people — Ross, Lynn, Rolf Kingston, Agatha, and I — were having a pleasant evening together.

Lynn has been with us now for ten days. His wound, received in the bloody fight of Fredericksburg, has healed rapidly under Mamma's nursing and the unlimited supply of petting afforded him by Agatha and myself. Until very lately, I have not been quite reconciled to the betrothal of my brother and my friend. Dearly as I love both, the news cost me a pang; it may have been of selfish regret for my prospective loss of his attentions, which were, in time past, rather lover-like than brotherly in their tenderness and constancy. It could not have been a doubt of her worthiness to fill the highest seat, even in his heart. I do not know a nobler girl than Agatha. If she is somewhat enigmatical once in a while, her peculiarities harm no one except herself. Latterly, her deportment has been beyond all praise. From the moment of Lynn's arrival, weak, pale, suffering, at his father's door, she has thrown aside the mask of maidenly coyness, and manifested toward him the calm, steady affection of a faithful wife.

"I am inexperienced, and I will not interfere with your duties. It is your right to have the nearest place; but, surely, it is my privilege to work with you, and perform such offices as you are willing to intrust to my unskilful hands," she pleaded with Mamma that night.

Since then, the understanding between them has been perfect, and their joint task performed harmoniously. For three days past, Lynn's convalescence has transferred the care of him almost entirely to Agatha; and very happy they are under this order of things. On this evening, he lay upon the sofa in the parlor, and she sat on the cushion at his side. We had voted, unanimously, for the exclusion of lamps, while the blending of twilight and fire-light was so bewitchingly provocative of con-. fidential talk and pleasing, yet sad, reverie. We, upon the opposite side of the hearth, were careful not to observe the clasped hands resting in the shadow of the invalid's pillows, or to overhear a syllable of the low-voiced conversation that under-ran the stronger current of ours.

"The atmosphere of this place is enervating," complained Ross, in mock dissatisfaction, throwing himself at half-length upon the lounge, and, uninvited, laying his head upon my lap. "I don't blame you, Lynn, for spinning out your recovery at such length. I would be willing to bargain for a flesh-wound myself upon the same terms."

"Hannibal and Capua!" said Rolf, smiling.

"I resent the comparison," I returned. "I prefer to think of Washington and Mount Vernon, in this connection."

"I wish the analogy were perfect in all respects," he said, feelingly. "I do not believe that any of the present company will accuse me of indolence or cowardice, when I say that I wish, from the bottom of my heart, the war were over, or that it had never been inaugurated."

I looked up in interest that had in it a large admixture of surprise. I have greatly modified my old opinion of Rolf Kingston. Within a year, he has ripened in true manliness of character, gained stability of thought and principle. Ross, who has had unusual opportunities for studying his disposition and conduct, in the daily association of their camp-life, has come to esteem and like him far more sincerely and heartily than he once thought possible. It is inevitable that this improvement, marked, and, so far as we can judge, radical, should be accompanied by increased breadth and justness of sentiment upon subjects that, from their importance, challenge grave considera-

tion. Yet the expression given above was so foreign to any
other I had ever heard from him, that I was incredulous as to
my correct apprehension of it.

"Is Saul also among the prophets?" I said, indiscreetly.

I was sorry for it when I noticed the pained pause that preceded his reply.

"Like many others, I took leave of my wits for a season. I
have had enough to bring me to my senses."

I remembered that he had seen his favorite cousin and two
of the dearest friends of his boyhood fall upon the battle-field,
and my heart softened with pity.

"It is too late now to regret past errors," answered Ross,
decidedly. "We have not only drawn the sword, but thrown
away the scabbard. My views, too, have undergone a change
since the beginning of the war; but my conversion is not akin
to yours. I have seen so much of Federal injustice and outrage — cold-blooded vandalism, resulting in the ruin of the
fairest land the sun ever shone upon — that I have come to
detest the cause for which these creatures in the shape of men
are fighting. I am fast learning to hate the sight and name
of a Yankee as virulently as does your 'original Secessionist.'"

"There have been excesses on both sides," said Rolf, temperately.

"I grant it; but let me tell you of what befell a friend of
mine, — a messmate of yours likewise. Robert Campbell —
you know him — lost a sister last summer, a beautiful girl of
eighteen. Her father's house was within the Federal lines;
and the day after her burial, a party of cavalry searched the
plantation, professedly for concealed arms and ammunition.
They smashed the china and mirrors, split up the piano and
bureaus into kindling-wood for their camp-fires, carried off and
destroyed provisions and clothing, beside pocketing all the silver
they could find, and consummated the sum of their atrocities by
opening the newly-made grave in quest of buried plate. They
dug down to the coffin, and opened it!"

"Horrible!" I cried. "And you can believe this of civilized men?"

"I had it from Campbell's own lips, that the invaders did just what I have said. This is but one of many similar instances of their fiendish spirit. I was a Union man once—Unionism learned at the feet of him who, in all other respects, has proved himself the wisest of Gamaliels. I declare calmly now, that were the invading army withdrawn to-morrow, and peace proclaimed, I would not cast my vote for a return of the separated States to their former relation to the Federal Government. I am not a lover of the Confederacy; still less am I a partisan of her rulers; but Virginia is my mother! To her, as a sovereign, and, if need be, an independent State, I owe allegiance. I would shed the last drop of my blood to save her soil from desecration. It is no poetical figure, to say that we —

> 'Strike for our altars and our fires,
> Strike for the green graves of our sires,
> GOD and our native land!'"

"Our unofficered bands have been guilty of many outrages — of shameful disregard of the rights of private citizens," rejoined Rolf. "I could match your story, sad as it certainly is, and truthful as you assert it to be. Have you never heard of rings, and charms, and watch-chains made of the bones of Federal soldiers slain in battle? If not, I have; ay, and seen them displayed exultingly by southern *ladies* as trophies of their lovers' valor. No, no, my dear fellow! we are not yet qualified, by principle or behavior, to set our enemies an example of moderation and magnanimity."

"War is a cruel, cruel thing!" I burst forth; "and these acts of plunder and sacrilege, that would disgrace a race of barbarians, are perpetrated by men of kindred blood and the same religious faith."

"You are right," was Rolf's reply, uttered gently and sadly. "These are a part of the fortune of war; and war is a cruel, abominable relic of the barbarous ages — the times of ignorance

at which GOD winked. The chariot of civilization has rolled a
fearful distance backward into the darkness since the guns
of Sumter proclaimed, 'Choose ye this day whom ye will
serve!'"   •

"Where's the sense in croaking?" asked Ross, impatiently.
"We have made our choice; or, rather, the pressure of events
forbade us to make any other. You have the blues to-night,
Captain."

"You are far from the mark there: I have not been so comfortable, in mind or body, this winter, as I am at this moment.
Still, I do not hesitate to confess, that, for me, the glamour of
this glorious strife is pretty thoroughly dissipated. Like Chris-
topher Sly, I am ready to sigh, 'An excellent piece of work:
Would it were done!' And until it is done, I expect to do
battle for Old Virginia, if my life is spared."

"What is all that raw-head-and-bloody-bones talk with which
those sons of Mars are regaling you, Nellie?" questioned Lynn,
from his sofa. "Are they fighting their battles over for your
edification?"

"Rather wishing they had no more to fight," I answered.
"To which desire I add my fervent 'Amen.'"

"And I mine," murmured Agatha.

Lynn dropped his voice to reply, and I spoke to Ross, to
cover the resumed *tête-a-tête* of the lovers.

"Do not talk to Papa in the strain you have just used to me,
Ross, dear. He would be troubled by it. I like to know just
how you feel and think; so you can express yourself to me
freely as you please."

"Does that signify partial conversion, little traitress?" he
said, playfully, pinching my chin.

I was so foolish as to redden angrily at the last word. He
could not see this; but my remonstrance was so quick he perceived that I was wounded.

"Don't call me *that!* It is not *I* who have changed my
creed —" I checked myself, and added, more humbly, "Forgive me; I did not mean to say so much."

" You are consistent: no one can gainsay that,' as my brother's reply as he returned the pressure of my ha .d ; " and we will not begin to quarrel at this late day, provided you do not insist upon my loving your pets, the Yankees. Hark ! "

He started up, as did Rolf. Lynn would have arisen, but Agatha prevented him. The silence in the room was so intense that we could hear the tinkle of the ashes dropping from the burning logs in the fireplace upon the embers beneath. Down the avenue leading to the house came the measured beat of many hoofs, evidently of a considerable body of horse. Not one of us stirred or spoke, until the nearer, louder tramp ceased suddenly at the clear shout, —

" Halt ! "

As if we had waited for the signal, there was a general movement.

" Nellie, you will stay here with Lynn and Agatha, while Kingston and I make a reconnoissance ; not in force, — I wish it were ! " Ross ordered, in a tone of attempted gayety. " We will not remain long in ignorance of the character of our visitors."

They left the room, and there was another interval of trying suspense. I shut my eyes, and prayed for strength to endure the ordeal I feared was at hand. In imagination, I saw my brothers dragged from their home, prisoners, their parents' anguish, Agatha's desolation, my own grief. Oh, it is moments like these that have made rebels of southern women ; not the arguments of politicians, or the conviction of wrong suffered at the hands of the old Government !

Irrepressible was the relief which we all sustained, when, following close upon a knock at the front door, and the subsequent parley with the servant who opened it, Ross' tones rang through the hall in cheery salute, and a great tumult of questions and welcomes ensued. The door swung back, and our two captains entered with a third gentleman between them. He wore the Confederate gray. His overcoat was buttoned up tightly to his chin ; his high cavalry boots were splashed with mud, and his hair was in disorder; but he was, notwithstanding these disadvantages of external appearance, a frank, soldier-like personage, with a bright eye, pleasant smile, and courteous bearing.

"My sister, Major Hart," said Ross, leading him up to me. "A young lady, who, if never firm in the southern faith before, is now, I'll engage. Own up fairly, Nellie: isn't the sight of the gray the most delightful that has blessed your eyes for a long while?"

"I cannot say that I am sorry to see Major Hart," I replied; "and since the gray is an inseparable accompaniment, I will accept it."

He was well known to me, by reputation, as one of the bravest and most dashing of the band of ubiquitous cavalry that is now scouring the country between the two rivers, — the Rappahannock and Potomac, — and which may yet, for anything we can predict to the contrary, be heard from to-morrow at Harper's Ferry, or in Maryland, or, more likely still, thundering at the gates of the National capital.

In ten minutes more, the hall was filled with soldiery, and a group of officers sat and stood about the parlor fire. The whole plantation was alive with the bustle of preparation for the refreshment and lodging of the new comers. Impromptu beds were placed in every apartment except the parlor and dining-room, and for these was held in reserve a plentiful supply of materials for pallets — mattresses, blankets, and the like. Mammoth boilers of coffee were hung over the kitchen fire for the privates, and loaves of bread, of proportionate size, with huge piles of rashers of bacon, were also destined for their consumption; while the store-room and pantries gave up their best treasures to furnish a repast for the weary and hungry officers.

"They are my friends and guests, Mother," said Ross, in bespeaking for them a hospitable reception. "I ask, as a personal favor, that you should treat them, for a single night, as if they were yours."

Major Hart objected, strenuously, for a while, to what he

called "this extravagance of generosity." His force numbered about a hundred men, he stated, and he could not consent that they should be quartered upon a private family. The utmost he asked for the rank and file was permission to bivouac within earshot of the house, and that Mr. Lacy would sell them a little forage for their horses, provided he could spare it without inconvenience. For himself and brother officers, he accepted the proffered hospitality, most gratefully. They had had a hard day's ride, and they must be in the saddle again before daylight.

Looking out of the window as our late supper was announced, I saw the gleam of camp-fires in the field beyond the lawn, and heard, borne upon the night air, the merry voices of the troopers. The officers were gentlemanly and agreeable, and the supper hour was a pleasant one, with the trifling drawback of the occasional allusions from some of the party to the object of their present expedition, and the success that had crowned it, thus far. The force of which they were a detachment, had been, for several days, busy destroying Federal stores, fighting Federal troops, and burning bridges that might offer facilities for the Federal advance. They were in high spirits, and inclined to talk over their exploits at length. And here Rolf Kingston gave me fresh reason for surprise and gratitude. Without putting any visible and unwelcome curb upon the communicative disposition of the strangers, he interposed repeatedly, with kindly tact, introducing different and yet enticing topics to lead them away from that which threatened to prove obnoxious to Papa, Mamma, and myself. When he could not do this, he tempered their boasting into harmless bravado, pardonable in consideration of the exhilaration attendant upon recent prowess. Whether or not the rest understood his aim and motive, I saw that Papa and Mamma did, and that, like me, they appreciated it. The tone of the party was gayer, and their talk of lighter themes, when we returned to the parlor. Agatha was the belle of the evening. She looked every inch the queen, enthroned in her arm-chair, as the cynosure of a knot

15

of obsequious and delighted attendants ; her face, sparkling with mirth, so beautiful, and her repartee so happy, that Lynn's eyes betrayed his proud satisfaction to all who chose to look at him. I was not neglected. Major Hart and Rolf were my devoted cavaliers. We chatted and sang together, without discord of opinion or voice, and really enjoyed ourselves as much, if not more, than did the more demonstrative company on the opposite side of the room. At last, Major Hart, at my request, sat down to the piano alone. He has a rich bass voice, and although, as I fancy, not a thoroughly educated musician, has excellent taste and a fair execution. He had sung twice when Agatha called out to him, —

" Major Hart ! do you know ' My Maryland ' ? "

" Quite as well as I care to, Miss Lamar," he answered, meaningly.

There was a general laugh, all comprehending the allusion to the late unsuccessful advance into that State.

" I mean the song ! I am dying to hear it. May he sing it, Nellie, dear ? We need not indorse the sentiments expressed therein, you know. The door is shut, and your Father and Mother will be none the wiser for the gratification of my idle curiosity."

At first, the proposition seemed to me unkind. An instant's reflection showed me that gayety had only rendered her inconsiderate ; that she could not wantonly have singled me out for the disapproving notice of those present. However this might be, I was the target for a battery of eyes — some inquiring, others suspicious, others displeased, although their owners withheld verbal comment. Not that I am ashamed of my principles. If need were, I believe I could die for the Old Flag. Next to my GOD and my betrothed, I love the land which GOD gave to my fathers, and the banner which symbolizes that country. But a weak, powerless girl, I can only pray for the restoration of peace and union to all her borders. Agatha intimated to me, once, that patriotism was but another name, with me, for the love I bear Harry. She is a close observer and a shrewd analyst of character; but I think she judges wrongly here. I did feel embarrassed, then, at the general notice fixed upon me by her remark. Before I could summon words to my relief, Rolf had taken up the matter.

"Even those who once lauded the production are tired of it now—nauseated as people usually are with false promises. It was very fine to sing,—

> 'See! she spurns the northern scum.
> She lives! she breathes! she burns! she'll come!'

But when we recollect that she didn't 'come,' or show the least inclination to do so, the whole affair is too ridiculous to be popular. Major! will you not give us the new song, with which you favored us at Colonel Raymond's in Richmond—that one about the solitary picket?"

The Major complied without demur, falling willingly into Rolf's plan of changing the subject. He sang the ballad well and feelingly. The music was simple, even commonplace, but the words had a power of pathetic description that touched every heart. At my request, the singer wrote them down for me after he arose from the instrument. I insert the leaf here as he gave it to me, partly because of the poetic worth of the song, partly as a memorial of this eventful night.

> "'All quiet along the Potomac to-night!'
>   Except here and there a stray picket
> Is shot, as he walks on his beat to and fro,
>   By a rifleman hid in the thicket.
> 'Tis nothing—a private or two, now and then,
>   Will not count in the news of the battle;
> Not an officer lost—only one of the *men*
>   Moaning out, all alone, the death rattle.

> "'All quiet along the Potomac to-night!'
>   Where the soldiers lie peacefully dreaming,
> And their tents, in the rays of the clear autumn moon,
>   And the light of the camp-fires are gleaming.
> A tremulous sigh, as the gentle night wind
>   Through the forest leaves slowly is creeping;
> While the stars up above, with their glittering eyes,
>   Keep guard o'er the army while sleeping.

"There is only the sound of the lone sentry's tread,
   As he tramps from the rock to the fountain,
And he thinks of the two in the low trundle-bed
   Far away in the cot on the mountain.
His musket falls slack — his face, dark and grim,
   Grows gentle with memories tender,
As he utters a prayer for the children asleep,
   And their mother — ' May Heaven defend her ! '

"Then, drawing his sleeve roughly over his eyes,
   He dashes the tears that are welling,
And gathers his gun close up to his breast
   As if to keep down the heart's swelling.
He passes the fountain, the blasted pine-tree,
   And his footstep is lagging and weary,
Yet onward he goes through the broad belt of light
   Toward the shades of the forest so dreary.

"Hark ! was it the night wind that rustled the leaves ?
   Was it the moonlight so wondrously flashing ?
It looked like a rifle ! ' Ha ! Mary, good by ! '
   And his life-blood is ebbing and plashing.
' All quiet along the Potomac to-night ! '
   No sound save the rush of the river,
While soft falls the dew on the face of the dead ;
   The picket's off duty forever ! ' " *

"All quiet along the Potomac to-night," hummed Ross, leaving the Major and myself at the writing-table, and sauntering over to Lynn's sofa. "Human life is so cheap in this market that a ' private or two,' or even a score of privates, make up a sorry return to the War Department."

"Yet they do the fighting !" I could not help saying. "And their mothers, sisters, and wives mourn them long and sincerely as if their shoulders were bestrapped and sleeves were embroidered. If your fighting machines were heartless and soulless, it would be of less consequence how soon they were knocked to pieces."

The words were still on my lips when a single musket-shot split the air to the north. A volley followed, and then a hubbub of yells, cheers, and shouted orders made a Pandemonium of the night. There was a simultaneous rush of the officers to the door. By the time I reached the hall, I could distinguish Major Hart's voice as he rallied the troops to sustain the

* Words by Ethel Lynn Beers.

attack. Through the door I had a glimpse of a confused mass of men, — some mounted, some on foot, — and of horses pluuging wildly about the field — all seen by the red flash of the musketry. Then, Rolf caught me about the waist, and drawing me back into the shelter of the wall, sprang through the doorway, closed it as he went, and was gone to join the combatants.

Lynn stood in the middle of the parlor floor, struggling vainly to unbind Agatha's arms from his own.

"Help me, Elinor!" she cried. "He is mad! He is not fit to go."

He felt it now, as he reeled in the faintness of reaction after the transient frenzy. Together we bore him to the sofa, and kneeling, one on each side of him, listened to the rain — I can call it nothing else — of the bullets against the wall. In two minutes the carpet was strewn with broken glass. We were untouched; but the sharp rebound of the leaden missiles from the bricks upon the piazza floor kept us in mind of the possibility that this security might be of short duration. It would have been sheer desperation to attempt a change of position. Agonizing fears for Papa and Mamma's safety racked my soul, but I could not seek them. I was thankful to think that my little sister's bedroom was at the back of the house, out of the reach of the deadly balls. But over all other thoughts, exceeding every other anxiety, was the one idea that my beloved brother was a participant in the affray, and perhaps himself the messenger of death to others. If I never prayed earnestly before, I did then, although my lips were dumb — my heart swooning with mortal dread.

The tumult without grew less loud, the combatants apparently receding from the house. Then the firing became irregular, and each discharge fainter than the preceding.

"They are retreating!" said Lynn, who had arisen to his elbow to listen. "We have beaten them off!"

"Thank Heaven!" ejaculated Agatha. "But I felt from the first that it would be so."

Lynn raised her hand to his lips. "My brave girl!"

15 *

I stole away, unnoticed. Papa and Mamma were in the dining-room, unterrified and self-possessed, trying to reassure a crowd of frightened servants, who pressed about them, some kneeling, some actually prostrate upon the floor and clinging to their mistress' feet and dress; many sobbing and praying in audible snatches; a few—and among these were Uncle Will and Mammy—emulating the calmness of their owners, and urging the rest to be composed. One glance showed me this scene, and I ran up to Carrie's chamber. A candle burned upon the table, and there was the imprint of another head than the child's upon the pillow. I understood, immediately, that the mother had knelt beside her latest born, while the deadly hail was falling around her manly boy; besought the protection of the Father for his precious life, as I had done in my unuttered prayer. Carrie slumbered soundly. In her innocent dreams, the din of battle, that seemed to me loud enough to rouse the dead, had no place. Her sunny curls were put away from her brow—I guessed by whose hand, and whose fond lips had been pressed to her cheek, before mine touched it, and my tearful blessing was whispered above her.

Ross met me upon the stairs, on my return to the lower floor.

"Here you are!" he cried, catching me in his arms, and kissing me. "And here are we all! safe and sound, and the Yankees scampering away like scared sheep. Hurrah!"

His cheer was echoed lustily from below. The parlor door was open, and there was passing to and fro in the hall and porches.

"All!" I repeated. "Was no one hurt?"

"On our side, nobody seriously, I believe. There are a few scratches, and the surgeon is looking after them now—but, see here! I felt the wind of the shot that did this!"

A ball had torn through the collar of his coat, and passed on without so much as grazing his neck. He laughed at my shudder, and gave me another kiss, "to bring back the color to my lips," he said.

"Why, who would have thought that you were such a coward? A miss like this is better than a mile. There is a spice of excitement in it that warms one's blood."

We were upon the bottom stair, when Rolf Kingston entered hastily from the front porch.

"Miss Elinor! you had better not stay here! There is a wounded man out there, who, your father insists, shall be brought into the house and cared for."

"Who is it?" asked Ross, anxiously.

"Only a Yankee, and a private at that!" returned a Lieutenant, who had followed Rolf. "He would do well enough out of doors. He deserves nothing less than he got."

Agitated as I was, I had nearly spoken the words that arose in my mind, —

> "Not an officer lost — only one of the men,
> Moaning out all alone the death rattle!"

"Elinor!" I had not seen Mamma until now, but she was standing at my side. "I want you!" she said, in quiet command. "Gentlemen! may I trouble you to let me pass? My son, will you invite your friends into the parlor?"

This was all she said, as she trode on, with her stately step, up the staircase; but Ross looked embarrassed, and the others, within hearing, abashed, at the dignified rebuke conveyed in her tone and expression. I went with her to her room. It was warm, and bright, and delightful, with that nameless air of elegant comfort she contrives to impart to' all her surroundings.

"I wish you could help me arrange this bed for that poor young man," she said. "You can sleep with Carrie to-night, and give us your room."

We wasted no time in talking; but rapidly as we worked, the heavy tramp of the bearers of the wounded private was upon the threshold, as we drew the folded sheet over the oil-cloth covering the mattress.

Mamma looked tenderly into my eyes.

"You can go, love! Thank you!"

"I had rather stay, if I can be of any use," I replied.

She said "Thank you!" again, and directed me to look in a certain closet for a roll of old linen for bandages. When I reëntered the room, the bearers had laid their burden upon the bed, and the surgeon was bending over him.

"He has only fainted from pain, or loss of blood," he pronounced. "Have you cologne or hartshorn in the house?"

Both were at hand, and as I passed them to Mamma, I caught sight of the poor fellow's face. He was ghastly pale. But for the surgeon's assertion, I should have believed him already dead. He was a mere stripling — not more than twenty, I should say, with delicate, handsome features, bronzed complexion, and a slight mustache, shading a mouth that would have been girlishly beautiful but for this manly ornament. Private or officer, he looked the gentleman; and in bathing his hands and wrists with cologne, I observed that they were well shaped — not the coarse members of one used to manual toil.

He revived with a groan, and looked wildly around in bewilderment he was too faint to express. Mamma's gentle voice reassured him.

"You are among friends. Do not be alarmed!"

"Friends!"

His eye turned doubtingly to the gray-coated surgeon, whose fingers were upon his pulse. The doctor smiled grimly.

"You see he recollects how he came to be my patient, Madam. Having some remnants of humanity left in me, young man, I will do my best for you."

Mamma motioned to me to leave the room as the surgeon commenced his examination of the wounds. I had no heart for the renewed hilarity of the company down stairs. Their bursts of laughter and animated voices ascended to me through the flooring, as I sat by the fire in my chamber, and mused upon the events of the past half-dozen hours. A new and terrible era had come to our quiet country home. Violence and bloodshed had desecrated the fair domain. Who could foretell the end of the chapter thus begun? Up to last night, we have seemed to bear a charmed life, environed, as we have been, by robbery, arson, and battles. My father's high character has been our security with both parties. The passing Federal bands have invariably treated him with respectful courtesy, while my brother's decided partisanship of the other side of the political question has been an additional guarantee to us against injury and insult at the hands of the Confederates. But Sunnybank is no longer neutral ground. I acknowledged the fact with a chill horror I cannot explain or account for; a sense of helpless loneliness, that drove me to my knees. I remembered Him whose are the few sheep in the wilderness. A crisis in our destinies might be very near us. It was for Him to avert disaster, and to impart His strength to those whose wall of safety had been blown down by the fierce blasts of war. Soothed, and almost hopeful, I was still dreaming over the embers, when Mamma came in.

"My child! are you up still? It is two o'clock!"

"I could not sleep, Mamma, if I were to go to bed. How is the poor wounded soldier?"

"His case is a very critical one. The doctor thinks his wound is mortal. His wounds, rather — for his right arm is shattered by a bullet, in addition to the more serious injury in the region of the lungs. Poor boy! he bore the probe bravely, and he is so grateful for our attentions, that it is a pleasure to wait upon him. Papa and Rolf Kingston are with him now. The surgeon has gone to his room."

She had sunk into an easy chair, as if worn out by fatigue.

"Mamma!" I said, uneasily, "you are wearied out. Let me help undress you; and lie down upon my bed."

But when I approached her, she threw her arms about my neck, and cried out, in a passion of tears, "Oh, my darling! but for the great mercy of the Lord, this might have been *my* boy, wounded and dying among strangers! GOD help and comfort his poor mother."

Everything is still in and about the house on this afternoon,

as if the alarm of the past night had been an ugly dream.
Major Hart and his troops were in the saddle by sunrise. Ross
and Captain Kingston left us after breakfast. Before going,
they paid a visit to the sick prisoner — for prisoner he is, my
father having given his promise that he shall not escape. It is
a mere form of military speech — this pledge; for there is but
one mode of escape from the chamber where he lies, and that
will probably be opened to him before many days have gone
by. He was awake and sensible when the two Confederate
officers entered. But his eye glittered with fever, and his hand
trembled as my brother took it kindly within his own. Warmly
as he resented the attack of the Federal party upon his house,
and bitter as is the animosity he professes to feel for all who
wear the National uniform, there was no room for ungenerous
enmity in Ross' heart, as he saw the pitiable plight of the sufferer.

"We met as enemies — let us part friends!" he said earnestly. "I am glad you have my mother to take care of you.
There is not another nurse like her in the world."

The bronzed cheek of the youth was flushed yet more deeply
than the fever had stained it, as he thanked him.

"And should you ever be in my condition, — a stranger and
wounded, — which Heaven forbid! do not fail to write to *my*
mother, and tell her where and how you left me. She will
never forget the kindness showed to her only son."

Ross' eyes were not the only ones in which there were tears,
as this was spoken. There was a refinement of feeling and
language, and a wondrous pathos in look and tone, that beto-
kened no mediocre heart and mind. He dictated an address,
which Ross wrote down on his tablets — "Mrs. Ruth Dubois,
Westfield, —— County, New York."

"I wish I could write it myself, but ——"

A glance at his crippled arm said the rest.

The young officers bade him a cordial farewell, mingled with
wishes — they could not say hopes — for his recovery, and they
parted. Strangers and foes but yesterday — friends to-day,
yet to be strangers still forevermore!

But for the trampled lawn and the remains of last evening's bivouac in the adjacent fields, the scene from my window is the same I looked upon twenty-four hours ago. The weather has changed, however. The December clouds, low and leaden, have shut closely down upon the hills; the smoke from the servants' quarters struggles upward, and falls heavily to the ground. The river is muddy and sullen; I hear a sound like the breaking of far-off surf upon a rocky beach, which is the moan of the rising wind through the pine-tops. There will be a storm before morning. Agatha is with Lynn. Papa is abroad upon the plantation. Fences were thrown down, and gates torn from their hinges, during the late skirmish. The carpenters have been busy, all day, in repairing the damage done to windows and palings. I have prevailed upon Mamma to prepare herself for her second vigil, by a long nap, and I have taken her place in Mr. Dubois' room. My task has been an easy one. For three hours he has slept heavily. The surgeon prophesied this, and said it would be an unfavorable sign. From my inmost soul I repeat Mamma's prayer, —

"GOD help and comfort his poor mother!"

CHAPTER XIV.

AGATHA.

January 7, 1863.

WE have had stirring times here for three weeks past. Incident the first was the arrival of my gallant knight and liege
lord with a bullet-hole in his shoulder — the unhandsome keepsake of a Yankee sharpshooter. I was pining for the lack of
excitement, and this event had a touch of the tragic about it
that recommended it to my mental palate. I was born with a
love for the sensational, and since then have developed a genius
for the dramatic that tells me what a grand actress was spoiled
when I took to very private life and toad-eating.

I have been upon double rations of this edible of late ; have
eaten humble-pie with manifest relish and incomparable grace.
Because? For the simple and sufficient reason, that I was
moved to the consumption of this unpopular species of food by
a combination of motives, all of them powerful. Primarily, I
was determined to disarm Prejudice, in the guise of my august
Mamma and right-worshipful Papa-in-law-that-wouldn't-be-if-
they-could-help-themselves. It is politic to shut my eyes to the
circumstance, that they are not enchanted at the prospect of my
union with the lesser of the twin scions of their house. Since
the announcement of·my engagement, they have treated me
with a scrupulosity of attention that would be intensely gratifying to a weak-minded girl. (And an immense majority of the
women in the world, old and young, *are* weak-minded.) Not
being either a novice or a simpleton, I have been amused, instead of delighted, at this obedience to the rules prescribed by
the " Rubric of Etiquette" — " To be used in times of Betrothal

in the Family." Following diligently in their wake, I have comported myself, at great cost of patience and wear and tear of nerves and temper, like an amiable, commonplace young lady whose market is made, and "from this date, the books for proposals at this office are closed."

I believe I have mentioned that I was getting tired of this part, when my "bowld sojer boy" was brought home with an unseemly wound so near the cavity of the chest that his fond Mamma has not yet done turning pale and shuddering when the subject is discussed. *Pour moi*, I too shivered and grew white ; but for all that, I kept my wits up to the occasion : and when Mamma-in-law was most nearly unnerved, the beauteous angel of Opportunity beckoned me to throw myself into the breach. I craved the post of sub-nurse, and I got it ; I asked for instructions in the divine art of healing, and these my Lady imparted with rare condescension, freely applauding my poor imitations of her acknowledged skill. Her son, dutifully sec-onding these plaudits, had, at length, the bad taste to prefer my ministrations to the maternal offices. Little by little, I wormed myself — apparently pushed by him, and hoisted by circum-stances — into her place ; until, when he was declared able to descend to the parlor, to be petted, entertained, and made much of generally, mine was the post nearest to, and most constantly at his side. If Mamma superintended the cooking of his meals, — a business for which I have no vocation, — and set out her delicacies, in ravishing array, upon the invalid's tray, it was I who hovered about these, like a humming-bird over a flower-garden, and buzzed musical praises of Mamma's talents as a cateress, and honeyed entreaties that he would make me happy by tasting her jellies, supping her soups, and devouring her cakes. He ate moderately well, I may observe, *en passant*, for a man in love, and with a lame arm. The repast finished, Mamma might retire to the background : I, and no one else, must read, play, and talk to him. All this came about gradu-ally, and by the natural gravitation of events, and created no

16

symptom of envy or other uncomfortable emotions in the demeanor of my patrons and their daughter.

Lynn had been domesticated here for ten days, or thereabouts, when Captain Ross Lacy and his now devoted messmate, Captain Kingston, joined our family group, upon furlough. The former, whose Secession principles at the outset of the war were decidedly *quasi*, has bloomed into a full-blown pink of southern chivalry — hates the Yankees, and abjures all their works as heartily as if his whilom Damon did not belong to the accursed race. Meanwhile, my particular friend, Captain Kingston, " draws" his patriotism, as the Cockneys have it, " uncommon mild." There is no longer a question in the mind of every intelligent Southerner as to the truth of the theory, that His Satanic Majesty had his birthplace north of Mason and Dixon's Line, and that he holds now his highest court in the city of Washington. But so benevolent and catholic has become the spirit of this *ci-devant* fire-eater, — I allude to Captain Kingston, not to His Majesty, — that, should this crowned imp of darkness, or, to go a step further, should Abraham Lincoln himself, appear, uninvited, in the presence of the brave officer, when his Dulcinea was looking on, he would receive him as a man and a brother, whose frightful lapse in political faith could not destroy his (Captain Kingston's) confidence in his moral worth and signal abilities. The stratagem is a capital one, — worthy, let me say in all modesty, of the brain of her 'who suggested the love-lorn warrior's adoption of it. I have well-nigh suffocated several times with secret laughter at overhearing the grave and temperate discussions held upon the other side of the room, while I appeared to be engrossed, ears and thoughts, by my interesting convalescent. Miss Elinor no longer avoided war-talk and political theories. There were palpable satisfaction and agreeable disappointment in her manner and address at hearing the Captain's sensible and conservative discourse. She was flattered and touched by his delicate deference to her opinions, his humoring and almost sympathizing with her heretical views, — respect and sympathy thrown into bold relief by Ross' outspoken denunciations of the enemy and their style of warfare.

The unanimous verdict of the household is now, " How Rolf Kingston has changed for the better ! " Ross openly declares him to be " one of the finest fellows alive ; " and Elinor says, with engaging frankness, " I did not imagine once that I could ever like and esteem him as I do. Military life has brought out all that is estimable and manly in him."

The consummate ninny ! Yet she reads her Bible, and ought to know that it is not an every-day, or every-century occurrence for the leopard to renounce his spotted hide in favor of the innocent sheep's wool. Nevertheless, I agree with her in saying, that he has displayed more manliness in speech and action than I thought was in him. He is playing for a high stake, according to his valuation of it, and the importance of the game has sobered him into a semblance of lofty respectability. He deserves to succeed ; and I begin to discern a dim probability that he may, if he has tact and perseverance, and, by and by, a vigorous dash of — I was about to say deviltry, but it isn't a ladylike word : I offer, as an imperfect substitute, unprincipled hardihood.

Enough of this. I must learn to tame my speech before *I* turn respectable in the character of Mrs. Lynn Holmes Lacy of Hayridge. This is the not over-euphonious appellation of my betrothed's inherited estate. This brings me to treat, in due course, of the main-spring of my ultra-wifely devotion to this gentleman during his confinement within his patrimonial halls. Human life is so uncertain that one becomes stupidly and tritely axiomatic in alluding to the dubiousness and brevity of what is commonly accounted as precious beyond gold and diamonds ; but a soldier's life is so unsafe that he might about as well have none at all, so far as society at large rears any calculations upon its durability. And if our matrimonial compact *is* "binding and sacred as marriage," — I quote my *fiancé*, — the law is so outrageously practical, so incorrigibly unsentimental, as to set aside this indissoluble union with a contemptuous whiff that

demolishes air-castles, and puts to flight lovers' dreams of solid
profit to be derived from verbal contracts, sworn to under "the
sweet, silver light of the moon," and sealed by kisses of Cupid's
most approved manufacture.   I omit a detailed account of the
gently persuasive measures by which I induced my amorous
swain to view the subject in a right aspect; by what process of
moral induction he arrived at the conclusion, that, if I were in
truth his by every law of honor and affection, it was his duty to
provide for me in the event of his untimely decease, as he
would have done had I been his wife in name.   I never put
forward so much as a hint of the advisability of this arrangement.   The wound that had instigated him to serious meditations upon his mortality had also its lesson for me.   It had
showed me how dear he was to me, and in a vague, dim, awful
way impressed me with the thought of what would be my desolation were he to return no more to me.   I said only this,
seasoned with obstinate tears that would gush between my
struggling eyelids, and punctuated by tender sighs.   This done,
I left the leaven to work.

He was pronounced well enough to leave us yesterday.   The
previous evening we were together, at twilight, in the parlor;
he reclining in his accustomed attitude upon the sofa, I upon
the hassock beside him.   His head rested upon my shoulder;
his hand held mine.   He is a lovable boy, and I mind petting
him less than I should any other man whom I had pledged myself to marry without having one atom of such attachment for
him as a woman should feel for her husband.

"Agatha, darling!" he said, "I do not wish to sadden you
more than our separation must in itself do; but there is one
thing I must say to you before I leave you.   I may never come
back, dear.   The next bullet may do its work more thoroughly
than this has done."

· I uttered a stifled cry, and hid my face among the clustering
locks I had been threading with my fingers.

"My poor girl! you would mourn me, I know."   His voice
shook   "But will you try and hear me through, sweet?"

Would I? Say, rather, what would have tempted me to miss a word?

"Perhaps you are not aware, dear, that I have property independent of my father—a bequest from an eccentric relative, who conceived a violent fancy for me when I was a boy, and made me his heir."

"That was unaccountable,—the fancy, I mean," I said, demurely.

He smiled, and continued:—

"This legacy, consisting of the plantation of Hayridge, a dozen servants, and a few thousands in money and stocks, will be yours, should you outlive me, whether we are married or not."

I commenced a passionate expostulation, which he checked at the third word.

"It is but just, my darling. We belong each to the other, and whatever is mine must be yours also."

"But your parents, your brother and sisters,—theirs is the prior claim."

"By no means. They are already amply provided for; and if this were not the case, my widow should still be thought of first. My father agrees with me fully upon this point. At my request, he drew up a formal will this morning, which was witnessed by my mother and sister. I can leave you with a lighter heart since this has been attended to. It is not a magnificent bequest; but you will accept and use it, in the event of my decease, as a slight testimonial of the love that will outlive death."

I am ashamed to recall the weakness in the cool, cynical mood that holds me to-day; but real tears were coursing down my face, and the sob that broke up my reply cost me no effort.

"Dear Lynn, I am not worthy of this devotion, this generosity."

"Never speak of generosity in connection with my conduct toward you, my own, or of unworthiness in the same breath with your name. You are a pure-hearted, noble woman! I

16 *

do homage to you as to a queen, while I cherish the hope, as I do **my** existence, that you will one day sit down at my fireside, my household angel, my wife! We may yet be very happy together, beloved, should Heaven spare my life."

"If you were taken from me, there would be nothing left worth living for," I answered brokenly, and, I am inclined to think, sincerely.

Love him I do not; I never can: but there is refreshment in his earnestness of belief and emotion, his fervor of attachment for me, his generous impulses, the stainless truth of his manhood. I am not good; and, I may as well add here, I never expect to be. But he *is*; and he is the one person upon the habitable globe who really and truly loves and trusts me. Elinor had something of this feeling once; but, since Harry Wilton's departure, the gulf between us has been steadily widening. I cannot always be mistress of my accents and looks, however I may watch my words; and when she has aggravated me up to the pitch where partial expression of my sentiments is necessary, if I would not expire of bottled spite, I have seen her great eyes fixed upon me with a solemn stare that signified suspicion; of what, I cannot exactly affirm. I imagine, however, of my sanity. I ask myself sometimes, "Can it be that Wilton deemed it his duty to put her on her guard by an account of the last interview he had with me?" True, he promised to keep my secret; but, pshaw! what is the value of a man's promise? Elinor did care for me formerly, and for some reason she would have me credit the profession of her continued affection for me, — which I don't. I had rather she disliked me, as I do her.

Au reste, that is, the rest of the people in my small world, I may chant the roundelay of the celebrated Miller of Dee: —

> "I care for nobody — no, not I!
> And nobody cares for me," —

xcepting this foolishly-fond boy. Thus it is plain, that, in one sense, I spoke the truth when I said that if I were robbed of his love, I should lose everything.

I am tired of sketching love scenes. They are very tedious in their enactment; that is, when all the love is upon one side, and on the other there is shallow mockery; and I find writing about them stupid work. It engenders uncomfortable reflections; unfits one to cope with realities; and I am growing to be a very consistent utilitarian.

Money is useful — *par exemple* — and so are houses and lands, and so were the sable sons and daughters of Virginia soil before the promulgation of the Proclamation which the paper of to-day describes, as the " most startling crime, the most stupid political blunder yet known in American history." I coincide with that editor's views thus fulminated; for am I not a slaveholder in prospective? What right has the Federal Executive to meddle with *my* property? Heretofore, I have not espoused the cause of either party, to my private self. But now, I cast in my lot with the oppressed South. " One touch of nature makes the whole world kin," and it is human nature to keep a bright lookout for one's worldly wealth. I have read " Vanity Fair " aloud to Lynn, recently, and I confess to genuine admiration for Becky Sharp. I am reminded, just here, of her soliloquy at beginning her governess-life.

" I am alone in the world ! " said the friendless girl. " I have nothing to look for but what my own labor can bring me ; and while that little pink-faced chit, Amelia, with not one half my sense, has ten thousand pounds and an establishment secure, poor Rebecca (and my figure is far better than hers) has only herself and her own wits to trust to. I must be my own Mamma."

If Rebecca were a flesh and blood entity, instead of a very real-looking paper she, she would reciprocate my complimentary opinion of herself, when she should learn to what purpose I have played the managing mamma to penniless Agatha Lamar. I wonder what put it into my god-parents' heads to have me christened " Agatha." Lynn is never weary of telling me that it means " good," in the original, whatever the original is. It seems to me he said it was taken from the

Greek.   As I remarked, a little way back, I am not a bit good,
and am never likely to be, unless I were to become very rich
and very happy.   To cite Rebecca again — " I think I could be
a good woman if I had five thousand pounds a year ! "

Next in importance to the will-making, among the events of
the past month, I place the night attack upon Sunnybank, that
has set all the tongues on the plantation and in the neighborhood to wagging.   A party of Confederate cavalry, one hundred in number, had tethered their horses, for the night, upon
the grounds in front of the house.   My Lady had dealt out hot
coffee by the gallon, and corn-meal hoe-cakes by the peck, to
the common soldiers, and the officers — a set of gallant gentlemen — had eaten and drunk of the best the larder could offer,
and were making themselves delightful to us in the parlor, when
the Yankees undertook a reconnoissance of the premises ; bent,
no doubt, on quartering themselves upon their Union compa-
triot, and were fired upon by the pickets.   A skirmish ensued,
in which Captains Lacy and Kingston lent active assistance,
and the Yankees were beaten off.   So say our valorous defenders.   Rode off at their leisure would, I dare say, be as correct,
leaving some half-dozen gray-coats slightly wounded as tokens
of their friendly intentions toward those whom they must have
regarded as usurpers of their suppers and beds, and one of their
own number, badly hurt, in the hands of the enemy.

" We must have done them more mischief than that ! " said
Major Hart, when I exclaimed, " One wounded private ! ' Oh,
lame and impotent conclusion ! ' "

" Of course ! " chimed in Lieutenant Grey.   " But they
carried off their killed and wounded with them — the rascals ! "

If they did, — and Lieutenant Grey ought to know better.
than I what is the Yankee custom in these little affairs — he
being a soldier, and I a woman, — if they did, I am exceedingly
obliged to them for their attention to our comfort ; for the one
man they abandoned to our tender mercies kept everything in
a ferment until. death relieved him of bodily pain, and me of
the annoyance of hearing him talked about.   The Lacys —

father, mother, and daughter tended him as if he had been a prince of the blood. I kept clear of the state chamber — my Lady's own — while it was thus tenanted, my excuse being the care of Lynn, who was cast into the shade by this new aspirant for bandages and jellies. According to the hourly bulletins issued orally by the trio of nurses, the sufferer was an Adonis in beauty, a Sir Philip Sidney in breeding, a triune St. Paul, St. John, and Daniel in piety and resignation — babbling, in his delirium, about "the good fight that he had fought," and quoting, still deliriously, Warren's hackneyed saying, that it was sweet to die for one's country. He repeated it in Latin, correctly, said Elinor and her Papa, who were mightily moved by these ravings. I cannot even remember the English of it, which proves me to be no blue. Elinor played scribe, and took down from his lips a long letter to his mother, which will, I suppose, be framed in black wood, and hung alongside of the old woman's school-girl sampler over the kitchen mantel of some Connecticut farm-house. To this epistle the weeping amanuensis appended a postscript, on her own account, after the demise of her charge. I had a chance of reading it, as I shall state presently, and it was a gem in its way. The Yankee private was interred — if not with the honors of war — yet with the stars and stripes wrapped over his bosom — a home-made banner, upon which Mamma Lacy and Elinor wrought secretly the night after his death. Lynn was not invited to look at the corpse. Nor was I, for that matter; but I was prompted by natural curiosity to interrogate my maid as to the funeral ceremonies, and was informed that "he looked like a gin'ral — all dressed up in de Union flag."

If the knowledge that her son drew his last breath upon the bed and under the roof of an F. F. V., and that his last days upon earth were solaced by the affectionate offices of three attendants of noble pedigree; that he lies buried within the consecrated bounds of the family cemetery, and that the bones of the deceased aristocrats already mouldering there did not turn uneasily at the plebeian intrusion, — if all this does not set that old Connecticut farmeress up in gentility for the remainder of her insignificant existence, where is the use of further attempts to preserve the wholesome laws of distinction of rank that govern Republican society?

Elinor was apparently inconsolable for the loss of her patient. She went about the house on tiptoe, murmuring little snatches of funeral chants and fragments of a song she had caught by ear, from hearing Major Hart sing it on the evening of the skirmish.   One stanza has gotten wedged into my memory through her incessant humming.

> "All quiet along the Potomac to-night!
> No sound save the rush of the river,
> While soft falls the dew on the face of the dead;
> The Picket's off duty forever!"

I wish her songs did not haunt me so impertinently. If she has any artistic talent, it is for music.

She moped, after this fashion, for two or three days, when a diversion arrived in the form of a call from Captain Kingston. He had leave of absence for forty-eight hours, that he might attend to some business in this neighborhood. His brother resides but four miles from us, and the Captain is, in these days, a most loving relative, judging from the frequency of his visits. He rode over to Sunnybank, one afternoon, to inquire after the welfare of the Yankee prisoner, and, as a matter of secondary importance, to see how Lynn's recovery was progressing. He was too sage a strategist to slight this opportunity of deepening the favorable opinion entertained by the family of his amended morals and manners. It was edifying to see his handsome face gather a look of melancholy interest as Elinor expatiated to him, in a corner of the room, upon the concluding scenes of her patient's life. A stranger would have been tempted to arrest him, on the spot, for sympathy with the invaders. The thrilling narrative over, he addressed Mr. Lacy.

"There will be a general exchange of prisoners within a few days, sir. One of my objects in visiting you, to-day, was to inquire if this poor young fellow had any message or letter to send to his friends. I am truly grieved that he did not live to see them again. If you will intrust to me the packet designed for his mother, I will place it in the hands of some responsible bearer, — a chaplain, or an officer in the Federal army, — and exact a pledge from him to deliver it safely to her address. You understand, however, that all flag-of-truce letters must go unsealed."

" Well done ! " I said, inwardly, as the father spoke the thanks the daughter was too much moved to do more than look.

This was a tremendous stride towards preferment with both. There passed from one to the other a meaning glance — on her part, of entreaty — on her father's, of comforting assurance — and Mr. Lacy arose.

" May I trespass further upon your kindness, and ask you to take charge of a letter from myself to a friend in New York ? "

Rolf bowed his acquiescence, and Elinor, first handing the dead soldier's letter to the Captain, followed her father to the study to assist in inditing the more important one.

" A formidable document ! " said Rolf, coming off his pious stilts when left alone with wicked me.

" Do you really mean to send it through ? " I inquired, taking it from him and slipping off the envelope.

" I do ! I could accomplish nothing by intercepting it. I don't care to cheat the old lady out of her son's last will and testament."

I had opened the sheet, and was skimming over Elinor's postscript.

" Which I commend to your perusal ! " I remarked, giving back the letter. " It is a neat sample of the respectfully sentimental."

" She couldn't do anything that was not perfect of its kind," he answered, seriously. " By Jove ! how lovely she is to-day ! It would pay a fellow to kill a Yankee under her window every night in the year, it adds so to her beauty ! I grudged that one his quarters One wouldn't mind a bullet in the heart or brain so much, after all, if he could die upon her arm, her glorious eyes shining down into his."

"Rolf Kingston!" I said, calmly contemptuous, "you are no nearer finding your wits than you were two years ago!"

"That may be! but I am nearer another consummation to be desired yet more devoutly!"

"I begin to think that you may marry that girl yet, if that is what you mean."

"I shall! Yankee iron and lead permitting," he rejoined, iu smiling confidence.

I succumbed to the temptation of dampening his provoking self-complacency — his silly satisfaction with the prospect of his fool's paradise.

"You design, also, of course, to play the trusty bearer to the letter which is now being written up stairs? You have no conception of the destination of that!"

The sneer did not disturb his equanimity.

"I am willing to wager that I can match the address!" and he took out his pocket-book.

From an inner compartment he produced a soiled scrap of paper, and held it toward me. It was the torn envelope Miss Hetty Stratton had picked up, the October night she passed here.

"Where did you get it?"

"From the person who found it. She values it highly, — next to her hopes of matrimony, I verily believe, — and I am to return it to her when it has wrought out its mission."

"Which is —— ?" I said, inquiringly.

"The punishment of treason!" he returned, in a would-be tremendous tone.

I laughed. "Very well! But don't summon me as a witness. All my information is second-hand."

"I question that! But you shall not be annoyed, if I can help it. We cannot afford to quarrel with each other. Moreover, it would nearly kill my friend, the Lieutenant, were you to appear against his father."

Then we talked of other and indifferent things in a louder and more lively tone. Parlors are dangerous places for conferences such as we are obliged to hold, now and then.

Mr. Lacy returned to us, in half an hour, bringing the promised epistle. As Captain Kingston received it, he dexterously turned the outside of the envelope toward me.

As I had expected, it was directed to " Harrison M. Wilton, Esq., New York City."

17

CHAPTER XV.

ELINOR.

In Camp. May 14, 1863.

MY DEAR MOTHER: I forwarded yesterday, to my father, a full account of the late severe engagements at Chancellorsville, resulting in the disastrous defeat and retreat of the enemy. One incident of the battle I purposely refrained from relating to him, hoping that I might obtain leave of absence shortly, and preferring to tell the story by word of mouth. I find that this was a vain expectation — no furloughs being granted just at present.

On the night after the first day's engagement, my company was detailed to guard a number of Federal prisoners who had just been brought into our lines. Some of them were wounded, and my instructions were to see that these did not suffer for want of care. Accompanied by a surgeon, I accordingly went from rank to rank, inquiring as to the whereabouts and condition of such as had been injured, and appointing them to a sort of temporary hospital improvised for their reception. I had little taste for the task, when I thought how many of our own brave fellows might be lying upon roadside and field, longing vainly for the like attention; but since it was duty, I resolved to perform it conscientiously. At length I came to a small squad of men collected about one who had lain down, or fallen upon the ground. A blanket had been spread under him, and his head rested upon the knee of an officer. The latter was bending over the wounded man, trying to pour spirits from a pocket-flask down his throat. By the torch-light I could see that both wore a Lieutenant's uniform. As I stopped, and was about to question the kneeling figure, the head he supported fell back, the jaw dropped, and the man was dead.

"It is all over with him!" said a bystander.

The kneeling man did not speak at once. He closed the eyes of his comrade, laid him down gently, and crossing his arms upon his breast, folded the blanket about the corpse in reverential tenderness. I could not but observe and respect, impatient as I was to complete my unpleasant work.

"Perhaps you would prefer that he should be buried by your own men, sir?" I said, respectfully, moved to unusual interest by the little episode. The Federal officer arose to his feet, giving me the military salute.

"You are very kind! I accept your offer gratefully!"

I had started back at the voice, and now, as our eyes met, the recognition was mutual.

Mother! this blue-coated invader of our State, this volunteer in a service that counts it no crime, but patriotic virtue and duty, to pillage and destroy peaceful homesteads, and devastate plantations inhabited by inoffensive old men, helpless women, and children,—in one word, this Yankee Lieutenant was Harry Wilton! My first indignant impulse was to strike him to the ground where he stood; my second, to pass him coldly by without a word of greeting. He evidently divined both feelings, for his manner was dignified, yet not deprecatory.

"Can I have a moment's conversation with you, Captain Lacy?" he asked.

I bowed, gave an order relative to the removal of the dead body, and we stepped some paces apart from the others.

"Your parents, sisters, and brother are well, I hope," he began.

I answered stiffly that they were.

"You are displeased at meeting me here!" he said next. "I do not blame you for this feeling. It could not be otherwise. To most men I would not deign to offer an explanation of what requires no excuse. But we were friends once, and on my part that friendship exists unchanged. I entered the

United States service last Fall, soon after the battle of Antietam. Do you understand, now, what urged me to this step, as no other consideration — and others were not wanting — had done?"

"You refer, I presume, to the new policy of warfare adopted by the Confederate Government," I replied.

"I do. While the South stood on the defensive, while her armies claimed to be fighting upon their own territory in defence of their homes and State rights, I, in common with many other Union men, while I did not justify her original appeal to arms in support of these rights, yet recognized a certain degree of consistency in her conduct. But when she imitated the very course she had all along unsparingly condemned, when 'Invasion,' and not 'Defence,' became her war-cry, every loyal citizen of the United States felt himself bound to resist, by every means at his command, the advance of the hostile forces. The question involved then was nothing less than National existence. It was a dark era for the Union cause. Defection and dismay were doing their evil work among all classes of society. There were whispers of treason in the highest offices in the Government and the army. No faithful lover of his country could, at that crisis, withhold his support from the tottering fabric. Many could, and did, give lavishly of their means to swell the National army. Thousands, who could not contribute in this manner as their wishes prompted and the exigency demanded, offered strong arms and stout hearts to accomplish the same end. Of this number I was one — and I am here. You would have done the same had my position been yours."

He said all this with no haste or parade of self-vindication, but as a dispassionate statement of facts it was best for me to know, and to weigh well before I judged him. Angry as I was, and indisposed to accept any explanation of his conduct as satisfactory, — sophistical as I felt his arguments to be, — I could not but yield a little to his olden influence over me.

"Perhaps I might," I said, unwillingly. "Yet I was unprepared to see you in the character of an enemy. Our relations, in times past, were so different, it is not surprising that I should be wounded and offended at this encounter."

"Had I listened to the pleadings of self-interest, or purely personal feelings, you had never seen me thus," he rejoined, mournfully. "It is the peculiarity of this war that the patriot is so often called upon to sacrifice his individuality, with its desires, and loves, and seeming expediencies, and labor with a single eye to his country's good. The first and often the hardest battle that he has is with himself."

"I am not so philosophical!" I retorted. "We have not learned, in this section, to dissociate men and the principles by which they profess to be guided. He who seeks to wrest from me home, property, citizenship — life itself — can be nothing but an enemy, and a deadly one. Nevertheless, Lieutenant Wilton, while you remain under my charge, I shall esteem it my duty to do whatever I can to render your situation endurable. Pleasant, I cannot hope to make it."

He raised his hand to his cap, as I did mine, and we parted.

Two or three hours later, I was passing near the spot where I had last seen him, and was arrested by the sound of a voice reading or praying. It was Wilton reading the burial service above the grave of his brother officer. At two o'clock in the morning my company was moved forward, and the prisoners consigned to the custody of another. The position we resigned to them was considered strong, yet it was attacked successfully by the enemy early in the day, the Confederates driven back, and the prisoners — two or three hundred in number — recaptured.

This is the exact history of an interview than which few others could have angered and distressed me more deeply. In reviewing it, instead of repenting my harshness, I wonder at my forbearance, while I do not withhold from Wilton credit for his admirable temper and manly bearing. I considered then, as I do now, that his course in joining the Federal army was inexcusable, and in view of his connection with our family,

17*

basely ungrateful — not to say unfeeling. According to his confession, he enlisted voluntarily. He was not the victim of conscription, or even public sentiment. The cause of the oppressors was never so unpopular since the beginning of the war as when he took up arms, with a probability amounting almost to a certainty, that he would be obliged to use them against those who were formerly his associates in business and social life — his intimates, his brothers in all save blood. Mother! it is monstrous! My heart grows hard and bitter when I think of it. Yet how I loved and trusted this man! How scrupulous and affectionate has been my exception of him from the invectives I have constantly been provoked into uttering against the detested race among whom he had his birth! There is much in birth, after all — and more in breeding. To borrow a parodied text from a jovial messmate, "Though thou bray a Yankee in a mortar with a pestle, yet will not his Yankeeism depart from him." *I believe it!* Yet, in the blindness of the ignorance that preceded the wholesale and abominable development of their true natures — before I knew all Yankees to be Yankees, whatever disguise they might assume — I was willing, yes! glad to have my sister betrothed to this one of the accursed tribe! I would as soon, now, give up an only pet lamb to the guardianship of a red-mouthed wolf.

I write excitedly, but it is less warmly than I feel. I have had a double hurt — to friendship and to pride. If I had ever conceived the imagination of Wilton's enrolment in the enemy's ranks, I would have repelled it as an aspersion of his love and good faith to Nellie and to me.

Lynn, who has just come into my tent, reminds me that you and my father may take a more lenient view of the case that has wrought me up to such a pitch of righteous wrath. I do not believe that this will be so. In any event, I do not think that you will consent to give your daughter in marriage to one who is a sworn foe to her nearest of kin; whose hands may, to-morrow, be dyed in her brother's blood.

Choose your own time and way of telling Nellie what she

must learn in some manner at some day. If I might advise you in so delicate an affair, I would recommend that the news oe broken to her, tenderly, by yourself or Agatha. Nellie is a warm-hearted, faithful little creature, and this will afflict her sadly, let the blow fall when it will.

We are well and in high spirits over our recent victory. There is but one cloud in the southern sky — the death of our matchless Jackson. All the blood in Lincoln's army was not worth one hair of that man's head.

Tell Brownie not to hate me when she hears all !

Affectionately,

Ross Lacy.

This is the entire letter. I have begged it of Mamma, that I might preserve every word of that dialogue upon what must ever be to me " the dark and bloody ground " of this most bloody and cruel war.

Providence did not leave to Mamma's option the means by which the terrible intelligence should be imparted to me. Letters from the army are common property with Papa, Mamma, and myself, and I chanced — no ! not that ! God does not afflict His children idly — it was ordered that I should be the only one of the three at home when Ross' communication arrived. I opened it in eager haste — my heart throbbing with sisterly love and longings. Every word was a drop of hot poison, and withered up my soul.

My parents and Agatha are very good to me.

" Regard all that your brother has written of his personal resentment as if it had not been said," Papa told me to-day. " His temper is hasty, and this incident has touched him nearly. When he is cooler he will repent of much that he has said and done. Listen to the voice of your own heart, the advice of your own conscience ; remembering, meanwhile, that Harry is guilty of no new heresy. He has but carried into practice the principles he held and asserted, two years since, and which your parents encouraged him to hold and to profess. I do not dictate

a line of action for your adoption. But this much I owe it to Mr.
Wilton to say ; — also, that your mother and myself do not see,
how he, while stanch in his present faith, could have acted
differently."

"I do not censure him, Papa! Do not imagine that for an
instant!" I returned. "In what he has done he has not been
actuated by caprice, or yet want of attachment to his Virginia
friends. My confidence in his integrity and truth remains firm."

But to-night, in the loneliness of my chamber, I have read
and re-read that letter until my spirit is utterly broken, and my
heart, too. It was sad enough before to quake with fear at
the arrival of every mail, or the sudden appearance of a visitor,
lest evil tidings had come of my brothers ; to fancy that each
gale might be freighted with the tumult of combat and the
dying breath of one or both of the beloved sons of our once
happy household. Another and more dreadful picture must
ever be with me now — my betrothed husband receiving his
death-wound from my brother's hand, or himself being that
brother's murderer. Oh, merciful Father! Thou hast bound
a heavy load upon thy fainting child! I have no articulate
prayer to offer, only a blind cry for mercy and strength! * * *

Agatha has been sitting with me for three quarters of an
hour. She knocked at my door as I was writing the last line
above. I said, "Come in!" when I had thrust my journal into
a drawer, and tried to smooth away the haggard look of wretchedness I knew was depicted upon my features. She was in her
night-dress, her hair unbound, and a great scarlet shawl
wrapped about her, although the night is warm, and she still
shivered, at intervals, as if suffering from cold.

"I felt lonely and 'blue' in my room," she remarked, "and
I have come to beg for a short chat with you."

I said that I was quite ready for it, and seated myself with
my back to the lamp. It was not envy that made my heart ache
the more in the thought of her happy engagement, while storms
had lowered above my path from within the earliest weeks of
mine, — each cloud darker than those that had gone before. I

did not grudge her her bliss, — but sometimes the unshaded sunshine is painful to eyes weak and sore with long weeping.

"I had a letter from Lynn, to-day," she said, after some commonplace observations upon the dampness she detected in the night air, and the neuralgic symptoms this never failed to excite in her system.

"Did you?" I asked, trying to shake off my listlessness. "Is his arm quite strong again?"

"No. He still has pain and weakness in it, at times, and he was seriously indisposed for a day or two after the battle, although he forbade Ross to mention this when he wrote. I am afraid that many months must elapse before he is entirely himself — if, indeed, he should ever recover. The shock to the nervous system may be irreparable."

"I hope not. His health has improved wonderfully during his camp-life. His constitution seemed nearly as vigorous as Ross', up to the date of his receiving that wound in the shoulder."

She shook her head, despondingly.

"It is sweet in you to seek to comfort me — but I have marked many signs of failing health in Lynn, of which I have never spoken to any one — not even to his mother. It is my conviction that let the war end when and as it may, it has left a life-long token upon him. Bear with my sadness, Nellie, dear! I have many miserable days and sleepless nights on account of these forebodings. I cannot rid myself of them, and I believe that the like torment him."

This startled me — principally because there occurred to me, as corroborative evidence of the existence of this feeling in his mind, the fact that he had made his will, last winter, and left it in his father's hands, with instructions how to proceed in the disposition of his property, should he die away from home.

"If that be so, he ought to get leave of absence, and come home, without delay," I said, earnestly. "He is not needed in the army, and we cannot afford to have him risk his precious life recklessly."

She smiled — sadly still, but proudly.

"Right and wrong both, my love!' We cannot afford to risk his loss — but the army does need him, and every other brave man who can wield a sword. The worst is not over, if the newspapers do announce the speedy coming of peace. The real struggle — to which all previous fights have been but child's play — is yet in the Future."

I had no answer. The vision of that conflict, and who were to participate in it, passed before me, veiling eyes and impeding utterance. Weak and worn with misery, I dropped my head upon my knees, and cried bitterly. When I recovered myself, Agatha's hand lay upon my head, but she had not spoken.

"I did not mean to distress you by my foolish tears!" I apologized, looking into her kind, grave face.

She appeared so much older and wiser than I, in that moment of unrestrained grief, that I felt humbled and ashamed.

"I am glad to see you weep, Nellie! I have feared that the unnatural repression of feeling would injure your mind or health. You do not confide your joys and sorrows to me, as you once did; but my love and pity are the same now as then. Nor is it my design to beguile you into a show of answering confidence by my exhibition of trust in your affection and discretion. I tell you of what grieves or delights me, because it is my nature to be frank to those whom I call friends. Heaven knows these are few enough!"

"You wrong me, Agatha!" I said, with feeling. "If I am reserved toward you, it does not arise from distrust. The sorrows which have visited me are not such as can be lightened by discussion. And" — for this sounded ungracious — "you know them already, without my telling them over. Dwelling upon them does me no good, and it would sadden others."

"Yet I could wish you were more frank!" she persisted, wistfully. "You are growing old and grave under your secret trouble."

"It is not secret!" I returned, unreasonably irritated by her continued attack. "Papa, Mamma, you, Lynn, Ross — every-

body who knows me well, understands why I am suffering —
why I must ever suffer, unless a miracle be wrought in my behalf."

"And that miracle?" interrogatively.

"Should be annulment and oblivion of all that has happened
since the 14th day of April, 1861!" I cried, writhing in spirit,
as under innumerable pin-pricks. "I am mad and wild whenever I think of my thwarted hopes and the slow torture of my
daily life. I can only keep down sinful repining and worse than
useless regrets by living out of myself——"

"And by forgetting that Harry Wilton ever lived!" she put
in, abruptly, with a strange gleam of eye and inflection of
voice.

I was sobered instantly.

"I had rather die than forget, or cease to love him!" I was
fully conscious now of what I was saying; felt that I threw
down the gauntlet at her feet — not in defiance, but with deliberate, steadfast resolve never to give him up.

She set her chair back as if to avoid my touch. After a
moment of silence, she resumed the conversation in soft, changed
accents.

"My poor child!"

"Don't pity me because I love him!" I retorted, hastily.
"That is the greatest happiness I have, except the conviction
that he loves me!"

No reply except that mournful motion of the head and another sigh, —

"Poor, poor child!"

I was growing angry again, and I held my peace.

"Has it not occurred to you —" she commenced very slowly,
apparently choosing her words with caution. There she stopped,
and began another sentence. "Lynn — both your brothers
think, with me, that it is singular Mr. Wilton did not refer
once to you in the conversation he had with Ross. The marked
omission could hardly have arisen from forgetfulness. It looks
to us as if he appreciated the truth that his enlistment in the

Yankee army had severed the connection between you more
effectually than any other event except death could have done."

She paused, and her inquiring tone demanded a reply.

"I should have been more surprised had he introduced my
name in a conversation like that repeated in Ross' letter," I said,
evenly and tranquilly as I could speak. "He inquired after
the health of the family, including Ross' sisters. He learned
from the answer to this question that I was alive and well. He
needed no assurance of my fidelity. He knew better than Ross
could have told him, that while we live, we belong to each
other — are united in heart, and that it is not in the power of
any man to put us asunder. Our betrothal was no light holi-
day pledge, but a vow to one another, to ourselves, and in the
sight of Him who made me for him and him for me."

"You would marry him, then, if, as Ross writes, he offered
you a hand stained with your brother's blood?" as horror-
stricken at the idea.

"The Lord is very pitiful! He will not bring this thing
upon me!"·was my reply. "He may see that it is best to fill
my cup to the brim with anguish; but this overflowing drop
will be spared. I will trust Him."

"Now, you *do* talk wildly! Child! do you believe that the
GOD of nations and of battles concerns himself with the petty
love-scrapes of foolish girls?"

I had a simple answer. "I am of more value than many
sparrows."

"In your own estimation! I tell you He does often fill the
cup of human anguish to overrunning — drowns the soul with
woe! Don't trust to that frail straw of hope! I repeat, —
if Wilton were to become the murderer of your brother, as well
as the enemy of your native State — what then?"

"And if my brother were to kill him — what then?" Was
I possessed of an evil spirit, that I turned upon her with this
speech? "You have tried me to the utmost, Agatha! I could
not respect or love you, if I thought that you had wantonly put
me to this test. You have complained of my reserve upon this

subject. I will tell you all that I know myself, and then you may rest content. I have promised to be Harry Wilton's wife, and when he claims me, I shall fulfil my promise. He may come to me with blood upon his hands, but there will be none upon his soul. If it is lawful for Ross to fight for State rights, it must be a duty which no patriot would shirk, — a glorious privilege no patriot would willingly forego, — to fight for National existence. I do not account Harry guilty even of ingratitude, which is the least sin Ross charges home upon him. I am as sure that he has acted right and worthily as that I live and breathe, and, living, love him more than State or brothers, or aught else except my Creator. Next to my duty to my GOD comes my obligation to trust, love, and serve my betrothed husband. This I have never doubted. If I have suffered, it is because Providence has placed me in circumstances that entailed trial and grief upon me — not that I have ever wavered in my faith in Harry, or my resolve to cleave unto him, and him only, until death parts us."

She sat perfectly still, while I went through this statement, eying me fixedly, and seeming in no wise agitated by my excitement and plain speaking.

"You have more spirit than I gave you credit for," she said, at length. "There is no danger of my misunderstanding you hereafter. And this answer I am at liberty to repeat to your brothers?"

"If they wish to know my decision, I can give them no other. It is not I who have raised the issue."

"No! it is Mr. Wilton!" she rejoined, dryly.

"I deny the imputation! His behavior has been manly, honorable, consistent, throughout. Be just, Agatha! You have never had a truer friend than is the man you three combine to condemn. You should know him to be incapable of a base or a mean deed."

"You do well to allude to our ancient intimacy. I would not lose the memory of it! Still, while I am the promised wife of your brother, I cannot reconcile it with my sense of

18

duty to communicate with his open foe, or in any manner to
palliate the enormity of the action that has arrayed the two
against one another. I thank you for your candor, and overlook
your unusual warmth of temper and language. I regret the
necessity that led me to provoke this — but it *was* a necessity.
I can say no more!"

She has gone — with her glittering eyes, weird smile, and
more mysterious words. I breathe more freely. The room is
brighter; and my passion is rapidly subsiding into amazement
and perplexed questionings.

What brought her to me with her pitiless catechism and more
unfeeling innuendoes? Was she my brothers' ambassadress?
No! they are true and gallant gentlemen, and could not press
this decision upon me while my spirit is yet faint with the pain
of the disclosure contained in Ross' letter. And she was Harry's friend and favorite before he ever saw me! But for him,
she might have toiled through years of ill-paid drudgery, surrounded by the coarse and vulgar associations which laboring
women, who are not themselves inherently vulgar, esteem the
greatest hardship of their lot! All that she has of ease, comfort, and refinement, and the education that fits her to adorn
her present station, she owes to him, — yet she would have me
forget that he ever lived, — for herself repudiates him as an
acquaintance! This is a lesson in human nature I would
gladly have been spared.

I have not been so angry since my childhood. I could not
have believed, three hours ago, that I could ever be so angry
with her. Nor am I entirely sure how it happened, that our
talk glowed so suddenly into a wordy combat. I but comprehend that she attacked my darling, and that I defended him.
Yet my brain is clearer, and my heart no heavier, — that could
scarcely be, — for the storm. I have asserted my position,
assumed my right place in her eyes and those of my brothers.

My brothers! "Tell Brownie not to hate me," says Ross;
and the forced levity of the message tells me more truly than

he suspects of the real sadness he experienced in the thought of my unhappiness when this injunction should reach me.

Is it always wrong to pray for death, I wonder? —

" The sooner 'tis over, the sooner to sleep ! "

Sleep, with no such horrible rumors of wars as must henceforward affright me in dreams, as they torture every moment of my waking hours. Thou, who art touched with a feeling of our infirmities, is there succor with Thee for a spirit so tossed and torn as mine?

CHAPTER XVI.

AGATHA.

August 15.

WE have had a raid.

Raids have been all the fashion this summer, and we may now claim a notable place among the fashionables of the region. And ours was no such pitiful affair as was the arrival of a scouting-party last December, when a band of perhaps fifty — our brave defenders swore there were treble that number — stumbled upon the outposts of the Confederates, who had encamped over night upon the lawn.

To proceed systematically with the history of the event, let me begin with yesterday morning, when I had taken a rocking-chair and a volume of Bulwer to a shaded corner at the west end of the piazza, and settled myself lazily for a quiet fore-noon, and nothing in particular to do. Presently, Elinor came out with Carrie, armed with spelling and reading-books, and sat down upon the upper one of the front steps, to hear the child's daily tasks. At first, I was inclined to change my quarters. It makes me nervously ill-natured to listen to the sing-song monotone of lessons. I suppose it has the opposite effect upon the voluntary schoolmistress; for she is punctual and assiduous in the performance of this duty, or pleasure, whichever she considers it. But I was very comfortably fixed, and, if the truth be told, too indolent to move, unless it should become necessary. The day was bright and breezy. Rain had fallen during the night, accompanied by sharp lightning and loud thunder, and the atmosphere was the better for the excitement. I often experience a kindred change myself after I have had a rousing, wholesome "sensation." The lawn was an expanse of emerald velvet, bespangled, where the tree-shadows still rested, with diamonds; the creeping roses and clematis upon the trellis at either end of the long porch, and trailing along the eaves, were full of blossoms; and every breath from the garden was aromatic with newly distilled essences from the flower-beds. I did not open my book for a while, but inhaled the perfumes, gazed out from my bower upon the green hills, upon fields of tall corn tossing tasselled heads in the sunshine, the grand old woods to the right, and upon the left the swift river, that had caught the spirit of universal jubilation.

There are two large acacia trees at opposite corners of the house, and the murmur of bees and humming-birds in their branches fairly drowned the sing-song I had dreaded. I amused myself by watching the coquetting of the happy creatures among the feathery foliage, chasing one another in and out, above and below the tufts of flowers, that resemble nothing else so much as they do the whitest and clearest of spun glass tipped with pink, — a matutinal quadrille, in the airy mazes of which the revellers appeared like so many living emeralds and opals. I mused, idly and pleasantly, over old tales of genii and elfin balls, and then of Eastern fables and songs, mingling diamonds, rubies, and acacias in sweet, bewildering confusion that suited my taste well upon this ripe August day.

> "Our rocks are bare, but smiling there
> The Acacia waves her yellow hair," —

I repeated, dreamily.

"Elinor, why does Moore call it 'yellow hair'? It is silvery, — more like Burns' 'lassie wi' the lint-white locks.'"

She raised her eyes gravely to me, then glanced at the tree. A look, part pain, part surprise, flitted over her features. I had not remembered until I saw this that the song from which I had quoted was one she used to be fond of singing with Wilton. But I cannot be forever upon my guard against reviving these tender souvenirs.

"There is a species of acacia that has yellow blossoms," she

18 *

rejoined, quietly; and her eyes went down again to the book in Carrie's lap.

I fell to studying her instead of the humming-birds and butterflies after that. She wears white this summer weather, morning, noon, and night. On this morning, she had on a white muslin with full waist and sleeves, a crimson belt, and, at her throat, a red rose-bud. It is one of her affectations, to consult neatness and becomingness in her attire, to please her father's taste. No other white man, under sixty, ever comes near the plantation now, unless it be a foraging party of rough Confederates, or ruder Yankee scouts. But the artful minx's brown locks were put up decorously, and her draperies smooth and pure as if she had arrayed herself for a ball. I suspect that she is never free from the hope that her lover may appear, unheralded, at her side some fine day, brave and gay in his Lieutenant's livery. She has read enough novels to incite her to dream of such a *dénouement*. All her care and circumspection, however, cannot conceal the marks of mental anguish she has undergone this summer. Her eyes are larger than ever, because her face has grown thinner; her lip has lost its spirited curve, and there is, instead, the tiniest imaginable droop of the corners; and she never sings now. I hated to hear her carolling, senselessly and ceaselessly, from top to bottom of the house; yet the place is unnaturally still without her voice. I asked her to sing a favorite air for me the other night. She hesitated, stammered, then made the attempt, fluttered feebly through a few bars, and broke down lamentably. She suffers intensely, — there can be no doubt of that, — as much as it is in her puny, undeveloped nature to suffer. Well, let her: the law of compensation ordains that this shall be so. Shall my teeth be forever on edge from the sour grapes which my forefathers have eaten, and all the sweet be given her?

While these thoughts, and others like them, were passing through my brain, a negro, mounted upon a bare-backed mule, came tearing down the avenue, and dashed around the house-yard toward the servants' quarters.

"Sister, that was Albert!" exclaimed Carrie. "What do you think is the matter?"

"I do not know, dear. Probably he forgot something when he went to work this morning. Well, Susan, what is it?"

A colored girl had run out to us from the hall, in complexion the color of ashes, her teeth chattering, and eyeballs protruding with terror.

"De Yankees is comin', Miss Elinor, — de whole army!"

"You are a deceitful creature," I said, coolly. "In your heart, you are delighted. You had better go to work and pack up your best clothes, and whatever you like of Miss Elinor's and mine, so that you can be off with your deliverers and friends at the earliest possible moment."

"Agatha," said Elinor, rebukingly, "you should not say such things to a good, faithful girl. There is no cause of alarm, Susan. Where is your master?"

He was nearer at hand than we had supposed. As his daughter spoke, he stepped out upon the porch.

"I have questioned Albert," he said, with no appearance of disquietude. "From his statement, I think that a large body of cavalry must be bearing down upon us from the river road. As you say, Elinor, there appears to be no occasion for fear. It is doubtful whether we have a nearer view of them than we shall get as they march by the upper gate. I apprehend nothing from the approach of disciplined troops, if their officers are with them, as must be the case with these. Albert tells me that Will, at the first alarm, ordered the horses to be taken from the ploughs and wagons, and sent them off to the maple swamp. It was a prudent step; but I do not know that the precaution was needful."

Pretty soon, the head of the dark-blue column became visible at the top of the rising ground toward the river. At this point, the highway forks into two roads, one leading past the gate, which is the outermost entrance to the plantation; the other diverging toward the village and railroad depot. Our suspense did not last long. Within ten minutes after we had our first glimpse of them, the avenue was filled with mounted men, riding at a slow trot in the direction of the house. Elinor and I had left the piazza, as it became evident that we were to be favored with a visit, and joined Mrs. Lacy at the parlor window. None of us offered any remark upon the scene before us; but the thoughts of all must have been busy. The quaint homestead with its aspect of peaceful comfort, the well-kept grounds, fine trees and rich fields surrounding it, appeared to win the admiring or covetous regards of the foremost of the troop, judging from their gestures and so much of their faces as we could see beneath their caps and above their beards. Next the vanguard was borne a broad, gay, flaunting Yankee flag — a sight that gave a strange thrill to those who had not seen one thus boldly displayed in many months. The double-leaved gate of the yard stood open, and the leaders of the line rode straight through it up to the steps where Mr. Lacy was yet standing. He bowed in reply to the slight salute of the principal officer — a Colonel — who, without offering to alight, made his business known. He wanted food for man and beast; was willing to pay a reasonable price for what his men ate, if Mr. Lacy would accept it, — if not, they *must* have the food. The men and horses were hungry, and they had a long march before them.

I could see that the manner, even more than the terms, of the proposal irked Milord. He made answer, that he had not the power to prevent them from appropriating the contents of his storehouses and barns to their use, if they were disposed to do this, but that it was impossible for these to satisfy the wants of so large a force. There must have been three or four hundred of them.

"Very well," was the response; "we can make it go as·far as it will."

He threw his leg over the pommel as he spoke, and dismounted slowly; stamped his boots upon the gravel walk to rid his feet of the numbness caused by long riding, and walked stiffly up the steps, followed by his staff.

"You are a Union man, I have been told?" he said, addressing the master of the house.

"I am, if you mean by that one who did his utmost to prevent the secession of the Southern States from the Federal Union, and who must ever regret that separation."

"Exactly!" sneeringly. "If the appearance of your plantation speaks truly, your Unionism has been a first-rate speculation. But how did it happen that a party of National troops was fired upon last winter from behind your lawn palings, from your very windows, too, I have been told, — several wounded, and one or more left prisoners in your hands? My information is correct — is it not?"

"I had nothing to do with the attack or the repulse," answered Mr. Lacy. "A company of Confederate cavalry encamped over night upon my premises, as Federal troops had done before them. A reconnoissance was made during the night by the party you have mentioned, and a fight ensued. No man deplored the mishap more sincerely than I did."

"And the prisoners: you forwarded them dutifully to Richmond, I suppose?"

"But one Federal soldier was left behind by the retiring party. He was mortally wounded, and died within the week, in my house."

"More likely he was starved to death in your dog-kennel," retorted the other, offensively. "We begin to understand by this time what are the tender mercies you of the chivalry show to wounded men and captives. Another question, Mr. Unionist! Have you, or have you not, two sons in the rebel army?"

"I have."

"Officers — are they not?"

"You are right."

"They entered the service with your permission?"

"They did not."

"Indeed! But you entertain them and their comrades during their furloughs? You do not forbid them your house, because they happen, unluckily, to be traitors?"

"I treat them as any other father should treat two sons who have never failed in filial duty, whatever may be their political errors."

"All very fine — entirely satisfactory! That is a neat way of saying that you give all the aid and comfort you can to the rebels, while you play loyal to keep out of our clutches. It is wonderful" — with a laugh and an oath, turning to his staff — "how many Union men we find, where the rebs have not been able to scare up one. Sly old foxes they must be, or they would have seen the inside of Castle Thunder months ago. Why, if we are to credit one half of what they say, the ordinance of Secession would not have stood the ghost of a chance, had the people been allowed to vote for it. That is your opinion — isn't it?" again to Mr. Lacy.

"You would not believe me if I were to assert it," rejoined that gentleman, with no show of temper or abatement of dignity.

Another oath, and, —

"That's the truest word you've spoken yet! Well, my good Union brother, we are here for the express purpose of affording you an opportunity of proving your love for the old flag. You should be willing to spend and be spent in the service of your country. My men want a lunch, and you will please see that it is gotten ready, for they are deucedly impatient; and they have an awkward trick of helping themselves, if they are not waited upon promptly."

He drew forward my rocking-chair as he spoke, and threw his unwieldy frame into it with a force that made it creak and groan again.

He was a coarse-featured man, flashy as to uniform, impudent as to bearing, and was, I more than suspected, two thirds drunk. His staff, with a single exception, imitated their chief, and sought their ease in various postures, more comfortable than graceful; some sitting upon the porch steps, others upon the railing, others still upon chairs abstracted from the hall. The honorable exception was one whom I had singled out, at sight, as the solitary gentleman of the party. He was about forty years of age — tall and fine-looking, and wore the neat dress of an army Chaplain. While the foregoing conversation was in progress, he had remained silent, although deeply interested, — his countenance showing plainly in whose behalf his sympathies were engaged. When Mr. Lacy reëntered the house, he followed him, overtaking him at the parlor door.

" Allow me a single word, sir?"

Perceiving our presence, and divining from our position that we had been unseen witnesses of the scene without, he bowed, removed his cap, and directed his apology to us more than to the host.

"I can make no reasonable excuse for the gross insult offered you, Mr. Lacy! It is dastardly and infamous! The only extenuation of the conduct of my superior officer is his condition. You must have observed that he is partially intoxicated. I beg you to believe, however, that low as may be the state of morals among the subordinates of such a commander, you will not be subjected to personal violence, or your house to robbery, other than the wholesale order for provisions and forage already issued. If I could protect you from this, I would do so; but this is beyond my power. Whatever influence I have with the regiment shall be exerted to spare you further trouble."

Mr. Lacy held out his hand, which was taken as frankly.

" I believe you, sir, and thank you! I was not altogether unprepared for the treatment I have received. The few remaining Union men of the South occupy an unfortunate position in this war. Like the cloth under the shears, they are the spoil of both sides. Allow me to introduce to you the ladies of my family — Mrs. Lacy — Miss Lamar — Miss Lacy!"

The Chaplain saluted us with more ease and grace than I had expected to see in a Yankee parson; and after briefly renewing his assurances of protection, he returned to his comrades.

Another survey of the outer scene showed me the soldiery falling, pell-mell, upon the cornfields; tearing off the unripe ears for roasting, and the green fodder for their horses; thronging the barn-yard, in quest of other provender; and leaping the garden palings, in squads of twos, threes, and fours, in predatory excursions after the fresh vegetables, which were not daily luxuries in their camp life. The negro quarters had given up their population — from the blind patriarch of ninety to the latest baby — to hang around and stare at the lawless crew. A trusty band of about a dozen — headed by Uncle Will, the white-haired sachem of the ebony tribe, and Mammy Rachel, Mrs. Lacy's own maid — collected around the back porch to ask counsel of their master, as to what measures could be adopted to rescue some scanty portion of the lately bountiful produce of the plantation from the horde of blue-coated locusts. The conference was interrupted by the approach of the Chaplain, at sight of whom the discontented servants drew back sullenly. It was clear that they regarded the cordial respect with which Mr. Lacy listened to what he had to say, as unmanly conciliation of the oppressors. The Chaplain's advice was sound, nevertheless. He had been talking with the inebriated Colonel, and others of the staff, and was prepared with the draught of a proposal by which the house and all that it held should be preserved from the general ransacking. The superior was a glutton as well as a wine-bibber, and the Chaplain had his promise that, beside himself and his immediate attendants, not a soldier should enter the mansion during their stay, if a liberal meal were provided for the privileged few without loss of time.

The airs that brute gave himself, that forenoon, were ludicrous and disgusting beyond any description I can offer. When the sun got· around to the porch, he retreated to the parlor, where he held his court, until dinner was announced, smoking, drinking, and talking boisterously with the choice spirits he had convened about him. Mr. Lacy had ordered us above stairs, before this invasion of the interior; but from the upper landing I had a tolerable view of all that passed below, both within and outside of the house. While the commanding officer recreated himself in the drawing-room, plunder and rollicking were the order of the hour, in lawn, orchard, meat-house, and servants' quarters. Some of the incidents which I observed from my lookout were pitiful, — more amusing. Each of the larger, or family-quarters, had a small garden and hen-house at the rear, kept, under Mr. Lacy's strict rules, in good order, and yielding, in many instances, a considerable revenue to the owners thereof, — the village offering a fair market for eggs, chickens, sweet-potatoes, ground peas (which benighted Yankees call peanuts), and the like. These petty domains the so-called deliverers of the oppressed race took especial delight in ravaging. Dusky faces grew grim, many tearful, as the necks of their pet poultry were wrung by the score, and their pigs squealed their last under the knives of the Yankee butchers.

Presently there strutted across the yard a burly Irishman, with a hoop-skirt buckled about his waist, and hitting his knees at each step, a many-colored shawl drawn over his dirty jacket, and upon his head poor Susan's best bonnet, which had been worn by herself, for the first and only time, the previous Sunday — a smart, dressy affair, purchased with a pocketful of Confederate bills — the hoardings of a whole year. At his heels hung the disconsolate mistress of the millinery, crying bitterly, and holding out the empty band-box, in vain supplication for the return of her treasure. While this pantomime was being enacted, a comrade of the gay Hibernian passed, leading his horse, with a bag of stolen oats lying across the saddle. Without the form of parley, he snatched the band-box from the girl, set it upon the ground, and filled it with oats for his horse's dinner. Susan gave a scream, and would have launched herself bodily upon her desecrated property, but the wearer of the bonnet prevented her by passing his brawny arm about her waist, retaining her in his grasp, until her shrieks drew the attention of the Chaplain. One stride from the porch brought him within speaking distance of the trio, and while the rescued girl fled to her mother's cabin, the indignant divine harangued

19

the sulky pair of National defenders, with gestures few, but sternly expressive. His interference in other cases was prompt, and sometimes salutary; but what could one man do, let his character or position be what it might, among a gang of ruffianly soldiery, the principle of whose Colonel was, that it was not only lawful, but praiseworthy, to do the enemy's territory all the mischief practicable?· The ice-house was entered, and shining blocks of the precious hoard were scattered all over the yard, leaking away their life under the August sun; the flower-borders were overrun, in the hot race for fruits and vegetables; choice peaches, and early apples, and bunches of unripe grapes, were stripped from bough and trellis in a spirit of wanton destruction that would have disgraced a pack of vicious schoolboys.

And all this while — as I kept thinking, ever and anon — the dead Yankee soldier, who had been nursed like a son of the house, slept in the family burying-ground, within hearing of the rude merriment of his former comrades, had not his ear been dulled for all time! Then I speculated amusedly, whether, in beholding this spoliation of his worldly goods, Milord did not repent him of his Union experiment. It was as if the destroying hosts of Egypt had overtaken the murmuring Israelites, just when they were whining for the leeks and onions of the goodly land of their captivity. Whatever were his private meditations, he showed the robbers an undaunted front. Whether he paced the back porch in company with the Chaplain, or passed from room to room to second his wife's orders for the entertainment of the self-invited party, or summoned a servant to perform the behest of the burly Colonel, when his roars for ice-water, mint, tobacco, and brandy sounded through the staid old hall, and awakened astonished echoes upon the oaken staircase, — everywhere, and at all seasons, his step was firm and equal; his voice calmly authoritative, as when surrounded, as of yore, by loving and obedient subjects; undisputed lord of the estate and those who dwelt thereupon. I was never partial to him, nor he to me; but his behavior upon this trying day would have done credit to a Lacedæmonian Chester-field.

At last, dinner was served, and, as I heard from Susan, Mr. Lacy sat at the head of his table and carved for his guests well and generously, as if he had been feasting a select company of friends. The Chaplain—"the Captain," Susan insisted upon dubbing him—sat at his right hand, and, aided by two or three officers, who preserved some show of good manners, prevented the meal from degenerating into a greedy scramble for food.

"But dat Colonel! he beats all!" said Susan, her black eyes saucer-like from the excitement of the day. "He is settin' at de foot of de table, wid a brandy bottle on each side on him, and for every mouthful he eats, he takes two drinks. He must be pretty nigh soaked through by dis time, big as he is. I hope he won't be able to set on his horse, when he starts; and as for dem two fellers what took my bonnet and band-box, there's a rope growin' somewhar for dem — sure! Low-lived white folks always was despisable in my sight, and I hates 'em wuss'n ever now! I done had 'nuff of Yankees — I has! Talk 'bout freedom! What I want wid freedom, ef I got to live long sech as *dem!*"

It was four o'clock in the afternoon before horses and men were pronounced fresh enough to proceed farther in the service of their country. Elinor and I overlooked the rabble from the upper hall window. I was busied with the inspection of some of the more distant scenes, when a low exclamation from her made me start. An orderly was leading a horse into the yard, which I recognized as Elinor's pet, Elfie — so named by Miss Morris, on account of a fancied resemblance between her and her mistress. She was a spirited creature, — not large, but elegantly formed; brown and silky of coat, perfect in gait, irreproachable as to pedigree. Elinor loved her as if she had been human, and I saw that she was deadly pale at sight of her in a stranger's custody. We leaned from the window to hear what followed. We gathered that the Colonel's horse was sick in consequence of an overfeed of green fodder, and incapable of carrying his master. The latter raged, and blustered, and swore at the stupidity of the groom, at the orderly who had witnessed the feeding, — at everything and everybody, excepting himself and his drunkenness. He had, it appeared, made a personal examination of the few animals standing in the stables — to wit, the carriage-horses, a restive colt, and Elfie, and decided the last to be the only thing worthy of bearing his illustrious corporeality.

I had not heard Mr. Lacy utter a remonstrance against any trespass, however aggravating, until now — but he pressed forward to the spot where the tipsy brute was getting himself sufficiently steady upon his feet to mount his new steed, and accosted him. We could not catch all he said, but we gleaned the sense of his proposition, which was to furnish the Colonel with a larger and more serviceable animal, if he would relinquish the idea of taking Elfie. The offer was scouted disdainfully.

"I know a capital bit of (hic!) horseflesh when I see it, if I am a (hic! and an oath) Yankee!" said this image of his Maker. "And this is the (hic!) nicest thing I have seen upon (hic!) hoofs for a month of Sundays. Bring her closer — can't you!"

Another volley of objurgations at the orderly, who tried to drag Elfie up to her future proprietor. The mare planted her fore-feet firmly in the turf, and pulled back — her intelligent eyes showing dislike and revolt, plainly as words could have done. Finding her obstinate, the orderly raised his heavy riding-whip, and struck her sharply upon the flank.

A stifled scream escaped Elinor.

"O, my poor pet! my gentle, loving little Elfie!" she cried; and kneeling at the window-seat, she covered her eyes with her fingers, to shut out the sight, and sobbed as if her heart were breaking.

Before she ventured another look, the entire line was in motion; the head of the train already winding into the village road, the star-spangled banner flaunting insolently beneath the giant Virginia oaks, that seemed to contemplate the pageant with solemn contempt. I think that I could go down to my grave in perfect peace of mind and heart if the only thing denied me were the boon of once again living beneath the folds of that gaudy rag. A raid or two more, and I shall become a ravenous salamander, in comparison with the most rabid of my fellow fire-eaters.

They were gone — and Mr. Lacy's voice was heard in the lower hall, — sorrowfully compassionate.

"Ida — love! where is our poor child?"

Elinor sprang to her feet and hurried down. I peeped over the balusters at the meeting, anticipating a renewed burst of sentimental lamentation — a second edition of Sterne's jeremiade over the dead donkey. I was cheated. She went bravely up to her father — head erect, and a smile upon her face.

"You are grieving over Elfie's loss — are you not, Papa? She was a dear little thing, and I was fond of her — but in reality, she was the least useful horse upon the plantation. She could not work, and nobody ever rode her but me; and I so seldom go on horseback nowadays! You must not be distressed on my account, for I am bearing it very well. Our lives and home are spared. We have much to be thankful for."

Her father kissed her, drew the brown head to his bosom and stroked it, smiling down at her, while his lip quivered.

"You are the bravest girl living! We have had a severe ordeal to-day, dear, but the gleam of light is not wanting to the cloud. Our kind protector, the Chaplain ——"

At this point, old Rachel came up the stairs, and not choosing to be detected in eavesdropping by a servant, I abandoned my post of observation. I lost nothing, I fancy, beside the recital of the Chaplain's good deeds, which, after all, were but acts of common humanity, intensified into shining benevolence by contrast with the double-dyed rascality of his associates.

The sun set in purple glory, rounding off a perfect summer's

19 *

day ; but the serene beauty of cloud, sky, and river made more
repulsive the blight, and havoc, and cheerless disorder pervading
the premises.   Personally, I have not been injured, nor are the
sufferers from this ruthless vandalism so dearly beloved by me
that I must needs be afflicted in their afflictions.   But were I
their bitter enemy, — and I do not say that the supposition is
far-fetched, — I must have sighed over the waste left in the track
of the invading host.   Not a stalk of corn remained upright in
the broad acres rolling down to the river's brim, and on the
hill-side, upon the other hand, an extensive field of tobacco had
shared the like fate — a piece of malicious mischief, done for
mischief's sake, since not even a Yankee, or a Yankee's horse,
can chew green tobacco.   The barn-lofts yawned emptily ; the
meat-house had been thoroughly cleaned out ; all the butter and
milk carried off from the dairy ; churns broken and milk-pans
crushed into uselessness.   The garden was cut up as by the
hoofs of a herd of wild horses, and the fine orchard, on which
the labor and care of many years have been expended, looked
as if a tornado had swept through it.

The Lacys are remarkable people in their way, and one of
these ways is a *penchant* for self-devotion, — the immolation of
one's own likes and feelings, that the comfort and happiness of
others may be secured, — provided these others are of their
name and kin.   They delude themselves into the belief that this
is very noble — touching the sublime, indeed ; but I, a dispassionate looker-on, pronounce it to be nothing better than ethereal
selfishness, refined humbug, and exalted foolery.   For example,
when we gathered around the tea-table, in place of a decorous
seriousness under the calamities that had befallen them, there
was an elaborate effort after gay nonchalance, while they recounted their losses.   My Lady led off.

" What was the name of that old lady — one of the heroines
of 1776, who, after her farm had been visited by the British,
found, hidden in a snug corner, an ancient rooster, the sole relic
of her populous poultry-yard, and forthwith mounted a negro
upon a horse, and sent him after the foraging party, with the

fowl and her compliments, saying that they had overlooked it? Rachel tells me the oldest duck on the plantation secreted herself under her bed at the earliest onslaught upon the fowls, and did not quit her shelter until sunset. Would the plagiarism be too · barefaced, if I were to despatch Albert with it and my respects to our acquaintance, the Colonel?"

"You might try it, if you could be sure of not losing negro and horse along with the duck, by your witty experiment," said her husband. "It was a happy circumstance that the cows were sent to the far pasture, this morning, and so escaped notice."

"And that Uncle Will was so prudent as to conceal the horses," remarked Elinor, lightly; as if I had not witnessed her grief at the maltreatment of her favorite, and it cost her no pain to refer to the horse-thieving proclivities of her compatriots.

"We are deeply indebted to the Chaplain for the security of the house and contents," was Mr. Lacy's next thanksgiving. "He is a noble fellow! It is a pity he is condemned to such uncongenial associations."

I deemed it time for me to have my say.

"His ministrations do not seem to have been blessed to the moral improvement of his flock. I should recommend a course of practical sermons upon the eighth and tenth commandments, profusely illustrated from life."

And, as a further contribution to the general hilarity, I supplied an embellished description of the scene of Susan and her bonnet. They all laughed, and then ensued more praises of the Chaplain. It transpired, in the course of this, that he had promised to call and spend a night here on his way back to headquarters. The main portion of the expedition will return by another route. His Reverence is no simpleton. The efforts he put forth in our behalf have elevated him to the dignity of heroship — a cheap price to pay for the honor.

Reports have been arriving all day of the doughty doings of our knights in blue. They supped and spent the night at James

Kingston's.   Wouldn't I like to see and hear Miss Hetty upon the event?

"They picked up everything that was loose upon the place!" said the old man, who stopped at the gate to tell the tale.

"Then Miss Hetty's teeth had no chance of escape!" I remarked, *sotto voce*, to Mrs. Lacy and Elinor; whereat they laughed, as I have never succeeded in making them do at more refined sallies.

They do not like Miss Hetty.

CHAPTER XVII.

ELINOR.

December 25, 1863.

MONTHS have elapsed since I opened my journal. I hardly know myself for the girl who used to confide her trifling joys and griefs to these pages, who looked upon this safety-valve for youthful enthusiasm and sentimental fancies as a friend and comforter, whose patient sympathy was unfailing, and akin to human companionship.

I am out of the habit of writing or talking freely. The last letter I ever wrote was to Harry. I intrusted it to the Chaplain, Mr. Emory, who was kind to us in the time of the raid in August. Papa, mindful of my happiness amid the distressing circumstances of his situation on that day, asked this gentleman if he would take charge of letters to a friend of his, an officer in the Federal army. He consented cheerfully, and although we were ignorant of Harry's exact address, we made up a package of three letters, and intrusted them to the friend and messenger at his second call, two days after the raid. I wrote unreservedly and at length. I felt that Harry stood in greater need than ever before of all the affection and confidence I could bestow. I told him that my love was not lessened, nor had my faith in his integrity swerved on account of his enlistment; that my prayers attended him continually in the persuasion that he had not engaged in a work upon which he could not ask the blessing of Heaven, and that my parents united with me in deciding that the hearts God had joined together were not to be put asunder by any arbitrary issues of man's devising. I affected no girlish shyness. I wrote fondly and solemnly, and more hopefully than I really felt when I reflected upon the thousand chances that might delay our meeting.

"For meet we shall in GOD's own good time," he had written in the one precious letter that reached me last year.

And we shall — only — how long? how long?

It was a month — just a month to the day — upon the 17th of September — when we received a communication from Mr. Emory. I was unusually blithe in spirit that day. The weather was fine, and I had been at work among my flowers during most of the forenoon; had just gathered a bouquet of wall-flowers and tea-roses to take in to Mamma. I was walking slowly toward the house, looking down at these, and, now and then, burying my face in their fragrant clusters, when Papa spoke my name. I shall never inhale the perfume of roses again without a return of the sick, dizzy feeling that rushed over me, as I saw him, within reach of me in the path, pale and sorrowful, gazing at me with loving eyes that could scarcely see me for the tears. I could not utter a question; but he put his arm around me, and supported me into the house, where Mamma met me, and took me to her bosom. By and by they showed me the Chaplain's letter. He had been at great pains to discover Harry's address, that he might forward the packet confided to his care. He "could hear nothing of him for a long while, but finally met an officer who belonged to the same regiment with, and who had been an intimate friend of, Lieutenant Wilton." From this gentleman he learned that "Harry had fallen, fighting bravely in the battle of Gettysburg."

"Shot through the heart" — and "Died instantly." This was the writing I saw for many nights inscribed in black characters upon my chamber wall — this the irreversible, hopeless sentence that drove me back when, madly incredulous, I resorted again and again to the fatal letter. Harry had never failed in his word to any one alive — I reasoned in my delirium, — and he had said that the hour of joyful reunion would come to us. I loved him so, I was so dear to him, that had he died that weary while ago, he would have come to me and told me. Dead in his nameless grave, while night and morning, in each hour of the tedious, shadowed days, I prayed for him, firm in the trust, through absence and evil report, and his long silence, that his arms would yet again enfold me, my head rest upon his breast in peace! There was some horrible mistake — and thus deluding my shattered senses, I would fly once more to the fighting lines, and read anew how he had fought and fallen, and " died instantly."

One night I came to myself. I had been ill for several days, dimly conscious of what was going on about me, and partially oblivious, during some merciful hours, of my deadly hurt. Mamma sat near my bed, reading by the lamp, whose rays were shaded from my eyes. As she read, the tears dropped upon the book; and when they flowed so fast as to blind her, she put her hands before her face, and prayed lowly and weepingly for me. This is what she said: " I *know*, O Lord, that Thy judgments are right, and that Thou in faithfulness hast afflicted her. Let, I pray Thee, Thy loving kindness be for her comfort, according to Thy word unto Thy servant. Let Thy tender mercies come unto her, that she may live. My soul fainteth for Thy salvation, but I hope in Thy word. Mine eyes fail for Thy word, saying, ' When wilt Thou comfort her?' "

" I *know*, O Lord, that Thou in faithfulness hast afflicted her!" I closed my eyes and repeated the words to myself, until something of the holy comfort of her reliance upon the Father's loving kindness stole into my soul — the loving kindness in which my darling had trusted, which had sent to him, at the last, a swift, true messenger of release from the pains and sorrows of this present evil world, instead of lingering torture. I could not yet say, " Not my will, but Thine, be done! " but I did feel a feeble stirring of gratitude that since he was appointed unto death, he had " died instantly." And thus did our Father's merciful kindness begin to be for my comfort.

It is a blustering Christmas night — a Christmas that has been no festival to us. There are sounds like the moans of the dying and the shouts of the victors upon the wind, as it howls in the chimney and shakes my windows.

> " And it saith to my spirit,
>   'No more! nevermore!'"

Am I resigned? Not if that implies that I would not have my beloved back if I could win him from Heaven. *There*, peace flows as a river — the peace which seems farther off than ever from our distracted land — and love without dissimulation — and his heart was grievously wounded here by the cold unkindness of those he accounted his friends. There are joys forevermore, and all these are his, and things precious that have not entered even into my heart to conceive as elements of his blessedness — yet — yet I can say no more than I am thankful my prayers cannot recall him to share my lot; that the Lord hath put it beyond my power to bid him return to comfort me. For I want him! I want him!

I learned every one of his last words to my brother Ross by heart, long ago. I study them oftentimes, now, weighing every sentence, and continually finding in them new cause for love and pride in him. He lived a patriot-hero. He died a brave man's death, battling for the land he loved, which he believed, and I believe, his GOD summoned him to defend. The day will come when it shall be accounted an honor to me that my betrothed belonged to the noble army of Union martyrs. I may not live to see it, but it will come! Does this console me? I am a sorrowful woman, mourning for the beloved of her youth. It is almost three years since I saw his face, felt the fond strain of his embrace; and I shall never look into his living eyes again!

Lynn has come home to pass his Christmas with us. Ross could not be spared from duty. I think he does not care to see me yet a while. He wrote to me, in September, a short, affectionate note, begging me to forgive the harsh things he had said of his best friend, and paying, in his sincere sorrow at his death, a feeling tribute to his character as man, friend, and

Christian.   He repeated his former request — " Don't hate me,
Brownie ! "   There is no room in my sad spirit for hatred, did
he deserve it, which he assuredly does not.   Sectional fury
spoke the words that stabbed Harry's faithful heart, that May
midnight, as the two parted on the banks of the swollen river,
the dead thronging their footsteps, — parted with a cold, silent
salute, in anger and scorn upon one side — who can say with
what repressed anguish upon the other?   Sectional fury — not
my brother's frank, generous nature, that, untouched by this
baleful fire, would have disdained to insult a captive foe, much
less refuse the friendly hand of one whom he had known and
trusted in other days.   I could not answer his letter, but Mamma did at my desire.

Lynn's considerate tenderness is an inexpressible comfort to
me.   This morning was mild, and we walked down to the burying-ground together ; sat there until near noon, talking, first,
of the poor soldier who had perished so far from home and
mother ; then, of the thousands of gallant men sacrificed in
this wicked, causeless war — finally, of Harry.   Whatever may
have been his sentiments respecting our engagement, after the
discovery that Harry was in the opposing army, now that he
has gone, Lynn praises him heartily, and with emotion.

" Oh, this war ! this war, Nellie ! " he said.   " We may
arrive at a rough computation of the lives lost upon the field,
in loathsome prisons, in hospitals, and in such pestilential
camps as were those in the Chickahominy Swamp, where more
were poisoned by malaria than fell before the enemy ; but who
can write the history of the broken hearts, the wrecked hopes,
the scattered families, that are the outer circles of the shock
of battle.   In these latter days, the pen of the recording
angel should be dipped in blood and tears.   It may be that
this is a nation's baptism into a new and higher life, but to
me it seems more like judgment than mercy."

Leaving this theme, he went on to tell me of his plans for
Agatha, should he be taken away from her and from us.

" You will be very kind and forbearing with her — will you

20

not?" he asked. "She loves me very dearly, and she would
be very desolate without the hope of my return."

I promised, and I mean to struggle with the doubts of her
rectitude and sincerity that will sometimes press in upon me..
For weeks after the news came of Harry's death, she did not
enter my room, alleging, as the reason of her apparent neglect,
that she was herself far from well, and dreaded the agitation
of an interview for us both. I hardly missed her, until one
day, when they thought I was asleep, I heard Mamma re
mark severely upon this indifference to my distress, and Papa
answer, quietly, " It is not indifference, my dear."

Since I have been able to join the family circle, her behavior
to me has been fitful, cordial, and cold by turns, without any
apparent cause for these changes. Since Lynn's arrival, I have
seen very little of her. He engrosses a good deal of her time,
and Aunt Ellen, whom Lynn escorted up from Richmond, engages Mamma's attention and mine.

Dear Aunt Ellen! her visit has done me good already. She
met me with a smile of mournful sweetness, and while she
spoke no phrase of consolation, there was that in her caressing
voice and touch that brought to my memory the bereavement
of her youth, her years of fidelity to her first love, and unselfish efforts for the happiness of others. This afternoon I have
spent in her room, my head upon her knee, while she confided
to me the events of that one year of her girlhood that changed
the whole of her after life. And in hearing it, I saw, dimly
still, but better than before, that there are points of light, like
trembling stars, in my night of sorrow. While Harry was alive
no breath of estrangement blackened the brightness of our
mutual affection. Our trust in each other was perfect. The
gulf that severed us was the effect of untoward circumstances,
not the result of our rash words or angry jealousy. Aunt
Ellen's latest parting with her lover was a stormy one. She
was a spoiled child, a vivacious coquette by reputation — really
a warm-hearted woman, loving him with all her soul and
strength, but vain of her power over him, and girlishly fond

of the admiration of others. He was proud, sensitive, and exacting. Words ran high between them, and they separated in displeasure. She left the city upon a pleasure trip of a week, and returned just in season to attend his funeral. He had sickened, and died upon the third day after his seizure. As the betrothal was unacknowledged, no one thought of summoning her to his death-bed. Passion had given place to repentance before she came home. During the journey she was dreaming only of reconciliation and renewed happiness, and while still at the depot in her native city, she learned through the chance remark of a passer-by that Lynn Holmes was dead.

I am thankful that Harry's eyes never gave me a reproachful look to haunt me until our next meeting in Heaven's eternal sunlight; thankful that I did not imbitter our farewell, or make his difficult duty yet more arduous by my weak wailings; thankful for the strength that supported me through the last days and hours of our companionship; thankful that I kept his image pure and untarnished in my heart until the picture of the mortal was exchanged for the vision of the beatified spirit; thankful that I wrote that last loving letter, although his hand was never to break the seal!

CHAPTER XVIII.

AGATHA.

January 1, 1864.

NEW YEAR'S DAY, and the year has commenced rarely. Owing to the intensely cold weather, none of us showed any disposition to stir abroad after breakfast. Milord retired to his study, and my Lady had domestic concerns to superintend. This left of the original party of grown people "us four, no more," as the old rhyme runs; to wit, Miss Morris and Elinor, Lynn and myself. My devoted's furlough expires to-morrow, and he has expected and received a double share of petting, to-day, in consequence of the agonizing anticipation.

This was the order of the tableau in the parlor.. At one end of the hearth, Miss Lamar and her soldier lad. I eschew mock modesty, and set down the names according to their comparative importance in my sight. Miss Lamar then, and her *fiancé ;* she leaning back in the most comfortable easy-chair the apartment afforded, in the complacent consciousness that she could appreciate its luxuriousness quite as well as any body else present — her supple fingers gleaming whitely among the coils of a mass of gilt braid she was manufacturing into an epaulet for her warrior's wear; her black eyes misty, yet lustrous, dividing their regards impartially between the shining threads and the softer brown orbs that studied her face and movements with undisguised pride. Lieutenant Lacy sat at' my feet. I cannot manage the third person well when I mean myself. He sat at my feet upon a convenient ottoman, which was constructed to suit his sister's whimsical fancy for low seats.

She is always dropping her dwarfish figure down upon a stool or cushion, or the carpet, and looking, as much as she can succeed in doing, like the picture of Evangeline one sees in every print-shop, and upon the wall of next to every farm-house in the country, until one feels — or I do — as if I should fly into a frenzy if she did not take her clasped hands off her knees, and her eyes off vacancy, and herself off that uncomfortable stone bench, and put up her hair like a sane woman (which she wasn't), and go about her business.

Very different from this lack-a-daisical figure was the hand-some youth now basking in the liquid radiance of my eyes, and looking all manner of adoring things to me in return. The primitive customs of camp life have not altered one of his fastidious habits of dress and personal daintiness. His hair and luxuriant beard are trimmed as by a professional tonsor; his hands fine still in outline, and unhardened by much handling of artillery and bridle. He wore the Confederate gray, — a new and stylish suit he had procured on his way through the city, — and without the risk of being mistaken for a mere parlor-knight, was a goodly sight to behold, and a winsome charmer to an ear that seldom hears complimentary sayings addressed to the owner of said auriculars when he is not here. He was chatting rather gayly this morning, usually to me, although, once in a while, he cast a pleasant word to his patroness, Miss Morris, who has chosen this inviting season of the year in which to visit her dear cronies, the Lacys. I verily believe that woman will never wear out, or grow older than she is at present. Her system, mental and physical, is made of vulcanized rubber. She softens down invariably when she speaks to Elinor, and as invariably hardens when she turns to me. To-day she looked wicked, and I felt so.

A week is a weary period when one is on her best behavior without an interval of refreshing naughtiness thrown in for the relief of fallible feminine nature. Lynn has not been home before since September, and I am out of practice in the exemplary line. It is not so hard to be all smiles and honey — a kind

20 *

of vitalized sweetmeat for forty-eight hours or thereabouts;
but my nerves are less sound than in lang syne, or my temper
less manageable.

For three days back I have been chafing ominously at the
necessity of prolonging the farce of " The Contented Betrothed."
It is a nauseous pill to Miss Morris to see me enacting this *rôle*,
supported by her adopted son ; but, as my luckless cavalier let
slip to me last night, she is under bonds to him to keep the
peace in public while she remains his mother's guest.

He expressed it thus : —

"She is the soul of candor, you know, dear, and she owned
that she had had her prejudices against you ; but she has promised to try and overcome these for my sake, and to love you as
my future wife."

There is a specimen of a man's wisdom for you ! to reveal to
one woman the true spring of another's forced cordiality — the
resolute intention to make the best of a bad bargain for the sake
of the divine youth who designs conferring upon this inferior
bit of goods the distinction of his name and possessorship ! I
nearly bit my tongue through while he was telling me of the marvellous fortune in store for me, in his patroness' toleration ; but
I held the imprudent member in its place, and bided my time.

Beside Miss Morris was the favorite of the day with this dis-
criminating lady, looking more diminutive than she used to appear
in her black dress, and prettier, with her delicately-oval face and
clear, unfathomable eyes. She has grown into a refined beauty,
instead of fading under her trial. I might better call it her bantling, for she broods over it and pets it, and levies upon others for
contributions of sympathy — all in dumb show — but unmistak-
ably, until my blood boils in my veins at the shameless parade.

Since that black September day, one name has never escaped
her lips in my hearing. She kept her chamber for at least three
weeks, and a doctor came and went, and there were cautious
steppings about the house, and carefully modulated voices within
the retirement sacred to widowed grief, and I might go my
ways, and nobody vex his or her wits about my moody turns,

and solitary sick days, and lonely rambles into the forest where no human eye could mark my wasted tears! The same old story, — "Unto her that hath shall be given." Given — the right, though her betrothed sleeps in bloody, unconsecrated ground, to mourn him without shame or fear of scorn ; to call herself, if she will, by his name, with no dread lest another should dispute her right to assume the title ; to feed her craving fancy upon the betrothal vow, the love-words spoken to her alone, and now never to be annulled by the utterances of another and a later love ; given — all that friendship and public sentiment can bestow in alleviation of a mighty loss.

Elinor was always an angel in the sight of her doting parents, and — I had nearly written — dotard aunt. Now she is a demigoddess, and requires close watching, lest, like the sainted Miss Betsey Gwin of tomb-stone celebrity, she should

> " Break the outer shell of sin,
> And hatch herself a cherubim."

She was sewing this morning upon a braided apron for Carrie. Another ingredient in her consummate counterfeit of self-abnegation is her increasing devotion to this child.

" Behold in me, all ye my acquaintances, and ye my possible lovers, a disconsolate widow ! " says her deportment. " To the world at large I am henceforth as if I had never lived. But lest your bereavement should crush you utterly, I have resolved to form my infant sister into a faint copy of what I once was, and set her in the niche left empty by my voluntary nunhood. Look at her as your rising star, and let me sink in peace ! "

She and Miss Morris were not silent while sitting for the pictures I have drawn. Indeed, there was a tolerably brisk patter of dialogue at that corner of the chimney, kept up mainly by Miss Morris, Elinor adding a tender treble of assent or inquiry, whenever the other paused to take breath.

" It delights me to see your sister so bright again," I observed softly to Lynn. " Miss Morris' visit is a real cordial to us all."

"Aunt Ellen is a great woman!" responded my auditor, loudly enough to be heard across the room, like the great clumsy animal a man is, where by-play is desired. "She could coax Patience off her monument if she cared to make the attempt."

I saw Miss Morris prick up her ears, and Elinor raise her eyes from her work, at this remark, which was uttered during a pause in their talk. There were needed only a swift, embarrassed glance from me, a lifted finger of caution, and a whispered "sh —— sh!" to emphasize and point my admirer's thoughtless repartee.

"Which is equivalent to saying that I could beguile you to quit that ottoman, I suppose!" said Miss Morris. "I believe I do *not* care to make the attempt. We should not know what to do with you on this side of the fire."

"That is fortunate!" answered the gallant Lieutenant, playing with an end of my gilt cord; "for I have not the remotest idea of removing from my present quarters."

"You would do capitally for a tableau of Hercules and the distaff!" was Miss Morris' next dart, flung with her usual air of playful humor, but aimed, as I divined, in anything but a playful mood.

Lynn laughed and dropped his plaything. "I owe you one, Aunt Ellen!"

So did I — one multiplied beyond my ability of numeration.

I smiled innocently, and asked, with careless simplicity, "Hercules? Wasn't he the god whose lady-love wrapped him in a poisoned mantle he couldn't get rid of, and which, at last, killed him? I wonder what is the significance of that fable? A *habit* of jealousy, I imagine, to which he was provoked by the fair murderess!" with a musical laugh at my pun.

Lynn espied no hidden meaning in my sally, but the two ladies did. Elinor's eye warned me that I was, unwittingly, as she believed, approaching dangerous ground. Miss Morris' flashed keen suspicion.

"Viewed in that light, one has less compassion for the charming widow," Lynn said, lightly.

"And more for her victim," rejoined I, seriously.

He took the cue. "It has always been a mystery to me how any woman, who really loves and is beloved, can trifle with the feelings she has inspired, and which she professes to reciprocate. I have no pity for the sufferings brought upon a coquette by her levity or deliberate scheme to try the constancy of her lover."

"True-hearted, good women are never coquettes!" I announced, with the aspect of a mentor.

"You are right there!" responded Miss Morris, composedly. "And coquetry in due time brings its own punishment. Whether, in a majority of cases, this is disproportionate to the offence, or not, I do not pretend to decide."

"A girl's love of teasing and fun is often styled flirtation, by prudish censors," said Elinor. "It would be hard were such playfulness to be visited by the loss of self-respect, and by public contempt. It is natural and pardonable for girls to love admiration."

I smiled again, covertly and sneeringly, averting my face as if to conceal my amusement.

"If there is one being more utterly abominable in my eyes than anything else in creation, it is a sly woman!" exclaimed Miss Morris, so energetically that Lynn wheeled his stool around, to get a better look at her.

"Heyday — Aunty! what has set you off?"

"Agatha understands me, and Elinor does not!" she answered.

I stared amazedly. Elinor stitched away, her cheeks flushing gradually.

"You are a riddle to me," pursued the gentleman. "What sly woman is the common detestation of yourself and Agatha?"

"Nobody. I know and despise one. If Agatha desires to make her acquaintance, let her come to me in private, and I will tell her a pretty story I once heard about a very Jesuit of a girl, with a broad, active streak of diabolism in her making up and daily behavior."

"I acknowledge a broad, active streak of curiosity in *my* making up," I returned pleasantly. "I shall certainly claim the fulfilment of your promise at as early a date as may be convenient. May I come to your room after dinner?"

"You may. I shall enjoy telling the tale to you."

"And if you are a very good boy, I will take you into confidence," I said to my betrothed, with childlike glee. "Aunt Ellen's stories are always charming, always graphic, sometimes thrilling. Yet they make one afraid of her, too. She is such a subtle anatomist of human nature, and has, withal, so vivid an imagination, that a *tête-à-tête* with her is like an hour spent in a picture gallery, filled with 'scenes from life by our best artists.'"

In saying this, I was ingenuous as a babe, sportive as a kitten, and the hazel eyes regarding the play of my countenance were eloquent of exulting fondness — the gaze of appreciative proprietorship in a mettled, but thoroughly-broken-in animal. "Aunt Ellen," upon whom I now bestowed this title for the first time, looked stilettos and poison-bowls at me, and my supple fingers did not intermit, or bungle, in their weaving while I sustained her scrutiny.

This spirited passage-at-arms did wonders toward relieving the monotony of a long morning in a country house, where the company was small and so familiarly acquainted with one another as to breed satiety, if not contempt; when the inclement season forbade walking or driving, and there was no prospect that the afternoon would be more favorable to out-door recreation. I need incessant stimulants and sharp excitants at that — to keep my system strung up within an octave of concert pitch. This argues a morbid condition of the moral liver, but I cannot help it. The anticipation of the battle in store for me affected me spiritually as cayenne pepper and quinine would have done bodily. I have longed to measure lances with Miss Morris ever since our acquaintanceship was five minutes old, and I resolved that the approaching encounter should be no child's play.

Yet, when I repaired to my chamber, after the strictly and lugubrious family dinner, to gird up my loins, — *id est*, my wits for the fray, — a qualm of heart-sickness laid hold of me. An Ishmaelite from my infancy — were peace of mind and concord with my fellows to be unknown to me through all my career? I waited, for some minutes, for the spasm to spend itself, and my courage to rise again to the requisite degree for the occasion — waited, sitting upon the rug with my back to the fire, looking absently around upon the comfortable room — in size, appointments, and situation desirable as that appropriated to the daughter of my host — and the thought started up before me, how it would feel to be innocent and lowly of mind, unambitious, unenvious — in one word, contented. I levelled the tempter with one blow of will and common sense.

"None of your dinner of herbs for me! Nothing venture, nothing have. If the tastes and temper which the Lord has moulded into my composition lead me out of the safe, old, respectable, beaten path, I am not responsible. This woman is my enemy, and she knows something about me which others do not. I have read it in her face dozens of times during the past week. She shall tell me what it is, make known all her grounds of dislike, and then I will return the compliment with interest."

The pungent spice of my ancient aversion having restored the tone of my mental stomach, I got up, surveyed myself critically in the mirror, saw that I was in high feather as regarded general appearance, and that my gypsy visage was both brilliant and wicked, and stepped out into the passage, humming a merry bravura all the way to Miss Morris' door.

"Come in!" she answered to my knock. I entered, and perceived, instantly, that I was expected.

She has a fashion of doffing her state robes every afternoon, assuming a wrapper and reading until dark, except when she coaxes Elinor to sit and chat with her instead. To-day, she had not removed her dinner dress — black silk, with a collar of old lace, and a small cap with lappets of the same material. She has unquestionably been a handsome woman in her day, and she is well preserved for her years. A noble fire of logs blazed upon the andirons, the hearth was cleanly swept, and a chair placed at the angle of the rug facing the window. This was plainly intended for my occupancy. She held the odds against me at the outset. I had not given the challenge, and according to the code of honor, mine should have been the choice of weapons and position. But I had accepted it with eagerness that betrayed my lurking grudge and my impatience to fight it out. Confident in my prowess, I did not shirk the disadvantageous place allotted me. I sat me down with the light from the west beaming broadly upon my features, and made the inevitable remark that it was growing colder every hour. She is impetuous, for a middle-aged lady, and her style of waiving preliminaries and going right at the subject in point, was comically like the manœuvre practised by the crew of boys who hang around the rivers and quays, during the bathing season — clasping the hands far above the head and then precipitating themselves, frog-fashion, into the water.

" You are engaged to be married to my friend, Lieutenant Lacy, Miss Agatha ! " I held my breath long enough to cause a pinky tinge to suffuse my complexion, and replied, looking bashfully into my lap, that I was.

" Do you love him? "

" That is surely a needless question, Miss Morris ! " plucking up a trifle of dignity.

" By no means — as women and society are now constituted. May I ask of you the favor of a reply?"

" If I had not loved him, I should not be betrothed to him. If I had not been willing to marry him, why should I encourage his addresses?" .

" There are a dozen ways in which the latter circumstance can be accounted for without the presupposition of affection on your part. He has the recommendations of family, wealth, and breeding. You are poor and ambitious. He is handsome and graceful, and you have an eye for outward advantages. Lastly, the engagement of Mr. Wilton to Elinor having removed him from the lists, you might not be reluctant to show him that the prize he rejected was not despised by another."

It was lucky I had steeled myself for any description of assault, or this would have unhorsed me — to alter slightly her trope of the tournament. I gazed straight at her with level, unblinking lids.

"You are prime authority in *les affaires du cœur*, Miss Morris. It would become me ill to question the accuracy of your deductions from appearances. Let us, for the sake of argument, admit that each and every one of the considerations you have named — including the climax — had a share in shaping my conduct in the formation of the engagement existing between myself and Lieutenant Lacy. What then?"

"I should say that you had spoken the truth, without expecting me to believe it. My opinion of your motives and character would remain unchanged. I am making no side-issues now, Agatha. I am in deadly earnest. This deception has gone far enough. I know you thoroughly. I believe yours to be a corrupt nature; and like all corruption, however skilfully its existence may be concealed for a while, it will show its abhorrent qualities eventually. Success has made you careless, or the crust of deceit is thinner and less specious than it once was. Your wiles impose upon fewer people every day you pass in this house. No girl ever had a fairer chance than you of making herself beloved and useful, had you chosen to walk in the straight path of right purpose and honest action. You preferred a circuitous course; have wheedled, and hoodwinked, and cheated; and to these practices there comes an end even in this world."

Her object was annihilation; but she had miscalculated the temper of the thing to be pulverized. I sat back easily and gracefully in my rocking-chair, and toyed with a hand-screen

I had taken from the table when she was midway in her harangue — tranquil and unsmiling, the embodiment of respectful
attention.

" You are general in your accusations," I ventured an objection at this stage. "I may be excused for feeling bewildered
by the rapidity and vagueness with which these are stated.
Will you favor me with a specific example or two of my baseness and double-dealing?"

"Willingly! While you were professing unbounded attachment for Elinor, you hated her for supplanting you in Mr. Wilton's regard. You nursed for him a sentiment he never asked
for, and which he could not reciprocate. Had you stopped
there, mine would have been the last tongue to utter the tale
of your unhappy love. But you overleaped the bounds of
womanly shame, as well as womanly pride, when you visited
him alone at his room, and pressed your unmaidenly suit upon
him. He kept your secret in spite of my repeated efforts to
extort from him an explanation of what I had myself seen and
heard. I was outside that room when my brother's knock for
admittance hushed your sobs and pleadings. Mr. Wilton unclosed the door very cautiously; but I had, through the wide
crack at the back of it, a glimpse of your dress, and knew it
for yours. I was behind you during that silent walk up to Mrs.
Dana's; passed you while you were still in the porch, and Mr.
Wilton was fitting the key into the lock. I charged all this
upon him next day, for I was very angry with him, while I
believed you were the greater sinner of the two. He refused
to give me any satisfaction except that he was true — heart,
intent, and deed — to his betrothed. Still, when he went away,
he must have been aware that your reputation was at my mercy.
The dead tell no tales, and you hoped, doubtless, to establish
yourself creditably in life without hinderance from the past you
thought was buried out of sight. For the sake of the family
whose worth and good name protect you, and out of mistaken
compassion for my poor boy, whose fate is so miserably entan-
gled with yours, I have hitherto refrained from exposing you.

I was so foolish as to hope that some miracle of love had wrought reformation in you; that you really valued the heart your guile had won. I find you unchanged, unless it be for the worse. I have listened without reply to your covert taunts, the unfeeling sneers directed at one the latchet of whose shoes you are unworthy to unloose. So far from respecting the depth and holiness of the great sorrow she bears so meekly, you let no opportunity escape without slyly probing the wounds of that pure, loving heart. Your deportment to Mr. and Mrs. Lacy, when their son is not by, is disrespectful under a lame ostentation of servility. I repeat — corruption will testify to its presence sooner or later, and I have cited but a few of the tokens of your real disposition and designs which I have marked during my short stay here. I have alluded to these in the hearing of no one excepting yourself. I wish to act honorably while I may seem unmerciful."

Here she halted, and rested upon her arms, before she delivered another volley.

I waved the painted screen gently to and fro, traced out the pattern with my forefinger, and once, when she was most energetic in her invective, turned it over in my hand to examine the reverse, and ascertain whether the handle were fastened in securely. Whatever might follow this tremendous preamble, my policy was clearly chalked out for me. She was warm. I must be cool. She dealt in sweeping assertions. I would contradict none of them. I could gain nothing by forcing her to prove a single one of these, for she had voluntarily told me in what manner she had gained her information. The story of her dislike was an old one, as was also her opposition to my marriage with her favorite. Yet I should marry him all the same as if she urged on the match.

"Now, Miss Lamar," resumed the virago, "I offer you two propositions. Break off your engagement with Lieutenant Lacy, upon whatever pretext you may choose to give him. Your inventive genius will not fail you at this juncture. You may then retain your home and respectability. I pledge myself to profound silence upon the matter I have laid before you this afternoon. It is not my mission to go about the world to correct abuses at large. But I will save my dearest friend from the miseries that would be entailed upon him by a union with a heartless, unscrupulous woman. Elinor you cannot injure now, good as is your will to ruin her happiness. Mr. and Mrs. Lacy are above your reach. I had rather have cut off my right hand than that Lynn should have been inveigled into this match. I shall use every effort to break it off. If you decline gratifying me in this particular, I shall forthwith repeat to Mr. and Mrs. Lacy, and leave them to tell their son all that I have said to you."

" Do it," I said coolly, " and I will marry him to-morrow. You know your power, Miss Morris. I do not over-estimate mine."

She stared at me blankly, as if uncertain whether she had understood me. I smiled slightly — a gleam of calm superiority — and twirled my invaluable toy. The short winter day was hastening to a close. The windows showed increasing duskiness without, and the fire roared more loudly within. I saw her bite her lip before she spoke again. She had changed her mind as to something she was on the point of saying.

" Lieutenant Lacy is not a silly boy, however fervent may be his attachment to you," she continued. I could see it hurt her whenever she admitted his love for the outcast, and I marked the weak joint of her harness. " His confidence in my veracity and in my friendship dates back to his infancy. He will believe me when I assert what I myself know to be true."

" You can try it!" I answered, imperturbably. " I would willingly avoid an *éclaircissement* which would involve unpleasant revelations to all who are mixed up in it; but if you are bent upon it, I do not shirk it. I do not question the strength of his confidence in his mother's oldest friend; and please remember that it was not I who impugned your veracity, but you, who charged me with falsehood. I have not opposed a denial to one count of your indictment. When the case is tried in open court, I shall privately instruct my counsel how to plead. I have no fear lest I shall fail in convincing him of my innocence. To drop the legal figure — if you make my residence here undesirable, I shall seek one elsewhere, and Hayridge is open for my reception as its mistress and the wife of its owner, whenever I think proper to return a favorable reply to his entreaties for a speedy marriage."

I lied here — for the Lieutenant would as soon leave me the solitary occupant of a wigwam in the trackless forest as install me at Hayridge during his absence upon military duty. The situation immediately upon the river, and in the track of the passing and repassing armies, renders it an unsafe abode for any woman, especially one young and beautiful. Nor has he ever intimated to me a desire for an early union. "When the war is over" — "when peace is declared" — are terms perpetually upon his lips in connection with our marriage. But I learned — a hundred years ago, I think — to utter a lie with a better grace than the truth, and very sensibly — since, if moralists are to be depended upon, Truth needs no dress except her native fairness. I am not prepared to contradict this ethical theory, for I don't happen to know anybody who indulges in exhibitions of the naked truth. It is not considered decent.

"It is superfluous to assure me that Lieutenant Lacy is not a fool," I said. "He is a high-minded, honorable gentleman, who would uphold the cause of his betrothed wife against a legion of slanderous mischief-makers, were this composed of his father, mother, sister, and every disinterested elderly friend he has upon earth. Mark me! I do not wish to balk your plans for his disinthralment. But, having the pleasure of a tolerably intimate acquaintanceship with him, it is but fair in me to warn you how he will deport himself in our nice tragi-comic drama. I would not be outdone by you in honorable behavior."

I *had* balked her. I saw it in her musing gaze into the red-hot coals, and the slow tap of her fingers upon the arm of her chair. She was considering whether it would be worth her

21 *

while to push me to the end of the plank. If she did, and I
maintained my hold upon her adopted son, she must go under,
for good and all. She was not cowed. She was too true metal
for that. But she was staggered by my hardihood.

"It would be useless to appeal to her sense of the justice due
the man she means to marry!" she said, interrogatively, more
to herself than to me.

"Quite useless!" I rejoined. "For our ideas of justice may
be totally different. I hold that he deserves all the happiness
he covets in a union with me. You would break his heart,
turn him adrift upon the world aimless and loveless. It is not
a light sin to rob a man of the hope he has cherished as the
brightest blessing fate has ever bestowed upon him. And hearts
like his *can* break!"

A swift shadow went over her countenance, and her lip trembled momentarily.

"I seek his true good!" she said, earnestly. "I wish I
could believe in you, girl!" ·

I bowed respectfully. "I second the wish!"

"But I cannot! I will not see my poor boy sacrificed
to ——" She checked herself.

"I can imagine the epithets courtesy withholds you from
uttering while I am in your chamber as your invited guest," I
said, rising. "I leave the decision of this knotty case entirely
with you, Miss Morris. I cannot say with truth that I regret
my failure to win your regard, since I have never been tempted
to desire your favorable opinion of myself or my conduct. I
shall not remonstrate against your resolution, let it be what it
may. But I shall take excellent care of myself in any event.
I have had some practice in that line. Have you any further
commands for me?"

"I have finished all I meant to say. In my plans for future
action, I shall not be influenced by needless consideration for
your sensibilities. You have set my mind at rest upon that
score. Good evening!"

She nodded coldly, and I returned a profound obeisance. I

had played my part well, and she had mangled hers by injudi-
cious effervescence of emotion. She had talked hurriedly, and
with heat, and I had been cautioned by this very warmth to
practise self-control.

I sought my chamber without meeting any one in the halls.
It was quite dark now, and the fire had burned low, as I
crouched once more upon the rug, and laying my throbbing
temples within my palms, sobbed in dry, hysterical gasps that
seemed to rend my lungs and swell my throat to strangulation.
I was helpless, forlorn, miserable! I almost persuaded myself,
in my rage against my tormentor, that I would be good and
happy with my intended husband, if she would let me. She
had insulted me grossly; driven me, with my fierce, vindictive
temper, to the verge of insanity; and I had no alternative but
submission. The one being who would have resented an injury offered me was the last person to whom I could relate the
scene I had just passed through. Oh, would the day never
come when it should be my turn to trample, and the turn of
my oppressors to be trodden upon! I could not go below,
although I heard Lynn strumming upon the piano, playing stray
chords and fragments of love-ditties that partially expressed
the unsettled state of his wits, and I knew he was impatiently
expecting me for a twilight confabulation. When, at last, a
servant knocked at my door to bring in wood and water for the
night, the fireplace was black, and I shivered with cold as I
dragged up my stiffened limbs from the floor.

"I fell asleep there, with my head upon the chair," I said to
the girl, who exclaimed at finding me in the dark.

I lighted my lamp, and carefully readjusted my toilet, sending the girl out upon an errand while I touched my olive-pale
cheeks with something taken from a secret drawer. I gnawed
my lips on the journey down stairs, that they might be dewy
and bright. No woman can afford to look ugly, however miserable she may wish to appear. My direct route did not take
me past the study, but an inward presentiment of evil to myself
did. Streams of rosy light shot through the keyhole and the

crack under the door into the dark hall. There were suppressed murmurs within, and I stooped to spy out the interior. Mr. Lacy and Miss Morris were closeted. I listened until I heard my name and Lynn's twice repeated, and withdrew softly as I had approached. My next essay was to look into the dining-room. As I thought, my Lady, Elinor, and Carrie were there, pulling long ropes of sugar candy for the delectation of the last-named.

"Come in," said they.

"No, thank you," I said, sweetly. "Lynn is waiting for me in the parlor. I have had a nap, and overslept myself, besides taking cold, I am afraid. This is a Nova-Zemblan night. How beautifully white your candy is, Carrie! I wish you had called me to help you pull it."

The parlor was ablaze with firelight, and Lynn was stalking up and down like the "lone picket" of whom Elinor used to be forever singing.

"Don't scold me, dear," I said, plaintively, as he began a remark about his impatient waiting. "I hadn't the spirits to come down stairs earlier: I have the vapors to-night."

With manly modesty, he assumed that I was grieving over the approaching separation, and I owned that this redoubled the original weight upon my heart. By this time, he had established me upon the sofa by him, and I leaned my head upon his shoulder, and cried a little. Thereupon, by a lawyerly cross-examination, he wrung from me the admission that the colloquy with Miss Morris had depressed me.

"She will never like me, darling," I sighed, pathetically. "I am weary with trying to conquer her prejudice, and her influence with your parents and sister is unbounded. Is it singular that these thoughts should sadden me? that I sometimes debate the question with myself, whether it may not be my duty to sever our engagement —— "

"Agatha, you drive me mad! What are parents, sister, the whole universe, to me, compared with one smile from you?"

The door creaked on its hinges behind us, and Mrs. Lacy spoke : —

"Lynn, Uncle Will wants to know if you put the stable-key into your pocket to-night."

"Here it is, Mother!"

He went forward to meet her, rendered up the missing article, and she retired. But there was a note ajar in her full, even voice, and I was assured that she had overheard the hyperbolical outbreak of her son. Fortune had, by way of change, tossed up a lucky card into my hand. Milord never moves in important affairs without consulting his better half; and she will think twice, after hearing this impassioned question, before she risks the banishment of her best-beloved child. I could afford to soothe my gentleman now with reiterations of my unabated affection, and the like emollients. I pleaded Aunt Ellen's jealous partiality for him, and her disinclination to be supplanted in his esteem by a younger and later acquaintance ; which he declared was "absurd in the extremest degree."

"I honor her candor," I said, generously. "She does not feign love where she cannot feel it. She has many noble qualities, which I can see and acknowledge, although she views all that I do through a distorted medium."

In conclusion, I won him to promise that he would not betray, by word, look, or behavior, what he had gathered from me.

"It would but widen the breach," I alleged. "I trust to time and your loving diplomacy to heal it. You are so dear to us both, that this antagonism cannot be perpetual."

"You are an angel of forgiveness!" he ejaculated. "But I warn you, that, should a crisis arrive, — should she, or any one else, compel me to declare my sentiments in this matter, — I shall not stay to weigh any claims beside yours. I would believe your lightest word in opposition to the oaths of a thousand others!"

Which, if it was a stereotyped love-speech, was exactly what I had intended he should say from the outset.

The evening passed by very soberly. Lynn had no private

conterence with any member of his family; for I sat with him, according to our custom, until the rest of the household were in their beds. He will be off betimes in the morning, which must be very near at hand. I have not slept a wink all night. I shall be sick after this New-year day's work; but, when that fond, foolish boy has gone, nobody will care whether I am well or ill.

CHAPTER XIX.

ELINOR.

March 16, 1864.

A STRANGE thing has happened — so strange and unlooked for I cannot convince myself that I am not dreaming when I begin to write of it. One night, three weeks ago, I had gone to my room, and had drawn up my desk to the fire, to begin a letter to Aunt Ellen, when Mammy tapped for permission to enter. She shut the door carefully, and crept toward me on tiptoe, wearing an air of mystery that amused, while it startled me.

"I have something to tell you, honey," she whispered, stooping to my ear. "It's right that somebody besides me and Uncle Will should know it, and it mightn't be safe to let on to Marster."

"Mammy! what can it be, that would not be safe with Papa?"

"Nothing, dear. He's close as wax, and wise as Solomon: but we colored people hears things that all white folks doesn't; and 'tisn't safe, upon his own account, that he should know everything that's going on in these days, which ain't a bit like old times. They might suspicion him, and get him into trouble. *You* wouldn't be thought of, nor harmed, if they did happen to find you out."

"Very well; what is your secret?" asked I, smiling. "I will keep it, if you still wish it, after we have talked it over together."

She lowered her voice until I could just hear her, and proceeded to relate, that Uncle Will had made an excursion into

the maple swamp that day, in search of certain roots and bark
that are considered medicinal by the negroes at this season of
the year. In passing a thicket of juniper-bushes, he fancied
that he perceived a movement within it, and parting the
branches, looked in.

"And thar, on the bare ground, dear, — all soaking wet
with spring rains, and not fit for a pig to wallow in, let alone a
white Christian creatur', — was a man. His clothes was
hanging in rags, his beard had growed 'way down below his
breast, and his bones was fa'rly poking through his skin. Says
Uncle Will to him, 'How did you get here? and what's the
matter with you?' And says he, 'I'm a-starving; but don't
tell whar I am.'

"As the Lord would have it, Uncle Will had put an ash-cake
in his pocket when he went down to the low grounds, thinking
he might be kept out late, and want his dinner. He sot down
'pon a log, and drawed the poor fellow up alongside of him, and
fed him, little by little, as he would a done a baby; and then
he takes his own coat off his back, and wraps the shivering
bones up in it; and 'Stay here,' says he, 'till dark, and I'll
take you to a comfortabler place.' For you see, honey, he mis-
trusted right straight off what he was, and how he came to be
hiding in the dens and caves of the yarth. And with that he
comes up home, and brings the story to me; and I got ready a
pot of warm tea and some chicken-broth, and made up a bed in
a dark corner of my up-stairs room; and nigh 'pon three hours
ago, he and I sot out for the swamp, — I taking along a little
tin bucket with a mouthful of soup in it, and Uncle Will had a
'tickler' of whiskey, which, being a member, he never touches
'cept for medicine; and leaning against the log, with the thick,
dry coat 'pon him to keep off the damp, we found him; and
says he, 'I was afraid you would never come.'

"We got him up on his feet, and took him betwixt us, he
a-resting all his weight 'pon our shoulders; and by walking
slow, and stopping to rest about a dozen times, we managed to
bring him up to my house. I washed him with warm water,

dear, from his head to his feet. Ah! the sight of *them* was pitiful enough — all cracked, and festered, and bleeding; and Uncle Will changed his rags for a shirt and pants of hisn; and he swallowed his tea, and a sup or more so of his soup: but he's a rack to look at, and I'm afeared he may not live through it. We 'cluded — Uncle Will and me — that some white person ought to see him, and take down his name, and where he lives, and the like of that. It's all the time in my mind, how that poor wounded man that died here last winter kept a-talking about his mother; but *this* one's mother wouldn't know her own child if she was to see him now."

I lost no time in questioning whether I should do as she wished. She had judged wisely, that this was not a matter to be brought before my father, if it could be helped. I did not inquire what discovery she had made touching the unfortunate stranger's previous history. I guessed immediately that he was either a deserter from one of the two armies that lie to the north and south of us, or an escaped Union prisoner. This war has made us familiar with tales of dungeons and summary retribution visited upon fugitives from military duty or imprisonment.

I found the wanderer lying upon the comfortable pallet which Mammy had made up for him in her upper room. A candle burned upon a stool beside him, and there were cavernous shadows in his face that made him look unlike a human being. His kind nurse had combed out his matted hair and beard, but their unshorn raggedness heightened his resemblance to some wild creature of the forest — less than man, and higher than beast. His wasted hands were crossed upon his breast, and he was sleeping peacefully as a happy child. Mammy and I sat down near him, Uncle Will keeping guard below until eleven o'clock, hardly daring to breathe, lest we should break that healthful slumber. Then he stirred, groaned deeply, and awoke. His hollow eyes glared first upon me, and he lifted his head with a smile that did not lessen the ghastliness of his appearance.

22

"Am I at home — or in Heaven?" he asked; and before we recovered presence of mind to answer, he added, more faintly, "Not in Heaven! I am weak and sick still!"

His head fell back, and he groaned again, in pain or feebleness.

I had brought restoratives, and salve, and soft linen, for bandages, from the house, and while Mammy renewed the dressings upon the wounded feet, I fed him, at intervals of ten and fifteen minutes, with wine and broth, until his pulse was full and regular. I did not catechise him at all, but Mammy asked for his name and place of residence, in order, as I understood, that I might communicate these to his friends in the event of his death. I spoke to him, occasionally, when the sunken eyes scrutinized me with wild questioning, — bewilderment he was too weak to put into audible language, — but I confined myself to reassuring phrases and hopeful predictions of his rapid improvement. It was after midnight when Mammy advised me to leave him alone with her.

"He is better already!" she said, cheerfully, "and I'm easier in my mind. His pulse is coming up steady, and his voice is stronger. You go back to the house, honey, and don't fret yourself any more to-night. And, Miss Elinor, dear, don't you be thinking 'bout sending for the doctor! '*Twouldn't do!* not ef he was a-dying, which he ain't going to do, this time!" This was smiled at the patient. "I'll bring him 'round, ef the Lord is willing. I've done some nussing in my day, and that's all he needs, 'cept the right kind of vittles, and not too much at a time!"

"I shall be in to see you in the morning," I said to the sick man. "This was my nurse when I was a child, and she has taken care of us all in our sickness ever since I can recollect I could not leave you in better hands."

He raised his hand, when I would have turned away.

"One word! Do you know what I am?"

"A suffering fellow-creature," I answered, "who is entitled to all we can do for him, while he suffers."

"I was a prisoner of war in Richmond. I escaped. I have wandered in the woods for a week and more. I thought I must die — or go back. I meant to die!"

"Say no more!" I interposed, as he gasped for breath. "I suspected all this before. You are safe here until you are strong enough to travel. Then you may go home. I promise you this."

"And you are a southern woman!" The burning eyes were fixed upon me.

"I am a Virginian, and I love the Union as I do my life!"

I saw him put his hands together and his lips whisper a thanksgiving; then I hurried down the stairs, my heart too full for speech. Uncle Will attended me to the house. I had left the side-door unlocked, and I mounted with soundless foot-steps to my chamber. There, my first act was to kneel and thank Him who had intrusted this poor fugitive to my care. It is little I can do to stem the tide of blood and tears that is wasting our land, — but what is permitted to me I do with a solemn gladness, a devout gratitude to the merciful One who has not made my life to be wholly a waste. As I prayed, it seemed as if Harry were with me, encouraging me by his approval, counselling me by his wisdom. When I fell asleep, his spirit still smiled on my dreams. I had never dreamed happily of him before, since I heard of his death. I had seen him fighting, wounded, or dead, — the fatal bullet lodged in his heart, — and had awakened, night after night, with a real phys-ical pang in my own that left it sore for hours afterwards.

But in this vision he was with me at the bedside of the stran-ger, ministering with me to his wants, and talking, in his brave, loving way, of the war, and the scenes in which he had been engaged since our parting.

"Thank you for this act of mercy, Brownie!" he said, lay-ing his hand upon the sick man's forehead. "Remember! you do it for my sake, and for love of the Union!"

It was a strangely vivid dream, and it never leaves me.

My charge was marvellously better next day, and on the

second, which was the Sabbath morning, I found him propped by clean pillows; himself arrayed in fresh linen that had once belonged to my father; his ragged beard and hair trimmed by Mammy's clever fingers, while Uncle Will, sitting by him, read aloud from his well-worn Bible.

"Good morning, Mr. Merrill!" I said. "I am glad to see you looking so well and bright! You do credit to your physician"—nodding at Mammy.

But, looking more narrowly at her, I saw that she had been weeping. I must have appeared frightened, for she hastened to correct my impression that she considered her patient worse.

"He's getting on finely! couldn't be doing better!" she said, confidently. "But we've been having some talk with him, my poor child,—Uncle Will and me,—and ef I had misbelieved till now that the Lord sent him to us, I should be ashamed of my doubtings. Don't break down, my lamb, if you can bear up—for it's a comforting thing that *he*, of all the other poor pris'ners that got away at the same time, should 'a been laid at your door."

The tears were streaming down her dear old face, and she had me in her arms, as she used to hold me when I was a hurt or terrified child. My dream had been very present with me all the morning, and as she spoke, I seemed to be living in it again.

"I think I know what you mean," I replied. "I shall not break down, Mammy. But I should like to speak with Mr. Merrill, alone."

She and Uncle Will went down stairs, and I took the vacant chair by the soldier's bed.

"Aunt Rachel tells me you were a friend of Lieutenant Wilton, of the —th New York," he began, diffidently, looking past—not at me. "I was a sergeant in the same company with him, and saw him every day, from the time we left home until Gettysburg."

I did shiver at that word—stamped upon my memory in

characters of blood. But I would not show that I was moved, lest he should keep back something from me I ought to hear.

"Were you near him when he fell?" I asked.

"I was not. But I saw him just before we went into battle. I had occasion to consult him about some order which had been passed to me. We non-commissioned officers and the men liked him best of all our superiors. He was patient, and kind, and merry, no matter how the day went, or how tedious the march was. He put spirit into us when we were clean fagged out, and if there was fighting to be done, he never said, ' Go in, boys!' but, ' Come on, my brave fellows!' There was no shirk in him.

" That morning, he was talking with our Captain, when I came up and saluted them.

" 'Well, Mr. Merrill,' says he, pleasantly, ' have you anything to say to me?'

" I stated my business.

" ' Why,' says the Captain, with an oath, ' what a thick skull you must have not to understand that! The thing's as plain as the nose on your face! Do thus and so!' explaining, after his fashion, what the order meant.

" The Lieutenant never said a word; only stood looking down, grave and quiet, until I was sent about my business. Then he followed and overtook me.

" 'Sergeant,' says he, ' I'm afraid our good Captain did not make matters quite clear to you.'

" 'You're right, sir!' says I. ' But I didn't dare say so to him.'

" With that, he put the case before me, in twenty words — made it easy as A, B, C.

" 'I am obliged to you, Lieutenant!' says I, heartily. ' You've done me a real favor!'

" 'It is nothing!' he said, kindly. ' It is a soldier's business to help his comrades in little, as well as great things. We are likely to have hot work soon, but we shall win the day, I hope. GOD defend the Right!'

"When the order to charge was given, which wasn't until near midday, I caught his eye as he turned and waved his sword towards the men. He smiled and shook it in the air over his head, as if he were repeating — 'GOD defend the Right!' I never saw him afterward."

Neither of us offered to speak again directly. I had not wept during this homely recital of an incident more precious to me in the hearing, than would have been the wealth of a kingdom. I could see, through the small window above the pallet, the green hills beyond the river, the belt of forest, and above these, the blue of the Sabbath sky, with the white fleeces sailing slowly across it. Just so brightly had shone the sun, just so blue were the heavens above those other hills and fields, far away, on that July day, when my darling looked his last upon them.

"GOD defend the right!" HE did! HE does!

From the room beneath ascended, in this death-like silence, Uncle Will's reverent tones, as he continued his morning reading.

"Therefore will we not fear, though the earth be removed, and though the mountains be carried into the midst of the seas; though the waters thereof roar and be troubled; though the mountains shake with the swelling thereof."

Our Father was near to him who trusted in His strength and protection amid the din and smoke of battle, as to me in my quiet communing with Him on this holy day.

"He died instantly, you know?" I said presently.

"So I heard, after reaching Richmond. A man who saw him fall, told me of it. He had a very fine sword, which was presented to him by his business partners before he left New York. The flashing of this must have caught the eye of a rebel sharp-shooter. The shot did its work thoroughly. He never moved after he fell. There were several members of his company in our room in prison, and two or three of them cried like children, when they got the bad news. Ah, well! ma'am! he was a brave soldier, and he fell in a glorious cause. 'Twas better he should die as he did, than endure what I have seen others suffer during my prison life. What with bad air, and bad food, and not enough of that, and cold, and homesickness — a man dies by inches in those filthy pens ! "

" You are right ! it was far better ! " I answered.

From this, we went back to the date of his earliest meeting with Harry, and he recounted many incidents of the wise care of the officer for his subordinates ; the courteous kindness of the gentleman to his brethren in arms ; the unflinching courage of the Christian patriot. My thirsty ears drank in all with avidity. I believed in every feature of the narration ; did not mar the enjoyment of listening by critical questionings into the authenticity of this or that portion. For me, each scene was painted with a fidelity to Nature that convinced me of the speaker's veracity. It was like gazing upon a roughly-drawn, but most striking likeness of the lost one.

" That was like him ! " was my only comment, and this I rarely made.

When he was through, — and I had to interrupt him at intervals, and oblige him to rest a while before proceeding with the story, — when he had finished, I thanked him, and bidding him try and sleep after his fatiguing conversation, summoned Mammy to stay with him, and betook myself, with my Bible, to my Sabbath chapel — the seat at the roots of the great willow, in our " God's acre."

Shall I ever forget the experience of that blessed forenoon? We seldom go to church now. Our neat house of worship has been twice used as a hospital, and latterly, as barracks ; the seats torn out for firewood and the window-sashes dashed from their frames. We have no pastor, and the little flock that once gathered in the beloved sanctuary are as sheep scattered abroad. But the shadow of that old tree was to me more sacred than temple consecrated by man's formal act. Those whom we call dead were nearer to my spirit than the living. Solemn peace held my soul, — a sweet benediction from Him who had chastened me for my good. I thanked Him, through tears that sprang from no bitter fountain, that He had not heeded my

ungrateful repinings, or punished my selfish indolence of grief
during the earlier days of my mourning. I accepted, as a pledge
of love and forgiveness, the keepsake He had sent me in the
mementos of my Harry's noble life and glorious death. I was
very humble, very tranquil — almost happy.

I did not know that I was singing as I strolled through the
garden to the house, until I met Agatha in the broad walk, and
saw her amazed look. I do know that my heart was one
hymn of praise and love, and I believe that my tongue was
busy with one of Mamma's favorites.

> " What if the springs of life were broke,
> And heart and flesh should faint, —
> GOD is the soul's eternal rock,
> The strength of every saint ! "

From that day Mammy's guest and mine recovered rapidly.
We had less trouble than I had anticipated in keeping his presence upon the premises secret from everybody excepting our
three selves. Mammy is a queen in her set, and since her husband's death, six years since, she has resided alone in her com-
modious cottage, and enjoyed, besides the distinction of Mamma's confidence, the post of head woman of the plantation, in
rank and authority inferior only to Uncle Will, who has been
Papa's manager from the day he married and took up his abode
at Sunnybank. Mammy's house is not to be rashly entered by
the other servants, and my visits to her excited no remark.
She was my nurse, and she is my friend. Whether she is sick
or well, I rarely let a day pass without sitting for half an hour
in her clean, bright room. She has chosen, lately, to prepare
most of her meals over her own fire ; and this habit afforded her
facilities for cooking such delicate and nourishing food as the
convalescent needed. It was difficult to refrain from taking
Mamma into our counsel, but we decided that she had better
be kept in ignorance until the upper room should be vacated,
and the prisoner again a wanderer. He bore his confinement
more than patiently. His spirits never flagged under the monotony of his daily life.

"It is Paradise, after what I have undergone since last July!" he said, once, when I expressed regret that he was debarred the enjoyment of out-door exercise, except upon dark nights, when Uncle Will attended him in his walks through unfrequented paths, and across lonely fields.

This could not last forever, however. We comprehended thoroughly the necessity of his quitting us so soon as he was strong enough to travel. Any day might bring discovery and danger to us all — death or captivity to him.

Rolf Kingston spent a night with us while Merrill was here. I was sorry to see him, and yet it seems ungracious in me to say so, for a brother could not have been kinder or more regardful of my feelings. Agatha was confined to her room with headache that evening, and the responsibility of his entertainment devolved mainly upon me. He gave me a deplorable account of the state of things in Richmond, the unscrupulous greed of capitalists for money; their speculations, and frauds, and oppressions, and the consequent sufferings of the lower classes. His hopes of the ultimate success of the Confederacy are few and faint. Papa has believed from the beginning that it would have an ephemeral existence. According to Rolf's statement, the ablest defenders of the new Government are far from sanguine as to its stability.

"Our star began to decline when Jackson died!" said he, despondingly. "Since then, our battle-fields have been slaughter-grounds upon which the best blood in the country has been poured forth in vain. While Lee commands, and Lee leads, we can but follow him to the end. What that end may be, the wisest among us cannot say."

I asked him, encouraged by his confidence in my discretion, whether there was any truth in the tales, darkly whispered among us, of the sufferings of the Federal prisoners in Richmond and other southern prisons.

He shook his head, sadly. "Only too much, I fear! It is the fortune of war. When our men in active service must perform forced marches for days together, without other subsistence

than a little parched corn and water, — when their blankets are
fragments of worn carpets, their coarse clothing is hanging
in tatters about them, and their naked feet are marking the earth
with blood as they walk, — the captives in our hands cannot bo
fed and clothed luxuriously. Yet the hardships of their situation might be mitigated in some degree, were it not that this
unnatural conflict has hardened the hearts of our people — rulers
and ruled alike — against the invaders. What a gigantic blunder the whole war has been !"

"A blunder the results of which can never be undone !" I
said.

He made a feeling response, and there the subject dropped.

"There will be another exchange of prisoners, shortly," ho
said, at another time. "Have you any message or letters to
send through the lines?"

"An exchange!" I exclaimed, eagerly. "I wonder if——"

The sense of my imprudence rushed upon me, and struck me
dumb with shame and fright.

"If what?" asked Rolf, kindly. "Is there any way in
which I can be of service to you?"

My foolish impulse had been to mention Mr. Merrill, forgetting entirely, for the moment, that he had, by his attempt to
escape, placed himself outside the pale of regular exchange, or
even of merciful treatment should he be recaptured. It was an
insane idea, and I trembled to think how nearly I had come to
exposing him. Had I divulged the truth, Rolf's duty would
have been clear. I believe he would have regretted the necessity of performing it — but my poor guest must have been
dragged back to his dungeon, and I borne the *onus* of betraying one who had trusted me with his liberty, if not with his
life. Self-convicted by these reflections of folly and criminal
imprudence, I longed to rush away and hide until reason and
judgment returned.

Rolf repeated his persuasive query.

"Will you not tell me what you were about to say? You
can trust me. Do you doubt this?"

"No," I replied, sincerely. "But I have no occasion to put your friendship and desire to oblige me to the test. I have no correspondent on the other side of the lines, excepting Uncle Charley. I may trouble you with a note to him."

For, although we have never spoken of his clandestine visit to us year before last, it is now generally known that he went North about that time. As I said this, I met Rolf's eyes fastened upon me with a mixture of perplexity and inquiry that confused me the more. I arose abruptly, and left the room. I hope he attributed my evident distress to the press of painful reminiscences, to girlish caprice — to anything but the real origin. It was a salutary lesson to me. Thenceforward I kept a vigilant watch upon my words and looks. I even forbore to go near Mammy's house that night, or the following forenoon.

The next evening, after Rolf had gone, I paid my customary visit, and found that my charge — no longer my patient — had taken a sudden resolve to set forth upon his journey northward that very night. Either the intelligence of Captain Kingston's arrival had aroused his anxiety, or he had a presentiment of approaching danger; for he was not to be diverted from his determination by any arguments I could bring to bear upon him. We accordingly began diligently to fit him out for his perilous undertaking. He had, by the help of a map of Virginia which I had lent him, and such additional information as Uncle Will and I could supply, made out a rude chart of the country through which he was to pass; and when he laid this down upon the table, and showed me how he proposed to avoid the outlying posts of the Confederate lines, and the more thickly-settled parts of the counties he must traverse, I partook of the cheerful confidence he expressed as to the success of the adventure. Our united resources were insufficient to provide for him as I wished to do, when I remembered by whose side he had marched and fought; and although he protested that he should want nothing more than we had supplied, I resolved to make an appeal in his behalf to Mamma. I attacked her boldly.

"Mamma, I want a suit of Papa's clothes — something decent and serviceable, but not too new or nice."

"As to that, my love," she replied, laughing, "his best suit does not come under your latter head. Unless he will wear 'butternut' homespun, anything new must shortly be an apocryphal term when applied to his wardrobe. But perhaps you may find what you wish in the closet of the oak-room. As to under-garments — look here!"

She opened a drawer, and laid out one article after another — strong, plain, and clean — even to two pairs of stout socks.

"Will these do?" she inquired, with affected gravity.

But there was a quizzical smile in her eye that betrayed her and overcame me. I threw my arms around her neck, and laughed hysterically.

"Dear Mamma! how you trust me! Indeed, I am doing nothing I need be ashamed of! You shall know all very soon!"

"Perhaps I am not so ignorant as you suppose!" she returned, kissing me. "No one has been telling tales out of school; but I have learned to read the signs of the times. Now — we will look in the closet!"

We selected a good suit — dark gray — such as any respectable farmer might wear on his way to town. Mamma added a pocket-book containing a considerable sum of Confederate money.

"He can use this until he reaches a place of safety. Other money, if he should be searched, would subject him to suspicion. It would be well to send Uncle Will with him on horseback for the first stage of his journey. I will furnish him with a pass to go to the Cross Roads and return. He can make an excuse of visiting his son there, and take Romp along to be examined by the farrier. Tom will have it that she is spavined."

Her easy tone, her smile, and the simple, well-digested plan of operations she had ready for us inspirited me to a liveliness of hope, that, in its first glow, dispelled my apprehensions for the traveller's safety. Taking the clothing to my room, I called Mammy to help me carry it to her house, and lingered behind her to put up a few trifles, such as scissors, needles, thread, and a small testament — a tiny package that he could carry in his pocket. Mammy had stocked his wallet with provisions, and fed him with an abundant meal preparatory to his starting. He was equipped for his journey, and with his strong, sensible features, iron-gray hair, and decent habiliments, looked as little like a man amenable to the penalty of the law, as if he had never stirred from his farm-house, or handled a musket.

"I should not dream of stopping you on the road and demanding your pass, were I a picket," I said, cheerily. "I predict that your honest face will serve you as well as a permit signed by all the generals in both armies."

He was standing in the lower room, hat in hand, and overcoat buttoned up to his chin; Uncle Will was near him, also dressed for riding, and Mammy — who had loved her late guest with the full fervor of her loyal heart since the eventful Sabbath on which she discovered that he was "one of Mars' Harry's soldiers" — was hovering about him, with parting injunctions and ejaculatory blessings, when she uttered a scream, and pointed to the window. A curtain was drawn across the lower half of it, and although we all turned in the direction designated by her finger and eyes, we could see nothing unusual. Uncle Will stepped quickly to the door, and went out.

"There is not a soul about!" he reported, upon his return. "I have been all around the house and the quarters. Who did think it was, Rachel?"

"It was a white face, with big, bright eyes, a-staring right at us!" she insisted, shaking with fear.

"More likely a big, white owl, or a cat!" said Uncle Will, laughingly. "The dogs would never let a stranger come into the yard without giving the alarm. You were mistaken, my good sister!"

She adhered stoutly to her assertion, however; and such is my faith in the accuracy of her statements, that, although I pretended to acquiesce in Uncle Will's explanation of the apparition, a chill fear crept to my heart as I lost sight of the two tall forms walking away in the faint starlight. The horses were awaiting them in the edge of the woods back of the house. Mammy and I watched and listened in the darkness outside her cabin, until they must have been a mile and more on their way; and nothing disturbed the stillness of the night except the hooting of an owl down in the swamp, and the distant bark of a watch-dog in the opposite direction to that the travellers had taken. There was a light in my room, and I knew Mamma was awake and waiting for my report.

"Everything seems to be quiet, Mammy," I said, arising from the doorstep where we had been sitting. "Maybe you were wrong, after all."

"I hope so, honey; but these are the latter days, dear, and in them it is written that your old men shall see visions, — and why not an old woman? I can't get the look of them eyes out of my head."

Nor could I the thought of them out of mine until Mamma made light of the occurrence.

"Rachel was always superstitious," she said "This is not her maiden experience in ghost-seeing she had some remarkable revelations in her youth. I hoped she had outlived such fantasies."

It was an unspeakable comfort to impart to Mamma all that had occupied my thoughts and heart since Uncle Will had played the Good Samaritan in the maple swamp, and Mammy opened her hospitable door to the perishing stranger. Her surmises had pointed to the truth, so far as she suspected that Mammy harbored a Union refugee, and that I was her accomplice in the charitable work; but she had no clew to the most wondrous part of the tale — Mr. Merrill's acquaintanceship and military association with Harry.

"The Father has granted you precious consolation, my darling," she said, when the story was told. "Let us both learn from it how to trust Him — if blindly, yet intelligently — for the future."

The following day, Uncle Will returned, leading Romp, and riding another horse. He had seen Mr. Merrill twenty miles on his way, — the few travellers they had encountered evidently mistaking them for a peaceful yeoman and his servant. It was a bold enterprise; but a week has elapsed without intimation that it will result in inconvenience to us, or recapture to the fugitive. So far as we can learn, the circumstances of his sojourn here, and our aid in forwarding him on his journey, remain in the keeping of our faithful quartette, unless — as I imagine is the case — Mamma has reported these to Papa. If ardent prayers can secure a safe arrival at his home to the wanderer, no ill will overtake him. Perhaps his wife, in the fulness of her delight at receiving him as one raised from the dead, may remember in her petitions her whose hero-love will be given back to her nevermore until her wanderings are ended in the land the name of which is **Peace.**

CHAPTER XX.

AGATHA.

June 20.

THE battle of the Wilderness has been fought, and won by both sides. For three days, Grant drove Lee through the jungles, and ravines, and tortuous bridle-paths, and treacherous morasses that go to make up that delectable region, capturing guns by the hundred, and men by the thousand; and the Commander-in-chief of the rebel horde is now, with his flying and demoralized troops, at the mercy of the victor. It is merely a question of time when the Confederacy shall collapse, like a cracked soap-bubble, leaving not a wreck behind. Its fate is sealed.

For three days, Lee, by an unparalleled system of strategy, led his adversary farther and farther into the trackless wilds aforesaid; halting here and there, as his matchless policy dictated, to despatch some ten, twenty, or thirty thousand of the undisciplined multitude, that could never have approached within striking distance of him had he not purposely stayed his triumphal march. Having extricated his magnificent army, with inconsiderable loss, from the waste and howling wilderness, he now has the Commander-in-chief of the Yankee herd *just where he wants him;* is playing with him as a cat does with a mouse before she opens her jaws for the fatal spring. It is merely a question of time with this greatest of modern generals when he shall put the finishing touch to the panic-stricken barbarians. Their fate is sealed.

If there are discrepancies in my account of the " situation," it is not my fault. I have compiled it, carefully and laboriously,

from the official reports of the leading newspapers of the day—
northern and southern.

From this mammoth battle-field, a cloud, no bigger than the
smallest finger-nail upon a man's hand to the optics of the Generals in command, has drifted in this direction, and the Sunnybank sky is black with storms. The twin-heirs of the estate,
the pride and hope of their parents' advancing years, were captured by an ungenerously early surprise, executed before breakfast by a wing of the enemy's forces. We have learned this
through a letter from Captain Kingston, addressed to Mr. Lacy.
Nothing has been received from under the brothers' own hand,
although more than a month has passed since their disappear-
ance from the Confederate ranks. My Lady was bowed to the
dust by the news. Milord rallied his fortitude to sustain him
under the stroke. It was reserved for their super-angelic
daughter to show them the silver lining to this murky curtain.

" It may be the means of saving their lives," she said, piously,
bending over the pale mother, salts and handkerchief in hand.
" They are beyond the reach of swords and bullets, and I believe the condition of the prisoners of war taken by the Federal
army to be far more tolerable than the newspapers and sensation story-tellers would have us believe. The appearance of
the exchanged Confederate soldiers shows that they are not
starved or ill-used " — with much more of similar stuff, that led
the afflicted parents to entertain more cheering thoughts, and to
talk, with some show of hopefulness, of the reunion of their
divided family.

I took my unsanctified spirit from out this saintly presence,
that I might seriously ponder—when the mental nausea excited
by this scene had subsided — as to the effect the new move on
the board of events would have upon my individual prospects.
After contemplating the subject from a variety of positions, my
mature conclusion is, that Dame Fortune has designed to do
me another amiable turn. It is so seldom she wears a benignant aspect toward me, I may be excused for not recognizing

her favors at sight. She has, indeed, separated me, for an indefinite period, from my only real friend and protector; but I enjoy immunity from affront and neglect by sustaining the character of his bereaved betrothed. My Lady is condescendingly compassionate; the Prince Consort gravely and graciously attentive to my actual or fancied wants; and the divine maiden, who has hushed her *De profundis* to chant consolation to others whose woe is more recent than hers, puts herself to a world of useless trouble to chase away my interesting melancholy, and revive my sinking hopes. I infer from these symptoms of public sentiment, that my counterfeited distress passes current without a question. Secretly, I own that Lynn's absence just now is the most convenient thing that could have happened. If I were a heathen, I would pour out a libation to Mars, in gratitude for his agency in accomplishing the desirable event. It has swept away a host of difficulties in the way of my advancing schemes, as the stroke of the housemaid's broom demolishes a spider's web.

Still the tidings did shock me, temporarily. I lack the comfortable persuasion cherished by Elinor, that the tenants of Fort Delaware and Johnson's Island lie upon beds of roses, and are fed upon turtle-soup and venison. My free, proud nature revolts at the idea of imprisonment, were the physical condition of the captive all she imagines, or feigns to believe, it is. I pity the two brave young men, who for three years have lived in the open air of heaven, and spent days and weeks at a time in the saddle; who have won honor for deeds of daring in the sight of their comrades; been caressed by their fellow-citizens as heroes and defenders of the faith, homes, and lives of the helpless non-combatants who people southern plantations. I pity them, I say, that, in one hour, one instant, they are snatched from action, distinction, and love, to be shut up in that most rigorous of confinements, a military jail, subject to the brutal will of a race they esteem as underlings. It irks me to think of Ross' haughty head bowing in servile obeisance to a Yankee corporal; of the high-bred Lynn, receiving his rations of coarse prison-fare from a surly, blue-coated private, who seasons the meagre supply with curses upon the " rebels."

I said as much as this to Rolf Kingston, who spent last night with us. I have called him "Captain," from force of habit; but he is Major now, having been promoted after the recent fights. He rejoices in a new and stylish uniform — gray, of course, and richly braided with scarlet. He is a splendid-looking fellow, and his demeanor to his diminutive flame is a pretty combination of deference and devotion. The devotion was in the ascendant last evening, and she detected it. The consummate prude widened her large eyes in a stare of sorrowful incredulity — as a pet fawn might, if one by whose hand she had been fed and fondled into tameness had suddenly tried to throw a noose over her graceful head. Then she bridled, and sat two inches taller — a manifest improvement to her appearance ; and as he continued his low-toned monologue, his fine eyes saying more intense things than his tongue dared syllable, she deliberately gathered up her sewing, and abandoned to his exclusive use the sofa she had deigned to share with him nearly the whole evening.

I laughed aloud from my piano-stool, where I was fingering over some music he had brought up from town — ill-printed scores upon frail, yellowish paper — the promising manufacture of our infant Confederacy.

" What amuses you? " he demanded, sharply.

" You must hide your hook better," I answered, still laughing, " and play your line more cautiously. You have frightened her away for half a year at least."

He kicked over the consecrated stool whereon her foot had rested, and said something very ugly under his breath.

" What is that? " asked I. " She and I together are — the _what_? I am flattered by the classification. Shall I repeat it to her? "

He was frowning sulkily, and made no reply. I grew serious too.

" Rolf," I said, walking over to him, and laying my hand

familiarly upon his shoulder (suppose my Lady had made an errand into the room at that second!), "this is child's play, or lover's foolery, which is sillier still. If you get that girl — and, as I have remarked before, I don't know why you should care to do it — you will have to bring heavier artillery into the field than you have yet deployed. She has grown into maturity and power that surprises me, and which should alarm you. I told you once that I thought you might win her in time. I have changed my mind. Her hand you may secure by the use of proper agencies. She has no heart to give you — she never will have."

"Do you mean that she is pining after that dead Yankee?"

I drew away from him. I wish I had struck him, as I was tempted to do. He who sneers at a brave rival in his bloody grave, deserves chastisement from a woman's hand: he is too mean an opponent to be touched by a true *man.*

"I meant what I said," I returned, with *hauteur.* "You may force Elinor into a marriage with you: she will never love you. Allow me to say, that she would be a fool if she did."

"She shall marry me!" he retorted, gnashing — not clinching — his teeth in tigerish ferocity, that ruined his good looks while the fit lasted.

"I believe you to be capable of making her do it." And I sauntered back to my piano and the saffron music-sheets.

He is to spend some days at his brother's, and he will probably do his best to enliven the gloomy quiet of this haunted old castle. It is refreshing to see a smartly dressed, handsome young man about the house, if he *is* in love with another woman. * * *

Night.

I had an adventure this afternoon. I rarely ramble out of sight of the house; but Mrs. Lacy and Carrie, convoyed by a train of sable attendants, were bound upon a berrying expedition to the edge of the swamp, where, upon a rocky shelf overhanging the morass, are to be found abundant store of black raspberries and early huckleberries, besides wild-flowers and mosses. Elinor looked pallid and drooping, and was advised by Mamma to stay at home. The sun was hot, and stooping over the berry-bushes would aggravate the headache, which, it appeared, had tormented the silent saint all day. Mr. Lacy instantly declared his disinclination to the excursion ; and we left the daughter comfortably established upon the settee in the airy hall, — the Venetian blinds, which form the day-doors of front and back entrances, closed, that the glare might not offend her eyes, — and Papa seated by her in his large straw chair, a favorite volume upon his knee, ready to read or talk, as his idol willed.

I, for whose complexion and general temperature nobody cares one jot, had to don my wide-brimmed " flat," and trudge at my Lady's heels down the lane, past the burying-ground through the pasture, — where the cows lay, with an aspect of malicious enjoyment in the shade of the willows, or stood above their knees in the stream, while we were panting under the fervid heat of a June sun, at four o'clock P. M., — up a hill and into a forest, where there was, at least, comparative coolness, and so on to the verge of the maple swamp.

" Your mother and I often took this walk in company," remarked my Lady, complacently, when we were midway across the unshaded meadow. " There is not another on the plantation that is more pleasantly associated with her in my recollection. She was fond of country sports — berrying, fishing, and rowing. It was a delight to be with her on such occasions. She entered into the pursuit of the hour with charming spirit. Her enthusiasm was artless as a child's."

A pensive sigh to the engaging qualities of her former companion put a neat period to this passage of her early history.

There were several salient touches in her speech, each of which I perceived, as she brought it out. It must be kept before me that my mother was, like myself, a humble retainer of the honorable house of Ross-Lacy, and that she had acquitted herself more to the satisfaction of her great friends than her degenerate daughter was doing, — my obedience being merely passive, while she clanked her chains and made merry music for the ears of her patrons.

"She was a very amiable person — was she not, ma'am?" I queried, in satirical meekness.

"She was very lovely in person and character," I was assured; and I drew the implied inference, that her child would do well to imitate her in respect to moral attributes.

"Do I resemble her at all — in appearance?" I next inquired.

"Very little — less than when you first came to Virginia. You are growing more like your father."

Which was a "settler."

I want to preserve the memory of all these pin-pricks. I would not forget one, or have them irritate me less burningly. I made a grimace in the shadow of my broad-brim, and trotted along behind my mistress, the dozen picaninnies behind me, until we gained the berry-patch. Then we scattered in groups, or singly, in the interest of picking the fruit. Carrie kept near her mother; the negroes and I went our several ways. I strayed off gradually out of sight and hearing of the rest, and preferring, at all seasons, to eat, rather than gather berries for others' consumption, I perched myself upon a rock, with my tired spine against a pine-tree, and began devouring the contents of my basket. This was naughty and greedy — above all, wasteful. My Lady was, in the halcyon days of her housewifery, a very Mrs. Rundle in the matter of preserves, and jellies, and jams, and sweet pickles, and berry-vinegars, and canned fruits, and everything else that could be concocted out of sugar and fruit for the titillation of the palate and subsequent remorse of stomach. But times have changed. With coarse brown sugar at forty dollars a pound, and refined loaf nowhere to be procured, the production of these delicacies is impracticable. Still, however, our notable feminine commissariat offers us a substitute in berries stewed in sorghum, the sirup being likewise of domestic manufacture. Every plantation has its field of Chinese sugar-cane, its mill for crushing the green stalks, and kettle for boiling down the juice.

"These have, at any rate, the merit of being wholesome," I heard her say to Rachel, her Vizier, to-day.

"And dried huckleberries make putty fa'r pies, when folks can't do better," added the sable oracle.

Thus forewarned that our excursion was not for present pleasure, but future profit, I had hearkened with inward sneers to the innocent encomiums upon my parent delivered, *en passant*, by my future Mamma-in-law. I was hot and thirsty; the berries contained a flavorous acid, which I expressed with the utmost gratification upon my dry tongue and throat, resolving, as I did so, to account for my empty basket, should I eat them all, by improvising a story of an upset and a spill-out. It was cool and still up where I sat, and I everlooked the swamp, with its mass of maples and tangled undergrowth. The natural features of the spot are singular. A ledge of rock in the form of a horse-shoe is the abrupt termination of the forest of larger trees — oaks, hickories, and poplars. Partially enclosed by this wall of earth and stone, which descends steeply twelve or fifteen feet, lies the sunken swamp, irreclaimable for tillage, and useless, except when frozen over in the winter. Then the noise of the axe is heard, day after day, through its dismal recesses, and many cords of fire-wood are piled upon the higher and firmer ground, to be hauled to the house. At this season of the year the place is lonely and quiet as a graveyard. The sunbeams were peeping through the boughs over my head; rejoicing the tiny flowers and the mosses — russet, crimson, and green — that carpeted the rocks, and every little while a gentle whisper ran from twig to twig, the zephyrs coquetting with the oak leaves and prim pine-needles. Below, the mists of evening were gathering in the thickets, and their chill creeping upwards to my seat. Not a spray quivered, not a bird chirped. It looked like an accursed region — the home, as it is said to be in autumn, of ague and typhus. Sunnybank stands too high upon the ridge, and is too far removed from this fever-nest, to be affected by its unwholesome airs; but a few plebeians, who till a limited number of acres on the other side of the swamp, have an annual visitation of the plague. My Grandfather Pinely lived just back of it, and his family were sufferers from malaria until he died, too tardily for their good. My Lady took the eldest daughter, and the rest dispersed to various quarters of the globe.

I was meditating upon these and kindred topics, munching my fruit the while, when a rustling below me called my notice to the foot of the cliff. There stood a man motioning to me to be silent, and not to move! I am sure there was not a drop of blood in my cheeks and lips as I obeyed the peremptory signal. It is questionable whether I could have moved had I desired to fly. He climbed the rock like a squirrel, until his head was on a level with mine. He had a small, wiry figure, keen eyes, and reddish hair. His face was shrewd, but not wicked, and his smile quieted my tremor before he bade me not be frightened. He spoke softly and rapidly, and his accent showed at once that he was a Yankee.

"And if a Yankee — a spy, or scout, which means the same thing!" said my quick wit. "Oh, for the strength and weapons of a man!"

"Miss Lacy?" said the spy, interrogatively.

I bowed.

"I am Miss Lacy. What is your business with me?"

"I promised a friend — Sergeant Merrill — to deliver this into your hands. I have been hanging around all day, looking for you. I knew you the minute I saw you, from his description. He told me to say that he was well, and again at work."

"In the army, I suppose?" said I, intelligently.

He nodded.

"Would you mind giving me a line, to let him know that his note was received? He would prize it very much."

I hesitated.

"Would it be safe?"

"Oh, for that matter, you won't sign your name in full. You'll find no direction or signature to this" — touching the envelope he had given me; "*that* wouldn't be safe, as you say."

"I have neither pencil nor paper here," I next objected. "You must take a verbal message."

He produced a slip of paper from his pocket, and the stump of a cedar pencil. Without further demur, I scribbled what he had asked — one line — using the rough face of the rock for my desk.

"I am in receipt of your welcome favor. E. L., Sunnybank."

"That is not **a bad idea** — that last word," laughed the spy. "It will pass as a surname, and bother whomsoever may happen to overhaul me. Am I to say you are all well? Is there anything he can do for you? He'd go through fire and water to serve you."

"We are well, and he can do nothing for me, thank you."

He tucked the scrap of paper into the lining of his cap, slid down the bank, waved his hand in adieu, and vanished in the dense underbrush.

I examined the envelope carefully. It was sealed, but not directed, and marked in one corner with hieroglyphics, that doubtless had their meaning to the bearer, but which looked more to me like a turkey's claw than anything else. The murmur of voices drawing near signalled me to pocket the missive and recommence my berry-picking. Mrs. Lacy and Carrie soon appeared with loaded baskets, and in excellent spirits at their success.

"I had quite as many," I said, mournfully; "but I tipped over my basket, and two thirds of them rolled down the bank."

"I don't see them," said Carrie, pertly, peering over the rocky wall.

"That is very likely, dear. They are not so easily seen as a certain little friend of mine would be, if she were to lose her balance, and fall in the same direction. But the birds will have a nice breakfast to-morrow morning. They have keener eyes than yours."

24

Mrs. Lacy had taken my seat at the root of the pine, and removed her bonnet. She was flushed with exercise and the summer weather; and this, with her bright eyes, dark, luxuriant hair, and changeful countenance, made her seem absurdly youthful, when one thought of her three grown children.

"I am a child again, in feeling, when I wander in these woods," she said. "Here there has been no visible change for forty years. I picked berries, and built grottoes of stones, roofed with moss, on this spot when I was no older than Carrie, here. The trees may be taller, and larger in girth; but they looked more gigantic to me then than they do now. It would try me sorely to have this forest levelled. I like the swamp, too, with its rank verdure, its poisonous-looking flowers, and the vines that used always to remind me of the story I had read of an enchanted forest, where the vines were changed into writhing serpents."

"What a conception!" I feigned a shudder. "I shall never walk under a wild grape-vine after this, without fancying that it may turn into a boa-constrictor. I have a mortal dread of snakes."

"The taste of the foolish countryman, who took the frozen one to his bosom, seems inexplicable to you, then?" smiled my Lady. "Yet one cannot help feeling a certain degree of sympathy for the poor victim of misplaced confidence."

Having aimed this polished shaft plump at me, she took up her bonnet, with the remark, that it was growing too late to stay in the neighborhood of the swamp, and marshalled her satellites for the return procession.

It is superfluous to observe, that, when I accepted the letter from the gallant sergeant's messenger, it was with no intention of giving it to his fair nurse. Yet it still lies before me unopened. It is late in the day for me to hesitate at committing deeds which the world in general would stigmatize as unfair. The weak and the fortunate can afford to be scrupulous. I have tramped over so many prejudices in my day, that my conscience is not sensitive about chimeras nobody really believes in, yet which it is the fashion to reverence outwardly. The difference between my practice and that of pious respectability is, that I am consistent in despising certain squeamish notions respecting the manner in which it is lawful to become acquainted with the private affairs of one's neighbors. I have seen scores of women who would show the whites of their eyes in holy horror at the thought of peeping through a keyhole, or listening behind a door, or reading, without permission, a letter addressed to another person. I never saw one who I did not firmly believe would do all three of these things, if she could thus gratify a lively curiosity without being found out. Still, something has held me back from opening this dingy envelope, which smells of tobacco, and which has probably lain in the pocket of that travel-stained spy for many days. Are the cabalistic characters in the corner a charm to keep off prying fingers? If I open it, will I be repaid for my trouble in secreting it, and tampering with what is honestly and truly the property of another? Since no names of persons or places are mentioned in it, what information can I gain from a perusal? Maybe, too, it is written in cipher, and that Elinor has the key, while to me it would be worse than Hebrew. This is likely enough. They had time to invent some such method of correspondence during the weeks he spent in Mammy Rachel's cabin. How Rolf raved when he heard of it! Had the flight been postponed until I had time to communicate with the Major, Sergeant Merrill — that was his name, according to the spy's pronunciation — would have enjoyed a safe and quick passage back to the Libby. It is the nature of his tribe to grovel and dig, and they turned their instincts to valuable purpose when they burrowed under the prison wall.

But the letter. Would I not advance my schemes by devising some way of transmitting it to the small conspirator, without my agency in the affair being suspected? Might not the circumstance be used with effect hereafter, or she be intrapped into some imprudent act. by the contents of the epistle that would involve others connected with her?

To cast aside subterfuge, something within warns me against making free with that seal. For, besides being fastened in the usual manner, it bears a big, green seal, with a motto upon it which I cannot make out, but which looks mysteriously aristocratic for a common soldier's use. There may be some meaning in it, which she would miss were I to open and re-enclose it.

Hark! Was that thunder? A shower is rising. My scouting friend will find his swamp a damp lodging-place. A dazzling gleam of lightning! I will throw this vexed question into the hands of Fate. My Lady says there is a Providence in all things, minute and great. I have laid my watch down upon the table. When the next flash comes, I will look at the second-hand, and mark the time that intervenes before the answering peal. Should it be less than two minutes, I will open the letter, and exercise my discretion as to the further disposition of it.

There it is! A whole minute, and all is hushed as death. Thirty seconds more — forty — fifty —— Great heavens! what a crash!

. Morning.

That was a terrific storm last night. I did not sleep a wink until dawn. As I stood at my window just now, I overheard one of the servants say that the big pine tree, under which I sat yesterday, was cloven from crown to root by the lightning. It would have been better for some people I wot of if the bolt had fallen while the stately tent sheltered me. But as for me, I am content to live. I am quite myself again. The fine, breezy morning has helped me arrange my wits. Only my blood still runs slowly and chill when I think of the risk I incurred in leaving to chance the opening of that letter. If I had not read it ——

I have burned it, and scattered the ashes to the winds.

CHAPTER XXI.

ELINOR.

Richmond, July 28.

IT is a hot, breathless night. The air is warm and humid, and my lungs labor in taking it in. The lamp does not flicker by the open window, where I have sat since I crept away on tiptoe from the adjoining room, leaving Mamma in a quiet sleep after her day of mental anxiety and bodily exhaustion. Without all is pitchy dark, save for the dull glare of an occasional street lamp, and in the north — where hung the glorious rainbow on that April day three years ago — the fitful play of distant lightning. The city is very quiet under this funereal pall — quiet that may be rudely broken up by and by, as it has been many other nights since we have been here, by the discordant jangle of the alarm bells and the boom of cannon — signals that the Federal army has accomplished some movement which threatens the beleaguered capital. These are often false alarms, but the effect is none the less startling on that account. No one can say when real danger may confront us.

I should not say " us." The entrance of the besiegers would bring blessed relief to our mourning souls. It is treason to write, or speak, or think this here; but what signifies circumspection on the part of a family already attainted as traitors?

What a dragging, wearisome summer this has been! What a dreary age has elapsed since that happy June evening that brought us letters from our absentees — news of their safety, and the kindness showed to them in their imprisonment by our steadfast friend, Uncle Charley! The letters arrived at sunset. We were all seated in the front porch, when the servant we

24 *

had sent to the post office rode up, and gave Papa a bulky package.

"From Rolf Kingston," he said; and out dropped two envelopes, each with the joyful inscription in the corner, "*via* flag of truce."

I screamed with joy, for I recognized Ross' handwriting upon one; and Mamma, catching up the other, cried out, —

"This is from Lynn! It is for you, Agatha."

Agatha changed color so rapidly I feared she was about to faint. But when I sprang to her side with offers of assistance, she pushed me away, and walked into the house, carrying her letter with her. Ross' was enjoyed by the rest of us. It was but a single page long, and every word was precious. His tone was brave and hopeful.

"Uncle Charley has been to see us," he wrote. "The sight of his face was worth all the boxes of comforts he has sent us, and that is saying much. Books, clothing, provisions, and money are never despicable. To be appreciated, one must be captured as we were, without a change of garments, and with our pocket-books filled with Confederate notes."

Papa read the letter aloud, — Mamma and I afterward, singly, with tearful smiles, and hearts overrunning with thankfulness. We were still discussing the glad tidings in the rosy twilight, when we espied several dark objects moving down the lane, and heard the tramp of horses.

"A visitation," said Papa, gayly, rising as the strangers entered the yard gate. "I am in such good humor to-night, that I could treat with civility the prince of the reigning powers."

We never said "rebel" or "secessionist" in Carrie's hearing. Mamma laughed in lightness of heart. She has never laughed so since.

The intruders were six soldiers, in Confederate uniform, headed by a Colonel, whom Papa knew and called by name, courteously, as he walked up the steps.

"Can I have a moment's private conversation with you, Mr.

Lacy?" asked the officer, when he had acknowledged the introduction to Mamma and myself.

His voice was grave, and, I fancied, agitated. I looked after
the two anxiously as they withdrew to the other end of the
long porch, and stood with their backs to us, engaged in low
conversation. The remaining members of the party had dismounted, and were awaiting the movements of their leader in
silence. But for the letters we had just received, my thoughts
would have flown instantly to my brothers; my sisterly fear
conjured up the darkest imaginations of evil that could befall
them. Free of this solicitude, I was nevertheless ill at ease.
There was a sense of constraint and discomfort in the proximity
of the soldiers, and I was pleased when Carrie said she wanted
a drink of water. It afforded me a pretext for taking her into
the dining-room, and ridding myself of the sight of those erect,
motionless forms, showing in the dusk like black marble statues.
Mamma followed us. There were lights in the dining-room,
and the table was already laid for our small family.

"Colonel Langdon will remain to supper I suppose," remarked Mamma, taking her key-basket from her arm. "And
since he has probably had a fatiguing day, we ought to have
something warm and substantial for him and his men. Will
you call Rachel, my dear?"

Before I could stir to obey, Papa entered. So devoid of all
suspicion was I, that my thought at seeing him was, what a noble, handsome man he was. The Colonel had attended him to
this apartment, and stood in the open door, within hearing of
every word spoken. Still I was not alarmed. What should
I fear for my father, knowing him as I did? He walked
straight up to Mamma with a mien of chivalric tenderness, such
as few men wear toward those whom they have called wives
for more than a quarter of a century, took both her hands in
his, and pressed them first to his lips, then to his heart.

"Ida, love! my brave, good wife! you have never failed me
in the hour of need. For my sake, and for the sake of our
children, be strong now. Trust in God and in your husband's

integrity. I am arrested upon a charge of carrying on a treasonable correspondence with the enemies of the Confederate Government. I am innocent. You believe this upon my simple assertion. I hope to clear myself in the eyes of those who will require other proof. Nellie, daughter! I wish that you, with Mamma, could have been spared this; but since it is otherwise ordained, you will show yourself the woman you are."

Anything like the wild, appealing terror, the love and agony of Mamma's eyes, as he mentioned his arrest, I have never witnessed in another countenance. But when he ceased speaking, she bowed her face upon the dear hands clasping hers for an instant — just one — then lifted herself, calmly, proudly.

"I will do as you wish, Morton. Must you go to-night? and to what place?"

Colonel Langdon advanced at this query.

"I lament more deeply than I can tell you, Mrs. Lacy, that obedience to orders has put this unpleasant task upon me. Whatever I can do consistently with my duty to render your situation comfortable, Sir, I will perform most gladly. There is no necessity or propriety in separating you from your family to-night. I shall be compelled to place a guard about the house and at the door of your room. The strict letter of my commands would oblige me to set one within your chamber, that no communication upon the subject of your arrest may pass unheard. But I will content myself with requesting your pledge that you will not speak to any member of your family with regard to the offence with which you stand charged."

"I thank you, Sir, and willingly give the promise you desire," replied Papa, politely and gratefully.

"It will be further expedient to seal up your private papers for examination before the Commissioner," added Colonel Langdon, with evident reluctance.

Papa bowed.

"I do not object, provided I have a guarantee for the safe return to my wife's care of such as are deemed irrelevant to the case to be tried. I will go with you to my study. Ida, dear! will you see that supper is prepared, and rooms made ready for this gentleman and his companions?"

I would not sit down to the table with the guests who were bidden to the family meal until Papa, noticing my absence, sent me a message to the effect that I would gratify him by taking my usual place at his right hand. Mamma presided — still pale, but calm; her tones clear and full, her demeanor to the Colonel and his companions that of the thorough-bred hostess and lady. Papa led the conversation to indifferent topics — the weather, the crops, different modes of farming, and the like. For aught that the servants or other mere lookers-on could discover, he was on a footing of friendly intercourse with his visitors, and had no occasion for special uneasiness growing out of their arrival. After supper he sat in the parlor with Colonel Langdon, while Mamma and I packed a valise with clothing and other necessaries. This was done in the presence of a guard, who, less gentlemanly than his superior, eyed each article narrowly as we put it in, and commented freely upon whatever struck his fancy.

"Reckon the raiders haven't been so hard upon you as they have upon your neighbors," he observed, when Papa's dressing-case was produced. "That 'ere article wouldn't have stood no chance if a Yank had happened to spy it. Most of us Confeds have forgotten the looks of a piece of soap, let alone such razors as them."

"Those are not the only decencies of life you seem to have forgotten," said Agatha, severely. She had come in unperceived by any of us, and heard this observation. "If it is not an essential part of your duty to make remarks upon anything and everything you see to which you are not accustomed, may we ask you, as the only favor you can possibly grant us, to hold your tongue?"

"Upon my soul, you're a sassy one!" blustered the enraged private.

"And upon my word, which is worth more than your soul in any market, if you open your lips again to insult these ladies or me, I will report you on the spot to Colonel Langdon!" retorted Agatha, coolly. Changing her tone completely, she laid her hand on Mamma's shoulder. "Dear Mother! you can do him more real service by staying with him during every minute he is spared to you than by this work. Nellie and I will finish packing."

Mamma submitted after a brief inward struggle, and committed the task to our hands. When the valise was locked and strapped, we left it in care of the guard, as he told us we must do, and went down stairs.

Carrie, who comprehended imperfectly that Papa had business that called him away from home on the morrow, had climbed upon his knee, and fallen asleep, leaning against his shoulder. He stroked her soft curls, from time to time; and once I saw him kiss the unconscious head nestled confidingly upon the pillow that was not to support it again for so long. At ten o'clock, the servants entered, as usual, for prayers; and after laying Carrie gently upon the sofa, Papa took his usual place at the head of the room, and, surrounded by his family, he read that glorious psalm that has been a watchword of sublime consolation to the Lord's afflicted in all ages:

"GOD is our refuge and strength, a very present help in trouble."

Then Mamma, who sat at the piano, struck a few grand chords, and her voice arose sweet and strong — Papa's joining in and sustaining it from the first note.

> "Our GOD, our help in ages past,
> Our hope for years to come,
> Our refuge from the stormy blast,
> And our eternal home."

Then followed the prayer — thanksgiving for mercies received; supplication for strength to meet what the morrow might bring to do or to bear; affectionate commendation of all those present to the Divine care for the night.

Papa remained standing when he arose from his knees.

"I have a word to say to you" — as the servants were about to withdraw. "I am compelled to leave you in the morning, perhaps for a few hours, perhaps for several days. It may even be that I shall not see you again for months. I am in the hands of a Father who will do whatever is best for me and mine. I leave you the only earthly protectors of my wife and children. You have been faithful to us in the past. Be very true and kind to your mistress while I am away, whatever scenes of trial and temptation you may have to pass through, and remember me in your prayers. God bless you all!"

Thus ended the last evening we spent together at Sunnybank. I would cherish the recollection while I have life and reason. Each utterance of our beloved father is a sacred treasure to his children.

His preliminary examination took place that week at the Court House, about ten miles from our house. He was not arraigned before a regular civil tribunal, but a military commission, a sort of Court Martial, as I understand it. Mamma and I were admitted to his room on the morning of the trial, and were allowed to accompany him into the Court House. My heart throbbed and ached to bursting, as I saw him take the place of a criminal in the view of the assembled crowd, most of them his neighbors and former friends. He exhibited no token of discomposure. His fine features were serious, but not sad, and as his eye passed from one familiar face to another, and settled scrutinizingly upon the witnesses, he appeared more like an intelligent and interested spectator, than one whose liberty, perhaps whose life, hung upon the transactions of that day.

The first witness summoned was our postmaster, a weak, well-meaning man, but an incorrigible busybody and gossip. He testified that he had on the 24th day of June found in the letter-box, into which mail-matter was dropped through a slit in the frame of the post-office window, an envelope directed, in Mr. Lacy's handwriting, to "U. S. F., Richmond, Virginia." It was unusually bulky, and had, as he imagined, a suspicious look. Moreover, when he began to study the address, it occurred to him that the initials might mean "United States Friend."

I saw Papa repress a smile as the man complacently brought

forward this proof of his sagacity. He had, in consideration of the reports in circulation derogatory to Mr. Lacy's loyalty, about made up his mind that it was his duty, as a good citizen, to intercept the letter, and submit it to the inspection of the proper authorities, when, in fingering the cover, he perceived that it was unsealed. It appeared to have been closed originally; but the adhesive gum used for this purpose was defective, and had not held the two parts of the envelope together. He thereupon took the liberty — precaution, he called it — of examining the contents of the packet. An inner envelope, which appeared to have several sheets within it, was sealed, and directed to " Mr. Charles Dana." There was no name of city or state appended to the address; but the postmaster knew that the gentleman for whom it was intended had removed to the North nearly two years ago.

" I had been warned repeatedly to look out for letters from Sunnybank to him," he continued; " and after seeing this, I could no longer hesitate as to the path of right. Instead of mailing it, I sent it to General B——, at Clay Hall " — the nearest military station. " I know nothing more of the matter from personal observation."

Papa had declined selecting a counsel for himself.

" I should only embarrass the one upon whom I called to perform this friendly office," he said to me, when I entreated him not to slight any means that could lead to his release. " I might endanger him as well, should he, in the discharge of his duty as my advocate, seem to express toleration for Unionism. I am competent to the management of my own cause — at least, in the preliminary stage."

He put a question as the postmaster was leaving the witness-box.

" Mr. Shipley, will you state to the Court by whom you had been warned to watch all letters sent by mail from my house?"

" By dozens of people! " the witness replied, doggedly.

" That is rather a vague answer," rejoined Papa, preserving his inimitable courtesy of bearing and tone. " Can you name the person who informed you that I was engaged in a treasonable correspondence?"

"Miss Hetty Stratton spoke to me about it several times, and so did Mrs. Riley and Mr. Coleman, but they had their information from Miss Hetty, they said."

Papa bowed, and sat down ; and to the postmaster succeeded General B——.

After confirming Mr. Shipley's statement as to the manner in which the letter he held had reached him, he read it aloud. It commenced, "My dear Charley," and purpor ed to be from Papa to our absent friend.

"Enclosed you will find a letter for my boys, who were taken prisoners, May 12, at the battle of Spottsylvania Court House. I leave it to you to discover their place of confinement, and to forward my epistle. Do not condole with me upon this event. None other since the beginning of the war has caused me such satisfaction. They are safe, and in the custody of their best friends, loath though the foolish fellows may be to acknowledge this truth. The end is not distant, and when the crash comes, they will be better off on the other side of the line. Nothing except my property and family has prevented me from following in your footsteps long ago. Situated as I am, I must stand my ground, and take the chances of convincing the army of deliverance that my wishes and hopes, my prayers and secret labors, have ever been with them. The horrible tyranny under which we groan would have made a Union man of me even if conscience had not kept me on the right side."

Then ensued a string of flippant abuse of the Confederate authorities, and allusions to sundry officials high in power, these being designated by their initials. Personalities gave way to a review of the military operations of the Confederacy during the past twelve months ; a sneering summary, that strengthened finally into savage exultation over the impending ruin of the "traitorous combination," and the suffering that already oppressed the masses who had refused to listen to the counsels of the opponents of secession. Next was a succinct sketch of the present condition of the rebel army, their assailable and impregnable fortifications, the number of available troops, etc. General B—— emphasized this portion of the document sternly, and the countenances of the Court darkened as they listened. The letter closed with a reference to information previously forwarded, and which, it was intimated, had been acted upon with signal benefit to the Federal cause.

Papa was graver as the reading progressed; but not a shade of inquietude crossed his face. He made a note occasionally upon a sheet of paper before him, but offered no remark when General B—— left the stand.

The third witness, to my amazement, was Miss Hetty Stratton. Not that I doubted her inclination to play the informer against those whom she openly reviles as " pestilential Yankee-lovers ; " but I was surprised that sensible men, like those who composed the board of examiners, should have allowed her this public opportunity of venting her spite. It was very hard to confine her to the pith of the narrative. She commenced very glibly by giving the precise date of a visit she had paid us — the day of the week and month — and enunciating in a solemn tone the words, " in the year of our Lord 1862." It was the night of Uncle Charley's farewell visit. From this she launched into a glowing exposition of her patriotism, and her repeated publication of the might and warmth of her zeal for the glorious Confederacy. At this point the Court caught up with her, and turned her back to the October night aforesaid.

Papa smiled two or three times; and some of the audience laughed outright at her characteristic oratory. Sometimes the question whether the patient examiner would ever get at the true drift of her harangue was apparently uppermost in the thoughts of all. But in the end he stripped the story clear of exaggerations, and digressions, and exclamations, and retailed it to the Court.

Miss Hetty had been on the alert during the evening she spent in our company, and collected enough suspicious material to justify her in sitting up all night, creeping through dark halls and empty bed-chambers, listening at keyholes, and eavesdropping at windows; the fruit of all which laudable labors in behalf of the holy cause of southern independence was the discovery that a "Yankee spy" was concealed under our roof at the very time it extended hospitable shelter to her loyal head; that he had conferred secretly with Papa, Mamma, and myself; been entertained in the most affectionate manner by us, and sent on his way before dawn the following morning.

There was a fine disdain in Papa's features as he arose to ask a question in his turn.

"You say that you heard and saw the supposed spy, Miss Stratton. Did you identify him as an acquaintance of your own?"

"I did, and am ready to swear to it!" she answered, defiantly. "I came here prepared with replies to whatever you might have the face to ask me, Mr. Lacy. I said to my sister, before leaving home, 'I am ready to be bullied and insulted——'"

Here she was called to order.

Papa resumed: —

"Will you please state to the Court definitely who the person was who talked with me in my study, slept in the chamber adjoining that room, and rode away from my side-door, next morning?"

"You will find his name there, just as you wrote it!" replied she, tossing a soiled, ragged bit of paper — part of a buff envelope — over to Papa.

The disdain was gone, and in its stead was a melancholy dignity that impressed the most thoughtless there as he examined the fragment. Then he handed it to the Judge Advocate, saying simply, "It may be needed."

Miss Hetty was dismissed, and four or five other witnesses were summoned; but they were to support the theory that the letter was in Papa's handwriting, and other minor matters. When he was permitted to speak, Papa's defence was brief and pointed. He denied the authorship of the document read by

General B——, showing that no one but a fool or madman would have penned this paper, environed as he was by hundreds of suspicious eyes. "Had my aim been to court discovery and punishment, to draw down upon myself and my family speedy and certain ruin, I could have chosen no surer method of accomplishing this than to trust a paper so singular in appearance and superscription, and so negligently sealed as was this remarkable composition, to the care of so stanch a friend of the Confederate government as I have long known Mr. Shipley to be."

Then he analyzed the subject matter of the epistle, showing the information imparted to his alleged correspondent to be useless as imprudent. Miss Hetty claimed his attention next. I could not sufficiently admire the gentlemanly forbearance, the freedom from everything like bitterness of recrimination, manifested in his review of her testimony. He stated the simple facts she had garbled into a mystery of iniquity; the visit of his friend, Mr. Dana, who, for reasons of his own, and unconnected with the Lacy family, requested that his presence in the house should be made known to none except himself, his wife, and daughter, and the two old servants whose services were required to provide for the wants of the guest during his stay.

"The envelope which I have passed to the Judge Advocate was found by Miss Stratton on the floor of the chamber occupied that night by Mr. Dana. It is the cover of a letter written by myself to a very dear friend then resident in New York city. Mr. Dana, as he afterward informed me, stripped off the envelope, deeming it more prudent that the letter should bear neither address nor signature."

"Because of its treasonable import?" interrupted one of the Court, rudely.

"The contents of the letter were strictly personal in their character," rejoined Papa, unruffled by the interruption. "There was no reference whatever made in it to political affairs."

"You say that this correspondent was then residing in the

city of New York?" said another inquisitor. "Where is he now?"

" He is dead, sir! "

" And unless we have been misinformed," said the man, brutally, "he fell in battle at Gettysburg, fighting in the Yankee ranks."

" He was, at the time of his death, an officer in the Federal army."

" Were you aware of that circumstance when you wrote the letter from which this envelope was removed?" asked the presiding officer.

" I was not! "

" When were you informed of it — and how?"

" I learned it through a letter from my son, written just after the battle of Chancellorsville! "

" Did you write to Mr. Wilton subsequently to this date, after you were apprised of his position in the invading army?"

" I did! I forwarded a letter to him by a Federal Chaplain who passed a day at my house."

" Will Mr. Lacy repeat as nearly as he can recollect what he said in that letter?"

" I cannot give a verbatim report of it. While I recognize such interrogatories as an attempt to make me criminate myself, and furnish evidence which every tribunal on earth demands should be produced by the prosecution, I will gratify the curiosity of the Court as to the general character of the letter. I wrote to inform him of the health of my family, and to assure him of our continued regard."

" *Undiminished* regard, perhaps Mr. Lacy intends to say!" remarked an examiner.

Papa took no notice of the sneer, and the question was repeated in a less offensive form.

" Did you ' assure' this Yankee officer that your esteem and attachment for him were unchanged by what you had recently learned of his association with the enemies of your native state?"

"I said nothing whatever of public questions. I did tell him that our love and respect for him were unchanged and unalterable."

I could have knelt and kissed his feet as he said this. It was the heroism of constancy to his lost friend, for there arose, from a distant corner of the room, a low but distinct hiss that grew into a murmur, then a roar of disapprobation, while furious visages lowered on the prisoner from all sides, even after the Court had restored silence. I do not think the comparison was blasphemous, when I thought involuntarily of another judgment hall, and the clamorous cry, "What further need have we of witnesses?"

The cruel farce treated moreover of Papa's kindness to the wounded Federal private, to which charge he made answer that he would have showed the same to his deadliest enemy, had he been left mortally injured at his door. I was relieved that no questions were asked respecting Mr. Merrill. Since Papa's arrest, I had pondered often and uneasily upon Mammy's fancy that he had been seen, just previous to his departure, by a "white face;" had resolved to offer my evidence to exculpate my parents from all complicity in my work of nursing and concealing him, and forwarding his journey. If need there should be, I was ready to suffer with my father for my fidelity to the principles that lay so near our hearts — which we dared name only in our prayers. There were moments during the trial, when, seeing him stand there in the majesty of innocence, baited by a set of angry foes bent on his destruction, blind to the clear reason of his replies, forgetful of the stainless record of a life devoted to the good of his fellow-creatures, — many of his beneficiaries being among them, who now hooted at him in the open light of day, — there were seasons when all this drove me to the verge of useless self-sacrifice; when, but for the remembrance of his injunctions to discretion, and the thought of Mamma's loneliness should I be included in his condemnation, I would have pressed through the raging crowd, and claimed a place at his side. For, I argued, but for me, but for the love and pity he felt for Harry and myself in our separation, he would never have written the two letters, the knowledge of which, it was apparent, had gone further toward settling the minds of his judges against him, than the one which was the primal cause of his arrest. Strange to say, they asked few questions relative to his correspondence with Uncle Charley. Having heard him say that he had forwarded but one letter to him, and that through Major Kingston's hands, to be sent by flag of truce, they wandered off to other branches of the subject. I have called it a trial, but it was a formal persecution, and acquittal was a conclusion unthought of in their iniquitous schemes. They talked and wrangled among themselves, and attempted to browbeat the prisoner through all the long, sultry day; and when night fell, the accused was remanded to jail to await the action of the morrow, and we went home.

All the ten miles back to Sunnybank. The proprietors of the two hotels at the Court House answered curtly to Mamma's application for rooms for the night, and so long as the trial should be in progress, that we could not be accommodated — their houses were full. After this rebuff, we would not ask for lodgings in a private family; and although we had many acquaintances in the neighborhood, not one invited us to his or her home. Carrie had been confided to Mammy's care when we left Sunnybank, and I was thankful that she formed an attraction to Mamma's sad thoughts, as we rolled along the fast darkening highway, silent and dispirited. In the morning, we had dared hope for and talk of having Papa with us on our return journey. Now we had no words ready, nor was there need of expressing what each knew the other was feeling. We were unattended, save by Uncle Will, who rode Papa's horse behind the carriage, and his son James, our trusty driver.

" I've never seen the righteous forsaken, Mistis! " was all Uncle Will said, as he tenderly helped Mamma into the carriage.

I saw the light come into her eyes, followed by a mist that

was not unmingled sorrow, as she thanked him. The text bore up my own heart mightily, whenever I espied his white head at either window of the carriage. Illiterate slave as he may be regarded, we had, in this trying hour of our misfortunes, no truer friend or wiser comforter.

We were within five miles of home, when, at a fork of the road, a challenge rang out sharply upon the night.

" Who goes there? "

Mamma uttered an exclamation of alarm or surprise, but Uncle Will was ready with a soothing sentence.

" It's only a scouting party, Ma'am! " he said hastily, riding forward to answer for his charges.

We could hear the intonation of question and answer, then of amazed comment, and a horseman rode up to my window.

" Mrs. Lacy! Miss Elinor! Can it be possible that you are travelling without a protector, at this hour and over this road? "

" We are not unprotected, Major Kingston! " was Mamma's steady rejoinder.

He thought she referred to her faithful servants. I understood the deeper meaning that commented upon Uncle Will's text. I, less courageous or less trustful in the Divine care, was unfeignedly rejoiced that we had met Rolf. He explained that he had been sent up from Richmond as part of an escort to an officer, who bore important despatches to General B———. He had embraced the opportunity of visiting his native county with the greater alacrity, because the news of Papa's arrest had just reached him. After a few words spoken aside with the rest of the party, of whom there seemed to be ten or twelve, he announced his intention of accompanying us home. Mamma expostulated; but he pressed his plea for permission to do us this " trifling service " with such earnestness that she yielded. This little proof of kindly interest in us and our fate was grateful as a cup of cold water to a thirsting tongue, after the series of slights and repulses we had experienced throughout the day. My heart softened toward him who had tendered the favor, and toward the human family I had just been describing inwardly as base, thankless, and bloodthirsty, while I heard Mamma draw a sobbing sigh, as she leaned back in her seat, and the carriage moved on.

We were not expected at home, and the great pile of buildings looked gloomy and desolate. If I was unutterably sad in returning thus, what memories and forebodings must have oppressed Mamma, as she entered the empty hall where the echoes sounded so strangely distinct that we unconsciously lowered our voices and trod softly!

She went immediately to Carrie, who had been put to sleep in my chamber; and the only tear that had escaped her eyelids all day, fell upon the pillow as she kissed the velvet cheek of the little sleeper. She was very weary and faint, and let me undress her; then lay down upon my bed.

"By and by I must go to my room, love!" she said, trying to smile. "Papa would not like to think of it as vacant tonight. I must keep it ready for him."

Mammy soon had tea and toast ready for her mistress, and more to please us than for her own refreshment, she partook of these. She clasped Carrie's dimpled hands in hers, and laid her head on the pillow, with the docility of a tired child.

"My daughters!" she said fondly, "my precious comforters!"

Darling Mamma! may I never forfeit my right to the title!

Rolf, Agatha, and I supped together. I had almost overlooked the latter during our ride, and quite forgotten her after our arrival; negligence for which my conscience smote me when I found that she had quietly slipped into the mistress' place below stairs, given orders for the reception of our guest and the evening meal, and taken from me the unpleasant business of recounting the events of the trial to Rolf. He was acquainted with every incident when we talked it all over after supper. His honest indignation flamed most hotly against his aunt, Miss Stratton, who, he roundly affirmed, had made more mischief in her life than all the other women in the state put together.

"She has been very careful not to take me into her confidence in this nefarious plot!" he said, warmly. "I believe she has gone crazy along with the majority of the southern people — the rulers included. We are living in a reign of terror. One expects tremblingly, every day, to hear of the Conciergerie and the guillotine! And this is a Christian land! These are brothers who prey upon each other's characters, and lie in wait for the lives of innocent men!"

"The Conciergerie and the guillotine!" "The lives of innocent men!" Words of dread that would not let me rest, that summer midnight — which come to me now with deadlier force than when they were uttered. Rolf would have been pained beyond measure had he guessed how his hasty speech troubled me. In assiduity, yet delicacy of attention, in lively sympathy for our sorrow and ardent desire to mitigate it by cheering words and thoughtful advice as to the expediency of retaining learned counsel in Papa's behalf, and bringing whatever of political influence he or we could command to bear upon the arbiters of Papa's fate, he was all that friend or son could be. I should have laid me down to rest in comparative peace of mind but for the imprudent ejaculation, which was probably forgotten by him so soon as it was spoken.

We hurried breakfast next morning, that we might be early at the Court Room. The sun was still near the eastern horizon when we drove out of the plantation gate. Uncle Will followed us, as upon the preceding day. But Rolf rode at the side of the carriage, and beguiled the wearisome way with quiet, pleasant chat — not oppressive hilarity, as many whose will was as good, but whose tact was less fine, would have done. Three miles from home, just opposite the yawning door of our little church, a courier met us, his horse covered with dust and foam. He drew rein and saluted Rolf, who looked startled at the encounter.

"Well, Willets! what is it?" he said quickly.

The man gave him a note, which he perused with his back to us. His eyes glittered, but his bronzed cheek was paler by many shades than it had been a minute before, when he presented himself at Mamma's window.

"My dear Mrs. Lacy, there is nothing in this change of arrangements to make you uneasy. On the contrary, I regard as a favorable omen — a security for a fair trial and ultimate acquittal — the fact that orders have been issued from the war department that Mr. Lacy shall be brought to Richmond for examination."

"When?" asked Mamma, huskily.

Rolf's averted eyes told me before his unwilling lips formed the answer.

"The escort having him in charge started this morning at sunrise!"

There was a dead pause. I can see the whole picture now — the dismantled church, with its shapely spire, lifted in mute appeal to Heaven; the brier-grown fences; the creek running swiftly between the fringe-trees and alders on the banks; the two soldiers sitting motionless upon their horses; Uncle Will leaning anxiously over the arched neck of Papa's splendid bay — poor Priam! and the hard, blue smiling sky, — all this my senses electrotyped before Mamma bowed her head upon her hands with a low cry that went through my heart like a knife.

She raised her face abruptly. "Were these the important orders you brought last night to the commandant at Clay Hall?" she demanded.

Rolf positively shrank back at her tone and air.

"Heaven is my witness, Madam, that I was ignorant of their purport! else I would have spared you this shock!"

"I hope you are speaking the truth!" rejoined she, bitterly. "It is a fearful crime to tear an innocent man from his home, to rob a wife of her husband, and defenceless daughters of the one protector God has spared to them. Heaven knows whether you have had anything to do with this outrage. I do not. James! drive back —" she was about to say "home" — but the dear word would not come, and she added with an effort, to Sunnybank!"

Even I saw no more of her until late in the day after I parted with her at her chamber door. She stopped there, and put
her hand confusedly to her head.

"I believe I was harsh — perhaps unjust to Major Kingston. If I was, say to him that I regret my heat, and ask him
to forget it. I have no room in my soul for human enmities.
I must inquire why the Lord has this controversy with me;
why these two things have happened to me in one day — widowhood and the loss of children!

At sunset, as I sat sadly in the porch with Carrie, who had
cried herself nearly sick for Papa, in my arms, I heard a firm,
light footstep upon the stairs, and Mamma came out to us.

"My poor children! did you think I had deserted you entirely?" she said sweetly, stooping to kiss us both. "I will
not be so selfish again."

I repeated to myself, "The clear shining after rain," as I
saw her countenance, so serene and elevated was her expression.

"Brownie," she continued, "we will go to town to-morrow.
Papa will expect us, and if we can help him anywhere, it must
be there."

To the city we came, accordingly. We went straight from
the depot to a hotel. Mamma would not compromise any of
her old acquaintances by quartering herself upon them. But
the next day brought a band of friends — not many, but true as
steel — to contest the wisdom of this independent proceeding.
Dr. Arthur Dana, the husband of the oldest and dearest intimate of Mamma's girlhood, is surgeon in a regiment stationed
very near town, and he accompanied Aunt Dana, his sister-in-
law, to see us. Carleton Dana, her son, also in the Confederate army, and, if last, assuredly not least, Aunt Ellen, made
up the number. Mamma was greatly moved by their affectionate entreaties, and after mature deliberation, she accepted
Aunt Dana's offer of a home in her house while we should
remain in the city. Her kindness is unremitting.

"You endangered yourselves by keeping Charley's secret,

and I have profited by your discretion," she says. " While I have a roof above me, it is as much yours as mine."

Her goodness is consoling, as are Dr. Dana's brotherly offices, and Aunt Ellen's warm advocacy of Papa's interests, and tender sympathy with ourselves — and we need all this and more. It is not that those who were once eager to claim our notice now pass us by with the chilliest of slight recognitions, or decline seeing us at all; that no one besides the faithful four above-named and Rolf Kingston has called to see us, or endeavored to gain admittance to Papa. These are but the scratches of tiny thorns, in comparison with this woful waiting from day to day, and week to week, for the deferred action of the proper tribunal in the case of our beloved prisoner; the knowledge that he is languishing in an overheated, fœtid prison, crowded almost to suffocation; denied the privilege of communication with us, except at infrequent intervals and in the presence of a guard.

Mamma has written to officials whom she knew in her happier days, and who are said to be potent in the councils of the Confederacy. Dr. Dana and Aunt Ellen have done the same, besides besieging these dignitaries with personal applications, while Rolf has devoted himself to this work of mercy and justice with zeal that has gained for him a firm foothold in all our hearts. Still, the trial is postponed upon one pretext and another, oftenest upon no pretext at all.

" It is inexplicable to me," said Rolf to-day, " how one so benevolent, respected, and beloved as was your father, could have made so malicious and dangerous an enemy as the writer of that letter. That he ever wrote, or even saw, it up to the moment it was produced in Court, nobody who knows him can believe — yet the trap was cunningly laid. Have you any suspicion as to the author?"

" None!" I replied. " I am glad that I have not. I would not suspect who it really is for the world, unless through my knowing it I could liberate my father."

He looked surprised at my energy.

" I do not quite comprehend!"

I answered frankly, " Because it would be wicked to hat
and despise any human being as I should do the person wh
devised this plot. It was the work of a demon, not a man!"

Agatha, who was sitting by, laughed — a low, musical ripple
that tingled queerly through my nerves.

" Why, Brownie! you have frightened Major Kingston mor
than a brigade of the enemy could do by your explosion o
righteous wrath!"

Rolf tried to jest, but he did seem shocked at my vehemence
Even he cannot know how much I have to bear — how difficul
is the attempt to keep alive hope in my own breast, and hel
another to see encouraging signs in the disheartening disap
pointments that beset our every step. Yet he is a loyal frien
— brave as loyal. May his need of such a one never be sor
as is ours!

CHAPTER XXII.

AGATHA.

I CAN image Rip Van Winkle's sensations with a vividness I should once have thought it impossible for any one to do unless he were a rural sexagenarian.

I was in Richmond two years,and six months ago, and to-day, I do not know the place save by certain natural features and some of the most aristocratic, and therefore least alterable streets. The city teems with population. It used to be a lively, well-to-do, complacent town. People were well dressed, and looked happy, and took their own time for doing all things, and were profoundly earnest about nothing unless it were in the persuasion that a born Virginian was but one remove from the nobility, and that to live upon one of the seven hills of Virginia's capital was equivalent to dwelling within a stone's throw of Paradise. But times have changed, and Richmond with them. The former inhabitants have vanished like scared birds at the approach of the hunter, and a multitude of aliens, rivalling a flight of locusts in numbers and rapacity, now swarm the thoroughfares in their stead. It was the wont of the old families (and what Virginia family is new?) to keep open house the year around. They enjoyed housekeeping principally because their friends could visit them, their tables and spare chambers be filled continually with a changing host of relatives, and acquaintances, and mere strangers, who came introduced by acquaintances, and were therefore entitled to the best welcome the establishment afforded. It was a disgrace, in their code, to suffer a friend to pass a night at a hotel if there were room in the family mansion for one more ; and to make this space, mine host would gladly vacate his own chamber and sleep upon the parlor sofa.

Now, these roomy mansions are indeed crowded, but it is with paid lodgers. Mr. F. F. V. finds that ready money comes hardly nowadays. His credit was boundless of yore — but a race of hucksters and shopkeepers has arisen who know not F. F. V. His credit doesn't go at all, and if he scrapes together a vast pile of bank-bills, they go a very little way.

Flour five hundred dollars a barrel; butter, forty and fifty per pound; coffee, sixty, seventy, eighty dollars; tea, one hundred and twenty; mint-juleps at the bar of the Spottswood and Exchange hotels, ten dollars apiece; and "gentlemen are requested not to eat the ice left in the bottom of the glass." F. F. V. tells his neighbor, with a ghastly grin, that he takes his money to the butcher's in a market-basket, and brings his steak home in his vest-pocket; and his neighbor, a lawyer, who was, before the war, in a growing practice, or a bank-officer, whose stand in society was eligible and maintenance more than comfortable, cannot grin in reply, although he makes an effort to do so — when he remembers that his wife is toiling at her needle, his eldest daughter an *employée* of the Treasury Department, and his lesser children shoeless and hungry. F. F. V. once owned a pair of magnificent blooded horses, which were wont, on fine days, to caracole before the family coach, up and down Franklin or Grace Streets, or through the winding avenues of Hollywood — there being a fashion, even in cemeteries. Mrs. F. F. V. would *not* give up her horses; and her lord, being one under authority, indulged her in this obstinate notion, although it was next to impossible to keep the bones of the pampered favorites hidden by a decent thickness of flesh, on account of the difficulty of procuring provender. On divers occasions, when their anxious owner had waylaid a farmer on his way to market, and purchased his load of hay, oats, or corn for a fabulous sum, the ubiquitous Government agent appeared at his elbow, cancelled the bargain with an authoritative word, tendered the countryman one tenth of the sum agreed upon between him and the chagrined citizen, and ordered the forage off to the Government barracks. Against such disregard of private claims there is no redress. Neither has Mr. F. F. V. been able to obtain any for the loss of his blooded span, which, just after Stoneman's dash upon the suburbs, was taken from his stables — *pro bono publico* — without the formula " by your leave," branded " C. S. A.," and sent, ostensibly, in pursuit of the fleet Yankee.

The once proud Old Dominion made a stupendous blunder when she elected to leave the shelter of the Eagle's wing, and consort with the birds of all feathers who are pecking her to death. She acted conscientiously, — of course, — and as she imagined, wisely, in steering clear of Scylla, but she is being abominably maltreated by Charybdis.

" We have come to fight for you ! Bow down to us as your saviors and masters," say the arrogant far-Southerners. " You kept out of our glorious Confederation so long as you could hang back in honor, decency, or safety. We admitted you upon sufferance. Treat us well, or we will withdraw from your defences, and you will be swallowed, at a gulp, by the ravenous Yank."

What is poor, cheated, famishing Virginia to do, but bow her hoary, discrowned head in base subjection, and, clinging to the gray skirts of her new masters, implore them not to leave her in the lurch? If I believed in human nature (which I never did, to the best of my recollection !) I should be terribly puzzled by the queer features of the life, foaming and bellowing on all sides of me. With Grant menacing Petersburg, and Sherman pushing his victorious legions westward and southward, and Sheridan everywhere except where the Confederate Generals want and expect to find him, and the Confederacy going to pieces generally (according to Yankee journalists), like a house built of cards — " going up the spout," is the choice phrase here for such demolition, — editors, capitalists, speculators, quartermasters, and Government officers, vapor loudly as ever of " breaking lights " and " final success " — while clergymen who, long ago, abandoned the publication of the Gospel of

26 *

peace as an unprofitable tale, bluster, and hector, and prophesy more blatantly than all the other classes combined. There are daily prayer-meetings for the encouragement of the masses, at which the principal means of grace employed are assurances from the clergy — their information being received, it is popularly believed, by special revelation — that the city will never fall into the hands of the enemy, and prayers that outdo what the old preacher called "David's cussing psalms," in invectives and anathemas against the universal Yankee nation. All this while, there is in high places — ay! and in low ones — a scramble for the spoils of office, — shameless favoritism, resulting in the enrichment of tens ; more iniquitous monopolies, that, profiting by the wants of the people, effect the opulence of hundreds. The thousands may starve or go naked.

None of these things move me. I should like to see that phenomenon of human depravity that could !

Apropos de bottes ! The topic of conversation at the tea-table to-night chanced to be Admiral Dahlgren's denial of the authenticity of the letter said to have been found upon the body of his son.

To the latter — a youthful Colonel in the Yankee army — was intrusted the business of taking Richmond in March last. The expedition failed — providentially — said the Confederates in their *Te Deums* over the deliverance ; — through the mistake or treachery of a guide, as the Yankee papers had it. Suffice it to say, it failed, and Colonel Dahlgren fell a victim to his rashness. His remains were brought into the city, and buried with every token of ignominy, in consequence of the appearance in the public prints, of a paper, taken, as was stated, from his pocket. This was an address to his troops, urging them to the liberation of the Yankee prisoners ; the destruction of the bridges over the river ; and the pillage of the doomed capital. The father of the deceased leader in this laudable enterprise, has, it appears, obtained a photograph of the original, and boldly declares the notorious order to be a slanderous forgery.

"Nobody pretends to believe this trumped-up tale !" said

Miss Morris, scornfully, this evening. "It bears falsehood upon its face. If Dahlgren did not write the paper, who did? No Yankee soldier would have dared trifle with his commandant's name, and no Confederate is base enough to commit such a fraud when he could gain nothing by it. Men don't forge signatures unless tempted to it by large promises of immunity from deserved punishment, or by the hope of reward."

Most of the company acquiesced in this judgment by silence or expressed affirmation.

"Yet," said Elinor, timidly, from her end of the table, "I had rather believe it to be a senseless, or mercenary forgery, than that it was the deliberate design of the Federal troops to cut off the retreat of the defenceless inhabitants of the city and then sack it. This would have been a piece of monstrous barbarity, unworthy of a brave soldiery and a great Government. If Colonel Dahlgren wrote the paper of instructions, he was empowered by his Government to do it. Better accuse one unknown man of perpetrating the libel upon humanity than cast the odium upon a whole Nation!"

"There is nothing incredible in the supposition that his masters would have borne him out to the utmost extent of his misdeeds!" said Carleton Dana, fierily. "They stop short of nothing that is diabolical. There isn't a man, woman, or child, born or bred south of the Potomac, who would have soiled his or her fingers with so foul a bit of writing as is that paper!"

"I am not sure of that. Other documents have been forged with the direct design of tarnishing the fame of innocent men — and have succeeded!" said Elinor, with spirit.

"I understand!" Carleton tempered his tone. "But you cannot prove that the one you refer to was not penned by some vicious, low-bred Yankee."

"It was not the work of an uneducated person, but of one familiar with the use of the pen and the language of gentlemen."

"I would stake my life upon the assertion that it never came from under the hand of a southern soldier!" cried the youth, bristling all over, to the tags of the Lieutenant's epaulets he has lately mounted.

"I have not insinuated that it did. It is certain that no brave gentleman wrote it, let him be soldier or civilian," was Elinor's reply.

My *vis-a-vis*, Major Kingston, had preserved a judicious silence while this discussion was pending, and now hurried to the rescue of both parties with a story he had gathered from a returned prisoner, of the humane treatment he had received in a Yankee hospital. It is my private belief that he manufactured it from Alpha to Omega, — but I joined in the remarks it occasioned, pleased, with him, to slip away from a disagreeable topic. It was lucky that I am buoyed above the risk of being dragged down by degrading suspicions; sustained, by conscious rectitude, in an atmosphere of beautiful equanimity of feature and feeling.

I was standing at the library window, just after supper, watching, across the valley, the kindling of the camp and hospital fires upon the hills, when Miss Morris pushed herself against my elbow.

"It is a beautiful evening!" remarked I, suavely, making room in the recess for the figure which is less sylph-like than it was thirty years back.

" I wish I knew exactly what you had to do with this wicked business!" she said, snappishly.

"Madam!" I opened mouth and eyes in stupid wonder.

"I mean this letter and the trial of your best friend!" she pursued. "I distrust you grievously, Agatha Lamar!"

"I do not feign to misunderstand you, Miss Morris!" I drew myself up haughtily. "Permit me to remind you of your sage and charitable observations: 'Men' — and by implication women — 'don't forge signatures unless they are tempted to it by large promises.' To make your charge plausible, you must discover a motive for the deed."

"It is killing Ida!" she said, passionately. "And her husband is guiltless of this deed as I am. He may be at heart a

Unionist, still. I suppose he is — and that is a pity ; but that he ever wrote that atrocious letter, or did anything else mean and clandestine, is preposterous ! I tell you no truer gentleman — no better Christian — ever breathed than he whom it is the fashion to revile as a traitor ! I get so mad with hearing the gabble about it — the lying rumors and scandalous hints flying around town — that I am ready to turn Union-lover myself out of spite ! "

" A desperate remedy ! " I said, coolly contemptuous.

I did not care to quarrel with her, but neither was I covetous of the honor of a confidential conversation. She drummed hard upon the window-sill — a girlish trick it is time she left off.

" Who wrote that letter ? " she demanded, wheeling short upon me.

For the life of me I could not have sustained her piercing eye. But I let my lids droop gradually in answering slowly and audibly, —

" I know no more about it than you do, and I do not insult you by the suspicion that you are an accomplice in the affair."

Then I turned away, more disdainfully than angrily, and left her to her cogitations.

Was there any significance in her attack other than the old story of inveterate dislike, and superadded to it the galling recollection of the duel between us on New Year's day ? Mr. Lacy was her confidant then. His wife of course shortly became a party to the secret. This I assumed as inevitable, although neither had ever approached me on the subject. The *sequitur* to all this gossiping would have been a general flare-up but for my precautionary measures. Had I not thrust forward my trusty knight in the nick of time, with his demonstration of boundless devotion to his hunted, cornered queen, she must have been swept from the board ignominiously. As it is, I make no doubt the *exposé* is but deferred until a convenient season. I am not positive that I care very much whether it comes or not. If other affairs prosper, the *éclaircissement,* even if it be an *esclandre* also, will perhaps be rather advantageous than disastrous to my prospects. For the present, Lynn and Hayridge constitute a pretty stout anchor to windward. I was a cipher on the wrong side of the heiress and daughter at Sunnybank. I might, by adroit manœuvring, depreciate her value in the estimation of a few impartial observers, but I did not thereby enhance my own. Here, I am less than nought — the most unconsidered of trifles.

But for Carleton Dana, I might pass whole days without a civil, i. e., a complimentary notice. He is young and gallant, and has an eye for the fine points of a woman — consequently he admires me. He has taken me to see the camps and fortifications, — down the river to look at the water above the sunken obstructions that hinder navigation; to Hollywood, to sigh pensively over the interminable line of ridges that hold the skeletons of a great army of southern braves; to Gamble's Hill, to overlook Belle Isle where the naughty Yankee papers will have it that some dozens of paltry Yankee Hessians were frozen to death last winter; to the Capitol Square, to see a review of the Home Reserve, — I counted twenty who limped, ten who could not walk without a cane, and forty with very white hair; — and most frequently of all other excursions — he has escorted me to Pizzini's. This Prince of Confectioners still welcomes visitors to his marble hall with beaming phiz and friendly bow; still dispenses from some mysterious cavern — stocked, people say, by means of Aladdin's lamp — incomparable creams, lucent jellies, luscious fruits and *bonbons* that would make a Parisian *artiste* in the sweet art tear his hair with envy. I have a sincere and growing regard for M. Pizzini. I have a childish love for confections, and he gratifies it.

Nobody disputes Carleton's right to ride, talk, and walk with me — *parce que?* Nobody gives the intimacy a thought. Major Kingston and I seldom exchange a word, except in general company. I severed our connection, formally, weeks ago. The understanding now is, that each is to shift for his and herself. He is doing this. His diplomatic skill really astonishes my weak mind when I bethink me of what a tyro he was when

I assumed the charge of his education. He has neither eyes, ears, nor thoughts for anything unconnected with his inamorata. He has offered himself as bail for the temporary release of Papa-in-law, and his application been testily refused. He has toadied this and that great friend, and done the state all sorts of service in order to procure tickets of admittance for his *protegées* — mother and daughter — to the cell of their imprisoned relative, and been only partially successful. His ardor of desire to serve them is not dampened by these repulses, but he boasts less of his influence and exertions. He is more prone to subside into dejected comments upon the hollowness of mortal promises, the fallacy of trust in rulers, and the undue, undiscriminating severity of the retribution which the hampered, thwarted — and, it is loudly whispered, increasingly unpopular — administration is inclined to mete out to real or presumed political offenders. His remarkably ill-concealed solicitude is telling upon Mrs. Lacy's strength and spirits. She has lost flesh, color, and appetite — disavow despondency as she may, and as she does; spends much of her time in her room, and only brightens into a semblance of her former animation when her daily note from her husband is brought in by Major Kingston. This gentleman is mail-carrier extraordinary to her Ladyship. It was he who wrung from the iron-hearted prison despots permission for the captive to correspond with his afflicted family, all missives to be scrutinized by some deputy Cerberus or other. He says he had difficulty in obtaining this concession. This may be — but he evidently thinks he has purchased the smiles and rapturous thanks of the devoted daughter very cheaply. What a showy sham is everything that looks well and everybody who affects disinterestedness on this great, hollow, dirty globe we are condemned to live upon!

" You do not believe that this arrest will culminate in anything more serious than protracted imprisonment — say, for three or four months?" I queried, confidentially, of Carleton to-night.

The others were clustered about a table in the front parlor,

looking over some papers — a scheme of defence to be put in
at the trial, or something of the kind, which had come to the
house in the pocket of the guardian-angel in " hodden gray " —
to wit, Major Kingston.   He was showman to the concern, and
his voice fell continuously upon my ear, as I sat at the back-
parlor window, trying to catch a mouthful of the river breeze,
and chatted soft nothings with my *preux cavalier.*

He shook his fair curls with owl-like wisdom.

" I have my fears — based principally upon the talk of out-
siders who pretend to be in the confidence of the Government.
It is time — these declare — that treason should be dealt with
as a crime, and a notable example, such as the rigorous punishment of one heretofore high in social esteem and once prominent in political life, would do more to awe other offenders and
restrain the growing turbulence of the disaffected than the execution of a score of obscure traitors."

" Execution ! " I repeated, horrified.   " They do not speak
of a penalty like *that !* "

He shook his head again.   " Not speak of it in so many
words, but they cloak the idea very thinly.   You see this is a
serious business.   The evidence is frightfully conclusive of his
guilt.   The Government can't afford to leave such dangerous
spies at large.   I *hope* he is innocent, but " —very confidentially, indeed, for he has, ere this, discovered the bias of my
political tenets — " the truth is, Miss Agatha, a man who is
false to his country in his heart is very apt to betray her in
act.   I would as soon trust Beelzebub as a Virginia-born
Unionist.   The Yankees are twice as respectable."

I surveyed the virtuously indignant visage of this incorrupt-
ible curly-pate with an air of profound edification.   Talk of
the Latter-day Saints !   A slow intellect like mine needs a daily
exposition of the latest patriot creed, outside of which there is
no salvation.   It is irresistibly comic !

How warm it is !   I pant, and fan, and muse longingly of the
breath of mown hay and clover-fields, and the babble of falling
waters, that enter my windows at Sunnybank.   The streets are

still, save for the distant shouts of some belated and quarrel-
some rowdies, who prowl abroad, like hyenas, as soon as night
falls. Gas is among the forbidden delights of the corrupt former days, and respectable citizens stay in-doors after dark, or,
if they stir out, carry a private arsenal of bowie-knives and
pistols. It must be insufferably hot in the lower portions of
the city; stifling in the crowded prisons, where languish men
with lungs made after the same pattern with those of their
accusers, judges, and jailers, and hearts constructed upon better
principles, according to Bible doctrines — *not* as they are ex-
pounded by the Richmond clergy. I am no Pharisee! I cannot say that I am not as other people are. I act in consonance
with the teachings of my religion, which are to keep the brightest possible lookout for my individual interests, regarding the
welfare of all others, of whatever name, degree, and profession, as secondary in importance. But I shall sleep better to-
night — if the heat lets me sleep at all — for the reflection that
I did not consign a single one of those suffering wretches,
thronging the noisome military jails, to a hateful confinement,
and a possible death of pain and ignominy.

Morning.

I broke off my description of last evening's proceedings at
Carleton's portentous summary of Mr. Lacy's "situation."

While I still lounged in the recess of the back-parlor window, — where is a divan fashioned exactly to my liking, and
Lieutenant Dana pleased himself, and would have bored me
had I troubled myself to listen, with stories of adventures in
the saddle and at the cannon's mouth; around the camp fire,
robbing Pennsylvania hen-roosts and Maryland shoe-stores, —
martial exploits all, that justified the delighted smile with which
I appeared to contemplate the budding hero, — while the group
about the centre-table in the foreground still rustled their
papers and laid solemn heads together over them, — there
appeared in the doorway a tall, gentlemanly personage. He
had a singularly prepossessing countenance, and was attired,

it is almost unnecessary to remark, *à la militaire*. When a man under seventy here wears citizen's clothes, it is the exception to the prevailing fashion. Even boys of fourteen dress in gray, with curlecues of scarlet braid upon their sleeves; upon their heads, truncated cones, pitched rakishly over the left eye; carry their shoulders very squarely and far back, their elbows very stiffly, and their legs knock-kneedly, and delude themselves with the conceit that they look more like mighty men of valor than galvanized manikins.

"Why! there is Colonel Copeland!" whispered Carleton, rising in a flutter of pleasure. "You know! the hero of Muddy Bottom!" and rushed forward to meet him with the respectful elation suitable to the occasion of a visit from a guest so distinguished.

Rolf was before him. He, too, had sprung to his feet, like a Jack-in-the-box, at the appearance of the renowned officer, calling his name, as he did so, in a tone of deferential delight. Mrs. Lacy was in the rear of the party, who were now all standing. Her eyes sparkled, and a glow overspread her matronly cheeks — emotion which I perceived did not belong to the class of sensations engendered in the young men by the arrival. The Colonel passed his subordinates with a hasty, but affable salutation, and sought my Lady. He covered the hand she resigned to the pressure of his right, with his left, and searched her face with a gaze of affectionate penetration.

"My friend!" he said. "My old, true friend! how happy I am to see you! It is a pleasure I have not had before in ten years. And this is 'Brownie!'" holding out a hand to Elinor, who stood next her mother. "A pocket edition of Ida Ross, as I first saw her! a trifle browner, perhaps, and with more eyes than the law of Nature allowed her mother — but very like, nevertheless!"

He paid his respects to Mrs. Dana; met Miss Morris as a boon companion of his young and wild days, and established himself upon a sofa between his early flame and her "pocket edition." I was not invoked to quit my cave. My Lady had

the grace, subsequently, to aver that she had forgotten my presence in the other room, and Carleton ungallantly protested that
his memory had been equally treacherous.

What else could I have expected? " What's Hecuba to him,
or he to Hecuba?" What possible community of interest can
there be between the hero of Muddy Bottom and a charity
girl?

Carleton did not return to me, and I had leisure for contemplation and reflection. Colonel Copeland sat with his back to
the folding-doors connecting the rooms, and I could not watch
his features so easily as I did those of his companions, who,
having the arms of the sofa to lean against, squared themselves
with their backs to these, their profiles to me, and full faces to
him, and listened as for their lives to all he said.

Mrs. Dana, in obedience, as I shrewdly surmised, to a signal
from the Colonel, presently arose, and left the room. From the
hall she privately signalled Carleton through the half-open door.
After a moment's absence he reappeared, and challenged Rolf
to a walk down town, promising to bring him back in half an
hour. There were left, then, the mother, daughter, Miss Morris, and the famous Colonel. There was no light in the rear-
room, and my dress did not rustle as I crossed the floor, and
lay down upon another sofa, placed on my side of the wall
dividing the parlors. If discovered, I had only to feign slumber. But I was certain nobody would think of looking for me
in the dark. Burning-fluid and bad lard-oil are indifferent substitutes for gas, and the obscurity accruing from the use of these
is favorable for ambushes. As I had divined, the topic introduced immediately after the winnowing of the company, just
described, was the one ever uppermost in my Lady's mind —
the incarceration of her husband. Colonel Copeland is a law-
yer of repute in his county and state, and the object of his visit
was to investigate this affair for himself, not trusting to Madame
Rumor.

He went into it with professional coolness and acuteness, and
Mrs. Lacy was his informant. Elinor and — *mirabile dictu !* —

Miss Morris sat by in mute attenton. My Lady has a clear
head and a ready tongue. If he interrogated like a lawyer, her
replies were those of a well-drilled witness, — concise, explicit,
— and so far as outward show was to be depended upon, dispassionate. Her testimony elicited a compliment from her interloc-
utor when he closed the examination bearing upon the leading
events of the arrest and trial.

"Candid to a fault, still, I see, and upright to fastidious-
ness!" he was pleased to remark, smilingly. "If I had not
confidence in your husband's word, I would believe in his innocence if you asserted it. Your conscience would not allow you
to screen even him from merited punishment. Our cause has
been the loser in not having you two to support it. Now that I
have had all the available evidence for and against him, do you
object to confiding to me any circumstances that might have influenced the decision of the Court, either way, had they been
known?"

Mrs. Lacy hesitated, in thought or uncertainty.

"You are afraid to trust a rebel?" asked the Colonel, playfully — yet in gentle reproach.

"I am not afraid to trust Richard Copeland!" she rejoined.
"I was trying to sift what might be useful to us from that which
may be irrelevant."

With this preamble she began the story of Elinor's concealment of the Yankee prisoner, asserting primarily, that her husband was ignorant of the occurrence until after the fellow had
left Sunnybank under the auspices of her favorite servant, and
enlarging upon the frightful appearance outside old Rachel's
window, of what the sable hag described as "a white face with
great big eyes," on the night of the flight.

"And this, you say, was not adverted to at the trial — was
known to no one excepting yourself, Miss Elinor, Mr. Lacy,
and the two servants?"

"I am positive that the presence of the sergeant upon the
premises was never suspected by another person, unless Rachel
were right in her fancy."

"In which event it would seem inevitable that the matter would have been reported at the examination," he responded, stroking his mustache thoughtfully.

"You mentioned just now another inmate of your household — Miss Lamar. What are her political principles?"

"She is engaged to be married to my son Lynn. Her sympathies are naturally with the southern cause."

Bravo! Mamma-in-law! Could the subtlest *diplomate* have sketched the case — as it should be, according to respectable, hymeneal laws — with fewer and more graceful touches? I could have liked her at that moment, had I not known what rank hypocrisy lurked beneath this fair pretence of maternal approbation of her son's choice, and justification of the "secesh" proclivities of his *fiancée.*

Colonel Copeland's next query was a rousing "feeler."

"Do you consider her entirely trustworthy?"

A blank and awful silence! What hindered me from rising and confronting the three base-hearted women with the array of sarcastic invectives that rushed hotly to my tongue? Significant reticence is the surest method adopted by prudes and demure-faced slanderers for blackening a sister's fame — and because the easiest and safest, the most popular.

Elinor recovered speech earliest. "She knows nothing that could injure us, if it were told. I do not think she would betray us if she were acquainted with everything."

"I wouldn't trust her!" broke in Miss Morris. "She is a snake in the grass — one of the slyest and most venomous sort!"

"May I ask your reasons for this declaration, Miss Ellen?" inquired Colonel Copeland, unperturbed by the announcement of my depravity.

"If you please, Ellen, we will not introduce anything into this discussion that cannot possibly aid us in discovering the real agents of the mischief!" said my Lady, in her tranquilly imperious manner. "Miss Lamar's interests are so nearly

27 *

identical with ours, Colonel Copeland, that the idea of associ-
ating her with any project for our ruin is absurd."

"It would indeed appear that you are right," was the response; "but these are odd times. A man's foes are oftenest
those of his own household. When fathers and sons are in
arms against each other, the animosity of daughter-in-law to
mother-in-law is the more plausible. The facts that Miss Lamar is the one member of your family — in the absence of
your sons — who inclines to the southern cause, and that
she is for this reason excluded from your family conferences,
dispose me to pry very narrowly into what were her movements and who her correspondents about the time of Mr.
Lacy's arrest. Every petty official is on the *qui vive* for treasonable symptoms — imagines himself Fouqué, Cicero, and
Brutus welded into one mass of human metal, and set for the
defence of a government that would be better off if a bayonet
were forced into the hands of each, and he put into the front
ranks with a *chevaux de frise* of bayonets at his back to prevent his running away. An indiscreet admission, a look or
gesture, from Miss Lamar would put these ferrets upon the
scent; and once fairly started, they would manufacture a rat
rather than acknowledge that they had been humbugged."

"Miss Lamar is never indiscreet," said Miss Morris.
"Whatever she does has been well conceived beforehand."

She did me bare justice thus far, and while doing it, heightened the unfavorable impression of me already existing in Colonel Copeland's mind.

He pushed his examination farther.

"Have you lived habitually upon good terms with one another? What is her disposition?"

"She has a high temper and a strong will. The one keeps
the other in check," said Mrs. Lacy. "There has never been
a quarrel between her and any of us during her residence at
Sunnybank. Her deportment is uniformly respectful, and usually affectionate."

"Is she quick — intelligent — clever?"

The answer came simultaneously from the three in varying intonations. Miss Morris said, "Decidedly!" emphatically, as she might have commended the ability of Mephistopheles. "More's the pity!" is what she would have added, had she completed her verdict in words.

Mrs. Lacy said, "She is!" in a studiously unremarkable manner, while Elinor replied, "Very!" with amiable heartiness.

"Handsome?"

Mrs. Lacy answered again, "Very beautiful!"

"And very much attached to my friend Lynn—eh! The scaramouch! Fancy his presuming to take to himself a wife! He wasn't out of jackets when I saw him last. Has this young lady many intimate friends—confidants—soul-sisters, etc.?"

"None!"

The monosyllable rang upon my ear like a knell. It was true! true! I had no friend, no adviser. Lone sparrow upon the housetop, I might chatter and make my moan, and none stay to heed and console. *Quoi donc?* There is the more reason why I should take care of myself.

"A remarkable woman, truly! No correspondents?"

"None except my sons, Ross and Lynn."

"And Major Kingston!" interjected Miss Morris, officiously.

"Aha! she writes to him then! Do you see the letters, Miss Elinor?"

"No, sir. They are very good friends, and I know that they do exchange letters occasionally."

"She makes no secret of this?"

"No, sir. She usually mentions to me when she has heard from him, often giving me messages he has sent through her to me."

"Does he write to you, too?"

"Never, sir."

"He shows bad taste there," said the gallant warrior.

" It is not his fault that he refrains," Miss Morris observed,
dryly.

" I see ! I thought him a sensible young fellow. I am
pleased to retain my original opinion of him. Excuse me, my
dear Miss Elinor, for asking your mother a question in your
hearing which may sound impertinent. We lawyers are used
to following out all sorts of unlikely trails, you know. Can
either of you ladies inform me whether Miss Lamar and Major
Kingston have any common grudge against a single member of
the Lacy family? Was there ever anything in their past intercourse with yourself, Mrs. Lacy, or your husband, or daughter, which may have implanted the germ of ill will? any slight
— real or fancied — any foiled scheme — any exhibition of
envy, or rivalry, or petty revenge ? "

I held my breath as the horrid creature spun out his list of
interrogations. Now for it ! for ripping up old wounds and
copying old scores ! I am confident that a whole hour passed
before any one offered a reply. I knew I lived an eternity in
what was probably, after all, not more than sixty seconds of
suspense.

" This is a singular question ! " said Mrs. Lacy, very slowly,
pondering each syllable and letter of her answer. " There
have been events in the life of both which might form the basis
of dislike toward one or more of us—but Mr. Lacy had nothing to do with these."

" Pardon me again, Miss Elinor ! you will think me a rough
old bear ! but — Mrs. Lacy, will you be candid with me, and
say if I am correct in suspecting that your daughter was the
disturbing agent in these *contretemps?* My dear young lady,
this is not the season for foolish reserve. Your mother and I
had delicate and sad confidences together years before you were
born. She did me a great service then, which I can never repay. I would show my gratitude by the effort to serve her and
those whom she loves. She would commit the life of her husband to my care if need were. You must bear with my med-
dling until I learn all there is to tell pertaining to this affair.

There has been villany somewhere. For that villany there existed a motive, and a powerful one. The foe incurred no little peril in putting his device into execution. I am interpenetrated with the idea that a woman is somehow mixed up in this mess — but a woman did not write that letter. There are strokes that show the soldier. General B—— told me, to-day, that no accomplished engineer could have described the defences of the river and the adjacent country with more accuracy than does that epistle. Here, then, lie two facts. The author of the forgery was cognizant of the internal operations of your family, knew that your father had written to Mr. Dana, and where this gentleman was residing; and was likewise familiar with the lines of defence constructed by the Confederate troops, for twenty or thirty miles up the river. I say there is strong evidence of joint work in this composition. Now, may Mamma answer me frankly, as I have talked to you?"

"She may."

I should have marvelled at Elinor's firm voice had I been less excited. This man, with his blandly protecting manner and invincible coolness, suggested things that curdled my blood. Yet what had I to fear? In calm retrospection, I can now defy him — laugh at his farce of detection, make jokes to myself, and be amused by them, about his resemblance to the immortal Mr. Inspector Bucket, and his scrupulous " Sir Leicester Dedlock, Baronet."

My Lady's response was straightforward and to the point.

" My daughter, you may go into the library for a minute." And when she had obeyed — " Elinor was betrothed to a young officer in the Federal army who is now dead. We have reason to fear that Agatha was, at one time, attached to him, and that his engagement to my daughter was the source of disquietude to her. With regard to Major Kingston — he addressed Elinor several years since, and was refused. But his conduct of late exonerates him entirely, in my opinion, from the charge of unworthy spite, or the desire for revenge."

And she expatiated upon his virtues and beneficent deeds

until I wondered why I had never guessed what an incarnation of angelhood was this flourishing sprig of the chivalry.

"You are a competent judge of character. I should be willing to accept your conclusion," commented the Colonel. "I was prepossessed myself in Major Kingston's favor by what I have seen of him in action. He has courage of a high order, and a brave man is seldom a rogue. I must dream over what I have heard before sketching my campaign. May Miss Elinor come back?"

Miss Morris got up to summon the shrinking damsel who could stab me in the back with her smoothly delivered implications, but who was too modest and tender to be allowed to hear a reference to her deceased lover. This was my opportunity for escape, since nothing was to be gained by waiting longer, and Miss Morris might take it into her crafty skull to spy out my whereabouts. I glided through the window which opened down to the floor of the portico, sped up the back stairway to my room, threw myself across the foot of the bed, and was sound asleep in a second. I am beginning to cherish a grateful belief in my angel of presentiment. I was barely settled to my satisfaction when a step was audible upon the stairs — knuckles struck smartly against the panel of my half-opened door. I was quiet.

"Agatha! Miss Lamar!" called Miss Morris.

No answer. She crept into the room, and a stream of light from the hall revealed my recumbent figure. She stood stock still — hearkening, I knew, to the regular rise and fall of my breathing — then went out again. Colonel Copeland had perhaps sent her for me that he might get a sight of the wicked conspirator. Animated by the thought, I jumped up; struck a light; brushed my hair; smiled at the mirror, to see whether I could execute the grimace without approximating a death's head, and walked boldly into the lion's mouth — that is to say, the Colonel's presence.

He bowed low and politely, when I was introduced, and not

to embarrass me by the scrutiny of a stranger, resumed his conversation with Mrs. Dana, who had returned to the parlor.

"Did you come to my room just now!" I asked of Elinor.
"Some one awakened me, or I dreamed that my name was
called."

"I went to look after you," said Miss Morris. "We thought
you had absconded."

I laughed — and Carleton entering with Rolf at this opportune instant, I rallied him upon his desertion of me.

"I should be implacable but for the excuse he threw over his
shoulder in his flight," I added. "The Hero of Muddy Bottom!" he uttered in a stage whisper — and I did what many
valorous men have done, at Colonel Copeland's approach — beat
a precipitate retreat.

The Colonel eyed me intently while the others applauded my
tribute to his prowess. Either he is indifferent to flattery, or
he was studying some other matter. For my pretty hit did not
tell. By and by he said, "Good night," and took Miss Morris
home under his renowned arm, and the company broke up.

I too have dreamed over what I have learned, and in my
humble way sketched my campaign. My tactics are simple. I
shall adopt Mr. Weller's favorite mode of defence, and "prove
a halibi."

CHAPTER XXIII.

ELINOR.

September 15.

WE have been at Sunnybank a month to-day. Carrie fell sick in Richmond with fever, and advised by the physicians, and urged by Papa, we brought her, by short and easy stages, home.

It was well for ourselves, and for the plantation, that we returned when we did. A deserted house is public property, liable to the depredations of both armies. While we were away, fences were levelled, growing crops trodden under foot of cattle and men ; and but for the kindness of our neighbor Mr. James Kingston, in soliciting a Confederate guard for the house, it would have been rifled of all valuables, and the furniture broken up or removed. The servants generally behaved well. Uncle Will's authority was sufficient to control most of them, and keep them at work. But two entire families left home and our service before our return. Mamma was pained by their defection. They were old family servants — there are none others on the place — whose parents and grandparents were in the employ of ours. Mamma was brought up with the heads of these families — superintended the rearing of the younger ones, and was sincerely attached to them all. It was an unkind blow — this abandonment of her and her children in the day of their misfortune.

She collected those who remained into the dining-room on the evening of our arrival, and offered to release them if they did not wish to stay with her.

" I am straitened for money," she said, " and I never needed wealth before as I need it now. Your master's trial will be expensive, but he shall be properly defended if I have to sell the house over my head to obtain the means. Not even to procure these would I consent to sell one of my servants. The oldest of you here will bear me witness that I have never parted with one of those whom my father left me, and my heavenly Father, who is also yours, designed, as I believe, that I should protect and provide for as for my own sons and daughters. I have no power to keep you with me. If you choose to go, I would not, if I could, drag you back. It rests entirely with yourselves whether you follow the example of Claiborne and Watt " — the runaways — " or stand by, and work with me. While I have a home, you shall have one. While I live, I shall care for you as I have done in the past. Dark days and nights of sorrow have overtaken us, but they have not come through your master's fault or mine. It is the will of the Lord that we should suffer at the hands of those to whom we have done no wrong. We look to Him for strength to bear it patiently, and trust in His promise that we shall yet find a path out of our trials."

She stood on the hearth at the upper end of the room, Agatha and I near her, when she made this address. Her eye was steady as an eagle's; her form erect; her voice not loud, but her articulation so pure that those most remote from her did not lose a word. My tears came unbidden, and I turned away to hide them as she finished. I did not marvel that the warm, impressible hearts of her servants vented themselves in loud weeping — that some threw themselves upon the floor at her feet, grasping and kissing her dress and hands, while all united in a voluntary promise to labor for her so long as she needed or desired to retain them in her service.

" I thank you all, and trust you," she said, when order was restored. " I shall write to your master to-morrow, and tell him what you have said and done. I could hardly send him news that would please him more. I thank you in his name as well as in my own. Now I wish to have you all pray with and

for me before we separate. Uncle Will! will you lead our
prayers?"

Papa has often said that Uncle Will was more gifted in prayer
than any other man he knew — but he never prayed before as
he did that evening, standing — like an Eastern patriarch, with
his dusky face and snowy hair — surrounded by our bowed figures. He loves Mamma better, I verily believe, than he does
his children; and his voice was choked by sobs when he poured
forth his soul in her behalf.

" She has walked before Thee humbly and in Thy fear all
the days of her life. She openeth her mouth with wisdom, and
in her tongue is the law of kindness; she stretcheth out her
hand to the poor — yea, she stretcheth forth her hands to the
needy. The heart of her husband doth safely trust in her;
her children rise up and call her blessed. Yet oh, our Father,
Thy hand is heavy upon her. The violent have come upon her
land, like a sweeping rain that leaveth no food; they have de-
voured her corn and vines like locusts; they have removed the
landmarks; they have taken away flocks and the food thereof.
The troops have come together, and raised up their way against
her, and encamped round about her habitation. Her kinsfolk
have failed, and her familiar friends have forgotten her. Those
that dwelt in her house, and her maids, have counted her as a
stranger. She called her servants, and they gave her no answer. Her children are far from safety — her husband is
carried away captive, and her sons lie like bulls in a net. Remember her, in all her afflictions, we beseech Thee, O Lord!
Let the sighing of the prisoner come up before Thee. Bring
him out from the prison, and him that sits in darkness out of
the prison-house. Attend unto his cry, for he is brought very
low. In the way wherein he walked they have privily laid a
snare for him. Grant not, O Lord, the desires of the wicked;
further not their wicked devices, lest they exalt themselves.
These Thy servants have not despised the chastening of the
Almighty. In all this, they have sinned not, nor charged Thee
foolishly. They have behaved and quieted themselves as a

child that is weaned of his mother. Wilt Thou not deliver them in six troubles, yea, in seven let no evil touch them! In famine deliver them from death, and in war from the power of the sword. Hide them from the scourge of the tongue, neither let them be afraid of destruction when it cometh. Our eyes wait upon Thee until that Thou have mercy upon us. Have mercy upon us, O Lord! have mercy upon us! for our soul is exceedingly filled with the scorning of those that are at ease, and the contempt of the proud. But our help is in the name of the Lord, which made heaven and earth."

De profundis clamavi! The subdued wail of the organ, the chanting of stoléd priests, the fragrant clouds swung from silver censers, could not have added impressiveness to the scene, as the quavering accents of the aged slave, untaught save by the Spirit of our God, arose in the summer twilight from the heart of that weeping band of the Lord's stricken ones.

Mamma's face was bathed in tears, when she arose, but she extended her hand to her loyal protector and servant, with a smile.

"You have done me great good! Our Saviour will reward you for it; for it was done in His name!"

Under her efficient management, the aspect of the estate has improved materially. In the hope of late frosts, we have sowed corn for foddering the cattle during the winter, and planted various vegetables that will not be injured by the cold weather, or which will mature before this sets in. Eggs are excluded from table use, and set to insure a supply of poultry, while a large proportion of the cattle are provided with hiding-places in the swamp, and rarely brought up to the house. Secret chambers have also been constructed under Mammy's and Uncle Will's houses for storing silver and other portable treasures, and a large pit dug and lined with planks and cement for the reception of our winter's supply of meat, when this shall be prepared. Most of the grown-up negroes are acquainted with these arrangements for the preservation of our property. We do not fear betrayal from them. Mamma has determined to show no half-way confidence in their honor and friendship. We have no communication with the neighboring plantations, with the exception of Mr. James Kingston's. He has been to see us twice — as he was careful to make us understand — at Rolf's earnest request.

From him we have learned that most of the planters around us have abandoned all effort to repair their losses, or to provide against future depredations. "If we die — we die!" is their motto. There are no young men left at home to win, by energetic labor, compensation from the earth for that of which they have been robbed. Only women and gray-haired fathers, or invalid sons and brothers, remain to provide daily bread for large and helpless families. Produce of all descriptions would command high prices in the market; but should they succeed in gathering their harvests without molestation from the raiders, they would not venture to send it over the roads, swarming with scouting parties and unlicensed highwaymen who commit robbery, and, if resisted, murder, under pretence of collecting supplies for one or the other of the two armies. Want stares in the face those who, prior to the war, lived in luxurious ease — want and starvation — not beggary; for those of whom they would solicit relief, in their extremity, are poor as themselves.

How often and portentously, as I hear of the privations, sufferings, and bereavements that have clothed our State in sackcloth, does the text, I once heard Uncle Will repeat in this connection, ring in my ears!

"Until the cities be wasted without inhabitant, and the houses without man, and the land be utterly desolate!"

And all for what? Will the next generation be able to answer this question?

Papa's trial is still unaccountably deferred. The prison rules are more rigid, too, than during the earlier period of his confinement. Our visits, never frequent, were divided by longer and still longer intervals, until, one day, Rolf came to us in deep dejection, bearing an order for our exclusion until further notice. We have letters from Papa yet, and can write in reply;

and this inestimable privilege we owe to Rolf. But for him, our situation, from the day of that shallow mockery of examination at the Court House, would have been pitiable indeed. He has been twice to see us since we reached home, bringing, each time, inspiriting news of our beloved absentee. His health has not suffered seriously from his protracted confinement, and he is serenely hopeful of final acquittal, more patient than we are of this needless, cruel suspense. It helps us to endure the separation, and the anxiety and dread accompanying it, to think of his uncomplaining courage, deprived, as he is, of wholesome employment for body and mind; his language, looks, actions, subject to ceaseless surveillance, while we have the blessed solace of free communion with one another, and of daily labor. We keep very busy in our secluded hive. Drones are inadmissible, for all must work for the common living. Mamma is conscientious in her resolve to husband such funds as she has been enabled to lay aside to provide for the exigencies of the wished-for trial. The plantation must support itself and us, and we must conform our tastes and habits to our means. I find in the necessity for constant employment alleviation of the heartache that has become a condition of my existence, without which I should not know myself. "Belittling cares," Agatha calls the duties that devolve upon us. They seem more to me like so many tiny conductors leading off in as many directions the surcharge of solicitude that would else press too heavily upon life and reason.

"'What GOD hath blessed, that call not thou common!'" said Mamma, when Agatha made this exclamation. "I thank Him hourly for the blessing of labor. It is often a brace, not a burden, which He fits to backs already bowed, that they may grow stronger and straighter."

Agatha laughed. "It may help the back, but it hurts the fingers. Look at mine!"

We were making up coarse blue and yellow homespun into servants' clothes. Papa set the example in the county, summer before last, of planting cotton for home consumption. Our crop

this year is promising, and has thus far remained unharmed.
Spinning-wheels and looms have wrought incessantly upon last
summer's supply, for several weeks past, and the progress of
the manufacture has been watched with lively interest by those
who hope for benefit from the result. I was myself pleas-
urably excited yesterday, when I helped Mamma unroll a
huge piece of, what Mammy styled, "real old-fashioned Vir-
ginny cloth."

"A step toward the achievement of southern independence!"
said Agatha, fingering one end of the stout fabric.

"A retrogressive step!" answered Mamma, pleasantly, "for
this is inferior to that made on the plantation forty years ago,
when manufactures were in their cradle."

A hundred times a day do I wish that Colonel Copeland had
never stirred up doubts in our minds of Agatha's truthfulness
and honest dealing with us. I wrestle with these as foes to my
peace and traducers of her good name. I am ashamed to catch
myself perpetually on the watch for a double meaning in her
talk; for mystery in her movements — the more indignant with
my own unfairness because I invariably fail to discover anything in these to feed my suspicions. She is gayer than Mamma and I. She has less to depress her, and even this seeming
lightness may be assumed to divert us from dwelling upon our
griefs. She is a little restive occasionally under the imposition
of unwonted cares — a natural dislike to what she esteems common and menial. If she were a hypocrite, she would have the
art to conceal these signs of rebellion; would study to cajole
and fawn that she might ingratiate herself into our confidence.
I have been convinced, all along, that our lawyer-friend has put
himself to a deal of trouble to no purpose; that the clew he is
bent upon pursuing is not only unlikely, but false. Mamma has
had but one note from him since he left Richmond in hot haste,
at an hour's notice, to meet Sheridan in the Valley.

"I do not forget your interests," he wrote. "I have used
my best endeavors both to expedite the trial and to discover what
unseen influence retards it. I shall not trouble you with con-

jectures and theories, but when I have run down the game, will make it known by word of mouth."

The same lesson repeated from every side — so easy to recommend, so difficult to practise — "Wait!" * * * *

I broke off here to pet Carrie, who presented herself in my room with the request that I would talk to her. "Mamma and Mammy were cutting out work and Cousin Agatha was asleep, and she" — Carrie — "was lonely and so tired." She is not strong yet, and is moreover a trifle spoiled by the attention and indulgence showed her while sick. I took her upon my lap, — the more lovingly that I felt what a light weight she had become, — and laying her head upon my shoulder, told her a fairy tale, then another, and for the third, the story of a little girl named Carrie, who kept a charm in her pocket that made everybody love her. She laughed, in childish glee, when good nature and sweet temper were discovered to enter largely into the composition of the amulet, and tugged at something in her pocket.

"Was it like this — do you think?" she asked, at last extricating from its close quarters a rusty-looking daguerreotype case.

"Not much!" I replied, and carelessly undid the fastening.

My head whirled madly for an instant; then I strained my dizzy sight to look again at the picture, which was a likeness of Harry — one I had never seen until now.

"Where did you get this?" I inquired, when I could speak.

"Cousin Agatha lent me a big box of ribbons, and feathers, and flowers to play with, and this was at the bottom. I put it into my pocket to take very good care of it, and forgot all about it."

"I will give it back to her when she awakes," said I.

Carrie sat upon my knees until she was sleepy. She is easily wearied in her weak state. I laid her upon my bed, and waited to see the heavy lids close fast. Then I sought Agatha. She was still stretched upon the lounge in her room, her eyes velvety black and her complexion fresh after her siesta.

"Don't think me the chief of sluggards!" she pleaded,

coaxingly. "But I did work dreadfully hard this forenoon, and I thought I had earned a right to 'laze' a tiny bit."

"Carrie found this in the box you gave her to play with," I said, laying the daguerreotype upon the stand by her.

Somehow, I could not give it into her hand.

"Ah!" with a scared glance at me when she saw what it was. "I did not know it was in there."

"So I supposed!" I replied, and turned to go out.

"Stop a moment!" she entreated. "Please sit down. You do not feel badly because I have kept that picture — do you?"

I was unwilling to confess that I *had* felt unpleasantly at the thought of its being in her possession; that she was not the custodian I should have chosen for the precious relic. I evaded her question.

"Why should I object? You were acquainted with the original before I was. You have a right to preserve such a memento of a friend if you wish to do so."

"But your secret thought is, that I, the affianced wife of one man, should not wish to keep the likeness of another. Speak out plainly! We have had a surfeit of partial confidences. They are childish and nonsensical."

I was displeased at her petulance, and my countenance showed it, although I said nothing.

"Now you are angry!" She pulled me down to the seat at her side. "I am the most unfortunate being alive! When I am reserved, I am suspected of 'treason, stratagem, and spoils.' When I utter my whole mind, I rupture where I would conciliate; alienate those whose love I long to gain. Do not go away under a false impression of Harry or of me. He was far more faithful to you than it is in the nature of most men to be."

"I do not understand what you mean by that!" I said. "If it is to assure me that he was true to me in thought, word, and act, from the hour he first loved me until his death, I know it already, better than any one else can tell me."

She scanned me with a singular expression — the same I had

noticed one night, more than a year since, when she came to my room to inquire what was my decision after learning that Harry was in the Federal army — a significant compassion that aroused me now, as it did then, to quick resentment.

"I ask no confirmation of this!" I repeated. "Nor would I credit the denial of it were my own mother to offer it!"

"Be still, my dear child!" she said softly — a cooing voice that caressed my ear even while I would have shrunk from her blandishments. "You are tilting with images of your own making. No one wants to cast discredit upon poor Harry's constancy to you — least of all, I, who was the first confidante of his growing attachment. You could have no better proof that all loverly passages were entirely over with us than his seeking me with the story of his later affection. Our engagement was a youthful weakness, the folly of which we both appreciated, before he transferred his addresses to you. I was poor, and he ambitious, and hoping to be rich. I told him this frankly when I asked a dissolution of this compact; and although he made a decent feint of opposition, I could see that my reasoning was not lost. He loved you very dearly. Never doubt it if it comforts you."

I was changed into stone as the poisonous words trickled into my ear. I could not leave her without a clear comprehension of the thing she hinted at, which she took for granted was a familiar tale to me.

"I had understood from you, as from Mr. Wilton, that you were friends — nothing more," I said mechanically.

"We were friends, dear, when he sued for your hand. But Harry was in fault if he did not tell you that he had loved me, or fancied he did, in his younger days. Perfect confidence in such affairs is the only foundation for perfect happiness. Before I engaged myself to your brother, I revealed to him every particular connected with this prior attachment. It was my duty to speak, and his right to hear of it. Harry erred in not treating you with equal candor."

"He had some excellent reason for the reserve," I said, more and more bewildered by her air of quiet assurance.

"Unquestionably! He was a man of singular discretion. I would not have reverted to the matter at all, even to explain my possession of the portrait, had I not believed that you knew all about it. He gave me the picture during our betrothal, and he would never take it back. I made a final effort to surrender it one evening just previous to his leaving Virginia. You may recollect, he wrote to you of his intention to go north, and left the note at Mrs. Dana's door for you. I had been out with Rolf Kingston, and we came up just as Harry turned away from the steps. He asked me to walk with him. He had something important to communicate. You know I told you next day that I had heard a rumor of his intended departure the preceding night. I was greatly concerned at the announcement, and did not try to conceal my regret. He saw my emotion, and misinterpreted it. His own heart was very full, and he said much that he would have scrupled to utter in a calmer moment. I was shocked and pained, and answered hastily. He grew warm, and so did I; and in brief, my dear, we had a very ridiculous scene! Poor, dear Harry! It grieves me whenever I reflect that my last interview with him was marked by bickerings and recriminations. His was a generous nature, and he repented himself of his unreasonable conduct when he recovered his senses. Here is the note he left with you for me. The excitement and the tearful night that ensued upon this quarrel with my old and cherished friend had induced a frightful attack of neuralgia, which confined me to my room. Moreover, I doubted the expediency of seeing him again. It was best for both of us that we should not meet just then. I have treasured the note of apology as a token that he did me justice in the end; that he did not bear away with him the heartburnings he had expressed upon that unhappy evening. I wish you would read it. You will see that it does credit to his cooler judgment and his warm heart."

She slipped the paper between my fingers. My eyes rested

upon it; my mind strove to receive the meaning of the characters — the import of the sentences. But in the review I see
that I was incapable of comprehending anything clearly. The
note was very kind, and, as she had described it, apologetic.
He was " disappointed and shocked " by what had passed at their
last meeting. " But since it *is* past, let it be forgotten by us
both. Life is too short, and real friends are too few, for us to
nurse unkind remembrances of those in whose fidelity we can
have faith." Then he alluded to " dear and lovely reminiscences of their intercourse ; " assured her of a continuance of
his " affectionate interest " in her, and prayed that she might
" be blessed with an abundance of Heaven's best gifts — hope,
love, happiness," and signed himself — " Faithfully, Harry
Wilton."

I could not dispute the genuineness of the note. It was the
identical envelope he had given me to be delivered with his
farewell to Agatha. I remember every incident of that last
day, as if it were but yesterday. I observed a peculiarity in
the superscription as I took the letter.

" You have written ' Agatha P. Lamar,' I said. " She
has dropped the middle name from her signature. She does
not like it."

" Ah ! " he said, indifferently, and began to talk of plans for
our correspondence — which were never realized !

His handwriting was marked, and, to me, unmistakable.
There was no space for questioning in this regard. He, and he
alone, had written these half-dozen lines, which I refolded and
laid upon the daguerreotype.

" You may have them if you wish," said Agatha, in kind
accents.

" I do not want them," I replied.

I stopped at the door with the confused idea that I must re-
iterate my trust in Harry ; defend his memory in the face of
apparent inconsistencies of profession and conduct.

" I am sorry you have told me what Mr. Wilton did not
think it best I should know. But nothing in the story I have

just listened to has altered my opinion of him in the least. I
was perplexed while you were narrating it. There is much in
it which is yet enigmatical to me. If he had lived, he would
have explained all to my satisfaction. Believing this, my faith
in his goodness, his honor, and his constancy remains firm."

This is the anchor to which I still cling in the storm of unrest
that drifts me to and fro, as I go over the strange tale I have
heard once and again, trying to separate truth from falsehood;
to reconcile Agatha's plausible statements with what I saw for
myself, and what Harry told me, and led, or suffered, me to
believe.

He loved her first and last; he would have married her had
her worldly advantages equalled mine: in the anguish of the
anticipated parting his true feelings asserted their supremacy;
he forgot his pledge to me; his ambitious dreams — everything
but the reviving glow of his old passion for her. Her persistent
rejection of his addresses inflamed him to madness, which was
repented of when sober reflection returned.

This, if not what she said, is the substance of what she
meant me to believe. Opposed to her wily insinuations, direct
protestations, and formidable array of evidence, I have but my
faith in him — his character and his word. By this I will
abide until our meeting where the wicked cease from troubling.

CHAPTER XXIV.

AGATHA.

November 28.

ROAMING, like an unquiet spirit, from room to room, from hall to staircase, of this old house, — hearing the echo of my footsteps behind me in the long, dark passages and on the broad stairs, until I was afraid to look over my shoulder, lest I should encounter the gaze of goblin pursuers ; hearing the wind scream and howl without and the rain dash, in rattling sheets, against the shaking casements, — I, last night, made my way to the lower story, in quest of human society that might dispel the sense of unearthliness that bewitched me. The parlor door was unlatched, and a slender stream of red light lay athwart the oaken floor of the hall. I heard a low, murmuring sound within the room, and pushed the door noiselessly a little farther back, that I might reconnoitre. I was never backward in improving such advantages. Now, I am ceaselessly upon the watch, for my next step may be upon a murderous torpedo.

There was no one in the great parlor except Elinor, and she was wandering up and down, talking to herself, or reciting in a low, sad monotone, it gave one the horrors to hear. She wears black still, and her dress, being of some soft woollen material, made no rustle as she walked, — only trailed upon the carpet in gloomy folds, precisely after the fashion of the figures of Grief one sees upon tombs, — these cowled women, who hang their heads like bulrushes, and hug funereal urns to their lacerated bosoms. Cold comfort — I should say !

This animated statuette of Melancholy had her arms crossed in true gravestone style ; head slightly depressed, and eyelids

29

drooping. The fire was bright, but unsteady, and the leaping flashes gave me uncertain glimpses of her features. She was repeating Longfellow's " Rainy Day."

> " The day is cold, and dark, and dreary;
> It rains, and the wind is never weary;
> The vine still clings to the mouldering wall,
> But at every gust the dead leaves fall,
> > And the day is dark and dreary.
>
> " My life is cold, and dark, and dreary;
> It rains, and the wind is never weary;
> My thoughts still cling to the mouldering Past,
> But the hopes of youth fall thick in the blast,
> > And the day is dark and dreary.
>
> " Be still, sad heart! and cease repining;
> Behind the clouds is the sun still shining;
> Thy fate is the common fate of all;
> Into each life some rain must fall,
> > Some days must be dark and dreary."

Miss Elinor seemed to find a deal of consolation in saying over this commonplace trifle; but to my notion, the comfort contained in the closing verse is of the same description as that of the funereal urns spoken of just now. If my neighbor comes to grief — or, as the poet has it, if rain falls into his life, is that any reason why I should be more willing to take a drenching? It doesn't satisfy me — it never did — to know that I am no worse off than other people. I don't want to be so badly off, by a great deal. I should like to be richer, and handsomer, and happier than all my acquaintances put together. If there is one small annoyance more hateful to me than another, it is to be told — when I am in pain of body or mind — all sorts of tiresome stories of how others have suffered from a like cause. As if I cared a snap if the rest of the world went supperless to bed, provided I was well served! "Misery loves company," is an adage old enough to be more true; whereas, the fact is, that thoroughly miserable people are so wrapped up in the contemplation of their own pet woes as not to cast a thought to the grievances of others. And so with the pretty figure of the sun still shining behind the clouds. I like better that deliciously savage snarl of the old rhymester —

> " If she be not fair for me,
> What care I how fair she be ? "

Do I walk any more contentedly and safely on a pitchy dark night for the reflection that the Chinese are warding off the sunlight from their yellow complexions with their bamboo umbrellas? I call such stanzas as these, balderdash — worse for all mental nutritive and medicinal purposes than sawdust pudding for the sustenance of the body.

It fretted me, therefore, to see the pained look pass from the girl's face, and one of mournful serenity settle upon it; to note that her fingers no longer chafed one another in nervous distress; to hear her commence softly, but more distinctly, another poem, the wind and rain beating time to the rhythmic measure.

> " Angel of Patience, sent to calm
> Our feverish brows with cooling palm;
> To lay the storms of hope and fear,
> And reconcile Life's smile and tear;
> The throbs of wounded pride to still,
> And make our own our Father's will!

> " O, thou who mournest on thy way,
> With longings for the close of day !
> He walks with thee, that angel kind,
> And gently whispers, ' Be resigned;
> Bear up, bear on : the end shall tell,
> The dear Lord doeth all things well!' "

It was a strangely pleasant picture. Her countenance, calmed and elevated, was tinted by the ruby shine of the flame, that burned more steadily in the partial lull of the storm. The long, old-fashioned room was lined with a double row of ancestral portraits, keeping watch over the solitary dreamer. Her voice is musical, her elocution good. The tableau suited my artistic taste, and I forbore to disturb it.

Elinor surprises me daily as she gains in ripeness and stamina of character. She has borne enough within four years to kill a dozen ordinary women. There is an exceedingly fine and slender wire, of Damascene strength and elasticity, running through her nature, that defies the accumulation of sorrows heaped upon her. Bend she may, for a season, like a willow before the gale; but the inherent power of spirit and mind is not impaired. Against my will I perceive, and to myself I confess, this; yet the growth of my dislike is commensurate with that of enforced respect. It would be cowardly to retire from the field because my opponent's intellectual calibre is more nearly equal to mine than I thought when I gave the challenge.

My heart hardened — not melted — within me at the scene I have described. Leaving her to quote as many volumes of Yankee rhymes as she liked, I turned to retrace my steps to my lonely chamber, when, above the gathering fury of the tempest, I distinguished a shout at the outer gate. I peered through the hall window, and saw a lantern move over the lawn from old Will's house, remain stationary for an instant, then pass toward the stables. A sharp knock at the door followed; and fancying I had recognized the tramp upon the piazza, I turned the bolt, and admitted no less a personage than Major Kingston.

Elinor ran out of the parlor at the sound of his salutation to me.

"We are very glad to see you! Are you wet? Have you letters?" cried the impulsive innocent, unconscious, apparently, that he was holding her hand while he answered, —

"I am a little wet; but it is a trifle."

He stepped back from her, and unbuttoned his water-proof great-coat, which was dripping with rain. She watched his serious face with manifest anxiety, and when the coat was hung upon the rack, went up and laid her trembling hand upon his sleeve.

"If you bring bad news, tell me first, and quickly," she said in a half-whisper. "Mamma will be down directly."

"Always unselfish!" — smiling down at her. "I have no letters, but your father was quite well yesterday; and I have little that is new to tell your mother."

" Is this sincere ? "

" It is."

She heaved a sigh of mingled relief and disappointment, and returned to the subject of his personal comfort. While she ran off to order a fire to be kindled in his room, I was left with him in the parlor.

" You must contrive to give me an hour's conversation with her to-night," he said, hurriedly. " It is not safe to postpone decisive movements any longer."

" What has happened ? "

" Nothing as yet ; but sundry things threaten us. That fox of a Copeland is pushing his impertinent inquiries in every direction ; and what may be of more importance ——— "

My Lady interrupted us. Her demeanor was slightly discomposed ; but she welcomed the visitor cordially.

" Elinor tells me you have no letters for us, but good news of Mr. Lacy's health. When did you see him ? "

" Three days ago. I applied for admittance yesterday, but was refused."

"Ah ! " — quickly. " Why was that ? "

" In consequence of the janitor's whim, I suspect. *He* said, in obedience to orders."

" And you disbelieved him ? "

" I did, Madam. He was half-drunk, and surly as a bear. I shall go in next time, if I have to get a pass from the President himself. I was telling Miss Agatha, when you came in, of joyful intelligence which does not rest on any uncertain basis. A general exchange of prisoners is determined upon, and will be effected within a few weeks."

My Lady's eyes filled with happy tears ; but she did not speak.

" You have brought us so many such rumors ! " I complained, wearily. " This may be no more reliable than the rest."

" The Secretary of War is my authority for this one," he rejoined, quietly.

I longed to seize and throttle him until I should be assured

29 *

that this was not fiction, invented to suit his selfish ends. I
sat perfectly still instead, the blood-red tongues of fire licking
my sight into blindness, the rush and roar of the storm seeming
like the tumult of waves in which I was drowning.

Suddenly some words of my Lady's pierced the confusion.

"Will they be ordered back immediately to service?"

"The South needs them, Madam. I believe, however, the
rule usually adopted in such cases is to allow them a month's
furlough. This, I understand, is the custom in the Yankee
army. The tale is, that they want men quite as badly as we do.
But for the unfeeling policy pursued by them in opposing all
reasonable proposals of exchange, our thinned ranks would
have been refilled long ago, and the fortunes of the Confederacy
materially changed."

The major part of this remark was directed to me, my interest in the fortunes of the C. S. A. being supposed to exceed
her Ladyship's. A summons to supper superseded the necessity
of a reply.

Our meals are unfashionably early now, and very tame affairs
compared with the jovial family-parties that used to circle the
table. Mrs. Lacy and I supported the heavy end of the conver-
sational burden. Elinor was subdued, and the Major *distrait*.
His appetite was indifferent; and he toyed with his spoon or fork
when his hostess was most urbane, and I most witty. We returned to the dining-room; and thitherward marched my Lady
when the evening orders were given to her garrison, and the
nightly round made by herself and her sable factotum, old Will.
I let the Major undertake the business of ridding himself of
her. He accomplished it summarily and graciously.

"I am afraid to promise too much," he said to her; "but I
have strong hopes of being able, through the help of a nameless
friend, to smuggle in a long letter to Mr. Lacy, if you can get
one ready before to-morrow morning."

"I will write it to-night. I am very grateful for the opportunity," replied the pattern wife, thankfully.

And impatient to set about the delightful occupation, she

tarried with us for the briefest possible space compatible with
civility. The strategist's next manœuvre was to send me to the
piano. I attacked a grand sonata, and tore it to atoms, playing
every passage *forte* and *ad libitum* — intent only upon making a
noise that should cover the advance of my ally. Without the
rest of a half-bar, I dashed off into a march, then essayed a
polka — a mad, rollicking thing — then let my fingers follow
the improvisation of my thoughts. It was raining in torrents;
the wind was shrieking and groaning like a legion of evil spirits.
But, in spite of piano-thunder and the turmoil of the elements,
I did not once lose the sound of the low voices at the farther
end of the room.

I had queer sensations while going through the easy part
assigned me in this act of the drama I had helped put upon the
stage. I thought of another rainy Autumn night, when other
lips had pleaded with me as Rolf's were pleading now with her
he had loved so long and desperately; of battle-grounds, and
burial-trenches, and prison-pens, with slow starvation lying in
ghastly ambush for those who had escaped the more merciful
sword; of manly forms and faces changing into the similitude
of skeletons and grinning skulls, incrusted with dank fungi,
while yet a feeble glimmer of animal life remained in the poor
carcasses; of the doomed girl's love for her slain betrothed, and
the filial piety that would eventually triumph over this devotion
to a bodiless memory; of the imprisoned father, and the sons
who would shortly be liberated; of their return, their indignation at the licensed persecution of their parent, their eager hunt
for the accessories to his downfall; of Lynn's rapturous greet-
ings, and his possible insistence upon a speedy marriage — all
these varied and apparently incongruous images passed in pano-
ramic march before me, while my tireless hands swept the keys
in majestic or fantastic movement, unheeded by myself, still less
by the absorbed pair at the fireside.

Rolf was the speaker for many minutes, interrupted frequently, by and by, by exclamations that had usually in them a
tone of pain, always of expostulation. After a pause ensued a

rapid flow of entreaty, argument, dissuasive reasonings — I judged only by the intonations; but these were most expressive — to which he rendered reply in a few strong sentences. Another pause, and Elinor again ended it. This time I caught a word here and there — twice a clause made up of several words — pointed sharply by anger or amazement.

"When I tell you I have no heart to give ——" and "You do not know what you ask."

Did he not? Had he perilled honor, reputation, maybe his life, — certainly his soul, — to secure the consummation of an idle dream? When the cup containing the coveted pearl — happiness — should be held to his lips, would he find the draught but seething vinegar? He held his ground. There was passion, deep and concentrated, in every tone; but resolution, undaunted and inflexible, pressed closely upon it. Entreat, wheedle, scorn, as she might, it was but the breaking of the spray upon a pitiless reef. Finally the door closed, and I knew the battle was ended in one way or the other; I was still in doubt which. I played on perseveringly, while Rolf strode heavily from end to end of the parlor, champing his mustache, his brows darkly knitted, and eyes bent downward. I would not interrupt his lucubrations, and at last he came to a standstill.

"For Heaven's sake, stop that hateful jingle!" he said, roughly. "It drives me distracted."

"Very well," I responded, obligingly, breaking off in the middle of a strain. "You asked me to play. Are you sure it is the music that distracts you?"

He made no reply until he had traversed his "beat" twice more.

"I wish I could leave her alone!" he burst forth, impetuously. "I feel like a murderer when I think of the wild, startled look of her eyes as I repeated the story I have been getting ready these two years."

"Why don't you 'let her alone,' then?" I asked, artfully careless.

"Because I have vowed to win her; because I worship her more madly this hour than I ever did before; because in less than two months she will be my wife."

"She has said so — has she?"

"No; but I have made her see that the happiness and comfort of her parents depend upon her doing this. I have told her what meshes are closing about her father; that his estate is already marked for confiscation, and fearful odds arrayed against his life. I have represented to her my relationship to certain great powers behind the throne, and the certainty that these will not suffer ignominy to fall upon one connected, however remotely, with themselves. I have engaged to purchase Sunnybank and the appurtenances thereof of the Government, should it be seized, and to settle it upon herself, — her parents and sister still to reside here, — until her father or brothers can buy it back. She loves the old homestead. It would kill her mother to leave it, and she loves her mother better than she does herself."

"Or you?" I interposed, mockingly.

He frowned yet more grimly.

"Be it so. But she does not dislike me. She owns that she has no dearer friend than I have grown to be. She may — she must — learn to love me in time. I will so adore and cherish her, that she cannot help it. Bad as I am, I would not marry her if I did not hope to make her happy in the end."

I sneered openly.

"Your scruples are late in their development. You have led her through a deal of trouble in order to secure her ultimate felicity."

I took a perverse delight in aggravating his tortures. He turned upon me as I expected he would.

"And *you* have studied to promote her happiness — haven't you?"

"Never, to my knowledge. On the contrary, finding that she stood in the path to mine, I have ridden her down without compunction. My revenge has been more consistent than your love. But a truce to quarrelling. What did she say to the neat little fiction you rehearsed to me just now?"

" Don't ask me."

He whirled on his heel, and tramped off to the other extremity of the apartment. I sat by the fire, smiling to myself in complacent superiority to this overgrown school-boy, who was ready to relinquish the prize he had toiled and panted to gain, because, forsooth, a terrified girl had turned up her eyes at him, as any other hunted thing might have done if driven into a corner.

" What an infernal hubbub the wind and rain keep up!" he said, pettishly, returning to the hearth, and stooping to warm his fingers before the scarlet blaze. He looked white and sick, and not in the least like a confident lover.

" This is a brutal business," he resumed, finding I did not respond to his complaint of the weather. "I am not devoid of feeling and conscience —— "

" Indeed!" I said, incredulously. " Now, I am."

" I believe you. You have no more pity for the sufferings of one of your own sex — an innocent, lovely girl, who has ever treated you with affectionate kindness — than if you were a graven image. Yet you look like a living woman."

" It is said to be wise policy to praise, not revile, the bridge that carries one safely over," I answered, in perfect good humor. " And, although our formal partnership no longer exists, I am still willing to aid you in gaining our common purpose. I am glad, for the sake of our success, that I am a woman. Were we both men, our soft hearts would be our ruin. Be sensible for once, Rolf, and tell me what she said, and what is to be your next move."

" She has asked for a week in which to consider my proposal."

" She who hesitates is lost," I quoted, encouragingly. " Well?"

" She stipulates that her mother is to know nothing of the dangers which threaten her father and the estate."

"Better still," said I, seeing I must coax every sentence out of his mouth. "I always thought she would some day display a wondrous genius for self-sacrifice. You see, she means to practise extravagance of generosity — not only to immolate herself upon the altar of filial duty, but to conceal this act of extreme self-denial from her parents. You could ask nothing more propitious. You will be received into the family without scruple, enjoy the position of a son-in-law freely elected by your divinity, instead of—— "

A gesture stopped me.

I ought to have felt sorry for him; for he was really undergoing an agony of conscientious visitation. The probability is, that, if any other woman except Elinor Lacy had been the object of his love and the cause of his agony, I should have been moved. As it was, I rather enjoyed the spectacle, and despised him all the while. The storm had reached its height. One might have believed that the ghosts of the quaint old ancestors staring at us from the wall were yelling outside — trying to get at us, and tear us limb from limb, for plotting against one of the chosen race; and that Uncle Kohlebörn — Undine's uncomfortable relative — had been pressed into their service, so heavy were the torrents dashed upon roof and shutters

I broke the silence with another query.

"Is it true that there is to be a general exchange of prisoners, or did you improvise the story to suit your own ends?"

"I repeated what was told me, and I believe it."

"Then — " I began, slowly.

He caught me up. "Then we had best lose no time. Brothers have a voice in settling the question of a favorite sister's marriage. Should they advocate my pretensions, what say you to a double wedding?"

His disagreeable smile was more hateful than his surliness had been.

"I have nothing to say in the matter, — being a woman!"

Then I got up, and went away to my chamber to recover my temper — a work of time, with the wind growling around my

end room, and the rain washing between the sashes, and
my nerves all out of tune.

My Lady was in the parlor when I returned. She looked
severely at me.

"I found Major Kingston with no company besides the fire
and his thoughts!"

"He could not complain of the lack of brilliant society then,
Madam!" I retorted, gayly. "I ran up stairs to look for a
paper I had put away to show him, but I could not find it. I
will hunt it up before your next visit. When are we to expect
you?"

"I hope to be in the neighborhood again in about a week. I
must ride early to-morrow morning, Madam, setting off at sunrise. I shall breakfast at my brother's. Is your letter ready?"

She produced the envelope directed, but not sealed. He
closed it.

"Smuggled letters are not examined," he smiled. "I like
to cut red tape whenever I can without chance of detection.
Please present my farewell regards to Miss Elinor!"

He shook hands with us, said, "Good night," and "Good
by," and bowed himself gracefully out of the room.

"He is one of the handsomest men I ever saw!" said my
Lady, approvingly. I responded with sisterly readiness, adding
an encomium upon his mental and moral worth that would have
electrified the subject of it, had he been at the keyhole. We
chatted a few moments longer, in delightful accord, of his numerous kindnesses to Mr. Lacy and ourselves; his high repute
in the army, the affection between himself and Lynn, etc. My
Lady is not the victim of blind prejudice. If I had not overheard Colonel Copeland's disparaging insinuations touching
Rolf and myself, I should never have surmised from her language
and demeanor that they had been made. Her manner, last
night, was very friendly, and I took a bold, unauthorized leap.

"Poor Rolf!" I said. "This waste of one's most precious
affections is a sad thing. I cannot persuade him that his years
of steady devotion are thrown away. I have imagined, some

times, myself, of late, that he might yet be rewarded by the attainment of that which he covets most fondly."

"He is not in love with Elinor still — is he?" blurted out my Lady, in undignified astonishment. "I hoped that was over and forgotten!"

"So did I !" I responded. "He says his love has never wavered for a second. It is a rare case. One's first passion is seldom the choice of his, or her more mature judgment," — smiling and coloring as I avoided her eye.

The adroit hint that complimented her son may or may not have passed unnoticed. She seemed absorbed in another thought.

"I am grieved to hear this — sadly grieved! On his account, more than on hers!"

This was the woman whose clearness of perception people extol as almost superhuman! A she-bear's instinct of danger overhanging her cubs would have been a safer guide than her boasted reason and knowledge of the world.

"Do you think his a hopeless case?" I asked, pityingly.

"Elinor will never marry!"

I smothered the glee that tempted me to clap my hands and shout with laughter.

"Yet she could be very happy with Rolf!" I said. "He comported himself nobly under her refusal, and while he believed her to be betrothed to another. We could not blame him, were he to renew his suit now. His conduct has been delicate and honorable."

"It has! I esteem him too truly to have him subjected to another dismissal, and she will never accept him."

"A girl's heart is a deceitful thing!" I ventured. "I have fancied recently, as I said, that hers was inclining toward him. I have great faith in 'the expulsive power of a new affection.' I long earnestly to see Elinor happy, as she deserves to be."

My Lady was thoughtful. My fervent manner and speech were working out their effect.

"It may be as you say," she remarked, at length, rising to

30

retire.. "But I think you are mistaken. I can hardly have been so far wrong in my judgment of my own child."

"It is the nature of youth to forget past sorrows," I observed, deprecatingly. "My dear Mrs. Lacy, you would not have this otherwise!"

"I would not! But Elinor's is not an ordinary nature."

I chuckled inwardly in bidding her "good night." She may alter the judgment she vaunted so pragmatically ere the week is completed. Rolf owes me another excellent turn — as does Elinor, although I am not likely to receive the thanks of either for the service. I have not convinced my Lady. But I have broken the ice — made her daughter's interesting revelation more easy of delivery, and more intelligible to the parent.

Elinor looks badly to-day. Her complexion is livid; her eyes heavy and lustreless. In reply to Mamma's solicitude, she pleads headache. I think sometimes that women's heads never do them half the service in any other way that they do by aching. The malady is a plea, the convenience of which is not lessened by frequent use, and one which everybody is bound to credit, while everybody is aware, that, in nine cases out of ten, it is a subterfuge that would be contemptible were it not in universal practice among our sex. My Lady watches over her offspring as a mother-bird might tend her wounded nursling. Perhaps slumbering instinct has awakened. Will it warn her not to open her arms to her fascinating son-in-law, to probe with exceeding nicety the inner recesses of her daughter's heart when she declares her intention of putting off the weeds of widowhood for bridal robes?

CHAPTER XXV.

ELINOR.

December 6.

' I WOULD count nothing a sacrifice which would purchase his release or acquittal!" said Mamma to me, this morning, in the course of one of our long talks about Papa. "This silence is wearing away my life! And I am helpless! bound, hand and foot — when, if the loss of my right hand and right eye would restore him to his home, I would cut off the one and pluck out the other!"

She has practised self-control in our sight so long and so successfully, that when her strong, earnest nature finds vent in words, it startles and impresses me as some great convulsion of Nature might do. I sat transfixed — gazing at the dreariness of longing in her eyes, the quivering nostril and tightening lips; and the conviction of my shameful selfishness flashed upon me with a vividness that appalled me. I — if what I had been told were true — I could end this living death — could give her back the husband she worships, restore to him home, wife, children, liberty. And I had hung back! had accounted the act which is the necessary preface to these glorious results a sacrifice too costly, a deed too irksome, for the weak spirit to meditate!

On my way across the hall from her room to mine, I met a servant with a letter from Rolf. He is at his brother's, and he wrote to ask when he might come to me. I answered at the bottom of the page, "To-morrow morning at ten o'clock," and returned the letter to the bearer.

So, I know when my fate will be sealed — how long it will

be lawful for me to linger lovingly upon the memories of my
dead Past; for how long a time I may still think of myself as
Harry's widow.   I have reviewed, to-night, those portions of
my Journal which chronicle the earliest days of our betrothal.
His portrait looked up at me from every leaf.   After to-morrow, I may not allow myself this sweet yet sad indulgence.   I
read there, among other girlish musings, a dissertation upon a
nun's life, springing out of a playful remark of Agatha's in
which she called me "little nun."   In the wiser meditations
of the care-weary woman, I could ask no happier destiny now,
than to be permitted to live single for the rest of my days, de-
voting my thoughts and energies to the service of the parents
to whom I owe everything of earthly weal that mortals can
secure.   Harry's picture lies by me, and near it the faded, blackened sprig of orange-flowers over which we plighted our troth.

"I shall never give you up till you send this back to me!"
he said.

I know that the companion-spray was crimsoned by the blood
that welled out with his heart's last sigh; that, if in that swift
passage from Time to Eternity, he had space for a thought of
the world he was leaving, my name arose to his lips with the
red tide.   I can never "send this back."   But, to-night, I shall
seal it up with his likeness and his few precious letters, and put
them away to be burned upon my marriage-day.   My marriage
— and with another than Harry!   I do not writhe in keen
anguish at the suggestion.   I am amazed at my coherence of
thought and firmness of purpose.   But for the dull misery far
down in my heart, I might beguile myself into the belief that
much weighing of the possibility, and latterly the certainty of
the event, had divested it of the power to terrify.   The finer
nerves of my spirit are numbed.   Is this exaltation above self,
or is it apathy?   Had Harry lived, my first duty would have
been to him.   Next, and now chief of all earthly obligations,
come those to my parents.   Secondary only to these stands my
debt of gratitude to him, who, since the captivity of my brothers, has been son and brother to parents and to daughter; who

has befriended us through evil report steadfastly as when we basked in the noontide of prosperity; who has endangered his own reputation in the eyes of his compeers by his efforts in behalf of a proscribed family; who prays now to link his fortunes with ours, earnestly as if honor and advancement to him were to be the consequence of the union.

Can I err with these considerations spread out fairly before me? Could my path have been defined more plainly had an audible voice from Heaven proclaimed to me, "Walk in it"? In my happier days I could not have wrought upon my inclinations to consent to this course — but in the shadow of the "needed cloud," resolution has strengthened into might of will — inclination waxed feeble. It is best so. "GOD always gives us light enough to see the next step." I discern mine beyond the peradventure of mistake. I am thankful I do not lack the strength to take it.

December 8.

Rolf's furlough was short. He left us this morning to rejoin his regiment. He brought us a pencilled note from Papa, secretly conveyed outside the prison by one of the turnkeys. He is brave and hopeful still. Nothing man can do, can daunt him, for his "heart is fixed."

Before going, Rolf had a conversation with Mamma. It was his wish and mine that he should impart to her the news of our engagement. She was less surprised than I had anticipated, and this has made it easier and more pleasant for me. She is ignorant — so we arranged it should be — of any benefit which is likely to accrue to herself from this alliance. Had she suspected the truth in this regard, her interview with me would have been marked by searching questions I would have found it difficult to parry, her consent to Rolf been less promptly given. To me, and I doubt not to him, she was kind and affectionate. She spoke of her love, gratitude, and respect for our new protector — not a new one, either — although but now formally acknowledged in his true character.

30 *

"He has won us all, it seems!" she said, smiling; and then followed a sigh.

I hastened to remind her that I was not to leave her — that the dear old roof-tree would still shelter us all, one family. I told her, moreover, that Rolf was sanguine of Papa's acquittal and return to us ere long. I did not attempt gayety; but there was no occasion for me to feign tranquillity.

"You are entirely satisfied, then, love?" asked Mamma, putting away the hair from my forehead — Papa's own gesture — and reading my eyes with hers — deep, loving, penetrating.

"Quite content," I answered. "And when Papa is restored to us, I shall be very happy. Rolf is thoroughly good and faithful, Mamma. He deserves all I can do to promote *his* happiness."

"He is all that you say, dear child; but he should not have my Brownie if she did not love him — did not elect him of her own free will and accord to the master's place in her heart."

"Never fear," I said, stoutly. "He knows what his standing is; and if he desires no higher, no one else has a right to complain."

She smiled again, and released me. Yet I had a passing fear that she was not altogether convinced of my sincerity. I have detected her watching me many times since with loving anxiety; and on these occasions I have studied to assume a calm, pleasant demeanor, to talk freely with those about me, — above all, not to yield to abstraction. I am not depressed. There is more room for thankfulness than for sadness in my heart, although I am of necessity thoughtful. Rolf has behaved nobly throughout the affair. His bearing to myself, in private and in the presence of others, was characterized by respect and delicacy that enhanced my regard for him. He made no demands upon my affection, he said, beyond what I could freely render. He but asked the privilege of teaching me to care for him as he would have me do. In all his sketched arrangements for the future we are to share was visible the same thoughtful attention to my tastes, my wishes, my comfort, and that of those I love.

We are to be married early in January. Mamma was startled at the early date; but Rolf says, with reason, that these are not the days for needless formalities, for conventional delays. He pleaded to her the uncertainties of a soldier's life; the chances that he may be ordered away, perhaps out of the state, and be unable to return for many months; and, lastly, the years during which he has loved and waited for me. To me, he spoke of our unprotected situation, and the guard his name would be when we should be visited by Confederate troops. However unfavorably they might regard Mamma, as the wife of one notoriously unfriendly to their cause, they would treat her with all respect as the mother-in-law of one of their own officers. I acquiesced passively in his reasoning. Thirty days, or thirty years, cannot remove the past farther beyond the reach of hope than it is to-day. It is well that I should, by one irrevocable act, make the backward glance impossible, because criminal. I have shut the door very firmly: this will bar it forever. I have few preparations to make. Rolf hinted at a needful trip to town; but the thought was so repugnant to me, that Mamma has written to Aunt Dana to make such purchases as she deems necessary. I must lay off my mourning garments so soon as I can procure others.

I spoke of this, last evening, to Rolf, as we were strolling in the yard.

"For the present," I said, "I have nothing else to wear."

"Do as you think best," he answered. "I can never love you better in any other dress than I do in that you have on this moment."

We were passing the holly-hedge as he spoke, and he plucked several clusters of the leaves and berries, which he brought into the house. With silk from my work-basket, he bound these into a chaplet, and laid it upon my head.

"It is an emblem of the love that glows most freshly in the

winter of adversity," he said, playfully, leading me up to the mirror.

For the sake of this thought, I let the wreath lie where he had put it, and tried to forget that the sight of the sharp leaves and the red drops had put me in mind of a crown of thorns.

I sent a letter to Papa, telling him of the new life appointed me, and asking his blessing upon it. It will not be withheld. His affection for me had never a tinge of selfishness. I would remember this.

CHAPTER XXVI.

AGATHA.

January 1, 1865.

THOSE who associate bridals with orange-wreaths, white satin, Brussels lace, and trunks full of embroidered, braided, and tucked *lingerie*, would stare aghast at the modest outfit which now engages the fingers of the feminine portion of the household.

About the middle of December, there arrived from Richmond, in charge of a military escort detailed by Major Kingston, a box of dry-goods, selected by Mrs. Dana from the very insufficient supplies of the Richmond stores.

"Fortunately," wrote Mrs. Dana, "a blockade-runner passed the Yankees safely the other day with a cargo of foreign goods; and happening to hear of the arrival within a few hours after they reached the city, I hastened down town to secure an early choice of the valuable articles. But for this opportune event, Nellie would have had a scanty *trousseau*."

It was curious and instructive to read the list of prices accompanying the case of haberdashery. For instance: One piece cotton cloth for under-clothing, containing thirty-seven yards, one thousand dollars; two pairs gaiters, one hundred and forty apiece; one dozen white cotton stockings, two hundred and fifty; one calico dress-pattern, three hundred; one *de laine*, four hundred and fifty; and so on. There was a pleasurable excitement in tumbling over new goods, however inferior in quality to what we should have thought fit for our wear in the corrupt former times; and while my Lady and I dragged them out, fingered and discussed them, enjoying as a favorite perfume of those olden days the peculiar odor of fresh, unhandled fabrics, a ring of ebony faces surrounded the box and us, at a respectful distance, agape with delighted curiosity.

"I had no especial *trousseau*," said my Lady, retrospectively. "I was married upon forty-eight hours' notice."

"That accounts for your consent to the brevity of this en-·gagement," I replied. "Long betrothals are an invention of the enemy of human happiness."

"I have known some that terminated happily; but the proportion of these to the whole number is not large," was the reply—an incautious one, for Elinor's head went lower and lower over a box of handkerchiefs she was counting.

My Lady, too, observed and felt this the next second; but it could not be mended. In her consistent habit of thrusting sly pins into me at every turn, she·had touched her darling's sore; and I was woman enough to relish the accident. This is the solitary occasion upon which I have marked any evidence of sensitiveness in Elinor on the score of her former ill-starred betrothal. Yet I scrutinize her narrowly. Whether chatting with her mother and myself as we ply our needles by the fire-side from morn till eve, from eve until our country bed-time, or assisting in the simple domestic duties that devolve upon the ladies of the family, or hearing Carrie's lessons, or reading her lover's tri-weekly epistles, she carries the same serene front. Her voice does not waver a semitone toward a pensive key. She does not shrink from allusions to the approaching nuptials, or hesitate to join in the praises of the gallant bridegroom as chanted by the conclave of maids, and less boisterously by their mistress and her white bondwoman. Even the great, sad eyes are no more dreamy; neither are they restless. They survey the coming fate with steadiness born of invincible resolve. In a monosyllable, she is "game." In the very far back times, concerning which Solomon was at least half right in pronouncing them to be no better than these, they used to manufacture martyrs out of such stuff as this whilom spoiled baby is showing herself to be made of. I find myself softening perceptibly from the rigor of my hate, the acerbity of my spite. When she is once Mrs. Kingston, I expect to grow positively sisterly in my sentiments and behavior. Why shouldn't I? Isn't she going to do the identical thing I have meant she should since I discovered Rolf's mad, determined passion for her? and in doing it, to render herself miserable as my best — by best meaning most energetic — wishes in her behalf could have made her, had each been accomplished fast as it was conceived? What more could an unreasonable rival want? And I am rational to a proverb.

We had one funny scene last week. The long parlor is the warmest and lightest room in the house at this season, and we sew there constantly without dread of being disturbed by company. It was early in the afternoon. I was hemming a ruffle, my Lady binding one skirt, and Elinor sewing up the seams of another, about one window; and Rachel, in the middle of the floor, was fairly "snowed under" by heaps of white stuff, — when enter to us, in awful parade, Mr. and Mrs. James Kingston and Miss Hetty Stratton.

The haughty Ross blood — hotter as haughtier than the Lacy — leaped to the brow of mother and daughter, aroused, I imagine, less by the tardiness of this ceremonious visit than by the insolent condescension expressed in the visages of the three. Miss Hetty frisked before the married pair, her lean arms extended like the attenuated frame of a windmill, and clasped Elinor to her very tight zone with such vehemence I listened to hear her lacings crack.

"You naughty, precious, wicked, dearest, silly, blessed darling!" she clattered, kissing the top of the brown head, that "ducked" instinctively as the salute was aimed at her lips. "And you are really converted, and are going to join the company of the elect! Don't talk to me about the age of miracles being past, as I said, not ten seconds ago, to Mary, here, if one of the Lacy tribe has come over to the right side. 'I don't despair,' said I to James, 'of seeing the father himself a good loyalist yet, if the right means are used.' You must know, my dear Mrs. Lacy, we count greatly upon our dear Rolf's influence. He is perfectly irresistible, as somebody besides his foolish Auntie has found out," — squeezing Elinor around the waist; "and whatever he sets out to do, he *will* do. I mean to make a clean breast of it, James. As I have remarked, at the lowest calculation, one million times, frankness between friends is the only safe rule. So when Rolf told us he was really, and actually, *and* truly going to be married, I said to him ——"

"Excuse me, Miss Hetty, for dissenting from your proposition," said my Lady, decidedly. "I think that candor, in many cases, is unkind and injurious to our friends and ourselves. Mrs. Kingston, will you not take this seat? It is warmer in this corner. We are having a cold winter, Mr. Kingston."

"Very," replied the relieved James, who had been casting forbidding glances at his volatile Aunt ever since she opened her mouth.

"Bitter, bitter!" cried Miss Hetty, hitching up her bony shoulders. "I can't sleep at night for thinking and weeping over our brave soldiers, lying upon the bare ground, or on heaps of prickly pine-brush, and toasting their poor, chilblainy feet by the watch-fires, while their pampered, dissolute, cowardly oppressors —— But, there! as I say with every other breath, where *is* the use of talking! I declare, as I proclaimed, openly, to our sewing-circle — our "Soldiers' Timely Relief," you know — I am ready to rob myself of my best blanket for the dear, valiant darlings' sakes! Rachel, don't clear those things away: I haven't seen a scrap of anything except homespun for so long, it does my eyes good to rest upon those pretty articles."

"Take them into the dining-room, Rachel," commanded her mistress. "Miss Hetty can examine them there. Agatha, will you go with her?"

To the dining-room we proceeded, pursuant to directions. Rachel "dumped" her load upon the table, and throwing an askant and venomous gleam at us, flounced out of the door, banging it after her.

Miss Hetty jumped almost out of her shoes at the concussion.

"I say," she whispered, "did you ever know the beat of this?"

"It is a nice article," I said, wilfully stupid, taking hold of the other end of the muslin, pinched between her thumb and forefinger as if she would nip a shred out.

"Pah! I don't mean this; although it is a fair quality, and I only wish loyal people could get half as good. If I had my way, no Yankee lover should have so much as a rag of clothing, or a pint of meal. But this match is the very oddest thing! Rolf Kingston — handsome, and rich, and distinguished — to throw himself away, when he might marry the President's daughter, if he had one old enough — which he hasn't, bless his soul! Rolf to throw himself literally away upon this traitorous little doll, that don't come up to my elbow! I say it is a scandalous shame!"

How I thought of the strained patrician blood of the lady-mother, and wished she were near enough to hear this!

"But it's no use talking to these men! If the country is saved, it will be owing to the pluck of the women — their pluck and their prayers!"

Association with the "dear fellows" has imparted an agreeable zest of slang to Miss Hetty's conversation.

"As I have remarked repeatedly to numerous ladies of my acquaintance, we have upheld the Confederacy with the points of our needles more than the men have with their bayonets."

"A bright idea!" I applauded the *bon-mot*.

"Yes, my dear — it has been universally complimented. Now, there's James Kingston, who dare not say his soul is his own, when Rolf disagrees with him. Between you and me, Rolf has made a fortune by the war. What with speculations in gold, and tobacco, and government stocks, he is ten times richer than when he went into the army; and they do say he has done the Government secret service, that gives him a hold upon it; and this, with his being nephew to one of the head men in the concern, and first cousin to another, is enough to make him a distinguished character — and yet he is about to ruin himself by a misalliance. Said I, 'James Kingston!

31

is the boy bent upon suicide? And will you stand by and see him destroy himself?' But James is poor. He has lost next to everything. All he is sure of is the money he has invested in Confederate bonds. I have put every cent I own in them — for, said I, 'What's the use of land unless you have negroes and stock to work it?' The Yankees don't leave a hoof, nor a horn, nor a woolly head behind them that they can carry off. Rolf laid his orders upon his brother, the last time he was at home, that he was to bring his wife over and play the pleased relation to Miss Brown-face. And when the trial comes off, — if I am called into court, which isn't likely, he says, — I am to 'modify my evidence.' As if I would perjure myself! But Rolf has an awful temper when his blood is up. You ought to have heard him blaze out at me when I endeavored to dissuade him in the gentlest possible manner from this fatal step! 'A good - as - convicted - and - condemned - and - who - knows - but - what - executed - for - high - treason traitor for a father-in-law!' I represented, mildly. 'Hold your vile tongue!' says he. 'I would marry Elinor Lacy, if her father had been hanged for sheep-stealing, and both her brothers transported for house-breaking! If you want me ever to own any of you again, you had better pay proper respect to her and her mother!' Such infatuation I have never conceived of! We had to effect a change of base immediately. He had flanked us by a broadside, and here we are, with conditions of truce upon our tongues and unconditional hostilities, the black flag, and no quarter, and all that, rankling in our hearts!"

"Dear me!" I said. "How uncomfortable you must be!"

This was no mere phrase of condolence, for she was obliged to settle her teeth with both thumbs, before she could articulate another syllable.

"Such a mercenary, basely interested scheme on their part!" she pursued. "To think of their playing upon his sympathy until he was beguiled into making an offer, and then catching it up, and naming the earliest possible day, for fear he might repent of his rashness! Oh! the impudence and unprincipledness of this world! And to cap the climax, the talk is now that the arch-traitor — that Benedict Iscariot and Judas Arnold, the father, will be released on parole — his trial be indefinitely postponed, which means that it may never come off. If *I* were the President's wife, he should guard the public peace better than to allow such iniquity to walk rampart" (rampant?) " through the land."

" What a pity you are not! " I returned. " I have not had a chance until now to thank you for not mentioning my name at the trial."

" I had my orders, child! Rolf ordered me — at least fifty times not to let it slip that I had ever opened my lips to you about the spy. He said it would make my testimony worthless, if I did."

She is more vain of her appearance in court, and the evidence there given in, than of any other event in her life.

" I couldn't begin to repeat the compliments that have been passed upon my conduct on that ever-memorable day. A friend of mine told me that General B—— remarked privately to some one near him, ' That woman is a second Charlotte Bronté!' (Corday?) ' If I had an army like her, I would besiege Washington in three days — sue for an armistice in a month! ' "

" How people lie! " I said, indignantly. " The story going the rounds is that, at the last Yankee raid, you crawled into a cuddy-hole in the garret, and staid there until they had gone; that you had to leave your hoop-skirt outside, and they carried it off at the head of the column as a trophy, elevated upon a bean-pole! "

She grew so angry I was convinced the tale had a truthful foundation.

" How any accountable human being can wilfully defame an innocent neighbor, is too mysteriously wicked for me to comprehend. It's a dreadful sin to take away one's character. But if slanderers and gossips don't get paid off here, they will be come up with hereafter. That's a consolation! "

" It must be to *you !* " with commendable gravity. " Hadn't we better go back to the parlor now? "

" Wait a minute ! "

She fell to work, pulling over the half-made garments, examining, criticising, and questioning. In the midst of this, Rachel reëntered, thinking, doubtless, that we had finished our inspection. Miss Hetty attacked her forthwith.

" Well, Rachel ! what do you say to *this* notion of your young mistress? "

" All Miss Elinor's notions are good ones ! " answered the woman, shortly, folding up the scattered clothing.

" But you were so fond of her old beau — and you are such terrible Unionists here — it can't be pleasant to you to have her marry a Confederate officer."

" She wouldn't do nothing that wasn't right ! If she's satisfied, we ain't got never a word to say."

" You don't object to Major Kingston as a master, then? "

Rachel dropped the gown she was busy with, and crossed her arms.

" *My* master's name is Lacy, and the 'Federates has locked him up in prison because he was upright and eschewed evil. The old Satan got holt of Job the same way. But I belong to Mr. Lacy and his'n. When he tells me to call another man ' Master,' I will do it — not till then ! "

" But don't you know, you stupid thing ! that if they prove him to be a traitor, you and everything else belonging to him will go to the Government? " Miss Hetty lost the last spark of discretion in her wrath at the servant's unexpected rejoinder. " You won't have the choice then, of a master."

" Maybe not. The wicked walk on every side when the vilest men are exalted. The servant is not greater than her master," rejoined Rachel, unmoved. " When that day comes, I belong to nobody 'cept the Lord ! "

" Which means she will run away to the Yankees ! " said Miss Hetty, as the victorious Rachel marched out again, her arms full of work. " If I were Rolf, I would never rest until the entire lot was sold off South ! "

" You talk of confiscation and a change of owners ! " I rejoined, nettled at her coarseness. " You forget the loyal sons ! "

" Who nobody believes will ever · come home again. Haven't you heard —I mean don't you know — it is the policy of the Yankees to kill the prisoners off — to starve, freeze, suffocate, poison them? This is why they are so slow about exchanging them."

" Both sides are playing at that game, if we are to credit the tales we hear of Andersonville and Salisbury," I remarked.

" They are dealing with gentlemen ! — we, with hired ruffians, low, drunken foreigners — the filth and offscouring of the earth. I would no more save a Yankee prisoner from starving than I would give a mad dog a bone to gnaw. I have a great mind to tell you — but Rolf would never forgive me — He was furious because the report had reached me, and charged me by everything that was sacred not to whisper it here ; but, as I often insist, you are not of the Lacys, if you are among them — and I have trusted you before, and if you are engaged to Lynn, that makes it all right, you know, although Rolf says the tale may be only a sensation affair, after all ; and that if it were breathed here it would nearly craze Mrs. Lacy. But as I represented to him, in the gentlest way, he is a rank fool to hope to keep it quiet long, for bad news flies fast. Ah ! well ! well ! if they are gone it was in a glorious cause, and as I shall always protest to my latest breath — it was better than to live traitors, and their country's thanks will be their epigram — "

I seized her by her lean arm. I think I shook her. I am positive I heard something bony rattle besides her teeth.

" What are you gabbling about? Can't you speak out the direct truth for once in your life? Who has gone? What have you heard?"

I was excited, and she was the color of a dingy pocket-handkerchief. I am sure she thought of Charlotte Corday in the

31 *

grasp of the *gens d'armes*, and that she would have screamed
had I not released her with a laugh.

"Hush! hush!" she said, under her breath. "Rolf will
murder me, if this get out through my indiscretion."

"You won't live to give him the chance!" I threatened, in
angry jest. "Out with it!"

"How impetuous you are, my dear!" with a sickly smile.
"Recollect — if I must indulge you — it is only a report. You
remember, that several hundred Confederate officers were
cooped up on Morris' Island, last summer or fall, — penned up
like sheep, and exposed to the fire of the Confederate batteries
— it was pretended, by the black-hearted Yankees, as a retalia-
tory measure for our putting two or three of their trumpery
Generals under fire in Charleston."

"Yes — but nobody was injured in either case. It was
mere foolery!"

"So some of the papers dare to say. Returned prisoners
and officers from the South tell another story. James talked,
the other day, with a man who escaped from the Island while
they were there. He says they were fed for forty days upon
corn-meal and pickles; were fired into by the mortars every
night; that the men caught cats and rats to eat to keep them
alive; that Ross and Lynn Lacy were among those devoted
martyrs to liberty, and that one of them was killed!"

I have strong nerves, but I staggered at this.

"Which one was named?" I faltered, when I could command my senses a little.

"Some say one — some another. This makes me say both
are dead."

"You were right to tell me this!" I said, thoughtfully.
"And wiser still to conceal it from the Lacys until the shocking news is confirmed. Now, we must really go back to the
other room!"

I led the way, smiling and self-possessed. If a breath of the
frightful intelligence reached Sunnybank, the marriage would
be postponed. I saw in this, certainly, Rolf's reason for hushing

up the story. Let him make sure of his bride, and his tenderness for the maternal sensibilities would evaporate with the dew of his marriage morning. I must stop thinking of what I had heard, lest my sober or absent mood should kindle suspicions that something was wrong.

I· dashed into the sluggish stream of conversation trickling from the lips of the Kingstons and Mrs. Lacy — Elinor sitting by, unsmiling and taciturn. I was lively and saucy to the embarrassed James, whose distaste to the projected alliance between treason and loyalty was kept under, only by his fear of his hectoring brother; was social and friendly with his insipid wife, who, like all other insipid women, can say and do a variety of spiteful things. She has exercised this talent upon all occasions when she had the opportunity to abuse and backbite the Lacys, and was itching to irk them now, in some way, but dared not wag her foolish tongue against them. In fine, I set everybody at his and her ease, and wound up the farcical visit agreeably to all parties.

Then I took myself off to the Growlery with my news, and revolved it at my leisure. The result of which operation was to beget a profound distrust in my mind of the whole narrative. I disbelieve it *in toto*. Yet, if it should be true, and Ross were the slain brother, this would in no wise affect my destiny. If Lynn — why, then, Hayridge and its appurtenances are not liable to confiscation. Am I unfeeling? Not more so than my most Christian neighbors. To Agatha Lamar I am unconventional — that is the difference betwixt me and them. There is, neither expediency nor wit in getting up sensational effects for one's private edification — particularly when there may be no cause for the exertion. I have learned one thing which this high and puissant Confederacy would do well to study; namely, not to squander my ammunition, or expend all my forces, upon an insignificant object. I have had a surfeit of wasted affections, unfounded apprehensions, useless tears, in bygone days.

Residence in this Scripture-quoting family — where, out of

the mouths of babes and slaves proceed oracles of Solomonic wisdom to answer fools according to their folly — has rubbed up my biblical lore. I have adopted, as my motto, St. Paul's capital rule, "Forgetting the things that are behind — *I press forward !*"

CHAPTER XXVII.

ELINOR.

January 12.

IT is a clear, frosty morning. My brisk little waterfall is spread over the rock below the lawn in twisted silver ribbons; the pointed crowns of the pine-grove are drawn sharply against the pale-blue sky; the smoke rises in straight columns from the village of servants' houses, and although there is not a breath of wind, I can hear the ring of axes, the pleasant confusion of happy voices from the frozen cove, between the hills, three quarters of a mile away.

The homestead is bright with sunshine, and great fires upon every hearth roar up the chimneys with a shout like the blast of a trumpet. There is a murmur of busy life in rooms and passages — much shutting of doors and echoing of footsteps, and calling from the house to the kitchen, and, once in a while, the uprising of a voice from dining-room, parlor, or chamber, in a song of praise, a " Hallelujah," or " Oh, be joyful!" Mammy, Aunt Becky, or Susan being the untaught musician. Mammy's favorite, " We are bound for the land of Canaan," seems most popular. As I write, she is bustling about the next room, getting it ready for Aunt Ellen, who is expected to-morrow; and the wild, sweet refrain breaks out at irregular intervals : —

> " We are bound for the land of Canaan,
> That bright and blessed shore;
> We are bound for the land of Canaan,
> There to part no more ! "

If the bliss of earthly reunion, after weary separation, fills the heart to overflowing, who can conceive the rapture of *that* meeting, in the full assurance of eternal companionship! Calm and brightness faintly, yet expressively, imaged by the still glory of this morning after the storm of yesterday — the piercing winds of the past night.

The darkness fell early, yet the day had hung heavily upon my hands and heart. I had not allowed myself a moment of relaxation from dawn to dusk, and the twilight found me very tired in body — cast down to the dust in spirit. For an hour before supper, the parlor is usually given up to my sole occupancy. Mammy peeped in to see that the fire burned well, readjusted the logs upon the andirons, lowered the curtains that swayed in the fierce wind, and advised me to lie down.

"You'll walk your feet off, pacing over that carpet, honey! I don't like your looks to-day. You are fairly fit to drop. It's bad for the flesh to be always lifting the heavy end of the cross!"

"Somebody must lift it, Mammy!"

"Yes, dear — but jest you ease it off upon the Lord! You couldn't overload Him, if you was to try!"

Left alone, I rested my aching head among the sofa-pillows, where my poor Lynn lay so long and cheerfully — shaded my eyes from the glare of the fire, and tried to obey her injunction. I had no power of connected thought to aid me in arraying remembered mercies and past deliverances into line of battle against fast-coming despondency and oppressing fears.

I but said, brokenly, and with tears, "I have tried to do and to bear Thy will, my Father! Grant me strength for what is to come, and let me not sink in dismay before my work is done!"

Then sleep overtook me — swiftly and completely. One moment I heard the roar of the flames in the fireplace, and the hoarse tempest battering the ancient walls until the house creaked and strained in all her joints — the next, I was a child again, playing with little Morton upon the grass in front of the door, making wreaths and chains of yellow jessamine, gathered from the vine overrunning the porch, while Mamma and Papa sat upon the steps watching us.

"Nellie is the stronger of the two!" I heard Mamma say. "The angels take pity upon the weak ones of the flock!"

Papa answered, tenderly, "Yet my baby-girl shall never dash her foot against a stone that I can remove from her path!"

As he said it, a torrent of passionate love and gratitude flooded my soul, and I broke out into loud weeping, in stretching my arms toward him.

"I would die for you, if I could, Papa!" I cried.

"I believe you, my darling!" he said, clasping me to his heart, and I felt other tears mingling with mine. "Thank GOD, there is no need for this!"

There rushed back upon my senses the roar of the fire and storm. I knew where I was, and that I had dreamed of my angel-brother; of the spring sunshine and fragrant blossoms; of infancy and Mamma's guarding care over her babes. But the strong arms enfolded me yet — there were tears falling upon my cheek, and kisses, warm and sweet, upon my lips; again a voice, tremulous with emotion, repeated, "Thank GOD!" — and oh! it was Papa's living, present self, upon whose bosom I lay!

He put his finger upon my mouth, when I would have screamed with joy.

"Mamma!" he whispered, warningly, "we must not startle her! Go to her, and say there is some one here with news of me — good news!"

I obeyed implicitly. I delivered the message without the alteration of a word — saw her face light up with sudden hope as she hurried along the hall to the door beyond which happiness awaited her; then I knelt where I stood, overwhelmed by the richness of this unexpected blessing.

Pretty soon Mamma called me. I have heard of voices full of tears. Hers was full of smiles.

"Where is Carrie?" she said, when I appeared. "She must welcome Papa!"

I rushed up stairs, and brought her down in my arms without a thought of her weight. Papa met us in the hall, and exclaimed at my imprudence, as he stooped to the child's delighted embrace.

"You must bear no more such burdens for me, dear!"

"All I can do is too little!" I answered.

I meant it honestly then. I echo the sentiment emphatically in the comparative calmness of this morning. Months of watching, waiting, and suffering were forgotten in the rapture of one hour such as we spent last night — Mamma and I on either side of him, and Carrie upon his knee, while he recounted all he knew of the circumstances of his release. This was not much. He had been waited upon by a couple' of officials, who informed him, that, in consequence of the representations and petitions of influential friends, the authorities having jurisdiction in his case, had resolved to liberate him upon his giving his parole not to communicate with the enemy, nor to quit the state until the charges against him could be fairly investigated.

"Rolf considers this equivalent to an unconditional release," said Papa. "He was waiting for me at the prison-door, having been cognizant of, and, I more than suspect, mainly instrumental in accomplishing, my deliverance.· He is a noble fellow, Nellie, and delicate as generous. He accompanied me to the gate to-night, but I could not induce him to enter, although he was drenched by the rain, which only abated about sunset. 'Your meeting should be without witnesses — however friend ly,' he insisted."

"But you have earned a right to participate in our joy!" I said.

He laughed. "If I have — which you cannot prove — I will ride over to-morrow, to receive my reward. Say to Miss Elinor — please — that this is the gift I promised her."

He wrote to me, a week ago, that he was having prepared a bridal present for me, which, he was confident, would suit my taste. And ungrateful I had never given the significant scu-tence a second thought! Can years of devotion to his interests and efforts to secure his happiness repay a service like this?

Papa resumed : —

"My momentary impulse, on hearing the message of release, was to answer as did Paul and Silas : 'They have beaten me openly, uncondemned, and cast me into prison ; and now do they thrust me out privily?' But visions of wife, children, and home arose between my eyes and my dignified exemplars, and I entered into the prescribed engagement."

"I am thankful you did!" responded Mamma. "Yet it was a cowardly method of extricating themselves from the embarrassing situation into which their folly had hurried them. We will not quarrel with the manner of your restoration, however. It is enough, and more than enough, that you are here — safe and well!"

More than enough! How often have I said it since my awakening in the dear arms that were the cradle of my helpless childhood! If I had not been reconciled before to the idea of the union, distant now but two days, Rolf's agency in procuring for us this inestimable boon must have won my consent. I have never said to him, nor to myself, that I loved him ; but my heart is very warm and full in the anticipation of his visit. If it is not love which I can guarantee him with the poor gift of my hand, the respect and affectionate gratitude that make up my regard for him, may prove a substitute worthy of his acceptance until warmer and fonder emotions shall supersede these. He deserves more — how much more, I will strive never to let him feel — than I can bring him.

The wind still raged around the house when I sought my pillow. Delicious slumber chained my thoughts and senses during the rest of the dark hours — such sleep as an exhausted child enjoys in his crib beside his mother's bed — clinging to that mother's hand. I did not dream of him again, but the perception of Papa's presence under the same roof with me abode with me until the keen rays of an unclouded sun awoke me. It was fitting that the world should be bright ; that Sunnybank should wear her gayest aspect to greet her returned lord. In consequence of the inclement weather, Papa did not summon the servants in to prayers last night. This morning, he rang the bell himself, and stood at the upper end of the room, — his arm resting upon the mantel, his Bible in his hand, his old place and old attitude, — surveying the familiar forms as they quietly trooped in and took their seats. His hair is bleached perceptibly by his confinement, and his complexion is less healthy than it used to be. His face is thinner, and his eyes seem larger from this loss of flesh and color; but their light is undimmed, and the finely-moulded lips, with their mild, firm lines when at rest, their strangely-radiant smile when he is pleased or engaged in lively talk, are unchanged.

When all were still and attentive, he read, very slowly, as tasting the sweetness of each word, a psalm that might have been indited by himself in commemoration of his perils and his deliverance.

"I will extol Thee, my GOD, O King! and I will bless Thy name forever and ever!"

We sang again, as we had done, the evening of his arrest, —

"Our GOD, our help in ages past!"

The entire service was like an earnest of the joys reserved for the inhabitants of the better, because enduring Home.

The breakfast hour was filled up with hopeful, merry conversation. Papa brought fresh, and, as we think, reliable rumors of a general exchange of prisoners of war. It really seems likely now that another month will see us, once more, a united family. Agatha, who had been, in a measure, put aloof from our happy circle, during our transports at Papa's return, was drawn within it by these tidings. She is ardently attached to Lynn. We hope that he may win back the olden trust and love we had in and for her, and she for us. His influence over her cannot but be for good. Her interest in the preparations for my marriage, and Rolf's regard for her, have, with me, partially effaced the recollection of what has been unpleasant and mysterious in our intercourse for several years back, and her sparkling eyes and speaking countenance, as Papa explained the probabilities of the proposed exchange, disposed him, .with Mamma, to forget the disagreeable passages that had warped their early favorable opinion of her. Our spirits arose into gayety in the reaction after our long season 'of depression. Mamma undertook to furnish Papa with a summary of her farming and housewifely operations during his absence, Agatha and I saucily supplying details which she saw fit to omit.

Mammy's favorite project, in which she is aided and abetted by her mistress, is the manufacture of a carpet woven of cows' hair and poplar bark. We had ridiculed the scheme at its inception, but under the combined influences of ingenuity and perseverance, the fabric is growing into a form so respectable as to silence our incredulity. The product of these will assuredly be a carpet — firm, pliable, possibly durable. But their difficulties about dyes are endless, and we amused ourselves and Papa by expatiating upon these. We related that whenever Mamma was missed from other posts, it was the habit of whomsoever wanted her, to repair, forthwith, to the weaving-room, where she and her coadjutor were invariably discovered discussing perplexedly the feasibility of making bricks without straw — i. e., dye without coloring matter.

"If you could hear Mammy's apostrophes to the departed shades of copperas and indigo!" said I.

"And Mrs. Lacy's suggested substitutes!" chimed in Agatha "To wit — yellow clay and wormwood leaves and stalks, which, being tried, result in a very sickly tint, that has the unpleasant quality of vanishing entirely when the cloth or yarn is dipped into water."

"The conferences always terminate in a very brave show of resignation and a very poor show of making a virtue of a necessity," said I.

"Well, Rachel, while we have madder and green walnuts, we are sure of an abundance of red and black!" says Mamma, philosophically. "We will try another stripe of each. After all, there is nothing that has a finer effect in furniture."

"For what state apartment is this marvellous piece of tapestry designed?" inquired Papa.

"What a question!" cried Agatha and I in a breath. "For the parlor, of course!"

"Nonsense!" laughed Mamma. "Our ambition does not aspire to loftier achievements than carpeting the dining-room. Wait until you have a warm thick covering over these slippery oak boards, and we shall see whose turn it will be to laugh. I do not plume myself so much upon my divers experiments at coffee-raising."

"What am I drinking now?" asked Papa, tasting his second cup of the smoking beverage. "It may be Java or Mocha, for aught I can say. The flavor is exquisite to a palate accustomed to that served out to the patrons of the Hotel Libby and Castle Thunder."

"The entire concoction is a deplorable 'sham,' with the honorable exception of the cream," answered Mamma. "The *coffee* is made of sweet potatoes cut into strips and toasted brown, and roasted rye, ground up together. The sugar is the residuum collected from the sorghum kegs after the sirup is drained off. It is sweet enough — too sweet, indeed — but I try to slip it into the cups when no one is looking at me, and keep the sugar-dish carefully covered while we are at the table."

"She tried to refine it by exposing it to the sun, but it changed back into sirup," Agatha supplied. "Then she racked her invention for some other method, but remembering nothing that bore upon the case, except that bullock's blood was an agent in the process, she gave it up as too costly an undertaking."

Papa made a slight grimace. "I am glad she encountered this obstacle — that there is nothing more in her sugar than meets the eye."

"I must tell you" — I took up the tale — "of a private

enterprise to which Agatha and I were incited by Mamma's notable successes. Following the illustrious precedent afforded by Michael Angelo when he hewed at a shapeless block of marble to liberate the angel imprisoned in it, Mamma espies household gods — or goods — in every herb, root, and tree. One day last fall, she was walking in the cornfield, and happened to put a dried black-eyed pea into her mouth.

" ' It tastes very much like a grain of raw coffee ! ' she said. ' I should not be surprised if it made an admirable substitute ! '

" Agatha and I took counsel of one another apart, and filled our pockets with peas. These we brought to the house, and intrusted, under seal of secrecy, to Mammy. She roasted the ' substitute,' · ground it, and next morning converted it into liquid *coffee*. Mamma tasted hers at breakfast, and added sugar, tasted again, and discovered that it lacked cream ; a third time — and replenished her cup from the hot-water pot. Still, something was amiss.

" ' I cannot get my coffee to taste right ! ' was her complaint finally, and our repressed amusement escaped in a scream of laughter. Then Agatha explained that it ' had a pea-culiar flavor.' "

" The war and the attendant domestic inconveniences have acted as an excellent school of philosophy in our household ! " said Papa, laughing. " There is no better way of taking the sting from a petty privation, or a great annoyance, than turning the dilemma into ridicule."

" Only those who have had no experience of real sorrow, fret over these paltry inconveniences," answered Mamma. " Now, if you have finished your breakfast, and these mischievous girls have no more stories of my failures ready, I invite you to make a tour of the premises, and judge for yourself of my successes."

It was so cold they did not linger long out of doors. They had just entered the parlor, where Agatha and I were seated with our needlework, when I saw, through the window, a gray-coated courier ride into the front yard.

"It is nothing, love!" said Papa to Mamma, who had turned deadly white. "My written parole is an effectual protection."

He met the messenger in the porch. He bore a letter for Mamma from Colonel Copeland, who, the note stated, was at the Court House.

"If it were expedient or possible for me to wait upon you in person, I would not trouble you to come to me," he wrote. "But important developments bearing upon Mr. Lacy's case have been brought to my knowledge since I last communicated with you. I mean to investigate these while here. I could not do this so well elsewhere. I may be compelled to change my quarters to-morrow. I can spare but a few hours from military duty to-day for any one — even yourself. The bearer of this is an honest, trusty fellow. Will you accept him as your escort, and ride over this forenoon? I believe the roads to be perfectly safe between Sunnybank and the Court House. They are well-picketed, if the intelligence brought in by my scouts is to be relied upon."

There was no time to lose. In less than half an hour after the receipt of the letter, the carriage was at the door; Mamma, enveloped in many wrappings, placed within it; Papa took a seat beside her, and with the courier bringing up the rear, they set off in the direction of the Court House.

"How inconsiderate in Colonel Copeland to send for your mother upon this fearfully cold day to aid in his wild-goose chase!" said Agatha, shivering, as we turned back into the house, after seeing them start.

"His business is probably urgent," I answered.

"I don't believe it! He has the reputation of being visionary and over-sanguine. What can he have discovered that will recompense her for her uncomfortable ride?"

"If he tells her nothing, she will not think of discomfort while Papa is her companion. Now that he is here, bugbears of every description have lost their power to terrify."

This is true. I seem lifted, as by one sweep of a strong arm,

above the reach of the fears that have preyed upon my spirits
since he was torn from us. His genial influence is diffused
throughout the plantation. New life has been breathed into
all, from the oldest to the youngest. Agatha did not return to
the parlor, and I came up to my room, arrayed myself as I
fancied Rolf would wish to see me — in one of my new dresses,
put a flower into my hair for the first time in a great while, and
sat down to write near a window that commands the road. I
have conned the vast debt I owe my betrothèd, and my father's
best friend. I strive to bear each particular in mind, that nothing may be wanting from my welcome. Against the dark
curtain of sorrows and reverses, his tireless goodness, his constancy, his daring adherence to our fallen fortunes stand out in
bold relief — compel my grateful affection. If I repeat this
often, it is to engrave it more deeply upon my heart and memory. In years to come I may review this record of the brightest
day that has shone through our four years' gloom, and marvel that when joy at Papa's restoration and thankfulness to his
deliverer were at their height, I could bring our benefactor no
worthier offering than such gratitude as friendship might know.

Unless I destroy my Journal with other precious relics that
must not outlast my wedding-day. One person, and one alone,
ever knew one tenth as much of my inner life as is revealed by
these pages. I shall feel almost as if I were burning a sentient
thing when they shrivel in the fire, so interfused are they with
my thoughts and feelings. Those other mementos — I shall ·
not look as the flame kindles upon them ; but in two days more
I shall forfeit the right to keep them. If I had my wish, I
know where all should be — journal, letters, flowers, and miniature. Upon a stilled heart, embraced by lifeless hands in the
National Cemetery at Gettysburg. ·

CHAPTER XXVIII.

AGATHA.

February 5.

IT was the day after Mr. Lacy's return to his home. I shall
always consider that Rolf treated me badly in that matter. He
ought to have paid me the compliment of forewarning me of
his premeditated and most startling move, not sprung the event
upon me suddenly, as it came upon the beneficiaries of his
charitable deed. I knew no more of the expected arrival than
did the wife and daughter of the late prisoner of state. A very
rotten concern this state must be if the release of her worst
enemies is so easily affected! The *furore* of the jubilation
attending the Master's return had not begun to subside, when
a ·despatch was received, per courier, from Colonel Copeland,
commanding, rather than requesting, Mrs. Lacy's presence at
the Court House. If Mr. Lacy's appearance had surprised me,
this message caused me serious perturbation. It looked as if
the wheel of fortune, having once inclined toward the interests
of the Tory family, were disposed to complete the revolution,
and bring them up in the world once more. Coupling it with
Rolf's sudden exertion of puissance in the case of his father-in-
law, I could not dismiss the apprehension that a screw was
working loose somewhere. It would have been more in accord-
ance with my ally's known decision and caution to make sure
of his fair one before paying the price for which she had bar-
gained ; to demand the ransom in full before delivering up the
captive. It was too much like the vulgar manœuvre of the
hunted thief, who drops the bag of treasure to divert attention
from his own tracks.

Ill at ease, therefore, I shut myself up in my chamber to ponder the signs of the times, and, in sailor phrase, make all weather-tight in case of a coming squall. I could have made more effectual preparations had the falling barometer indicated the quarter from which " the blow " was likely to attack me. There was a splendid fire in my room, the day being bitingly cold, and my blood sensitive to chilling influences. When I think, I *think!* no wandering thoughts, or discursive memories, or useless sentimentalizing — the rambling reverie·most women call a brown study. Nothing sharpens the faculties like the sense of personal dangér. I wrapped myself up in my shawl, let down my window curtains, drew up my rocking chair close to the hearth, put my feet upon the fender, and looking the glowing fire in the eyes, fell to work upon the problem. I commenced systematically at the beginning of the campaign, noted the stability of each position, the effect of every stratagem, the consequences of every pitched battle, as seemed to me reasonable and right, until I arrived leisurely — making clean work the whole way — at the moment of apparent victory. This accomplished, I was as much in the dark as ever as to the importance I should attach to the unfavorable portents I have named, or whether, indeed, I should continue to view them as portents of any description, malign or propitious. I had just made up my mind to do as common sense had dictated at the outset — to suspend inquiry and suppress foreboding until Rolf's expected visit to his Dulcinea should grant me an opportunity of getting the truth from headquarters, when a commotion below stairs, and out of doors, pierced the wall of my abstraction.

A reconnoissance from the windows on both sides of my room showed me negroes, in groups and singly, flying across the lawn with burdens of divers descriptions in their arms — clothing, baskets, and the like, while in and about the smoke-house a gang of six or eight were busy secreting meat, under old Will's generalship.

"A raid or a false alarm?" I asked myself, as I descended to institute inquiries, and bear my part in the laudable work of cheating the freebooters of their expected prey. I was not frightened. Nor was any one else, except the sillier of the servant women. The frequency of warnings that the Philistines are upon us had habituated us to the idea, and practice had made us experts in the task of clever concealment. I drew my shawl up over my head, and repaired at once to old Will. I don't like him, and he thinks me like my Grandfather Pinely, the pauper and drunkard; therefore entitled to an inferior quality of respect to that due his mistress' daughter. But he is a sensible fellow, and can give a straightforward answer. Hence my address to him.

"Who brought the news?"

"The boys from the cove, where they were cutting ice. Don't empty them hogsheads! Leave enough to make 'em think there's no more. And fill up two of 'em to the top with ashes. If they want meat, let 'em gravel for it."

"Where are they?"

"Crossing the river, a mile the other side of the cove. Dick! it's time the horses were off! Cut right across the fields. I'll send a boy after you to put up the fences."

"Were there many?" I persisted.

"They *say* five hundred! Maybe there's fifty!"

"A mighty long string!" said one of the laborers.

"Cavalry?" I asked of him.

"Yes, ma'am."

"And blue coats?"

"Yes, ma'am."

"I'd as lief see one as 't'other," said Will. "Kautz or Wheeler, Mosby or Stoneman, — they will all take whatever they can lay their hands upon."

Just here, Albert galloped down the hill, at the summit of which he had been posted by the commandant of the sable guard.

"Dey're comin' dis way — sure and sartain!" was his report to headquarters.

"How far off?"

"Just the other side of Tim's Creek," — which is half a mile from the outer gate.

"All right!" returned the Eboe Napoleon. "Shovel spry, boys!"

Above the excavation that occupied one corner of the meat-house, were fitted, at the depth of a foot, stout planks; upon these, dried leaves and straw were laid, and the whole covered with earth, which was kept in huge hogsheads for this purpose and no other. When the busy spades had beaten this hard, sand was strewed over it, to hide the marks of recent digging, should the flooring be removed; then the boards were nailed down, and boxes and barrels piled upon them.

"Now scatter!" ordered Will. "And don't one of you dare to cut his eyes this way, if he expects to get anything to eat for the next six months."

The bits of straw and leaves had disappeared from the floor and threshold before the brooms of the women, marshalled by Rachel, and another scout announced that the blue-coats were entering the upper gate.

"Let them come!" responded Will, imperturbably.

"Dar's a thousand of 'em!"

So added the scout, his limbs shaking, and his wool seeming actually to uncurl with terror.

"A big scare is a fust-rate magnifying-glass!" rejoined the head man. "If you're afraid of the face of man, Sim, I'll send your mammy with you down into the swamp 'long with the rest of the calves and feeble cre'turs. Miss Agatha, I'm thinking you ladies will find it more pleasant up stairs. I'll keep them down, if I can. Anyhow, they won't hurt you!"

"Oh! *I* am not afraid!" I laughed, going into the back door as he strode around the corner of the house.

In truth, I never felt more unconcerned in my life. My few articles of jewelry were done up in a little packet, which I easily pocketed, and sought Elinor. She was at her window, watching, from behind the bowed shutters, the advance of the raiders. There were, I should say, between two and three hundred in all, and I was immediately struck by the villanous appearance of those who were near enough for us to discern their faces. They were mostly foreigners of the lowest class, with unkempt beards, wild shocks of sunburnt hair, and their tanned visages were rendered yet more repulsive by their dress — the light-blue great-coats, worn by the Yankee army at this season — undeniably the ugliest uniform ever adopted by any body of civilized human beings.

Will met the foremost at the yard gate, and a parley ensued — loud and insolent on one side — respectful on the other. After the exchange of half a dozen sentences, the negro stood aside, and the calvalcade streamed into the yard.

"Is there no white person on the premises?" demanded the leader, as he sprang to the frozen ground with a prodigious clatter of sword and spurs.

"Only the children of my master and mistress, who are absent from home at this time," Will replied, dignifiedly, mustering his best English for the occasion.

Elinor smiled amusedly at the adroit answer.

"One might suppose us to be under Carrie's age!"

The front door was opened, and the lower story filled with a disorderly, loud-stepping, loud-swearing crowd.

"Hark!" said Elinor, as a blow and jingle arose above the din of coarse voices. "That must be the large parlor-mirror!"

Another crash — blending the discordant wail of many musical chords, violently smitten. Still another — and she clutched my hand.

"They are breaking the piano to pieces! What will they do next?"

Affairs were assuming a serious complexion. All former

visitors, of whatever political creed, were lambs in gentleness beside this turbulent crew. The ring and rattle of crockery and glass, dashed to the floor and hurled through the windows, followed; then the duller "thud" of falling chairs and tables; the shouting, the riotous laughter, and horrible babel of oaths waxing more deafening the while. Carrie had crept into Elinor's arms, and buried her face in her bosom. The elder sister, pale as a ghost, yet controlled features and voice, and tried to allay the child's fears.

"Oh! if Papa and Mamma would come home, and drive these horrid men away!" sobbed Carrie, in a paroxysm of fright and anger.

"It is better that they should not be here, darling! All this would only distress them. They could not hinder it."

Heavy feet were trampling up the stairs; the turmoil raged along the halls to the door of the room in which we were.

There Will's slow, determined accents said, "This is the chamber where my master's children are! There's no arms, nor money, nor silver in here! Will you please to pass on?"

"Stand back, you old fool!" vociferated a drunken voice, and a scuffle had begun against the very panels, when Elinor arose from the chair whereon she had seated herself, when she lifted Carrie, and, holding the child by the hand, walked across the floor, and unlocked the door.

"You can come in, gentlemen, and search for whatever you desire. We will leave the room to you. But, as we are two defenceless girls, and have, besides, the care of this little child, I shall be obliged to you if you will set apart another chamber for our use, where we shall not be interrupted during our parents' absence."

To save my throat from the knife, I could not have spoken thus, confronting, as she did, the throng of lowering faces that blocked up the entrance and the hall beyond. Old Will was at her side instantly; picked up Carrie, and stood ready to accompany them. To be candid, I had shivers of physical fear pinching up my flesh, and thrilling every joint of my spinal verte-

33

bræ. I would have given all my chances and hopes of worldly aggrandizement for a snug covert in the trackless swamp to which Will had scornfully directed his timorous scout. Those nearest the door recoiled instinctively upon the next following, and these pressed backward toward the staircase, causing an immense deal of grumbling and swearing among the impatient patriots there collected.

"Take them to the dining-room, Sambo!" said a fellow, with straps upon his shoulders, and, I inferred from this, an officer in the noble band. "We're through in there!"

A laugh — a genuine guffaw — ran through the crowd, but they opened their ranks, and let us pass in Uncle Will's track, as he bore Carrie down the staircase. We entered into the meaning of the officer's witticism when we reached the haven he had designated. The sideboard doors were split into bits like splinters of firewood, as were those of the fine old beaufet and the mirror set above these — an heirloom, greatly prized in the family; there was not a whole chair left, and from end to end of the table was a crack made by the stroke of an axe. The air came frostily through the broken panes; table linen, cutlery, and crockery bestrewed the floor; pots of preserves, jellies, and pickles had been taken from the adjoining store-room, and their contents either flung away, or smeared, in a spirit of wanton destruction, over the wainscotted walls. While we stood transfixed, surveying the scene of barbarous spoliation, the door was pushed rudely back, and a man glanced in. He was dressed like an officer of rank, and was, in fact, as we soon learned, the chief in command of the gallant troop. His beetle brows met in a frown as he espied us; but instantly comprehending what was the character of the group gathered thus forlornly in the desolate apartment, he showed his teeth under his bushy mustache in what he meant for a reassuring smile.

"Soho — my worthy Snowball!" he said, thickly, by reason of an overcharge of liquor and a foreign accent. "These are the children you spoke of? You deserve one rope's end for

slandering such deuced handsome women! Ladies, make yourselves easy. You shall not be molested in your retirement. I
will myself be your guard."

Thereupon he planted himself upon the hearth, his back to
the fire; put his hands under his coat-tails, and fell to whistling and staring at us. There had accompanied us into the
room old Rachel, bent upon keeping her nurslings in sight, and
four or five other women, scared out of their wits, or moved by
a feeling of devotion to their master's children. Ingratitude is
the crying sin of the negro race. We have too many exem-
plifications of this in these times to question the truth of the
oft-reiterated saying. On most of the surrounding plantations,
the venal wretches turn informers so soon as the Yankees
appear — assisting zealously in the disinterment of the treasures
they have helped their confiding masters bury; stripping the
families, that have counted them as a part of their number for
generations, of every piece of plate, every trinket, and, in some
cases, taking the last mouthful of bread and meat from the lips
of the foster-children who were dandled in their arms, and who,
in babyhood, hung at their breasts. The Sunnybank servants
have proved miraculously faithful among the many faithless of
their color and station. I attribute this less to their attachment to their master and mistress, than to the influence of old
Will and Rachel, and the superstitious reverence with which
the pair have contrived to inspire their disciples. Fidelity to
their owners has been inculcated simultaneously with the duty
of obedience to the Lord, whom they worship blindly, as did
their forefathers their Oboe and Fetish. "My heavenly Marster first! My earthly marster next!" is one of Will's senten-
tious rules; and woe betide the unlucky wight who transgresses
this tenet of his faith!

It was incumbent upon him, as his terrestrial lord's unworthy
substitute, to look first after the safety of his young mistresses;
secondly, to protect the property whenever he could. Committing us to Rachel's care, he sallied forth, leaving us huddled
miserably together in the centre of the room, unable to escape

the impudent stare of our "guard," but keeping at a decent distance from him. Fussy old Rachel bustled about us, with
cloaks and hoods, bundling us up until we looked like Laplanders
bound upon a sledding frolic. She muttered incessantly, —
phrases of endearment and consolation, mingled with uncomplimentary comments upon the "herd of cattle," as she styled
them — who were wasting the home she held in such pride.
The officer overheard as much as he liked of this, and she did
not care if he did. I suspect she intended most of her remarks
for his edification. By and by, he laughed and swore at her
in a breath.

"You are one great blockhead! We are your best friends."

"Then I hope and pray the Lord never to let me ketch sight
of my worst!" she retorted.

"Hush, Mammy!" said Elinor. "We cannot help ourselves,
but we can bear our wrongs in silence."

"Which of these young ladies hopes to marry a Rebel Major
in two days?" interrogated the officer, impertinently, still showing his teeth.

"I expect to, sir!" replied Elinor, with real dignity, eying
him firmly.

"Your father is a very good Union man — is this so?"

"He is so called, sir!"

"That is one old trick!" said the fellow, wrinkling up his
nose in an ugly sneer. "Ah! it is well! We levy upon
both parties in that we forage for supplies here. Do you
see?"

Elinor vouchsafed no reply; only turned her face again toward the window, and gazed at the line of bleak hills; the leaf-
less forests crowning them; the cold, blue sky.

An Aid-de-camp entered, at length, and held a low, excited
dialogue with his superior, of which little reached us except
the profanity. Waving his comrade to remain in the background, the Colonel, or Major — I do not recollect his precise
rank — advanced toward us.

"See!" he said, angrily. "My business here is to search

for arms and horses. Rebels have no right to hold weapons, and my troop want good horses. My men find nothing worth carrying off. There are but two old plough-horses in the stable. I will have more. The owner of this plantation has somewhere cattle and silver. Where?"

"If I knew, I should have no right to give up my father's property into your hands," returned Elinor, tranquilly.

"There is a way of finding these things out!" suggested the officious Aid. "If that old rascal of a nigger, who gives himself such airs, were tied up by the thumbs and flogged for an hour, we should hear of something to our advantage."

Elinor quailed. She shook from head to foot, and her lips took a bluish pallor. Then the fire of the Ross and the indomitable firmness of the Lacy returned to eye and feature.

"You say you are the colored people's best friend!" she answered. "The shame of such a deed would follow you farther and faster than would the murder of ten white men or women. Your Government has no quarrel with our servants. It protects *them!*"

I had never heard the least approach to censure of the Federal authorities from her until this implied reproach was uttered in mild mournfulness that would have appealed irresistibly to the heart of a true Unionist. The hireling brutes laughed.

"By Jove! she is two thirds right! We must keep our hands off the nigger!" said the Aid, who looked and talked like a Yankee. "More's the pity!"

"Do you know, bold young woman!" resumed the chief, again sneering vilely, "that I could *kill* you for not telling me what I want to hear?"

"I do!"

"And what if I say I will do it, unless you show me where are hid your plate and your horses?"

"Then you can kill me!"

She did not flinch now, although Rachel threw her arms about her with a cry of rage, horror, and pity. She was so small and slight, as she faced him — he, so huge and bloated

that I could not but liken them to a humming-bird and a vul-
ture. Her spirit was the braver of the two. He withdrew
his insolent gaze with a louder laugh and stronger oath. He
swore that she was "pluck! game to the back-bone, and ought
to have a better husband than a Grayback!" and walked back
to his Aid at the fireplace.

At this, the moment of her victory, Elinor espied — what my
sight had caught a second earlier — the figure of a man, walking rapidly up the main alley of the garden. He was in citizen's dress, and his hat was slouched over his brows; but we
both recognized the springing step, the lithe, elegant figure. I
saw through it all at a flash. Rolf had equipped himself in
this garb upon several previous visits — a token of consideration
of his betrothed's dislike to warlike accoutrements. On this
forenoon he had, in nearing the plantation, discovered who were
our guests, and avoided them by striking into a bridle-path
leading through the woods at the rear of the house. He had
tied his horse in the underbrush, and having probably learned
that Mr. and Mrs. Lacy were not at home, distracted by apprehensions regarding Elinor's safety, he had determined to
protect her in person. He would hardly be assaulted were his
real character to remain unknown; and for this he trusted to the
known sagacity and fidelity of the negroes. It was a mad enterprise, worthy of a lunatic or a lover.

I passed my arm involuntarily around Elinor, and drew her
up to me — not in womanly sympathy, but to remind her of the
need of silence and self-command. Rolf had his hand upon the
garden-gate when a voice shouted to him,—

"Halt there!"

It was a sentinel, who had been stationed in the back porch,
directly under our window. Rolf had unlatched the gate, and
pushed it outwards. As it swung open, he threw up his arms,
as a signal of surrender, or to show that he was empty-handed.
Simultaneously with this gesture, the report of a musket rent our
ears, and the unarmed man fell heavily backward. One wild,
woful shriek burst from Elinor's lips, and she had thrown up the

window and darted into the porch. The sentinel checked her there ; seizing her arm and asking, with a demoniac grin, what she "wanted with a dead Rebel."

"Let her go!" called the lesser fiend — the superior officer.

When I joined her, she had raised her lover's head in her arms, and was pressing her hand hard over the wound in his breast, the bright-red blood spouting up between her fingers. He spoke but once. All that was audible then was "Darling!" and "forgive!"

And as the dying eyes lost their hold of hers, and the blood gushed from his lips, I remembered how he had said, "One wouldn't mind a bullet in the heart or brain so much, after all, if he could die upon her arm, her glorious eyes shining down into his!"

It was all over in less time than it has taken me to write ten lines. Not five minutes had elapsed from our first glimpse of him, when Will and three other serving-men lifted the lifeless body, carried it into the house, and laid it upon the table in the dining-room. Elinor did not swoon. I wished she would, instead of keeping her stand beside that still warm clay, with her blood-streaked dress and death-like face, while Will opened the vest and felt if the heart fluttered yet. The commanding officer stood on the other side of the table, and eyed the movements of the servants in tipsy curiosity.

"Come with me, my poor lamb!" sobbed Rachel, plucking at her young mistress' sleeve. "You can't do him no good, now. The Lord has him, honey, and He is mercifuller than man!"

The murderer-in-chief appeared to regard this as an imputation upon his humanity.

"Upon my word, Miss Lacy," he said, clumsily, "I swear I am sorry this thing has happened! You must excuse my poor fellows. It is a cold day, and they have been drinking!" *

Elinor fastened her large eyes upon him — a weary, passion-

* A true incident, even to the officer's language.

less stare that ought to have frozen his veins; then raised her
hand and pointed to the door. The brawny ruffian motioned to
his Aid, and the two skulked out. Shortly afterward, we heard
the shrill bugle-call to the saddle, and the house was free of the
horde.

Mr. and Mrs. Lacy returned after dark, not having encountered a Yankee trooper, on their route, going or returning. If
the morning had been busy, the afternoon was busier. The last
blue-coat was hardly out of sight, when Will rallied his forces
to the work of restoration. The night closed in, freezing cold,
the wind having risen again about noon. Broken panes were
pasted over with paper and rags; the freshly scoured floors
dried by enormous fires; the *débris* of the various rooms removed; some of the least injured furniture repaired, and neatly
re-arranged. One apartment alone was made clean and bare,
and left fireless, the wind whistling shrilly through the closed
shutters and unglazed sashes. Rachel was the last to withdraw
when all was done, and she locked the door. The table, with
its burden, was covered with a fair, white sheet; the oaken flooring, lately slippery with gore, was washed. These homely services were the utmost tokens of respect and affection which the
simple-hearted dependants could render to the almost bridegroom
of their idolized young mistress. Old Will planted himself
outside the locked door, with the stern resolution of a Roman
guard, and did not quit his post until his master and mistress
entered the house. Rachel had met them in the outer porch,
and whispering caution, led them into the parlor. I had, an
hour before, in alarm at her dilated irids and rigid features,
administered an anodyne to Elinor. It had taken effect, and the
noise of the carriage-wheels had not disturbed her. Satisfied
that she slept, I left her in charge of her maid, and slipped,
with soundless feet, down the stairs. Rachel's tale had been
told when I entered. I read horror at the cold-blooded brutality
of the deed in the visages of husband and wife, — but not the
grief they might have been expected to feel at the murder of a
friend — a son. I understood, intuitively, what had been the

result of that day's investigations. My judgment said that the bullet which had cut short Rolf Kingston's life was not more fatal to his schemes of earthly happiness than would have been the parents' verdict had they returned to find him the living, exultant lover of their daughter. Mrs. Lacy prepared to go to Elinor's room, and her husband exchanged a meaning glance with her.

"Not a word, love!"

"Of course not!" was her reply.

At that I was sure of what I had hitherto but strongly suspected. Their subsequent discretion in my presence was exemplary; their deportment, during the tumult of consternation, indignation, and sorrow that attracted half the county to Sunnybank for the two days following, and went far toward reinstating them in the good graces of their neighbors — for the time being, at any rate. They attended the empty shell that had been a man to its last resting-place beside his mother in the Kingston burying-ground — his mother, who died when he was a baby! Poor woman! she had better never borne him, or, when she died, taken him to her cold bosom and colder pillow of earth!

Well! we laid him there, and drove back in decorous silence to Sunnybank — the rifled and desecrated home — and the shaken, turbid cup of daily life began to settle into calm and clearness. And still no word to me — or, so far as I could ascertain, to Elinor, of Colonel Copeland and his discoveries. Was I to bear this — racked as I was by conjectures and dreads? Miss Morris was, I was assured, Mrs. Lacy's confidante, as well as Elinor's comforter. One night, I conceived a scheme for making myself a participant in the coveted secret. There is no end to the closets in this house. In Miss Morris' room there are three. The most spacious of these has two doors, one opening into her chamber, the other into a smaller one beyond. The latter is always kept locked, and the key is one of a bunch that hangs beside the mantel in my Lady's own room. I feigned a headache, and while the rest were at supper, I possessed myself of the keys; tried them, one after another, in the lock I wished to open; took off that which fitted, and replaced the bunch without detection.

It is the habit of the two cronies to sit for an hour in Elinor's chamber before seeking theirs, Mrs. Lacy usually taking her friend's room in her way to bed. I chose this time for entering my hiding-place. It was a bitter night, the sleet tinkling fast against the one window of the anteroom as I crossed it; but there were mountains of bed-clothes upon the closet shelves. I appropriated a blanket, and deposited myself snugly upon the floor, my ear to the inner door. Thanks to the builders' carelessness, or the lapse of years that has warped the joints and shrunken the beams of this old edifice, it offers capital facilities for eavesdropping, as I have reason to testify. My lucky star ordained that my Lady should tarry late over Miss Morris' fire, and that their talk should run principally upon the topic I would have chosen above all others. If Rolf was crafty, Colonel Copeland was subtle. If the one had his spies and emissaries, the other had his trained detectives to scent out the trail these tried to cover. What were the consecutive steps of the lawyer-soldier's investigation, I could not discover. Nor did it matter much that I should. I gathered that Rolf had lodged the information against Mr. Lacy — not in person — but that he was the instigator of the proceedings against him whom he pretended to defend and serve; that the clever but needy debtor whom he had hired, under bonds of eternal secrecy, to copy a certain letter of his composition into a presentment of Mr. Lacy's handwriting, had betrayed his master for a yet larger bribe, or through fear of exposure and punishment; that Rolf's powerful friends at court had persisted in their opposition to Mr. Lacy so long as he plied them — still not directly — with arguments and proofs tending to criminate the Unionist; that they had readily changed their tactics when Major Kingston made individual application for the release upon parole of his future relative. But why do I continue the list of counts in the indictment against the departed strategist? If he had attained his ends, he would have remained a spotless hero to the pair

who now named him with loathing and self-accusations of stupidity and negligence in that they had become his dupes, and
pious shudders over the narrow escape, the providential preservation, of their darling.   He failed, not because he was not
skilful in cunning, but because the instruments employed in
furthering his machinations were of untempered material, and
another surpassed him in shrewd sagacity.   The unsuccessful
are ever the condemned — the doubly damned.

I guess the policy of her guardians to be to let in the light
gradually upon Elinor's ignorance ; to lower her late betrothed,
inch by inch, from the altitude he gained by his supposed services
to her father, and by his tragical end while flying to her relief
from the persecutions of her unmannerly guards.   For this, the
final act of a life stained darkly by passion, deceit, and cruelty,
he should have his award of praise.   With all his faults he
loved that girl with every instinct and thought.   Perhaps he
did not dream that he was perilling his existence for her sake ;
but I, who know him better, his failings and his crimes, — a thousand times better, — than do the censorious couple, believe that
he would have died for her rather than not live with her.   When
she hears all she will not credit this.   She will grow to think
of him as her advisers would have her do — to repudiate the
idea that a single one of his professions was genuine, to inter-
lard her orisons with ejaculations of thanksgiving at his untimely end.

I had plenty of leisure for meditation while Miss Morris pursued her preparations for retiring, and when in bed, composed
her nerves and mind to tranquil slumber.   I could hear her
breathing, and I muffled mine, lest her ears should be as quick.
The clock had told two of the small hours when I deserted my
lair, and limped off to my lawful lodgings.

I was not comfortless.   " All that a man hath will he
give for his life."   To a woman, the gem of reputation — let it
be a true diamond or a specious brilliant — is the thing of price.
I think of Rolf the more compassionately that his downfall has
not involved me.   I was not mentioned once in the fireside

conference. If I am to fight my battle unaided, I have no cause to dread the explosion of hidden mines. My future is yet in my own hands. A woman is a born conspirator — a man an artificial — more frequently than otherwise a bungler, who ruins himself in attempting to gain the pinnacle of his air-castle by trampling upon the hearts and vaulting over the heads of others.

Yet — poor **Rolf!**

CHAPTER XXIX.

ELINOR.

December 24, 1865.

MAMMA and I are left in charge of the house to-day. We were busy together all the forenoon preparing Christmas baskets of provisions and groceries to be distributed to-morrow among a few of our poorest neighbors. All are more or less needy, and the utmost assistance which our slender means justify us in extending to them will do little toward lessening the great aggregate of want and misery. There will be no festivities at Sunnybank. The traces of suffering and bereavement are too fresh in our hearts for us to think of merry-making. But there will be PEACE! sweetest word that ever comforted a mourner's spirit; that ever quelled the fierce surges of national strife; that ever passed a Saviour's lips! It thrills, yet soothes me like a strain of celestial music. We, the dwellers in this region, should know the wealth of blessedness bound up in that little syllable.

Mamma, who is more easily fatigued than of yore, is lying down for her after-dinner nap. I have consigned Carrie to Mammy's care, and spent an hour in looking over my Journal. I think no longer of destroying it. The record of the last semi-decade may in years to come interest others, as well as instruct me in hope, love, faith.

Papa was given back to us the second week in January. The raiders were here next day. Then all was quiet until the news of the evacuation of the Capital, and the surrender of the Grand Army ran like wildfire through the state. The end had come so suddenly that no one was ready for the news — not even those who had prayed for the day, as do the chosen people for

34

their restoration to the promised land. Aunt Ellen was with us still. We had begged for her society while the shadow of the awful event that clouded our joy at Papa's return enshrouded us. After the capture of Richmond, we rejoiced, ou her account, that she had yielded to our persuasions. We had suffered too sorely from the lawlessness of so-called disciplined troops not to tremble at the imagination of the military occupation of the city — the prize for which two mighty hosts had fought, month after month, and year after year, until both esteemed it impregnable. If not bombarded, until not one stone should be left upon another to mark the site of the place, we believed, as did the population of the doomed town, that it would be sacked, and probably burned.

The sun arose upon the 3d of April, through dense masses of black smoke ascending from burning warehouses, where were being consumed the hoarded stores for which a famishing people were vainly pining; from arsenals, with their bursting shells, and the louder thunder of explosions that shook the seven hills to their foundations, and filled the terrified inhabitants with dread of imminent destruction; from bridges, the stately piers of which, anchored in the seething current of the James, had stood for years among the proudest ornaments of that incomparable river-view — fired, lest the pursuing host should overtake the fugitive army. What sickly light could pierce this dreary canopy fell upon dismantled fortifications and deserted homesteads; upon a tumultuous throng of liberated slaves riotous with freedom, and laden with plunder; upon the pale, awe-stricken faces of their late masters, impotent to prevent the wasting of their goods and the conflagration of their houses — the crowning injury inflicted by the Government that to them had wrought only disaster from the day of its inauguration until this latest hour of final humiliation. Upon that morning, when Richmond the Fair, a queen in her woe, sat in sackcloth and ashes; when men's hearts were failing them for fear; when mothers clasped their infants to their breasts, and, kneeling beside their virgin daughters, besought the GOD they were ready to believe had forsaken them, to grant them the merciful boon of instant death rather than deliverance into the hands of the barbarous invaders; when the soldiery who had sworn to die in the last trench surrounding the beloved citadel had abandoned her to her fate; when the word-valiant patriots, once coveting the high privilege of riding to their saddle-skirts in Yankee blood, and each to oppose his single arm to the united force of five of the hireling robbers, now, forgetful of the very ties of natural affection, leaving their helpless households behind them, were crowding the outgoing thoroughfares in hot and frantic flight, — there entered the burning town an army, vast in numbers indeed, but in discipline so perfect that their progress through the streets was audible only by the clanking of iron heels and sheathed sabres. Looking neither to the right nor to the left, without the bray of trumpet or the triumphal music of patriotic airs, they marched in solid rank to t. t quarters appointed by their leaders; guards were set to protect the citizens against the depredations of the freed negroes, or unruly stragglers; active, capable bands were detailed to extinguish the flames kindled by the departing Confederates, and Richmond enjoyed the first night of safety and quiet she had known since Sumter fell.

To my mind there are not many events in history more sublime than this occupation of the heart of Rebeldom by the defenders of National integrity, the representatives of National power.

Our first thought after the delightful surprise of hearing that our friends in the city were safe, and that the dreaded foes were changed into benignant protectors, was of our imprisoned boys. Our postal arrangements were broken up. We could neither send nor receive letters; and this was no common privation, longing as we were for tidings of the missing ones. Aunt Ellen proposed a remedy for the grievance. I should accompany her to Richmond, and try every method of establishing communication with Fort Delaware, or, at all events, with Uncle Charley. Agatha sued for the privilege of going with

us with an earnestness of importunity which I ascribed to her
solicitude on Lynn's behalf. Aunt Ellen's insuperable aversion
to her could not blind her to the evident agony of expectation
Agatha underwent as the hour drew near at which Carleton
Dana, who officiated as our postman, was accustomed to bring
in letters. She would quit her lookout at the chamber or parlor window at the first glimpse of him, fly down to the door,
seize upon the packet,—if packet there were,—and bring it in to
us with a countenance that told, before she opened her lips, what
had been the issue of that day's waiting. At last she entered
to us, breathless and beaming, holding aloft three letters—
one for me from Ross, one from Lynn to herself, the third from
Uncle Charley to Papa. They were safe and well; they had
signified their willingness to take the oath of allegiance; they
hoped to be with us shortly. This was the sum and substance
of Ross' epistle. I did not see Lynn's; but Agatha said, with
a smile and a blush, "that I would learn nothing more
from it than I had done from his brother's." I did not open
Papa's. Since the fearful lesson I had learned from a former
liberty of this kind, I had recoiled from breaking open an envelope directed to another. I put it away carefully instead,
hoping for an early opportunity of sending it to Sunnybank by
private hand. Such offered four days later, but the letter had
disappeared! In vain I ransacked the drawer wherein I thought
I had laid it, and extended the search to every other in the
bureau; in vain interrogated each person in the household; in
vain cross-questioned my memory, to determine whether I had
deceived myself as to the place of deposit — the fact of its dis-
appearance was so stubborn, and my impressions of the locality
wherein I had last seen it grew so vague: it was nowhere to
be found! I could do nothing except write a note to enclose
with Ross', telling Papa of the loss I had sustained, and my
regret that I had suffered my ultra-fastidious or superstitious
scruples to prevent me from making myself mistress of the con-
'ents upon its arrival.

Then we began to watch for the coming of our beloved brothers, as we had done for their letters. Aunt Dana heard from her brother-in-law, as did Carleton; but he wrote respecting business affairs, referring incidentally to the circumstance that he designed making direct, special application for the release of the captives. Thus a fortnight went over. It is a weary time when one lives by the hour. One bland evening in May, when we were gathered about the open parlor windows, a carriage stopped at the door; slow footsteps came up into the porch; a pass-key clicked in the lock; and we rushed into the hall. Uncle Charley and Ross were there, and supported between them was another figure. Could that bowed, wan man be my once erect and handsome brother Lynn?

He tried to raise his head. He did say, " Agatha!" then he fainted.

We left him alone with Agatha, when he revived sufficiently to know and speak to us. From Ross we heard that his brother had taken a violent cold ten days prior to his release, which resulted in serious illness, aggravated by homesickness. When, in reply to his importunate queries, Ross confessed that the order for their liberation had arrived, the restlessness of the invalid knew no bounds.

" One breath of Virginia air! one glimpse of dear old Sunnybank! one kiss from Mother, Agatha, and Brownie, and I am content to die! " was his cry.

" Removal may be fatal," said the surgeon.

" Can he recover here?" asked Uncle Charley, who had joined his adopted nephews, meaning to accompany them home.

" It is more than doubtful," the surgeon answered. " Certainly not, unless we succeed in calming him."

They brought him around by steamer, avoiding thus the fatigue and changes of the land route. He was lifted into the carriage at the wharf, but when he reached the well-remembered door, he would stand and try to walk.

" Nothing but his invincible resolution to see home and friends once more has kept him up," said Ross. " It is out of the question to think of transporting him to Sunnybank. A trusty messenger has already been sent forward with an account of his situation. If all goes well on his journey and on theirs, we may expect Father and Mother to-morrow night."

Aunt Ellen and I watched by Lynn's bedside until morning. He suffered little, but several times I thought him dying from weakness, so faint was his breathing, so feeble his pulse. Even at these seasons, the dark eyes followed us with a happy light shining within them; upon the pallid face rested a smile of ineffable content. Agatha staid with us until one o'clock, when her lagging step and heavy eyelids admonished me that one of her neuralgic attacks would be the price of her vigil, and we persuaded her to lie down in the adjoining room.

"I shall not forget how near you are to me, dearest!" he said, in seconding my entreaties, and Aunt Ellen's more imperative orders. Poor Aunt Ellen! she never had much patience with Agatha, and on this occasion she was unusually energetic in her attempts to get rid of her. Lynn thanked her for her care of his betrothed, and I saw her wince. It hurt her to receive the unmerited praise, yet this was not the time for the avowal that the sight of the graceful form hanging over "her boy's" pillow detracted grievously from the satisfaction she would otherwise have felt in nursing him.

The best medical assistance which the city afforded was summoned promptly. There were three consultations of physicians held during the next day, the last at evening. Their opinion was unanimous. We must give him up. Long-mourned, hardly restored to our embraces, — he would soon, very soon, leave us forever. At midnight, Papa and Mamma arrived. Lynn was first to notice the distant rumble of the carriage upon the quiet pavements. As it stopped at our door, he folded his hands and closed his eyes; his lips moved in silent prayer. It was like — "Now lettest thou thy servant depart in peace!" When Mamma drew his head to her breast, the rest of us fell back. Her claim in that honest hour was before all others.

"My boy!" she said, with a smile of unearthly beauty; and

he answered as he had done in his childish illnesses, " Mamma, dear ! it is good to have you hold me."

His head nestled upon no other pillow while he lived. Others might put the cup to his lips, bathe his face, and adjust the coverings of his bed. " Mamma must hold him." The day was breaking when the unrest the doctors had predicted as the forerunner of dissolution overtook him. He stirred uneasily, tossed his arms from side to side, and muttered brokenly in his slumber. Yet he was rational when he awoke.

" Mamma ! " still the old pet name — " am I going ? "

" I fear so, my darling ! "

" But not alone ! You will be comforted by this — will you not ? "

" It is my only comfort, my son. His rod and staff are a sure support."

He bade us farewell sweetly and calmly. When Mamma would have withdrawn a little as Agatha approached, he restrained her with the invariable petition, " Hold me, Mamma — please ! "

" We might have been very happy together if GOD had let me live ! ", he said to his betrothed. " For I love you, and you have been true as the sun to me, dear. Father — Mamma — you will be kind to this poor child when I am gone, because of her love for me ! "

Agatha slid from his encircling arms to the floor, kneeling, or rather crouching there, her face buried in the coverlet until the sad scene was over. When Aunt Ellen's turn came, he drew her down to him, and kissed her affectionately.

" I shall see *him* sooner than you will ! I shall have much to tell him about you — my second mother ! "

His mind began to wander slightly. He fancied, for an instant, that he was at Sunnybank.

" I hear the robins sing, and I smell the locust blossoms. The trees are white with them. Do you know, Mamma, dear, that I had not seen a flower since I was captured until Harry Wilson brought me a basketful — mignonette, and violets, and heliotrope? They were like a gift from the gardens of Heaven!" He opened his eyes, which had been half shut in his dream. "I should like to say farewell to Harry! He has been very kind to me. But for him I should not be in your arms now, Mamma! I was his enemy, and in prison, and he visited me. I wish I could thank him once more!"

Why did Aunt Ellen put her arm around me to lead me from the room? Why did Agatha shake as with an ague fit? What meant the glances of embarrassment, doubt, inquiry, which others bent upon me, unless that they feared lest these incoherent murmurings might disturb the equanimity I ought to maintain while he could be distressed by any show of emotion? I quietly resisted the impulse of Aunt Ellen's kindly embrace.

"I will stay here!" I said. "I see how it is."

I believe it was Ross who stole so softly from the room, that I did not remark his absence. But at a movement in the doorway, and a slight change in the several positions of those surrounding the bed, I glanced up from the face of my dying brother, and saw my Harry's ghost! He was older and sadder looking than at our parting; there were unfamiliar lines in the forehead and about the compressed lips, and, here and there, a silver thread in his hair; he was ashy pale, and his eyes full of grief — still he was my Harry, for all these changes. But he never looked at me! Inclining his head in respectful salutation to all as he entered, he passed to Lynn's side, and grasped the poor, thin hands in his.

"Thank you for letting me come!" he said, huskily. "I shall never forget it!"

"I could not die in peace without seeing you again!" was the reply. "There has been a great mistake somewhere, Harry! We should never have fought against one another. I thought I was right. You believed honestly that you were doing your duty. Ah, well! God knows!"

"It is over now!" said Harry, gently. "Let our dead Past bury its dead. We will look forward!"

I lost not a word of all this. I did not faint, but I seemed changed to stone. Only my startled brain was preternaturally active, and teemed with ghostly fancies. We had gone with Lynn to the verge of the dark river, and a pitying spirit had crossed over from the other side to convoy him through the chill waters. Or were we all shades together? Or was this apparition and the greeting between him and his late foe the trick of a disordered imagination? Had I gone mad at last? Aunt Ellen has told me since that I betrayed none of these thronging conjectures in my features; that I stood perfectly still, my hands clasped on the head-board of the bed, and gazed steadily — she could have thought unfeelingly — upon the two friends. When the farewell words were spoken, the last hand-clasp loosened, and Harry left the room, I passed my hand over my eyes as if to sweep away a mist, looked up at her, and smiled.

Our Lynn died that evening without pain or struggle.

"I feel as if I could sleep now," he said drowsily and indistinctly. "Hold me, Mamma!"

And while he was speaking, his spirit escaped from her loving arms.

Beyond this scene I recall nothing clearly until I stood over his grave, and read little Morton's name upon the headstone of the next mound. Like a whisper from an Eternity past, there floated over my memory words once fitly spoken upon this spot.

"He is safe. Whatever may befall her other sons, our Mother has felt the last pang of solicitude she can ever know on account of him who sleeps here!"

I cried aloud, "Thank GOD!" and the hot, heaving brain was refreshed by a rain of healthful tears. When the paroxysm was over, I was too weak and worn for thought or conversation, and fell asleep, my hand in Aunt Ellen's. She sat by me at my awakening in the morning, in the dress she had worn at the funeral. Remorseful at my selfish cruelty, I started up.

"Dear Aunt Ellen! I have kept you up all night!"

"Not you, Brownie! The Lord does not give sleep to eyes

so overweary with tears as are mine. That I could watch over your rest was the one comfort of my night. You are all I have to live for. My Lynns are together now, but they have left me very desolate! very desolate!"

"God's will be done!" said Mamma's voice behind us. "I have lain awake for hours past, thinking of the blessed truth contained in one little clause of a text — '*who spared not His own Son.*'"

From that moment no one has heard a desponding word from her. Every duty is discharged with punctilious fidelity. She has loving tones and sayings for husband and children; kind counsel for those who, nominally free, are still her dependants and co-laborers; hopeful predictions for the discouraged and suffering. It matters not that many of the latter passed by on the other side, or, like poor Miss Hetty Stratton, lingered near only to upbraid and taunt, in our days of deepest affliction. There is no room for animosity in the large, tender heart of this Christian woman and mother. Nerved by her example, I, too, tried to make of sorrow a means for the attainment of higher Christian graces, to fasten, in this gloom of the night-time, upon the Chastener's hand, that I might be led whither He would have me go. I prayed, —

> "Nearer, my God! to Thee,
> Nearer to Thee —
> E'en though it be
> A cross that raiseth me!"

But I fainted daily under my secret burden. For, since Lynn's death, Harry's name had not been spoken in my hearing. I questioned myself incessantly as to the reality of his appearance. I might have persuaded myself finally that the interview I had witnessed was a hallucination, but for the changes I had noted in his face and figure — the imprint of suffering, severe and continued — whereas, until then, I had remembered him in the full strength of his manhood, alert and vigorous in health and spirits. He had returned from the dead, then! He lived, but he loved me no longer! Else, he would not have come and gone from my sight without look or token that he saw me, and rejoiced in our reunion. Else, those who loved me best would not preserve this significant silence with regard to his resurrection; the services he had rendered my brothers; the touching farewell of our lost one to him he had once esteemed his enemy. And I was starving — yet could not syllable an inquiry that might break the spell. I could not ask, "Has he ceased to care for me?" I said to myself that I knew already what would be the inevitable reply. Yet to have the truth confirmed by other lips would have killed me. I was very nearly mad at that period of my life — short in truth, endless in seeming — or I must have cleared up the dread mystery in some manner.

I slept in Aunt Ellen's room now. I had grown cowardly nervous of darkness and solitude. One moonlight night, when neither of us could sleep for thoughts of the grave on which the white light was shining, she began to tell me some incidents of her early life, with which recollections of her lover were intertwined.

Pausing abruptly in her story, she said, "Brownie! pride was the bane of my happiness! What made you cast away the last chance of yours?"

"Aunt Ellen!" I ejaculated, amazedly.

"There should be no foolish reserves between us, child! You would never have thought of marrying Rolf Kingston had you not believed Harry Wilton to be dead. Why then did you reject one who loved you, and whom you still loved when he wrote to tell you that he was alive and constant?"

I could not keep back the heart-breaking confession.

"Oh, Aunt!" I cried, clinging to her and bursting into tears. "He never wrote me one line! I did not know he was alive until I saw him at Lynn's death-bed!"

She tore my arms from their hold — pushed me from her that she might examine my countenance in the moonlight.

"Is this true, Elinor Lacy?"

"It is!" I answered. "And you — Papa — Mamma —

Ross — everybody — have nearly killed me by your silence when I was longing for the mere sound of his name!"

" I see it all!" she ejaculated, deliberately.

She arose, lighted the lamp, opened her writing-desk, and dashed off a note of perhaps a dozen lines; directed and sealed it, and looked at her watch.

" Four hours to daylight! Fool! fool and blind!"

I watched her in perplexity and some alarm. She acted and talked like one bereft of reason. Suddenly, she came back to the bedside, took my hand in hers, and knelt upon the floor.

" Brownie! look into my eyes. I am awake and sensible at last! Harry Wilton was carried off among the Confederate wounded from the battle-field. For fifteen months he languished in one of the pest-houses they called prisons, at Salisbury. He was released last December. He wrote to you repeatedly after his return to the North. It was not surprising that he should receive no reply to these letters, for it was a difficult and uncertain enterprise to send letters through the lines. I know they never reached you. But when the way was open, he wrote once more, asking leave to visit you. This letter was sent to Richmond, and he had an answer!"

" Not from me!" I said, eagerly.

" I believe you, and I mean that he shall! If I can unite two tried and loving hearts, it may atone — it may lighten my exceeding weight of anguish. Lay your head on my shoulder, dear, and let me tell you all you wish to hear."

I shorten the recital — not that I have forgotten any portion of it, but because I remember it so well. Harry was the instrument of my brother's liberation. He had petitioned for this in person, and himself been the messenger that bore to them the welcome tidings of release. He watched with Ross by Lynn's pillow during his illness; he helped carry him to the boat, and remove him from his state-room to the carriage that was to bring him to us. He was the messenger who volunteered to take that lonely night-ride to Sunnybank that Papa and Mamma might be apprised of the condition of their dying boy. At his request, the brothers and Uncle Charley had refrained from allusions to him in their letters to Virginia. He wished to announce himself, he said, when he first spoke of it. Afterward he told Ross that he had had an answer to a letter he had written me.

"Which"—to use his words—"has put an end to whatever hope I may have cherished of her continued regard for me. I only ask now that you will not annoy her by any allusions to me or our former intercourse. When she sees fit, she may tell you why she has rejected me."

Ross and Lynn, remembering their opposition to the union they now desired should take place, the report of Harry's death, and my subsequent engagement to Rolf, of which they had heard through our letters, agreed privately that they ought to have foreseen what would probably be the tenor of my reply, and prepared Harry for it. Yet Lynn had revealed the circumstances of Harry's visit and brotherly kindness to them in a letter to Agatha written the day before he fell ill, and Uncle Charley had dwelt upon the same subject at length in a letter to Papa.

"Which was lost, you recollect," said Aunt Ellen.

"But why did Agatha conceal the news she had received?" I asked.

"That is a question which remains to be solved," rejoined Aunt Ellen. "There are depths of villany which you are not expected to fathom."

This observation made me notice Agatha's startled expression at breakfast, the following morning, when Mamma replied to my query after Ross, "He has gone to Richmond, my dear."

"Ah!" exclaimed Agatha, glancing up. "Wasn't that a sudden movement?"

"It was a foolishly delayed one!" returned Aunt Ellen, shortly; and there the matter rested.

On the afternoon of the succeeding day, I walked down to the burying-ground with fresh flowers for Lynn's grave. It was a still, bright hour — the sunset of a lovely June day. The wil-

35

low tent was thick and green above me ; the grassy carpet soft
and rich ; the ivied wall a compact bank of verdure. I dis·
posed my flowers as ·I had intended to do, sat down upon the
turf beside my brother's grave, and rested my forehead upon it.
I was not happy even with the renewed faith in Harry's love
implanted by Aunt Ellen's story. I had walked in the shadowed
valley for so long that I had forgotten how to be glad. Whatever of delight the Future might have in store for me, nothing
could remove the sombre background of war and bloodshed,
and the tombs of the loved and brave. Misguided they may
have been ; sincere they assuredly were. To the merciful
Judge of all it belongs to say how many or how few were guilty
of wilful wrong-doing. My brother was not of this number.
His error was of the head. If he loved his State too well, it
was not that he did not love his Nation. Mourn over the unhappy issue between the two he did, even while he believed that
he ought to fight to save his Motherland from conquest, his
home from plunder, his sister from insult. Feeling thus, he
battled with those whom the war had made to be his enemies ;
feeling thus, he died, saying, almost with his parting breath, " I
thought I was right ! Ah, well ! GOD knows ! "

My brave, noble, gentle-hearted brother ! If I could have
died in his stead ! If this strong, beautiful staff could have
been spared to his father's declining years, to his mother's yearning heart !

I had not heard footsteps upon the velvet of the grass. Yet
arms were about me to raise my bowed head to another resting-
place ; kisses, and, at the last, a great tear or two fell upon my
brow, cheek, and lips. Harry had come, and he believed in
me now !

We were a long while in that sanctuary of the dead. It was
not profanation to speak there of love like ours. When the dew
fell heavily, Harry forbade my lingering longer out of doors.
We were leaving the enclosure when he perceived the grave of
the Federal soldier. Papa had erected a white head-board to
mark the spot, and written upon it the poor fellow's name, age,

and regiment. I had laid flowers there when I decked the mound above Lynn. Harry stepped aside to read the inscription, and to press his hand, in reverent affection, upon the swelling turf.

"Brother in arms!" he said; and then to me, pointing to the flowers, "Thank you for these! Merrill wrote to you of his discovery that I was a prisoner — not killed."

"I never received the letter!" I interrupted.

"No, love! Letters seldom reached their destination at that time. But the faithful sergeant did write, and exerted himself to the utmost to send his communication to you. His was one of the first faces I saw after my exchange. He was on board the transport that received us. I was in a pitiable plight — but we will not talk of that. He became my especial attendant. I owe my life, under GOD, to his care and nursing. The best cordial he gave me was tidings of you. For days he kept me alive — this is fact, Brownie! by stories of you; your sweet offices in his behalf, and your unabated affection for me. When I was able I visited the mother of him who lies over there, and she showed me your letter. I copied it for her, and she gave me the original, for I told her how I loved the writer."

We were in the garden now, in a retired walk, edged with rose-trees, white and red.

"Sunnybank holds its own!" said Harry, looking up at the belvidere, gilded by the latest yellow sun-rays. "How often, while in prison, I dreamed of this, our favorite path — inhaled the perfume of the roses and syringas!"

He stopped short, and took from his pocket an envelope.

"Can you guess who sent me this?"

It was a sprig of orange blossoms, dry and scentless.

"Is it the one I gave you?" I asked.

He replied in precisely the same words — "Is it 'the one I gave *you*?"

"No," said I. "I have mine still."

"Yet this was the reply to the letter in which I begged

permission to visit you.   Do you know, now, to whom I am
indebted for it?"

He showed me the superscription of the envelope.

"That is a poor imitation of my writing," I said.   "It is
more like —— "

I checked myself.

"So I think now!   So I ought to have thought when I received it."

"We will let it pass!" I said, hastily.

"For the present — yes!"

"Will you not throw that away?" I prayed, as he returned
the dried spray to the envelope.

"No, dearest!   It has a purpose to serve."

I did not press him for explanation. If more tender and loving than ever, he was still firm — still masterful. How naturally the old epithet came to my mind in looking at and hearing
him!   Oh! the exquisite sense of rest that stole through every
nerve, and fibre, and thought, as I leaned my whole weight
upon him, gave myself up once more to be cared for and guided
by his strong heart and will!   Another surprise awaited me at
the house.   Upon the piazza, talking with Uncle Will, with
Mammy hovering about him, as a mother-hen rejoices over a
recovered bantling, was Sergeant Merrill.   When our joyous
salutations were over, I observed another man, a stranger,
dressed, like Mr. Merrill, in the Federal uniform, standing some
paces off, and watching me keenly.

"This is my friend, Mr. Clark, Miss Lacy," remarked the
Sergeant.   "I intrusted a letter for you to him, but he blun-
dered in delivering it — an unusual thing for him to do.   Did
you ever lay eyes on this lady before, Dick?"

"Never, I am sorry to say!" was the reply, too curt to be
taken as a mere compliment.

"We will talk about that by and by," said Harry, leading
me away.

Agatha did not appear at supper-time.   Mamma sent up
to say that we were at the table, and had a reply to the effect

that " she begged to be excused. Her head was aching violently."

" Rachel," ordered Mamma audibly, as Mammy passed the door, " step up stairs, and say to Miss Agatha that I wish to speak with her after a while. If she is not well enough to come down stairs, I will go to her room."

When Harry and I went up stairs on our way to the study, soon after supper, we met her on the landing. She drew aside her black drapery, and stood still to let us pass. Her eyes gleamed luridly ; her cheek was crimson ; her head high and haughty. She looked steadfastly into Harry's face as he approached her, and he into hers. There was no sign of recognition from either. I was determined to speak, and I resisted his gentle impulse onward. She was lonely, forsaken, despised — I, affluent in blessings. She had wronged me cruelly, and without provocation from me ; but I could not dislike her while Lynn's pleading voice followed me. " Be kind to this poor child when I am gone ! " She had suffered ; she was in torment now, and direr humiliation awaited her.

" I am sorry to hear you are not well to-night ! " I said timidly — perhaps awkwardly.

She seemed to tower yet farther above me. The intolerable light of her eyes scorched my vision.

" Pity from you ! from *you* ! " she repeated, in intensest scorn. " I am not yet reduced to that ! " and swept down the staircase.

I could not sleep that night until Mamma came to my room with the particulars of the decisive interview. She had talked alone with the unhappy girl. She denied nothing of which she was accused ; admitted, in reply to Mamma's questions, that she had personated me to the scout Clark ; in this character obtained Mr. Merrill's despatch to myself ; and that she had labored sedulously, from that moment, to conceal from me the fact that Harry still lived. Carleton Dana had given her four letters, one of which she had concealed, and afterward read and destroyed. She had enclosed the faded flowers to Harry in reply, having kept them by her a long while in anticipation of this

35 *

opportunity. In pursuance of her system of concealment, she had likewise purloined the letter from Uncle Charley to Papa, foreseeing that its contents might frustrate her scheme. She had played recklessly and desperately, and she had lost all.

"What had Elinor done that you should hate and injure her?" inquired Mamma.

"She has done me the foulest wrong woman can endure from woman," she rejoined. "She has robbed me of all I cared for in life!"

Then she became inflexibly sullen, and refused to say more.

She kept her room while Harry remained with us. Before we were married she removed to Richmond, having engaged board in a respectable private family in that place. She has no maintenance except the rent of Hayridge. The few thousands Lynn possessed were invested in state and bank stocks, which up to this time have yielded no returns. Papa interested himself to procure a good tenant for Hayridge, and the nominal rent, paid over punctually in quarterly instalments to Agatha, far exceeds the real sum collected by Papa. Without suspecting it, she is still his beneficiary. He will not let her suffer want while he lives, for Lynn loved her.

Our marriage was a very quiet affair. The Danas were all here, with Colonel Copeland and Mr. Merrill. But none of the neighbors were bidden, and my white muslin was the only one in the room. Harry asked me to wear white during the ceremony. That evening, we left the company long enough to go down together to the enclosure at the foot of the garden, where I laid my bouquet of orange blossoms, with myrtle and pure, snowy roses, upon Lynn's grave.

We talk little of the events of the four years' war. Why should we, when the living present is thronged with duties, and Hope is ever pointing to the reward of labor done for the love of man and of GOD? Harry's health renders a residence in the country advisable; but were this not so, he would still seek out some employment near Sunnybank, that our parents might not be deprived of another of their children. Ross has returned to the city. Harry has taken Lynn's place here. He is a wise manager — says Papa. Mamma calls him " my son," as she does Ross — as she used to say yet more frequently and fondly to our " mother's boy." To me — wondering at, when I am not incredulous of the reality of, my great happiness — he is —

" Not half so good a husband as my peerless wife deserves !

(Signed) HARRY."

MARION HARLAND'S WORKS.

Uniform editions of the works of this favorite authoress are now ready.

ALONE. 1 volume. 12mo. Price $1.75.

HIDDEN PATH. 1 volume. 12mo. Price $1.75.

MOSS SIDE. 1 volume. 12mo. Price $1.75.

NEMESIS. 1 volume. 12mo. Price $1.75.

MIRIAM. 1 volume. 12mo. Price $1.75.

HUSKS. 1 volume. 12mo. Price $1.75.

NOTICES OF "NEMESIS."

" It is a story of surpassing excellence—its scene laid in the sunny South, about half a century ago ; its characters limned with a master's hand ; its sketches graphic and thrilling, and its conclusion very effective. Such a work is beyond criticism, and needs no praise."—*Troy American.*

" In all the characteristics of a powerful novel it will compare favorably with the best productions of a season that has produced some of the most successful books that have appeared for a long time."—*Courier and Enquirer.*

" ' Nemesis ' is, by far, the best American novel published for very many years.—*Philadelphia Press.*

" It is worthy of note that the former works of this authoress have been republished in England, France, and Germany—indeed, no other American female writer has the honor of a republication in the Leipzig issues of Alphonse Durr, which embraces Bryant, Longfellow, Hawthorne, and Prescott."—*N. Y. Home Journal.*

" Marion Harland, by intrinsic power of character, drawing and descriptive facility, holds the public with increasing fascination."—*Washington Statesman.*

GRACE TRUMAN;

OR, LOVE AND PRINCIPLE.

By SALLIE ROCHESTER FORD. With Steel Portrait of the Authoress.
1 vol., 12mo. Price $1 25.

" We have read the book with uncommon interest. The tale is well told, and its development is natural. It is intended to illustrate the trials and triumphs of a young wife, in maintaining her principles against the intolerance of the open communion friends of her husband; and this is done so as to preserve unfailing freshness in the narrative, and to throw a flood of light on the principles and practices of the Baptist denomination. We expect to hear that the book will have multitudes of readers."—*New York Examiner.*

" This is truly a delightful book. Mrs. Ford has thrown around a young bride—the Christian heroine of this fascinating romance—such severe, and yet such life-like trials, that we at once become deeply interested in her behalf, and watch, with great solicitude, the result of the struggle between Love and Principle, as we follow her through some of the most trying scenes."—*New York Chronicle.*

" This work, we predict, will create a sensation in this country such as has attended the issue of few books for a long time, and its popularity must exceed that of any other work of a similar kind that has recently appeared. What is more important still, it is a book which can not fail to do good wherever it is circulated."—*Western Watchman.*

" ' Grace Truman' is another religious novel, *founded on facts,* as any one may see who is familiar with denominational prejudice. It is written to show how many difficulties one may meet, and how much actual persecution they may endure, in the attempt to follow out what they conscientiously may believe to be *right,* when their friends, relatives, and social connections believe a different way. Mrs. Ford has skillfully drawn a picture of what she has seen and known. The work is true to real life, and therefore it will be read."—*Mothers' Journal.*

" We have been borne through the perusal of this book with unflagging interest. Like ' Theodosia Ernest,' it is designed for the illustration and defense of our denominational principles; and without detracting in the slightest from the enviable reputation of that work, we do not hesitate to pronounce this more ornate in style, more artistic in plot, more thrilling in incident. It can not fail of a wide popularity and an extensive circulation."—*Religious Herald.*

" We must not overlook, as occupying no minor position among the *dramatis personæ* of the story, *Aunt Peggy,* an old, pious, shrewd domestic, and a Baptist all over, inside and outside, with strong faith in the promises and providence of God. She talks, looks, and acts like a pious slave of an elevated Christian character, and is allowed great liberties with Christian people. Talk about the negro caricatures in ' Uncle Tom's Cabin !' The authoress of 'Grace Truman' was born and brought up with this race, and enjoying a chastened as well as a luxuriant imagination, has drawn truthful and life-like characters in all her portraits. This book should be extensively circulated. Pastors should see to it that it goes into every Baptist family."—*Rev. John M. Peck, D.D.*

SONGS AND BALLADS FOR THE HOME AND HOUSEHOLD.

By SIDNEY DYER.

1 volume. With Steel Portrait. Price 75 cents.

"A book of mark in the field of poesy."—*Correspondent of Watchman and Reflector.*

" Mr. Dyer is evidently a poet—not a poet on stilts—nor a poet without common sense brains, nor does he fly away from every-day life on the wings of imagination—but sings of things familiar—things of the household, such as come to the heart and affections of us all. Mr. Dyer has added to the stock of our literary wealth."—*Chicago Democrat.*

" Excellent of its kind. They grow out of the experience of life, and teach us to do bravely in the-battle of life."—*Chicago Tribune.*

" We have read with the keenest enjoyment many of the pieces in the volume, some of them with a tear standing in our eye."—*Western Christian Advocate.*

" These sweet lyrics of Dyer ought to be in every family. They are so pure and musical—so full of home affections and memories—that they renew within us the feelings and joys of childhood. Taking up this volume after the toils of the day, late in the evening, we went on reading and reading, unconscious of the passing hours, until, roused from a sweet reverie, we found it was past the hour of midnight. We most heartily thank the publishers for sending us this volume of songs and ballads."—*Lutheran Home Journal.*

THE BRIGHTHOPE SERIES.

By J. T. TROWBRIDGE, author of "Neighbor Jackwood," etc.

Tho Old Battlo Ground,   Iron Thorpe,
Father Brighthope,   Burr Cliff.
Hearts and Faces,

5 vols. 18mo, gilt back, uniform, in cloth. Price $4 00.

NOTICES OF "FATHER BRIGHTHOPE."

" The object of this charming little story is to show the beautiful effect of piety in the family. The moral lesson is pure and impressive."—*C. Herald, Detroit.*

" We have read no little homo narrative this many a day so delightfully interesting as this one."—*Toledo Blade.*

" There is a charm about this little volume which one does not easily forget."—*Wor. Palladium.*

" It abounds in passages of exquisite humor."—*Portland Eclectic.*

" A most valuable book for Sabbath School and Juvenile Libraries.—*Pathfinder.*

NOTICES OF "THE OLD BATTLE GROUND."

From the Boston Transcript.

" Mr. Trowbridge has never written anything that was not popular, and each new work has added to his fame. He has a wonderful faculty as a portrayer of New England characteristics and New England scenes."

From the Boston Traveler.

" It is an enticing little work, written in that pleasant style which has made the author one of our most popular public instructors. It will take high rank among books that should be bought at this gift-giving season."

From the Salem Register.

" Mr. Trowbridge will find many welcomers to the field of authorship as often as he chooses to enter it, and to leave as pleasant a record behind him as the story of Father Brighthope. The present addition to the series is worthy of his reputation as one of the very best portrayers of New England character and describers of New England scenes. It is not a story of war and bloodshed, but, as the author says, the daily struggle of love, and pride, and hatred, and despair, which never cease on earth, will interest those who accompany him in his walks about the Old Battle Ground. Every body who likes a wholesome book will be pleased with it."

THE SUNNY SIDE SERIES.

By MRS. E. STUART PHELPS.

Peep at No. 5,   Tell Tale,
Last Leaf from Sunny Side,

3 vols. 18mo, uniform style. Price of each 80 cents.

THE ROLLO BOOKS.

By JACOB ABBOTT.

Rollo Learning to Talk,	Rollo's Museum,
Rollo Learning to Read,	Rollo's Travels,
Rollo at Work,	Rollo's Correspondence,
Rollo at Play,	Rollo's Philosophy, Water,
Rollo at School,	Rollo's Philosophy, Air,
Rollo's Vacation,	Rollo's Philosophy, Fire,
Rollo's Experiments,	Rollo's Philosophy, Sky.

14 vols. Illustrated, uniform style. 16mo. Cloth, 60 cents each.
14 vols., uniform style. 18mo., cheap edition. " 50 " "

THE ROLLO STORY BOOKS.

By JACOB ABBOTT.

Trouble on the Mountain,	Georgio,
Causey Building,	Rollo in the Woods,
Apple Gathering,	Rollo's Garden,
The Two Wheelbarrows,	The Steeple Trap,
Blueberrying,	Labor Lost,
The Freshet,	Lucy's Visit.

12 vols. 18mo. Cloth. Illustrated. Price, per set, $3.

THE FLORENCE STORIES.

By JACOB ABBOTT. 75 cents each.

Vol. 1. Florence and John. 16mo. Cloth. Illustrated.
Vol. 2. Grimkie. 16mo. Cloth. Illustrated.
Vol. 3. The Orkney Islands. 16mo. Cloth. Illustrated.

From the Boston Journal.

" Mr. Abbott is always an entertaining writer for the young, and this story seems to us to contain more that is really suggestive and instructive than other of his recent productions. Florence and John are children who pursue their studies at home, under the care of their mother, and in the progress of the tale many useful hints are given in regard to home instruction. The main educational idea which runs through all Mr. Abbott's works, that of developing the capacities of children so as to make them self-reliant, is conspicuous in this."

From the New York Observer.

"Mr. Abbott is known to be a pure, successful and useful writer for the young and old. He is also the most popular author of juvenile books now living."

From the Boston Advertiser.

" This new Abbott story gives a description of a well-arranged home school, in which the children study with their mother. Minute and useful details are given, interesting to domestic teachers. The children's plays are also described in Mr. Abbott's own style. This opening volume of the new series gives excellent promise of what may be expected as it goes on. The scene is laid at a country house on the North River, and the volume is well illustrated."

From the Boston Traveller.

" No writer of children's books, not even the renowned Peter Parley, has ever been so successful as Abbott."